STARLIGHT
PASSAGE

STARLIGHT
PASSAGE

Anita Richmond Bunkley

A DUTTON BOOK

DUTTON
Published by the Penguin Group
Penguin Books USA Inc., 375 Hudson Street,
New York, New York 10014, U.S.A.
Penguin Books Ltd, 27 Wrights Lane,
London W8 5TZ, England
Penguin Books Australia Ltd, Ringwood,
Victoria, Australia
Penguin Books Canada Ltd, 10 Alcorn Avenue,
Toronto, Ontario, Canada M4V 3B2
Penguin Books (N.Z.) Ltd, 182–190 Wairau Road,
Auckland 10, New Zealand

Penguin Books Ltd, Registered Offices:
Harmondsworth, Middlesex, England

First published by Dutton, an imprint of Dutton Signet,
a division of Penguin Books USA Inc.
Distributed in Canada by McClelland & Stewart Inc.

First Printing, May, 1996
10 9 8 7 6 5 4 3 2 1

 REGISTERED TRADEMARK—MARCA REGISTRADA

LIBRARY OF CONGRESS CATALOGING-IN-PUBLICATION DATA
Bunkley, Anita R. (Anita Richmond)
Starlight passage / Anita Richmond Bunkley.
p.   cm.
ISBN 0–525–94009–X
I. Title.
PS3552.U4715S72   1996
813'.54—dc20   95–47908
                                                CIP

Printed in the United States of America
Set in Janson and Mona Lisa
Designed by Julian Hamer

PUBLISHER'S NOTE

To my Sisters of the Word—
writers and readers, you know who you are.
We raise our single voices, yet rejoice as one.

With thanks and appreciation to

My agent, Denise Marcil
and
My editor, Audrey LaFehr

You keep me afloat and pointed in the right direction.

Prologue

THE howl of a spotted hyena shrieked up from the floor of the densely forested valley, its maniacal echo breaking Ijoma's concentration. More annoyed than startled, she frowned, then placed her hands firmly against the wall, pressing her palms flat against the dark mahogany poles to create a sliver of an opening between the tightly tethered pieces of wood. Cautiously, she inched her small brown fingers inward, the golden bands beneath each knuckle scratching the wall as she forced the sections apart. With her shoulders locked rigidly in fear, she listened for the familiar sound of Tabansi's footsteps as she fit her right eye against the tiny peephole and stared.

"So many of them," she murmured in hushed surprise, her eye flitting over the gathering of bare-chested men squatting in front of bulging camel skin bags. Like a colony of scarabs picking through a dung heap, Ijoma thought.

With brazen delight she studied the pincherlike arms and chiseled faces of the *Wangara* traders as they meticulously weighed and measured their hordes of gold. A tall spire of flames, held in check by a circle of water-filled clay pots, roared in the center of the walled clearing, etching the fast approaching dusk a flat yellow hue. As the somber gold merchants prepared for the next day's trading, the hiss and crackle of burning wood was the only noise coming from the compound.

Ijoma grinned, delighted to witness a sight that no other girl in her village had ever laid eyes on, though a tinge of disappointment did flare as she assessed the scene in the rapidly darkening courtyard.

Why weren't the men dressed in white robes, turbaned and upright, draped in necklaces and armbands of gold, ambergris, and saffron? That's how Tabansi had told her the *Wangara* would look. But here they were, sitting on their haunches like fat tiger beetles, wearing no more than the shanti warriors wore to protect their private parts. Ijoma's heavy golden earrings brushed her wine-dark cheeks as she shook her small head back and forth in disbelief.

Suddenly, the strong shoulder upon which Ijoma sat shifted, threatening to throw her off balance.

"Hold still, Sekou!" she hissed, settling more firmly onto the smooth warm flesh of her accomplice. "You will make me fall."

The young man supporting her slight frame struggled to recapture his balance. Ijoma teetered precariously above his head.

"Stop moving!" Ijoma urged, her tense whisper resounding in the humid twilight. Reluctantly, she turned loose the poles to steady herself by grabbing Sekou's head. The pieces of wood snapped back into place with a crack. Ijoma froze, then jumped to the ground and ran.

"Wait!" Sekou called, the word no more than a frightened breath. "Wait, Ijoma!"

But Ijoma kept going, fleeing into the leafy forest as Sekou hurried after her, his bare feet making flat, muffled thuds along the path.

"What did you see?" Sekou asked, grabbing Ijoma's arm, forcing her to stop.

"Not much," Ijoma whispered quickly. "You should not have moved." She pulled Sekou beneath the low branches of a silk cotton tree, then leaned against its trunk.

"Was it beautiful?" the young man asked. "Were they dressed as kings? As the *Chibale* would dress?"

Ijoma straightened her brightly colored lappa, then replaced the gold-threaded head-wrap that protected her elaborately braided hairdo from the eyes of nonroyals. If Gram-Ma-Ma knew Ijoma had been out of the compound with her head uncovered she'd never hear the end of it.

"Beautiful?" Ijoma replied sharply. "No. Not at all. You should see for yourself how common they are. Half naked! Heads uncovered! The *Wangara* look more like the beetles we torture with sticks at Lake Volta than traders in gold."

"Common? The *Wangara*?" Sekou's full lower lip turned down in disbelief. Suspiciously, he tilted his flat ebony face to the sky, sniffing as if searching for a scent. "Maybe we are at the wrong compound. Maybe these are not the gold traders at all."

"Oh no," Ijoma said, now inching back toward the mahogany wall. "This is the right place. The gold is piled high. In camel skin bags. And I could see the salt blocks lining the courtyard. This is the place all right." Ijoma stepped forward, then turned to look at Sekou. "Let's go back. Lift me up again. I want to see them again, to memorize the sight."

Sekou raised one shoulder in question. "Why tempt our good fortune? I promised I'd take you to see the *Wangara*, and now you have seen them. Let's go, Ijoma. Please! Tabansi will pass by soon."

"Old Tabansi?" Ijoma intentionally injected disdain into her voice to remind Sekou of her royal status. "He does not frighten me. He is only a servant. My father would never allow Tabansi to punish me."

"Maybe not, but Tabansi has acquired much power through allegiance to the Kante clan. Your father allows him much control."

"True," Ijoma admitted, "but Tabansi is still only a servant and he is getting old. He takes his job of protecting the secret location of the *Wangara* much too seriously."

Sekou placed a long finger under Ijoma's chin and gently lifted her face toward his. "Just as seriously as he takes his job of protecting the *Chibale*'s daughter."

Now Ijoma squinted, weighing Sekou's remarks against her own knowledge of her father, the ruler of their village. The natives of Bwerani considered her father a just ruler, a patient soul with plenty of time to listen to their problems. Ijoma had witnessed his somber posture while he quietly received his people, but when it came to his only daughter, he had no time for her at all! He shut himself away, letting old Tabansi make all the rules, allowing him to hover over her like a wary lioness.

Sekou tries to be such a know-it-all, Ijoma thought, wishing she could put him in his place, yet not hurt his feelings. "Sekou!" she said, pulling back her delicate shoulders in courtly assertion, "I think you have forgotten that Tabansi must serve me, too."

"Ha!" Sekou threw back in a loud guffaw, playfully slapping his hands at her. In the dusky twilight, his richly beaded corset shimmered on his ebony chest. "Then why did I see you doing the picking of the rushes while Tabansi carried the basket when you were at Lake Volta yesterday morning?"

Scowling, Ijoma pushed past him, turning deeper into the forest that she knew as well as the network of lines on the back of Gram-Ma-Ma's hands. Taking long strides up the narrow trail, she clamped her lips shut, both angry and pleased by Sekou's question. "You spied on me at Lake Volta?"

Sekou fell in step beside her. "I wasn't spying. I only said that I *saw* you."

"You didn't make your presence known," she said, annoyed that he hadn't had the courage to step forward.

"Why get Tabansi all riled up?" Sekou replied. "He doesn't like anyone who is not Kante coming around. The word has traveled far across the lake. He will never accept me as worthy of your attentions."

"You worry too much, Sekou. I told you Tabansi has no say about who I spend my time with. You should not be so frightened of him."

Ijoma's haughty tone belied her inner joy that Sekou had come looking for her. For the past three moons they had been secretly meeting at the cove on the lake and her mind was made up—Sekou would be her husband.

If only he would show more courage, she thought. Who knew? The *Chibale* might be impressed enough to accept him as a son-in-law even though he wasn't Kante. Besides, she had already lain with Sekou, more than once, and her body craved only him. She couldn't imagine lying with any other man.

"I am not frightened," Sekou muttered in protest, easing his arm around Ijoma's waist. "I only wish I could be with you all the time, Ijoma. I'm not spying. Don't ever think that." He splayed his fingers along her side and stroked the warm flesh that peeped out above the waist of her lappa. His voice deepened as he told her, "I only wanted to see you."

Ijoma smiled, lids lowered as she stole a glance at the muscular young man beside her. "It won't be long. Only four more moons until my sixteenth season. Then my father *will* agree to our union."

"Did he say this?" Sekou asked warily, his grip tensing on Ijoma's waist. "Will he let you join with my tribe?"

"Well, I'm not certain . . ." Ijoma hedged, "but I feel he is coming around. In four days Asesima will speak for me. I am certain he will not refuse Gram-Ma-Ma's request."

Sekou hugged Ijoma closer. They continued up the leaf-covered path in silence, then bent low to duck into the bushy green ferns that camouflaged the trail to the *Wangara*. Emerging, they paused at a fork in the road. Sekou turned to face Ijoma, his eyes fastened on hers.

"Will you be at the lake again tomorrow?" he asked.

"Yes, and everyday until the harmattan ends. The royal basket weavers need many rushes. They are creating the most exquisite ceremonial pieces for the celebration of Asesima's fiftieth season. Gold threads will be woven with the rushes to create a most rare type of basket. More delicate than those created in any other village—far superior to those made in Bambuk. Everyone in Bwerani will attend."

Sekou nodded. "Then the rushes must be gathered before the rains are upon us once more." He let out a deep, contented breath, edging closer to Ijoma. "I wish the baskets were for our marriage ceremony."

Ijoma stroked Sekou's bare shoulder, facing him, almost dutifully lifting her lips toward his. At this same fork in the road he always kissed her good-bye before returning to his village on the other side of the lake. "Soon," she whispered. "Have patience, Sekou."

"Yes. Yes. Until tomorrow," he murmured, kissing her lightly, affectionately, with a great deal of respectful restraint.

Ijoma touched the back of Sekou's hand, lowered her eyes, then hurried up the path to the royal compound, hoping she hadn't been missed.

Morning came very quickly and Ijoma woke easily. Her eyes popped open, her mind cleared in the space of a moment, and she was immediately flooded with a sense of victory. She felt smugly grown-up to have seen the *Wangara*, and to have managed to slip into her sleeping chamber without running into Gram-Ma-Ma or one of her nosy servants.

The pale wash of daybreak nudged against the slatted window as Ijoma wrapped a fresh lappa about her hips and placed her heavy Cowrie shell collar around her neck. In quick movements, she twisted a length of white silk cord through her braids, then pulled a roll of thin banana leaf parchment from a waist-high basket near the door. Reaching deeper, she retrieved two small pots of indigo paste, a sharpened quill, and several long-handled finely tipped brushes. If she hurried she might be able to get in an hour of sketching before Tabansi rattled her door to drag her off once more to the thick stand of bamboo at the edge of Lake Volta. Why the basket makers insisted that the reeds be cut by the family of the *Chibale* escaped her. They *were* excellent artisans, but entirely too superstitious.

"High God of Patience remain with me today," she grumbled in prayer, making up her mind that this morning, *she* would carry the basket and order Tabansi to wade out into the murky water and cut the prickly rushes. No one would know the difference.

During the next hour, Ijoma practiced drawing the intricate designs of the Kante tribe on brittle pale banana leaves. The pattern of the horned dogs with their scrolling tails and tongues was her favorite. When the elongated animals were drawn very close together, the fluid shapes blurred into a circular linkage that made them appear to be moving. Ijoma had instructed the royal dressmaker to weave the dogs into Asesmia's new ceremonial skirt.

The diagonal blocks of bold stripes separated by tight little spirals was difficult, but not nearly as hard to master as the flat oval fish with their butterfly tails and tiny mouths bursting with sharp little teeth. There were concentric circles overlapping each other, triangles set closely together, and feathered sunbursts that represented cascades of shooting stars. And then there were the weeping gods with their sorrowful faces, flat and round, covered with plump, long teardrops.

Of the forty-seven traditional designs of the Kante, Ijoma had only mastered twenty-three and even those were not so easily drawn. No matter how hard she tried, her lines never came out straight and her circles were always wobbly. The weavers, she knew, would not welcome her into their chamber to work the golden threads until all the designs could be recalled and woven perfectly, and quickly. They would have little patience for her sluggish hand. If the gold could not be placed precisely onto the design, a piece could be ruined in the space of a second.

Sighing, Ijoma dipped her sharpened quill into the pot of rich blue paste, curled her tongue over her bottom lip, and began inscribing a series of eight-pointed stars with hollow centers on the blank banana leaf scroll. She was determined to master the royal designs—as Gram-Ma-Ma and her mother had done.

Soon sunlight streamed through the bamboo curtains, crept across the hard dirt floor, and touched the edge of her straw mat, signaling the end of her morning practice. Ijoma scanned her work, then nodded, the early-morning ritual was beginning to pay off—she had completed three more passable designs. Now it was time to meet Tabansi at the front gate. The smell of boiling peanuts and wild bananas drifted into her chamber, but Ijoma knew there would be no breakfast for her until the rushes were gathered.

With a towering multicolored basket atop her head, eyes vacant in regal indifference, Princess Ijoma made her way through the village of Bwerani. Proudly arrogant, Tabansi led his charge from her walled home through the dusty assemblage of thatched huts and meandering cattle, to the road leading out to Lake Volta. No one dared to call out or approach Ijoma as she proceeded on her royal mission, for all the people knew of her part in the upcoming ceremony for the fiftieth season of the *Chibale*'s mother. Excited speculation grew as the villagers discussed what might be fashioned by the secluded artisans who worked in gold, leather, and even glass.

Stepping briskly to the thumping cadence of Tabansi's finialed walking stick, Ijoma took two steps to each of his.

He is trying me, she thought, determined to say nothing until they reached their destination. Then I'll let him know who is in charge. Nearly giggling aloud, Ijoma imagined the old man's astonishment when she ordered him into the lake.

Emerging from the wooded trail Ijoma grimaced in disappointment to see a wispy fog hanging over the flat, still water. On a clear day Ijoma could see across the lake directly into the Oda village where Sekou lived and communicate with him using hand signals, letting him know how much she missed him. Not so today.

Lowering the basket to the ground, she inhaled, trying to settle the quaking sensation in her stomach. Hesitating a second, she summoned the courage to give Tabansi a royal command.

"Stay close to the shoreline, Princess," Tabansi began. "And be sure to cut above the waterline. The weavers have no use for soggy reeds."

Ijoma stiffened her spine and raised her chin until the flawless brown skin of her neck was taut and smooth. "Tabansi," she started, peering down her nose at him, "I think it is time you understood . . ."

"Listen!" the graying servant stopped her. "Do you hear?" He cupped one hand to his ear, leaning so far from the shore the hem of his white robe sank beneath the water's surface.

"Yes!" Ijoma answered, turning to look back at her village, then across the lake. She *did* hear the sound of drums—a faint and hollow resonance, the talking drums of her people.

"Shh." Tabansi put a finger to his lips and listened. "There are strangers in the area. Evil strangers. The white man's hunters have returned." He waded deeper into the water.

Ijoma gasped. "Those who raided Diomo last moon?"

"The same," Tabansi uttered lowly, motioning for Ijoma to stay put. He crept farther out—until the rush-filled water came up to his knees.

A thick curtain of milky white mist shrouded everything. Only the faint drumbeats coming across the lake penetrated the barrier. Ijoma began to shake.

"What do they say, Tabansi? What?"

Tabansi didn't answer, but quickly turned around, stumbling onto the bank to grab Ijoma by the arm. "We must go back!"

The look of surprise that came to Ijoma's face was not brought about by the rough manner in which Tabansi had spoken to her, but by the sudden appearance of a huge Sosi warrior who materialized out of the fog.

"Tabansi!" she warned as the hunter shook his arrow-tipped spear up and down, advancing on her servant's back. With a swift stroke, the slave hunter knocked Tabansi to the ground. Ijoma fell to her knees beside him, only to be jerked upright. The warrior tried to bind her hands with a length of jute, but she struggled, pressing against the hunter's slick, wet chest. Ijoma cried aloud, digging her fingernails into his arms. With a snap of her head she bit down on his sheening black flesh, tasting the warrior's bitter blood on her tongue. He tried to pull his arm free, but she clenched her jaws, holding on, her head lolling back and forth until her silken cords fell from her braids and landed in the dust.

The painful clamp of the hunter's hard fist over her skull forced her to let go.

"Stop! Turn me loose!" Ijoma plead. But the slave catcher wrapped her body in rough hemp, cutting her slender arms as he shoved her down on her knees. Raising his spear, he growled, then thrust it into Tabansi's chest. Withdrawing it, he waved the dripping lance at arm's length, spinning the old man's blood into the air, splattering Ijoma's face.

Sickened with fear, Ijoma doubled over, watching in horror as a band of slave catchers rushed from the forest and thundered toward her village. Within seconds, bright orange flames rose in the distance and the screams of her people clawed at the sky. Lowering her face to the ground, Ijoma let the soil of her land fill her mouth.

"Oh, Gram-Ma-Ma . . . oh my *Chibale*," she whispered, "help me."

But she knew that neither her grandmother nor her kingly father would hear her cries for rescue when a callused hand closed over the tender skin at the nape of her neck. With a grunt, the slave catcher pulled Ijoma to her feet, heaved her over his blood-soaked shoulder, then sprinted away from Bwerani.

The gentle splash of waves lapping against the ship calmed Ijoma and nudged her into a welcome half sleep. The slaver had docked hours ago and Ijoma's sensation of continual motion was finally beginning to subside. For weeks, the curling sound of the ever-present water had seemed like moving pictures inside her head, like the fluid Kante designs she had memorized. Into the never-ending darkness, she had mentally etched the swirls and points of the long-tailed dogs, the bold diagonal stripes of the Ghanaian sunset, the spirals and spinning circles of her ancestors' markings against the pitch-black span of her journey. She wondered if Gram-Ma-Ma had lived to wear her ceremonial skirt. Had Sekou survived the massacre? Only visions of the intricate Kante designs had kept Ijoma imagining, remembering, sane.

She pulled her left foot an inch forward, grimacing as the iron cuff scraped her flesh anew. At least the ship had docked—where, she did not know. And for the first time in ten weeks Ijoma no longer smelled the stench of death or the rancid reminders that some in the hold were still living. Her senses had, fortunately, become immune to the pervasive odor of rotting flesh, excrement, and fear.

After five weeks in the holding pen at Cape Coso and ten more weeks at sea, she was grateful to be alive, thankful that her body had been small enough to allow extra space in her eighteen-inch berth, leaving sufficient room to shift now and then and keep her circulation going. The woman chained to her left arm had not been so lucky and Ijoma wondered how much longer it would be before the captain ordered the corpse removed.

Now that the journey seemed to be at an end, Ijoma felt the grip of fear. A nervousness that she had managed to keep at bay during the passage resurfaced in galloping waves. What would await her in the bright sunlight of this far-off land? What manner of people would she now live among? Surely they must be a most savage tribe to have created this barbarous way of bringing others to their shores.

Ijoma swallowed dryly, tasting the foul odor of her fellow travelers in her mouth. A spasm of nausea surged up, but instead of frowning, she smiled. If she had been able to move her hands she would have lovingly stroked the swell of her belly, but instead, she offered up a silent prayer of thanks to the gods who had watched over her during the journey. Sekou's child had survived the trip.

"I will call you Adiaga, the first daughter," Ijoma decided, certain it was a girl struggling to grow inside her bone-thin body. "You will be strong like Mama, Gram-Ma-Ma, and all the Kante women of Bwerani. As soon as you can hold the quill, I will teach you every one of the Kante designs that I have brought in my head from my village, and you will never forget where you came from."

Chapter One

Tuesday, June 1, 1993
Houston, Texas

KIANA slid a trembling finger over the rough finish on the yellowed paper, embracing her mother's old-fashioned script. Her heart swelled with pride and her eyes misted over as she stared at the travel-worn notebook. The image of the haughty Princess Ijoma lying in the belly of the slave ship was seared like a cattle brand into Kiana's mind.

If only I had opened this box before now, Kiana thought, fanning the pages of the book. There were names, dates, cities, and historical references that she knew would be very helpful. Twenty years after her mother's death, Kiana had finally forced herself to sort through Louise Sheridan's research papers before relegating them to indefinite storage. And now, as she put her mother's narrative into her carry-on bag, she was struck by the relevance of her discovery: At a time when second thoughts had begun to plague Kiana, this book had surfaced to bolster her confidence.

She shoved the last two issues of *Essence* magazine, the current edition of *Houston Style*, and three newsletters from the African-American Genealogical Society into her flight bag, along with the journal. Her three-hour flight from Houston to Washington, D.C., would be a good time to catch up on her reading.

She reached for a pale blue envelope lying on her dresser. Before stuffing it into her oversized purse, she opened it, and for the third time that day, reread her letter of acceptance.

March 30, 1993

Dear Miss Sheridan:

Your application to join the Smithsonian's Summer 1993 Underground Railroad Tour has been accepted. You have been granted permission by Marla Sherer, the president of The Sojourners, to travel with their group. The Sojourners is a national network of amateur genealogists, all of whom are descendants of some of the most influential and prominent African-American families in the United States. There will be fifteen in your tour group. A suggested list of what to bring is enclosed. Each member on the tour is limited to one large bag and one carry-on, and you must be able to handle both pieces by yourself. Please contact your tour guide, Mr. Rexford Tandy, at the number listed here if you have any questions. We look forward to seeing you at the orientation meeting at the Museum of African Art, Room 301, at four o'clock on Thursday, June 3, 1993.

Sincerely,
Felton Mills
Tour Manager

Kiana slowly folded the letter, slid it into the side pocket of her purse, then climbed into bed and snapped off the light.

I will finish your story, Mother, she silently vowed as she plumped up her pillow, then sank down on it. Listening to the sound of Latino music drifting across the courtyard, she lay awake for nearly an hour, focusing on the pulsing beat, trying to visualize her neighbors' party—anything to keep her mind off the inevitable reunion she was about to have with Ida.

The silver bells on Kiana's charm bracelet tinkled as she handed the flight attendant her empty coffee cup. Rebuckling her seat belt, she reclined the back of her seat, snapped down the window shade, and closed her eyes. Though she'd finally fallen asleep last night and had really slept quite soundly, she still felt tired—not mentally exhausted as she usually was after a day of drumming important dates in American history into the heads of her tenth-grade students, but physically tired, as she ought to be after scrubbing, vacuuming, sorting, and packing the entire contents of her apartment.

Resigning her position at Robinson High had been easier than Kiana had expected, bringing to an end her six-year contract to teach history at the inner-city school. Her time there had been satisfying, though marred by a rocky relationship with her principal, Donald Thatcher. Professionally polite, though aloof, Thatcher had quickly branded Kiana as a radical, outspoken, troublemaker because she had dared to challenge his attempt to censor her lesson plan on the civil rights movement.

She had wanted to show her students a video of the Birmingham fire department turning fire hoses on black demonstrators. Thatcher had called the newsreel emotionally and racially inflammatory, convinced it would provoke violence between the black and white students, and erode racial harmony at Robinson High.

Kiana had taken issue with his statement, accusing him of not only having little faith in the students, but of trying to undermine her authority. Thatcher had reluctantly backed down, but later retaliated by refusing to grant Kiana six in-service credits for attending a conference on reparations. After that decision, Kiana had presented her case directly to the school board. Thatcher's ruling had been overturned.

Kiana grimaced at the memories. Donald Thatcher must have felt threatened by her support of the fledgling reparations movement, though he had never taken the time nor the interest to discuss the issue with her. Kiana believed that reparations could be the first step in a healing, not a destructive, process. Thatcher's stubbornness was insulting, but now that her resignation was official, she hoped he regretted not taking her seriously.

For twenty minutes Kiana tried to sleep, shifting restlessly in her seat as the plane floated toward Washington. Giving up, she checked her watch—ten-fifteen, eastern standard time—then raised the shade to a splash of sunlight that scalded her weary eyes. The trip was a godsend, she thought. Not only would she be able to finally advance her academic standing, but by leaving Houston, she could put Stanley Tregle firmly into her past.

The shock on Stanley's face when she had broken off their engagement still pained her, but the relief she felt after getting out of the one-sided relationship canceled out all of her guilt.

Why did I try to fool myself into believing he was right for me? she shuddered, ashamed to have fallen for a man with whom she had had nothing in common. A Desert Storm veteran, he had been content to live off a meager government check while waiting for a big payoff he was convinced he was due for the emotional hardships he suffered during the war. He had been so enthusiastic about his upcoming windfall, that for eight rocky months Kiana had believed him, supported him, even lent him money.

Humiliation filled Kiana as she chastised herself, again, for her poor judgment in men. With the treadmill dating scene behind her, she was determined to forget about men—at least until she finished her research project and completed her Ph.D.

After pressing a ten-dollar bill into the taxi driver's hand, Kiana refused his offer to help with her bag. She grabbed the oversized soft-sided suitcase on wheels and easily hoisted it out of the cab, then swept past the doorman and entered the lobby of the Quality Inn on Capitol Hill.

At the registration desk, she gave the attendant her name and handed over her American Express card.

"Good afternoon, Miss Sheridan," the sister at the computer beamed as she accepted Kiana's credit card. "Love your braids."

"Thank you," Kiana replied, her voice strong with pride. She touched the mass of softly woven hair cascading from the crown of her head, silently thanking her Nigerian neighbor, Cele Torouba, for doing her braids in exchange for a gaudy brass lamp. Traveling through the back roads of Tennessee without a hair dryer or a curling iron was going to put this new hair-do to the test.

The clerk shuffled some papers, then checked the card scanner.

"Um . . . Miss Sheridan. I'm sorry, but this card is no longer valid."

Embarrassment smoldered against her cheeks. "Not valid?" Kiana said, lips parted nervously. "It must be a mistake. Really. Try it again, please?"

"Certainly," the young lady replied, scanning the card again. She looked up, shook her head, then handed it back to Kiana. "Sorry. Do you have another one we could use?"

Digging into her purse, Kiana pulled out her Visa Gold and held her breath as she waited for it to clear, furious that the smooth-talking customer service agent at American Express had assured her that her late payment would cost her a fee but not cancel the account. Kiana clenched her jaws tightly. At one-nineteen a night she hoped there was enough credit on the Visa to pay the bill at checkout time.

"Thank you, Miss Sheridan," the clerk said, returning the card. "You are in room 2845. Elevators to the right. Do you need help with your bags?"

"No, thanks," Kiana said. "I can manage. I'm in training for a serious tour."

"Oh." The girl smiled. "Good luck."

"I'll need it," Kiana replied.

"Hmm . . ." The clerk was still clicking her way through the registration process. "There is a message here for you."

Kiana frowned. "Can you read it?"

"Sure." The clerk read, "Call me as soon as you arrive. Ida."

"Thanks," Kiana murmured vaguely.

After entering her room, she shut and bolted the door, then hoisted her suitcase onto the luggage rack. She removed jeans, sweat-shirts, a pair of high-topped hiking boots, and several pairs of thick white socks. She had packed only one dress—a printed wraparound affair she had purchased at a Pan-African festival last year.

At the mirror, Kiana attempted to repair her makeup with a light brush of nutmeg-colored powder to dull the shine on her forehead and a swirl of ruby-wine lipstick to brighten her lips. She ran an index finger over her thick straight brows, feathering the sleek hair above her chocolate brown eyes. Gently massaging her temples, she checked the clasps on the silver loops in her ears, then went to the telephone and punched in the number for Bering & Overton Advertising Agency.

"Hello, Ida," Kiana said, wishing her stepsister were not forc-ing this reunion. During the four years since Ida's release from prison, Kiana had called many times, written her letters, and even sent her stepsister several birthday gifts, but Ida had rudely refused any communication.

When Kiana's mother, a young widow with an infant, had married Ida's divorced father, Kiana had only been eighteen months old. Douglas Sheridan had immediately adopted Kiana and become the only father she had ever known. Ida, six years older and openly hostile, had shunned every overture Kiana had ever made to be a real sister, even a friend. So what could Ida possibly want now? After four long years of silence?

"My God," Ida blurted out in a clipped East Coast accent. "Why didn't you call me back last night? You hung up before I had a chance to ask about your flight. I could have met you at the airport. I left two messages on your machine."

"I was busy packing," Kiana replied.

"Well, I told you I could contact my friend at the Sheraton Premiere at Tyson's Corner and get you a real room. You really ought to stay in a nicer hotel."

"The Quality Inn is fine," Kiana managed tightly, not interested in benefiting from Ida's web of contacts.

Ida could produce the best hotel suite in the city, the best table in a restaurant, designer clothes at bargain-basement prices, or free tickets to any concert or event. She loved wheeling and dealing to get what she wanted, and thought nothing of living far beyond her means. Though her schemes had landed Ida in trouble many times, and she'd served six months in prison for a credit card scam, Ida had landed on her feet when Bering & Overton took a chance on her and brought her into the advertising industry.

"Let me see if I can't get you into the—" Ida started.

Kiana bit her lip, then stated flatly, "I'm happy where I am and, besides, I won't be in town that long."

"So I gather," Ida replied, a hint of disapproval in her voice. "What in the world are you thinking of? Giving up your job, closing down your apartment . . . to go off on a wilderness trek."

"A tour," Kiana corrected.

"Whatever. And this group you're going with? What's it called again?"

"The Sojourners," Kiana said.

"Oh?" The line was silent but Kiana could almost hear Ida's

agile mind scanning for a connection. "Marla Sherer, the president, and I are very good friends. Bering & Overton has her husband's advertising account. He's in high-rise condos, luxury hotels."

Before Kiana could make a comment, Ida flew ahead with Marla's credentials—as if Kiana cared.

"She's president of the Links, the Ladies of Distinction, and secretary of the district chapter of University Women. On the board of two museums . . . I forget which ones—"

Kiana stopped Ida's chatter. "Well, the next time you talk to her, thank her for me. The only reason I'm going on this particular tour is because Marla Sherer accepted my application."

"Tell me about it over dinner, okay?" Ida pressed. "I really want to see you. It's been too long."

Struck by the urgency in Ida's voice, Kiana relented. "Yes, it's been awhile."

"I have a design session with a client in Falls Church at eight. Why don't we meet early, say at six?"

"Sure," Kiana relented, her curiosity growing. This was not typical Ida talking. She wanted something, but what?

"How about F. Scotts in Georgetown. You know how to get there? Should I send a car?"

"No, Ida. That's not necessary. I can manage on the Metro just fine."

Ida clucked her tongue in disapproval. "You can be so provincial, Kiana. Why elbow your way through rush-hour travelers for a seat when you can ride in a limousine and relax?"

"It doesn't bother me. In fact, I rather like riding the Metro. We don't have anything like it in Houston."

"Suit yourself," Ida tossed back. "It's obvious you haven't changed."

"You're right, I probably haven't," Kiana answered. She paused, then as she replaced the receiver asked, "Have you?"

Chapter Two

AS soon as Kiana entered F. Scotts, she saw Ida sitting alone at a table for two on the far left side of the room. Thin, regal, and pale, Ida looked like a Fashion Fair model waiting to be discovered. She wore her hair in sleek ribboned fingerwaves that rippled up from a strong widow's peak and ended in a gentle fluff of black curls atop her head. Her navy blue Vittadini suit with Cartier accessories, contrasted with Kiana's beige-and-brown printed dress and clunky wooden jewelry like diamonds set against bamboo.

Kiana lifted her hand in greeting, then hurried over. After a quick peck on Ida's cheek, Kiana slid into her seat and appraised her stepsister's elegant dress, hair, and obviously real gold jewelry, impressed by Ida's radiant sophistication.

They had grown up on a farm near Centerville, Pennsylvania, and both had left the sprawling homestead at the same time. Kiana had entered Texas Southern University, then remained in Houston to get her masters and teach. Ida, who said she didn't care about a college education, had taken a job with a small community bank in Pittsburgh, and had eventually moved from minimum-wage teller to assistant comptroller. She did well, and had earned the confidence and trust of her coworkers and her boss, until all hell broke loose when it was discovered that Ida had juggled the books to embezzle close to two-hundred-thousand dollars from the bank's credit card accounts.

Someone, and Kiana still wondered who, had come up with the money to make a partial restitution. After serving time in a minimum-security facility, she was released on long-term probation. She had relocated to Washington, D.C., and after four short years was already a vice-president at Bering & Overton, one of the most elite advertising agencies in the country. Now Ida had an expense account, a tomato red Lexus, a spacious office on the forty-first floor of the Randolf Building overlooking the Potomac River, and an obsession to prove that she could amass more money with a high school diploma than Kiana ever would with a Ph.D.

Kiana ordered a Caesar salad and a glass of white wine. Leaning back, she settled into her chair and appraised her stepsister for the first time in over four years.

"You look . . . well," Ida said, forcing a stiff smile at Kiana as she pointedly observed her braided hair. "Interesting style."

"Thanks," Kiana replied, determined to take it as a compliment. "You look . . . prosperous, I'd have to say."

A self-assured smile came over Ida's face. "Can't complain," she said. "The agency is overloaded with clients. Everyone is working full tilt. I had hoped we'd get to spend some time together . . . shopping . . . the theater, but I'm afraid it's out of the question. I've just moved into a fabulous apartment in Chevy Chase, and if things weren't so hectic, I'd invite you over."

Kiana waved her hand in dismissal. "I understand. Maybe another time."

"So," Ida began, "you said you've finished your course work?"

"Finally," Kiana replied.

"Now your dissertation, right?"

"Right."

"What's the topic?" Ida asked, sipping her wine.

"A Study of the Nineteenth-Century Black Artists' Struggle for Economic Compensation—A Reparative Approach."

Ida's creamy smooth cheeks dimpled as she pursed her lips. "A reparative approach?" she repeated, eyes wide. "Like in reparations?"

"Exactly. And on this tour, I hope to dig up some information that I can use as foundation material in my dissertation."

Ida folded both arms, then laid them flat on the table, piercing Kiana with a reproachful expression. "I hope you aren't seriously getting involved with this reparations mess."

Kiana's lips parted slightly. A look of exasperation came to her face. "Mess? I'm afraid I don't see it that way. I've attended a few meetings, shown my support."

Ida lifted her chin, zeroing in on Kiana. "I remember when you were in high school. You were always protesting, marching, raising hell about something. I would have thought that you had outgrown the desire to make a public spectacle of yourself. Reparations? Why that?"

"Because I believe in the concept," Kiana tossed back icily, even though she wasn't sure yet how she felt about the issue. She was hoping her studies would help clarify it for her.

"Don't you realize how damaging it can be to align yourself with unpopular causes. *Those* people . . ."

"What people?" Kiana interrupted, taking umbrage. She and Ida had never gotten along and now it was painfully evident why. She'd been right to stay away.

"Those militants, that's who!" Ida hissed in a loud whisper, glancing around as if she were afraid someone she knew might overhear their conversation. "I've seen them on talk shows ranting and raving about what blacks are due. Excuse me, but don't you think black people ought to stop begging for handouts? If they've got time to go around the country spouting off, they can get busy and work . . . help themselves. All this talk about payback is alienating white people . . . driving them to keep us from economic opportunities. You'd better be careful, Kiana. You're going to run into people who don't share your views."

"I'm sure I will," Kiana agreed, not raising her voice. Trying to discuss any slightly controversial subject with Ida was as useless as trying to keep ice from melting in the sun. Her self-centered attitude was shockingly disturbing, and Kiana wondered if Ida was capable of having compassion for any cause other than her own. "I'm sorry you have such a narrow view of reparations, Ida, but don't worry. I have no plans of trying to convert you to my way of thinking. Right now, all I want to do is concentrate on finishing Mother's family history, and if possible, I want to use parts of it in my dissertation."

"Your mother's family history?" Ida blinked, her heavily mascaraed lashes fluttering in surprise. "What exactly do you mean?"

"I'm tracing Great-great-grandfather's artistic legacy and I want to incorporate what I find into my thesis. Then, hopefully, I'll finish the book Mother started."

Ida set her wineglass carefully on the table. "You're tracing the origin of Soddy Glass?" Her voice was taut with interest. "What prompted this?"

Kiana twirled a piece of lettuce on her fork. "You won't believe what happened to me, right before Christmas last year."

"What?"

"I was at an auction in Houston. Several pieces of glass, which looked exactly like Great-great-grandfather's work, were put up for bid."

"So?"

"So, each piece sold for thousands of dollars. One went for thirty-seven hundred."

"Really?" Ida stared wide-eyed at Kiana, then her eyes narrowed suspiciously as if she did not believe what she had just heard. "Thirty-seven hundred dollars? For that ugly stuff?"

"Yes. Can you believe that old glass we used to play with at Grandmother's going for such outlandish prices?"

"Well," Ida hedged, "I did read in *Antiques Today* that black art has become quite collectible, especially among wealthy blacks."

"Whites, too, let me assure you," Kiana said. "But thirty-seven hundred dollars for a vase?" She sat back, eyes level with Ida's, watching as her stepsister nervously stroked the tiny finger waves rippling up from her temples.

"Do you think it was real Soddy Glass?" Ida asked.

Kiana tilted her head. "Funny you should ask. No. I don't think it was. I am beginning to think the pieces were very good reproductions and I'm going to find out where they came from."

Ida suddenly shrugged as if no longer interested, flipped open her compact, and studied her bow-shaped lips. "Did you talk to the auctioneer?"

"Yes, but she knew little about the original source of the glass. She bought the pieces from a man named Marvin Watts, an antique dealer and glass expert in Nashville, Tennessee."

Ida snapped the compact closed with a loud click. "You're not going to Nashville, are you?"

"I sure am," Kiana said.

"So what do you expect this guy, Watts, to say? *If* you find him? I doubt he'd admit that the glass was not authentic. Sounds like a stupid wild-goose chase if you ask me."

"I didn't ask you, Ida." The words flew out before Kiana had had time to think. She grimaced. "I don't mean to be rude, but someone may be ripping off a legacy that belongs to me, to my family. This is important."

Ida sniffed and raised her chin, obviously insulted. "I can see it is . . . to you."

Kiana deliberately held her tongue for a second, angered by Ida's comment. "I'm sorry you feel that way. Your father adopted me, and we really are sisters. Grandma Hester and I may be the only surviving blood ancestors of Soddy Russell, but you shouldn't consider yourself an outsider."

Ida drew in a low breath, then let it out. "Sure," she said lowly. "Suit yourself, but you're probably wasting your time. Really! You can get so wrapped up in your crazy fights for justice."

Kiana bristled. "I can't sit by and let people illegally profit from Soddy Russell's work."

"I guess not," Ida replied, exasperation heavy in her voice. "When do you leave?"

"The tour orientation is tomorrow afternoon, then we have four free days for sightseeing and research at the Library of Congress, but I'm going to use those days to go see Grandma."

"You're going to Centerville?" Ida asked.

"Yes. I want Grandma Hester to help fill in some blank spots. Have you seen her lately?"

"No," Ida said. "It's been months since I even talked to her."

"Why don't you come with me?" Kiana asked, feeling bad that their get-together hadn't gone better. "It would be nice to get back to the old place, see Grandma . . ."

"I'm sure it would," Ida agreed coolly, "but I can't leave town right now." She paused, a secretive smile curving her lips. "You see, I'm engaged. My fiancé and I have plans this weekend." She held up her ring finger, flashing a large Marquis diamond.

"You're *engaged*?" Kiana was truly surprised.

"Yes. And he is wonderful."

"Who is he?"

"His name is Bonard Wilson. A very successful financial investor. He's also running for a seat in Congress. From Maryland."

"Congratulations," Kiana murmured, realizing that this made the third time Ida had made such an announcement. "When will I get to meet him?"

Ida lowered her chin and fixed a serious look on Kiana. "We're having a party to announce his campaign kickoff on Saturday. I'd like you to come but . . ." She made a tent with her fingers and pressed her lips to them. "But that depends on whether or not you can keep quiet about the . . . uh . . . difficulties I've had in the past."

"Keep quiet? Ida! What a thing to say!" Kiana was hurt by the implication of Ida's request. "I have no reason whatsoever to discuss your past. With anyone."

Ida gave her head a curt jerk to the side. "True. But I have to be sure. No one in D.C. knows about it and you can imagine what Bonard's opponents, or the press, could do with such information."

"Does Bonard know?"

"No," Ida said defiantly, "and there is no reason for him to ever find out. It's a closed chapter of my life. I was confused. I made a mistake. I paid for it. Bonard's campaign cannot be jeopardized. Understand?"

"I do, indeed," Kiana agreed coldly. "Face it, Ida. You and I move in very different circles. I doubt anyone would question me."

"You never know what to expect in politics," Ida murmured. "I know you. You can be so . . . so damned honest and impulsive sometimes. Be careful what you say and to whom, Kiana," Ida warned.

"You can trust me, but I won't lie for you, if that's what you're asking."

Ida looked visibly disgusted. "Fine. But don't go volunteering anything, you hear?"

"Okay. Don't get into a panic." Kiana signaled the waiter. "I won't be able to make your party, anyway, but thanks."

The tension eased when the waiter brought the check, and Kiana grew a bit envious to see the platinum American Express card Ida plunked down. Ida's drive to be somebody had pushed her up the social and professional ladders, and now it appeared she was about to mount the political ladder, too.

"Well. You can't say I didn't invite you," Ida muttered curtly.

"No, I can't," Kiana agreed. "Send me pictures of the party and of Bonard." She was anxious to end the evening before she and Ida found themselves parting under even worse terms.

"Send them where?" Ida said critically. "You don't even have an address."

"To Grandma's," Kiana replied.

"All right," Ida said, then hurriedly added, "Leave me your itinerary. Fax it to my office, okay? I'd like to know how to find you in case something comes up. With Grandmother."

"Sure, I'll do it first thing in the morning," Kiana agreed, giving Ida a quick peck on the cheek before leaving.

Ida remained in the restaurant, staring after Kiana, trying to decide what to do. Why was Kiana suddenly fixated on finishing her mother's book? And this determination to talk to Grandma Hester! Why, she was so feeble and locked in the past she probably wouldn't even recognize Kiana, let alone be able to carry on a decent conversation. Ida remembered her last conversation with Hester as a rambling, disjointed effort to communicate that had brought on a raging headache.

Ida sniffed her dismissal. Well, I'm glad Kiana won't be in town very long, she thought. She'd only complicate my plans. Bonard's campaign kickoff is too important to risk a slip of her tongue. God only knows what radical topics Kiana might bring up.

Ida rose from her chair and headed toward the ladies' room as she mentally clicked off the names of the society couples and successful black business people she had invited to the party.

Smiling to herself, she thought about those bourgeois types who had snubbed her at Bering & Overton when she had been the lowest paid secretary at the firm. They'd soon be scrambling for invitations to one of the most extravagant celebrations ever held in Washington, D.C. Just wait, she thought, I'll wipe those smug smiles off their faces when Bonard is elected to Congress.

Ida sighed. Catching Bonard Wilson had been easy, getting him to the altar had taken longer than she'd planned, but her carefully orchestrated strategy had been flawless. Literally bumping into him at the Black Artists of the Twentieth Century exhibit at the Museum of Art two years ago had been a stroke of luck. The fact that his interest in and appreciation of African art rivaled hers, had been destiny working overtime on her behalf.

Ida had been happy to chat with the astute collector and after only a few moments of conversation, had realized that the compatibility level between herself and the wealthy investor was high enough for her to overlook his coarsely attractive features and rather flashy dress to let her calculating mind rule her heart for a change. Bored by the good-looking wanabes who were great in bed but had little to offer, Ida had been holding out for just the right man: one with the financial wherewithal and obsessive drive to create the type of lifestyle she hungered for—and Bonard Wilson seemed fit for the role.

When she calculatingly, yet casually, revealed her ancestral connection (leaving out the fact that the connection was through marriage, not blood) to the glassmaker Soddy Russell, Bonard had quickly elevated their chance encounter to a higher level of intimacy. He had immediately invited her to lunch. One week later they made love, two weeks later he told her she was the woman he wanted to marry, but didn't offer a ring.

The waiting had dragged on and on, but Ida had hung in there until Bonard decided to announce his candidacy for Congress. His chances of getting elected would be more favorable if he had a beautiful, dutiful, competent Mrs. Bonard Wilson by his side.

Now Ida gazed at her five carat Marquis diamond, twisting it to allow the light to spiral off its faceted surface. She sighed, wishing she were truly in love and could feel that crazy fluttering sensation in the pit of her stomach whenever she thought about Bonard—as she had with so many others—but she told herself it really didn't matter. She was in love with Bonard's ambition and money, and the way he liked to spend it—on her and on the acquisition of beautiful works of art.

Why did Kiana have to come back into her life and stir things up now? Ida fumed. Just when everything was falling into place. She entered the ladies' room and went to the pay phone. Reaching for the receiver, Ida felt a nagging worry interrupt her thoughts, and her hand stopped in midair. She recalled an article she'd read in a magazine about how the elderly could remember the past but often forgot what they had done an hour earlier.

Ida lifted the handset, dropped in a quarter, and rapidly dialed, frowning to hear a recorded message.

"Marla. Ida Sheridan here. Please give me a call-back tonight. Any time. No matter how late. I need to talk to you about a tour I understand your group, the Sojourners, is sponsoring. It's very important. Thanks."

Ida slowly hung up the phone. Well, if Grandma Hester remembers, so what? Ida silently calculated. No one is going to take the word of a ninety-one-year-old woman as gospel truth. And if Kiana asks, I'll just deny it. She was too young to remember a thing.

Chapter Three

THE tufted leather chair was comfortable, the atmosphere quietly elegant. Kiana cast a wary eye down the length of the polished cherry table, then up to the square brass clock. Why was she the only person in the room?

Impatiently, she took out the letter and read it again. Today was Thursday, June 3, she was in the right museum, room 301. The receptionist at the front desk had greeted her warmly and given her directions. What was going on? If Mr. Tandy had changed the time or the place, why the devil hadn't he informed anyone?

Too restless to wait any longer, Kiana stood. She might be missing the orientation. As she started toward the door, a man entered. He was carrying a green canvas gym bag in one hand, and his eyes were riveted on a piece of paper held loosely in the other. Kiana stopped. Holding onto the back of her chair, she quickly sized up the man who appeared to be a member of the tour.

He wore an expensive-looking, though rumpled, gray Armani jacket that had been casually tossed over a plain white T-shirt. His faded stonewashed jeans were stuffed into cowboy boots that hugged his legs midcalf—the scuffs and scratches on the worn black leather contributed to a casual, nonchalant statement that was more attractive than shoddy. The overhead light sheened his curly dark hair that glistened with just enough hair oil to make him look well-groomed—without the greasy look of a jeri curl.

When the confident, good-looking brother stepped into the room, he looked up at Kiana in surprise, then without speaking, crossed the room in a long-legged stride, his scuffed boots thumping the carpeted floor.

"Hi," he said, pushing the slip of paper into his bag.

"Hello," Kiana said. She tried not to stare. The man was lean, ruggedly attractive, yet didn't have the unnatural swagger of the cowboy look-alikes who usually dressed as he was. This guy seemed very much at home in his clothes, and she was glad someone close to her age was going to be on the tour. She didn't know why, but she had assumed she'd be traveling with a group of ladies who might be old enough to be her grandmother.

His face was the color of rich sweet raisins—free of wrinkles, burnished by the sun, and a feathering of delicate lines came together at the corners of his eyes when he smiled and said, "A little early, aren't you?"

Tilting her head to one side, Kiana looked at him in question, noticing that the faintest shadow of a mustache curved above his lips and beneath a finely sculpted nose.

"Early? I thought everyone else was late." Kiana forced her eyes from his bronze hands and tried to smile. "I'm glad you showed up." Relaxing, she felt the taut muscles in her face begin to soften.

"Showed up?" he asked.

"Yes. This is room 301 isn't it?"

"Yep," he replied, nodding.

"Well I've been here since a quarter to four. I was beginning to think I was the only person going on the tour. You'd think a notice would have been posted if there were going to be a time change. Who the hell is this man"—she checked her letter again —"Rexford Tandy to leave people hanging like this?" Kiana expelled air from her lungs in a loud, impatient sigh. "I was starting to get ticked off."

"What's your name?" he asked, moving to sit sideways on the table, one booted foot braced on the floor, the other leg bent casually at the knee.

Kiana's gaze roamed the length of his jeans-clad leg, unable to miss the visible bulge of muscle that strained against the worn denim fabric stretched across his thigh. Lifting her eyes, she answered. "Kiana Sheridan. I'm here for the Underground Railroad Tour."

"Oh," he said, smiling, an interested flame lighting his eyes. "*You're* Kiana Sheridan?" He pointedly looked her over. "And I thought you would be some bespectacled little lady, wearing orthopedic shoes."

Unable to share in his joke, she frowned. "How do you know my name?"

"Because your name was on the list."

"For the tour?"

"Yeah, but this is the room for the landscape photo class. The tour you were registered for was canceled." He leaned back and pierced her with darkly confident eyes.

"Canceled? When?" Surely he was mistaken.

"This morning, I'm sorry to say." Bending closer, he extended his hand. "Let me introduce myself. I'm Rex Tandy, the guide who was scheduled to escort your tour."

Kiana's mouth fell slack. Pausing to take in what he had said, she started to reply, then held back as she accepted his outstretched hand. When her fingers closed over his firm dry palm, she knew that Rexford Tandy was a natural charmer; a man who made his living greeting strangers, gaining their confidence, winning them over in the span of a handshake.

"Well," Kiana said firmly, her anger gathering momentum, "why the hell didn't you bother to inform me of your decision to cancel the tour, Mr. Tandy? I'm a long way from home and I can't go back."

As if stung, Rex flinched. "That wasn't my responsibility."

Beads of perspiration crowned Kiana's silky brow, and a vein began pulsing at her temple.

Ducking his head, Rex pulled out a chair and sat down facing her, denim-covered legs slightly apart. He put his elbows on his knees, folded his hands, and centered them between himself and Kiana.

Gradually, Kiana let her eyes connect with Rex's. Defiance radiated from her unflinching gaze, making clear the strength of her resolve. She congratulated herself to see Rex shifting nervously in his chair.

"Don't be angry with me, Miss Sheridan," he started. "I didn't make the decision to cancel the tour."

She was not appeased. "Don't give me that 'it's not my job' cop-out." Kiana slammed the letter down on the table, her palm making a loud, flat crack.

Startled, Rex told her, "I'm not copping out! Really. All I know is that the Sojourners canceled. I don't know why. They probably couldn't get enough members to sign up."

"I doubt that." Kiana clucked her tongue in dismissal. "I was put on a waiting list for six weeks before I got a spot. That tour was booked solid months ago."

"There is a good possibility that the trip will be rescheduled for August," Rex offered lamely.

"You've got to be kidding. August! What good is that?" Kiana was furious.

"You have every right to be upset, and please don't think I take this cancellation lightly, either. I write for *Black Culture Watch*, in addition to teaching photo classes and taking out tours for the Smithsonian. I had set aside a block of my time for the trip. Now that it's canceled, I have to adjust my work schedule, too."

"How unfortunate for you," Kiana said sarcastically. "I gave up my teaching position, sold my car, and basically planned my future around this trip. I have quite a bit at stake here and I don't have the time or the money to be playing around." With the heel of her hand she shoved the letter back and forth, the reality of her predicament settling in.

She realized that she was more frightened than enraged by this turn of events. What was she supposed to do now? "I really can't sympathize with you, Mr. Tandy," she said. "You have no idea how disastrous this is."

"I'm sorry," Rex said, genuine regret in his voice. "I can see what a disappointment this is."

"That's an understatement," Kiana grumbled, crumpling the letter in her fist, jettisoning it across the room. Fastening an icy gaze on Rex, she asked, "So, Mr. Tandy, what happens now? Do

I get a refund? An apology? Or am I supposed to say, 'Oh that's okay' and catch the next flight back to Houston?" She folded her arms defiantly across her chest, waiting for his response.

Rex wiped his mouth with a nervous hand. "I wish I had the answers to your questions, but I don't." He cleared his throat, one hand to his lips as he thought. "I'm surprised you weren't notified about the cancellation."

"I flew in yesterday. I was at a hotel. I never got a message."

"Well, I'm sure your money will be refunded."

"That's a comfort. But when?" Kiana's financial state was already precarious. Easing forward, she said, "I'd better not have to wait weeks to get it."

Rex lifted his hands defensively. "Hold on. I'm not *certain* when your money will be refunded, but we can find out. You need to talk to Felton Mills."

Kiana clutched her purse to her stomach in stubborn refusal, glaring at Rex as if she were about to explode. "I'm not in the mood for a runaround—a lot of double talk."

"I know. I know," Rex urged, taking Kiana's hand.

She started to pull away, then relented and stood up.

"Mills is a pretty regular guy," Rex said. "Believe me, he's not about to let a dissatisfied customer walk out of here. He can't afford that. We'll get this straightened out. Pronto. His office is right down the hall."

The rich wood paneling in Felton Mills's office gave the room a warm cozy feeling. Rex left Kiana standing by the door and strode across the parquet floor toward Mills's raven-haired secretary.

"Rex!" She smiled, hanging up the phone as she glanced at Kiana, then back to Rex. She raised her brows. "You're teaching the landscape photo class this evening, right?"

"Yeah. Five o'clock." Rex turned to Kiana, motioning her closer. "Brenda, is Mills in? This is Kiana Sheridan. She needs to speak with him."

"Hello," Brenda said, shaking Kiana's hand. "You didn't have an appointment, did you?"

"No," Kiana said.

Brenda sighed in relief. "I didn't think so. Mr. Mills is out, won't be back in the office until Monday."

Rex frowned. "This is a mess, Brenda. Miss Sheridan came in for the orientation for the Underground Railroad Tour."

"Oh my," Brenda said vaguely. "That tour was canceled this morning." She opened a drawer and took out a folder. "My assistant was supposed to notify everyone. No one called you?"

"No," Kiana replied. Brenda riffled through some papers, then stopped when Kiana asked, "What happened? I went through extensive preparations for this trip. The Sojourners accepted me. I thought everything was arranged."

"I didn't get the details, Miss Sheridan. All I know is that Marla Sherer, the president of the Sojourners, called early this morning and said that the trip had to be postponed. Something about an emergency session of the group had been called and that was the decision."

"Great," Kiana grumbled. And just last night she'd been praising Sherer to Ida. "What about my refund?"

"Oh," Brenda murmured, perplexed. "It will be ready on Monday. As soon as Mr. Mills gets back. He will have to handle it."

"And what am I supposed to do in the meantime?" Kiana wanted to know.

Brenda raised her shoulders. "All I can say, Miss Sheridan, is that it *will* be straightened out, I assure you, but not until Monday morning."

"Well I can't sit around the Quality Inn running up my bill waiting for Mr. Mills to return."

"I understand and I apologize for this inconvenience . . ."

"Inconvenience!" Kiana was incredulous. "You don't have a clue how inconvenient this is. Not to mention how expensive! I want this straightened out. Now!"

Rex attempted to take Kiana by the arm, but she stepped away.

"Brenda," Rex asked, "can't this be settled before Monday?"

"I don't see how," Brenda said. "I don't have the authority to issue checks. It will have to be handled by Mr. Mills."

"I can't believe this is happening," Kiana said.

"Please, Miss Sheridan," Brenda said, "maybe we can pick up part of the costs at your hotel. I'll see what I can do. Okay?" She pulled out a form on which she wrote Kiana's name. "If you will please fill out this request for a refund, it will get things started right away. I apologize for this. Really. It's never happened before."

Kiana abruptly took the pen from Brenda, jotted down the name of her hotel, then signed the form, and put the pen down firmly. She turned to leave the room.

"Brenda, push this through ASAP, okay?" Rex pleaded, one eye on the door as it banged shut.

"I'll do what I can, Rex," Brenda said, shrugging her shoulders.

"Thanks." Rex rushed out the door, entering the hallway just as Kiana rounded the corner at the end of the corridor and disappeared. He heard the ding of the elevator's arrival, then a whoosh as the doors slid shut. He ran to the stairwell and dashed down all three flights, determined to intercept Kiana.

Chapter Four

JESUS, what a mess, Kiana thought, wishing she had the financial resources to go on the trip alone. Frustrated by the sense of helplessness that being strapped for money created, she was boiling mad when the elevator doors slid open.

Kiana stepped out and was startled to see Rex Tandy on the far side of the lobby. She glared at him, then turned away. What did he want? He was only a free-lance tour guide and magazine writer who sure couldn't solve her problems.

"Miss Sheridan!" he called out to her.

Kiana acted as if she hadn't heard him and continued toward the exit doors. "Let the museum deal with it," she muttered under her breath, walking faster, trying to keep her face turned from him. Her disappointment lay like a stone in her chest and she feared she might start crying. After months of planning and anticipation, it had all come down to this? The last thing she wanted right now was sympathy from a stranger.

"Please! Don't go!" he called out.

She spun around. "Why not?"

"Because I'd like to talk to you." He raced across the polished marble floor and stopped beside the front door.

"We have nothing to talk about, I assure you," Kiana said, stepping out of the way of a man and a woman who were exiting the building. When they had passed, Kiana pushed the door open.

Rex put out his hand and stopped her. "I can see how important the tour was and how disappointed you are. But don't leave angry."

Kiana's misery was so acute she felt a burning in her stomach. She swallowed dryly, then spoke. "I've got to go."

"Where are you going?"

"Back to my hotel."

"To sit and sulk and worry?"

Kiana shrugged.

"I thought so," Rex said. He stepped around to position himself in front of Kiana, blocking her path. "Look. I was supposed to be your tour guide through Tennessee, so let me be your guide while you're here in D.C." He gave her a glint of a smile and waited for her reply.

"I don't feel much like sightseeing," she said. "Besides, I thought you had a class to teach."

"I do. So, how about tomorrow?"

She hesitated.

"Hey, you can trust me," he said. "You would have been stuck with me for four weeks on the road."

Now Kiana laughed, feeling slightly ashamed. She was not concerned about going off with Rex, in fact he was a rather pleasant guy, but she was so distraught about the cancellation, she couldn't think about seeing the sights.

Rex took advantage of her hesitation. "You're stuck here until Monday, right?"

Kiana nodded.

"So, you might as well let me take you around to some of the historic sites in the city."

"That's true," Kiana admitted. She stared past him out the double glass doors and let her gaze rest on the sweep of manicured grass in front of the museum. Spending time with Rex Tandy might beat another miserable dinner with Ida, or a weekend of watching TV. "I can't get out of this, can I?"

"Nope," he said. "Where are you staying?"

"The Quality Inn on Capitol Hill."

"I'll call you tomorrow morning."

"Fine."

Grinning like a teenager, Rex kept his eyes on Kiana as he walked backward toward the elevator. "Gotta go. See you tomorrow. And be sure to wear your walking shoes. There's a lot I want you to see."

Sitting in the darkened room, clicking through his slides of the New England countryside, Rex tried to give his students as informative a lecture as possible, but knew his presentation lacked enthusiasm. He checked his watch in the stream of light coming from the slide projector, wishing his evening were free. If he hadn't already missed the first round of matches in the amateur boxing tournament, he'd call Lionel and cancel, but another broken date with his baby brother was more than he could afford. He'd better be ringside tonight.

When the slides came to an end he snapped on the light, asking if there were any questions. One student wanted clarification about night lighting. Another needed information about lenses to use when photographing water in bright sunlight. Rex answered their questions, dismissed the class, and hurriedly packed his gear.

It was dark and a light drizzle had begun to slick the streets. Traffic was so sluggishly tangled that the ten-minute drive to Pauley's Gym on Florida Avenue was taking twice as long as it normally would. The windshield wipers whipped back and forth, drumming up thoughts of Kiana Sheridan. She was strikingly beautiful and he loved the way her braids hung like soft curls around her face. And her eyes—like glittering pieces of jet. Rex considered himself a better-than-average judge of women and he took pleasure in impressing those who caught his eye, and Kiana certainly had.

At thirty-four, Rex Tandy had been engaged once, in love twice, and had recently evicted his live-in lover, Lashandra—a fashion model with whom he had shared his life and his town house on Capitol Hill for the past eight months. Now that she was out of his life, he felt relieved, but an emptiness persisted that he found hard to shake. Having Lashandra around had definitely been preferable to going it alone.

When Rex pulled to a stop in front of Pauley's Gym, he hoped the boxing match would not last longer than four rounds. After he dropped Lionel at his parents' house, he'd go home and call Kiana tonight.

The nickel-colored smoke hanging over the gym was about as annoying as the lingering odor of the sweaty youthful bodies that had trained at Pauley's over the years. Not much had changed in the cavernous hall in the fifteen years since Rex had donned his gloves and black satin trunks to challenge one of Pauley Rebatta's muscled protégés. The walls had been splashed with a fresh coat of paint and the overhead lighting was a little better, but the tiny roped-off ring in the center of the gym still sagged in the middle, its worn canvas floor a testament to all the young men who had danced over it.

Rex relaxed when the bell sounded to end round two. He slumped back from the edge of his seat and gave his brother a thumbs-up and a wink. So far so good, Rex thought, impressed, yet concerned by the raw, reckless way Lionel had gone after his opponent. Plucky aggression was an admirable trait, but Rex found the cool gleam in Lionel's eyes and the way he propelled his entire body into the fight disturbing.

As a teenager Rex had chosen boxing lessons at Pauley's Gym over hanging out on street corners and had wound up with a physique that the girls found impressive. Lionel was different. Almost twenty years younger, Lionel trained at the gym solely to perfect his survival techniques, to learn how to more effectively bruise the flesh and break the bones of those who challenged his turf. The hungry streets of Columbia Heights were Lionel Tandy's domain, and the hours he spent slapping the punching bag with his shiny hard gloves were his hours of combat training.

By round four Bubba, Lionel's opponent, was bleeding above the right eye and struggling to stand. The young men sparred, clinched, then fell against the ropes, tussling until Lionel managed to deliver a sharp left, and send Bubba reeling backward. He crumpled to the mat like a drunk man slipping on a wet barroom floor. Lionel stood panting in triumph over him.

The referee finished the count, then held up Lionel's hand in victory. A long-legged girl in a silver lamé bikini handed Lionel a gold trophy. With a nod of his head, both thumbs up, Rex saluted his brother, then began shouldering his way toward the locker room.

Later, on the way home, Rex realized that Lionel was unusually quiet. After the frenzied shouts of congratulations at the gym, the silence in the car seemed uncomfortable. Rex could feel his brother withdrawing, as he had begun to do whenever they tried to have a one-on-one conversation. Rex turned down the volume on the radio, quieting 2Pac's "Definition of a Thug Nigga," and braked to a stop at the light.

"When's summer school start?" Rex asked, trying to sound as nonjudgmental as possible. Lionel had a failed algebra class to make up.

"Dunno yet," Lionel replied, turning his chiseled face toward the open passenger window. As arrogantly handsome as any male model gracing the pages of *Ebony Man*, he had little concern for his appearance, preferring to dress in baggy pants slung low on his hips, oversized Air Jordans, which he never laced up, and any kind of shirt as long as it was black.

Rex frowned, infuriated by his brother's flippant attitude. Born when Rex was a senior in high school, Lionel had grown up to be a pushy, demanding adolescent who didn't appreciate the love and support his family tried to give him. Lionel shunned Rex's advice, ignored his parents, and generally did as he pleased, rarely discussing his comings and goings with anyone.

"What's that mean?" Rex asked, disgusted by Lionel's evasive reply.

"It means I dunno if I'm going. I might hang loose." Lionel toyed with the zipper pull on his jacket, face still turned from Rex.

"Well, are you thinking about looking for a job?" Rex asked.

"Doing what?" Lionel said curtly, swinging around, brown eyes narrowed in challenge. "What jobs you know about for sixteen-year-olds around here? Get real."

"You'll be seventeen next week," Rex said, determined to keep the discussion positive.

"No difference." Lionel's voice had no positive life.

"Oh, I don't know," Rex said. "I might be able to get you on at *Black Culture Watch*. Packing, delivering magazines. Things like that. I can check."

"Hey, man. Don't bother." Lionel laughed. "I'm gonna be busy at the gym. You know. Pumpin' up. Things are gettin' pretty raggedy in the hood. Gotta stay prepared."

Rex stepped on the gas and sped through the intersection of 13th and Irving, distressed by the lighthearted way Lionel alluded to his association with the Sharps—a loosely organized neighborhood gang that, as far as Rex had been able to determine, engaged in graffiti warfare and sporadic fistfights with their rival to the east—the Treps. The eight square blocks bounded by Kenyon, 15th, Belmont, and 11th belonged to the Sharps—turf that was hauntingly familiar to Rex. In the old days he had delivered newspapers in the community that was now a run-down, dangerous ghetto.

"I know it's tough out there, Lionel, but—"

"But what?" Lionel cut Rex off. "But you think I oughta stay out of it. Right?"

"Right," Rex finished bluntly. "You need to go to summer school, catch up on your math, and stay off of the streets. You'll get caught up in some dangerous situation if you don't watch out . . . if you don't get killed first, hanging with those thugs you call your friends."

"Oh! So now the homies who protect me are thugs, huh?" Lionel dipped low to better see Rex's face. "You know 'em. Momma knows 'em. They're the brothers and cousins of the same guys you ran with. They all grew up on Lamont and Kenyon, the same damn streets where you used to hang out."

"Right," Rex said. "*Used* to. Things have changed."

"Oh? Tell me something I don't know. You went off to college, got you a degree, and bought a three-story pad over on the Hill. Now everything is okay? You *just* got your ass out the hood, Rex, so don't go judging my friends and don't forget you got a momma and a daddy back on Lamont who still have to deal with the shit that goes down outside their door. Everyday, Rex. We gotta deal with this shit."

"You think I don't know what you have to put up with? Living like prisoners? I told Dad I could help you guys move to a better place. Someplace nice. Safe."

"What's Daddy gonna look like living over in Silver Spring? Alexandria? Please. He's lived on Lamont for forty years and he ain't gonna run away now."

"So, what can I do? Huh?" Rex asked, exasperated, tired of the guilt trip Lionel was determined to lay down. As long as his parents refused to move from the neighborhood that their friends had abandoned long ago, there was little Rex could do.

"You can't do nothin', that's what," Lionel said. "Leave them alone. Leave me alone, too."

"I won't do that," Rex threw back. "Maybe Momma and Dad are stuck . . . but it's their choice. You're too young to settle, Lionel, and I refuse to lose you to the streets! You don't need to be running around all night chasing after gangs, getting your kicks playing war." Rex was beginning to believe that the problems ran too deep for him to ever get through to Lionel.

"Hey, at least I'm doing something," Lionel said. "I live here. I'm not about to run away—like *some* people I know. I'd never turn tail and hide out across town." Lionel sniffed loudly, grimacing as he drew his shoulders back in an attempt to show how tough he was. The corded vein in his smooth brown neck pulsed in anger and frustration. "The Treps will be in for a fight if they try to take over my block. Let 'em show their ugly faces over on Lamont. I'm ready for their asses. Wait and see."

Wearied by the discussion that he knew would only go in circles, Rex forced himself to be silent. Yes, he had been fortunate enough to get a college degree. Yes, he had money in the bank and was able to support himself in his brownstone on Avenue C that he was working hard to restore. Why shouldn't he live in a safe neighborhood, live the kind of life he had worked hard to afford? But Lionel was his only brother. He had to try.

"Lionel," Rex began, "I understand where you're coming from. There *is* a war going on, but being in a gang isn't the way to win it. Spray painting everything, beating up guys. It's not going to solve anything. You need to finish school, really focus on your education. There are better ways to work on the problems around here."

"Yeah? And how's that?" Lionel asked. "You went off and got yourself educated. So what are you doing to change things in Columbia Heights?"

Rex sighed, unable to explain it. How could he make Lionel see that his work with the Smithsonian and *Black Culture Watch* were his ways of reaching out, of putting something back into the community to educate people about alternatives to violence? He paid his taxes, voted, and diligently worked within the system to get his messages across. But his accomplishments only seemed to inspire contempt in Lionel.

"All I can say, little brother, is that hanging out—planning revenge attacks—is not going to do a thing but get you killed."

Lionel sputtered in derisive laughter, one hand across the bottom half of his face. "I hate to break it down to you, bro, but if anybody's steppin' out in dangerous waters, it's you!"

Rex frowned. "What are you talking about?"

"I told you, man. Don't be walkin' around the hood takin' pictures, askin' questions. You better kill that story you been tellin' everybody you doin' on the Treps and the Sharps. If *Black Culture Watch* runs it, you're in deep shit, man. You're gonna be marked, if you know what I mean."

Rex rounded the corner of 13th and Lamont, pulled to the curb in front of his parents' narrow row house, and put the car into park. "Marked? Who said that, Lionel?" he asked.

"I dunno," Lionel said, averting his eyes. He opened the door, stepped out, then leaned back to warn Rex again. "The brothers are tense, understand? You got some shots they ain't too happy about. Anything could fly off . . . anytime."

"What's going down?"

"Hey, man. I don't know nothin'. It's just somethin' I heard on the streets."

Rex sat in the car after Lionel went inside, thinking about his brother's warning. An aimless parade of young men criss-crossed the street, strutting past in baggy pants, baseball caps turned to the side.

Am I fooling myself to think that my articles and photography can help turn this mess around? Rex wondered, sickened by the hollow realization that he couldn't even reach his own brother.

Chapter Five

By noon on Friday Kiana and Rex had already shuffled through the public rooms of the White House, visited the Treasury Department for an overview of the history of U.S. currency, and were strolling down Pennsylvania Avenue eating chocolate ice cream cones.

"What would you like to see next?" Rex asked.

"I'd like to drop by the Library of Congress," Kiana said, halting at Ninth Avenue. "There's some information I'd like to check."

"You're working on your dissertation, right?" Rex said.

"Yes," Kiana replied, pushing a slender braid off her shoulder. "I finally got the course work done."

"In?" he asked, lightly holding onto her elbow as they stepped off the curb and rushed across the busy intersection.

"In humanities—with a focus on American History," she replied, glancing over at Rex. He had removed his sunglasses and was wiping them with his handkerchief. Nice, Kiana thought, liking the warm flecks of gold that shimmered in his dark brown eyes. For some reason she instantly felt more at ease.

"Where are you doing your advance work?" Rex asked, resettling his glasses on his face.

"Texas Southern."

"Good for you."

"It hasn't been easy." Kiana ran her tongue over the dripping chocolate, laughing as she recalled. "For the past six years, I've been teaching full time . . . tenth grade social studies, taking night classes. It's been hectic."

"I can imagine," Rex empathized. "I remember being in a similar situation when I was working full-time selling radios and TVs at Circuit City, on my feet all day, going to school at night. Things got a little easier when I got a Carver Fellowship to Howard and only had to work part-time."

They paused to sit on the steps of the National Gallery of Art to finish their ice cream as they talked.

"What's your dissertation on?" Rex asked.

Kiana told him her topic, then quickly asked, "Do you know who Soddy Russell was? What Soddy Glass is?"

Grinning in obvious relief that he could truthfully answer in the affirmative, Rex said, "As a matter of fact, I do. His work was included in the Folk Art of America Exhibit here at the Museum of American Art during Black History Month last year. I believe he was noted as one of a very few black men who worked in glass before the turn of the century. The Porter Glass Works in Pennsylvania, wasn't it?"

"Yes. The story is that he was hired to do labor—shovel sand, tend the furnaces, clean the factory, but somehow he learned the trade and created pieces in unusual designs that surfaced and became very popular in the early 1900s. After his death."

Rex nodded. "I remember reading an old newspaper clipping about that in the exhibit. Russell's name was listed as an employee at the factory, and a picture of the vase in the exhibit was also in the paper. It was decorated with what looked like African tribal symbols."

Kiana nodded.

"What's your interest in him?" Rex wanted to know.

"Soddy Russell was my great-great-grandfather," Kiana said, finishing off her cone.

"Whew! No kidding?" Rex said, intrigued.

"No kidding," she said proudly. "The vase in the Black History Month exhibit was lent to the museum by my grandmother, Hester Russell."

Rex could only stare. "I have to tell you, I thought you were special when I met you yesterday, but this? I'd never have guessed this in a million years. Glass collectors and historians are rather curious about Russell's origins and the inspiration for his patterns."

"And I'm working on the answers," Kiana replied.

"Oh? Tell me more."

Kiana told Rex how she believed Soddy Russell got his inspiration from Adiaga, his wife. How her mother, who had a degree in anthropology, was an avid reader and was doing genealogical studies long before Alex Haley got blacks interested in searching for their roots. She and Kiana's stepfather worked for an international relief mission, so she traveled a lot and wrote extensively about her experiences. She had begun a narrative of her family's history and it included her research about Adiaga—the daughter of Ijoma, a Kante princess from the African village of Bwerani. Apparently the princess Ijoma brought the tribal designs of the ancient Ghanaian kings to America when she was brought over as a slave.

"What a story!" Rex said when she stopped. "Your mother did all the research?"

"Right, and I just recently found the book she was putting together before she was . . . killed."

Rex scowled. "Killed?"

"Yes, in a plane crash in the Nigerian jungle twenty years ago. I was only twelve when she died. My father . . . well, he was my stepfather . . . died in the crash, too."

"I'm sorry," Rex said.

Kiana nodded. "I plan to finish her book."

"So you are the descendant of a princess and an artist?" Rex teased.

Kiana laughed. "It's true!"

"I'm impressed." Rex chuckled, then stood. "I've never met a person with royal ancestors before."

Kiana got up, smiling at him. "You probably have, but you just didn't know it."

They laughed at the truth of her statement, then continued on their walk.

At the Library of Congress, Kiana stood among the giant marble columns of the magnificent entry hall, feeling small and insignificant next to the invisible stacks of books, manuscripts, and records that were stored in the most significant repository of the nation's written word.

"It's mind-boggling to even try to imagine how much information is stored in this place," she said, facing the massive pillars.

"If it's been documented, invented, or published, it's probably here," Rex agreed. He looked over at Kiana. "Once you finish your book, it will be here, too."

"Yes," Kiana murmured, strolling up the wide staircase. "I'd like to check and see if there might be a patent for glass patterns registered here under Porter Glass Works or Soddy Russell." She turned around and waited for Rex, who was mounting the stairs behind her.

"Good idea," he agreed. "It's possible."

At the search desk, Kiana and Rex filled out the proper forms and went through the computer checking, but after an exhaustive search, no records were found.

Disappointed, Kiana left the library more determined than ever to track down the source of Soddy Russell's legacy.

From the library, they headed to the Capitol, then to the Supreme Court Building, and wound up at Union Square, where they sat on the ground beside the Reflecting Pool near the exquisite equestrian statues.

"You mentioned having dinner with your sister," Rex said. "What does she do?"

"Ida is my stepsister," Kiana corrected. "She's in advertising. A vice-president with Bering & Overton in D.C."

"Oh? Up there with the big boys, huh?" Rex said.

"Sounds impressive, doesn't it?"

"Very."

"Unfortunately," Kiana began, "Ida and I don't get along very well. She is absolutely consumed with her work. I think she's trying to prove to the world . . . well, maybe just to me . . . that she can make big money in spite of having only a high school education."

"So it's just you and Ida?" Rex asked.

"And our grandmother Hester . . . my mother's mother. She raised us after our parents died. She lives in a little town called Centerville, near Pittsburgh."

"Do you see her very often?"

"Unfortunately, no." Kiana shook her head. "I haven't been home in years, but I'm going over on Sunday. I want to take this opportunity to spend some time with her while I rethink my plans."

"Yeah. I'm real sorry the tour was canceled, but it might be rescheduled. Don't write us off."

"Oh, I won't, and I know it wasn't your fault." Kiana hugged her arms about her knees and thought. "Coming to D.C. kind of forced me to see Ida. I'm glad. It's been a long time since we saw each other." Kiana pressed her lips together, trying to decide how to explain their relationship. She thought about divulging the nature of Ida's troubles, then changed her mind, saying only, "Ida's had some difficulties in the past." Kiana trailed her index finger across the surface of the cool blue water, then changed the subject. "You said you have a brother?"

"Yeah," Rex sighed. "Lionel."

"He's a lot younger than you, right?"

"Yes, and the generation gap seems to be short-circuiting our lines of communication."

"I'll bet," Kiana replied, familiar with Rex's complaint. As a high school history teacher she had often become frustrated by the ease with which some students tuned her out, as if she were so ancient she couldn't possibly understand their problems. It wasn't easy, but she persisted in her efforts to reach them. Sometimes she was successful, sometimes she wasn't, and it saddened her now to see tension begin to creep over Rex's features. "Lionel will change. Don't stop talking," she advised. "He needs you more than he'd ever admit."

Rex leaned over, resting one arm on the rim of the pool, turning his face to the sky. "It's a struggle. Lionel has this crazy notion that I live a fabulous, jet-set, carefree kind of life and that I don't understand what he has to struggle with back in my old neighborhood. A buppie, he calls me. I don't get it."

Kiana grinned knowingly, assessing Rex with exaggerated scrutiny. "Let's see. Black. Easy on the eyes. Upwardly mobile. An advanced degree. A town house on C Street, isn't it?" Kiana mocked his credentials.

Rex slowly shook his head, indicating she was probably on target.

"Well, brother-man," Kiana teased, "I'd have to say you fit the buppie tag real well." Kiana could not let that one pass. He had told her when he turned thirty-four last January, he had treated himself to a trip to Jamaica arranged by Soulmate Journey, an exclusive, members-only Club-Med type of travel agency for single African Americans. Surely he understood that he had all the attributes and was rapidly accumulating the necessary accoutrements to earn the buppie label, but so what?

"Hey, I'm just a working stiff," Rex defended. "Trying to stay afloat. I haven't forgotten where I came from. I just don't want to live there anymore."

Kiana detected a hint of humor in his obvious frustration, and was glad Rex didn't take himself too seriously. It was a relief to spend time with an intelligent black man who wasn't totally engrossed with himself. After Stanley's narcissistic behavior, talking to Rex was a refreshing experience. "I know exactly what you mean," she said.

Rex nodded. "I can't be there for him all the time, but I'd like to keep Lionel from making mistakes he'll regret."

Kiana listened as Rex expressed his concern about Lionel's attitude and his allegiance to the Sharps.

"Rex," she started, "you shouldn't feel guilty about your choices . . . your lifestyle. Your brother *is* impressed by what you've done with your life and what you continue to do. But expressing it, well, it's probably terribly hard for a seventeen-year-old to do."

Kiana spoke from experience. Her six years at Robinson High had given her the background to offer such an assessment, and she didn't want Rex to give up too soon. "At that age, it's easier to act unimpressed by everything and everybody, than to admit that your big brother is your hero. Don't let it get to you," she counseled. "He'll snap out of it. And when he does, you'll be glad you stuck by him. You're setting the right example, and your efforts *will* pay off, though you may not see results for years."

"I hope you're right," Rex said. "I don't want to come off like a know-it-all busybody, or something like that, you know? I'm not his keeper, and don't want to be. I'm just his brother. I love him. I try to accept him for who he is, but we argue all the time. It's very discouraging."

"He's young. Give him time." Kiana thought for a moment, then added, "Rather like my relationship with Ida. After I went off to college, she was bitter. My natural father had provided money for my education before he died, so I had financial resources. Ida didn't. She is six years older than me, and had already settled into a secretarial position at a local meat packing plant by the time I graduated from high school. My leaving home to go to college hurt her, I see that now. Back then I had no idea she had assumed that I was going to stay around Centerville, like she did, and settle for a job at the local Wal-Mart. But now that we're older, I can see how resentful she's always been of me. I wish we could have been close, like real sisters, but it did not work out and it doesn't look like that will ever be the case."

Kiana had begun to rethink Ida's invitation and regretted not accepting. She wanted to meet Bonard Wilson, not only to see what kind of man Ida had chosen, but what kind of man would put up with her. Was he as greedy and self-centered as Ida? Was he blind? He could hardly be more than a tool for Ida to use to hasten her climb up the political and social registry.

Rex tugged a blade of grass from the lawn, twirling it as he spoke. "My situation with Lionel is not really so different. I know I have every right to live where I please, I've just got to stop letting Lionel make me feel guilty about my decision." Abruptly, he tossed the blade of grass aside, then stood. "Enough about family. Let's enjoy the rest of the day. There's still a lot to see. If you're up to it," he prompted, extending a hand to Kiana.

"I'm with you," she said, gripping his strong fingers, allowing him to pull her up beside him. When she stood, she faced him squarely and let his eyes capture hers. Without saying a word they started walking, shoulders nearly touching as they circled the Reflecting Pool and entered the Botanic Garden.

Chapter Six

IDA pushed her pink peignoir off her shoulders and let it fall to the floor. Standing naked, she admired her trim figure in the bank of full-length mirrors that doubled as closet doors. She smoothed her manicured fingers over her prominent breasts, then eased them to her newly liposuctioned stomach—now as firm and flat as a plaster wall. Worth every bit of three thousand dollars, she decided, lifting both arms overhead, then bending to touch her toes.

After a perfumed soak in her sunken tub, Ida hurried to get dressed. The doorbell rang just as she was slipping her feet into her soft gray pumps. Patting the high crown of her finger-waved hair, she gave it one more spritz of hair spray, then clipped a pair of pearl and diamond earrings on either side of her face, in no hurry to greet her visitor. Leaning toward the mirror, she dusted her cheeks with plum-colored blush, lowered her lids, and layered one more coat of jet black mascara over her feathery lashes.

The bell chimed again. Ida pursed her pouty red lips, shaking her head. Usually Cora answered the door, but Friday was the housekeeper's evening off, so Ida was left on her own to prepare and serve dinner. Not much preparation was needed: The scallops were marinating in the refrigerator, the water was boiling for the angel hair pasta, and a bottle of champagne was chilling in the ice bucket on the bar. There was really little left to do, yet Ida, who could cook as well as or even better than Cora, secretly hoped that she and Bonard would never fall into the dismal rut of eating at home very often.

After a quick once-over in the full-length mirror, she strode down the art-filled corridor that linked her bedroom to the spacious living area of her high-rise apartment. With the assistance of Clodette, one of the most talented and sought after decorators in the district, and an unlimited draw on a bank account that Bonard had insisted on opening for her, Ida had managed to transform a rather nondescript six-room apartment with a fabulous view into a jewel of a place—as elegantly appointed as any upscale Fifth Avenue apartment of any wealthy New York socialite.

Ida had restructured the flat white walls of her sleekly modern residence into warm muted alcoves with nooks and crannies to hold the burgeoning collection of decorative objects and original art Bonard so eagerly bestowed on her. She was an eclectic collector who boldly displayed fragile Czech-Baroque glass alongside Benin masks and terra-cotta figures from the Yoruba tribes. Resting on an ivory base was a marble sculpture of the Sleeping Eros, and next to it stood a bronze bust of Harriet Tubman.

The dim yellow lights in every room of the apartment illuminated tables that were graced with exquisite art glass vases and bowls in a variety of colors, and her walls were hung with paintings by well-known artists from Andy Warhol to Jacob Lawrence. A huge John Biggers mural dominated the wall opposite the entryway.

In her tiny, but well-appointed study was an astonishing collection of early hand-worked pieces; quilts, lace doilies, finger towels, and pillow slips—all documented as having been hand-sewn by slaves for their mistresses. They were displayed on the walls, protected by thick sheets of glass. By Ida's estimation, Bonard had already spent close to a quarter of a million dollars indulging her decorative fantasies, refining her artistic tastes.

As Ida passed her newest acquisition, a rare Tita Rubella bronze, she ran a finger lightly over the sculpture of a man and woman locked in an embrace, then frowned at the bit of dust she picked up. Cora would have to do better, she thought as she reached to open the door.

The wide pinstripes in Bonard's Giorgio Saint Angelo suit made his shoulders appear two inches wider than they were. A man of medium height and build, he had a blunt nose, flat planed cheekbones, and a thick bullish neck that might have been considered sexy on a member of the Washington Redskins. Though he spent lavishly to dress in a manner that would deflect attention from his less than attractive features, his custom-made suits and shirts did little to slim his barrel-shaped body or give his jawline a better edge of definition.

At forty-four, despite his girth, Bonard looked closer to thirty-four—his youthful genes the result of his rather unusual heritage. His mother had been an exotic Afro-Puerto Rican beauty, his father, a small dark man who was purportedly one-third Cherokee. Born into the familiar poverty of life in the inner-city projects, Bonard had grown up in the foggy shadows of the capitol's shimmering monuments. He managed to escape when, as a young man, he took a job delivering parcels and envelopes to merchants in town on a secondhand bicycle he had rescued from the dump.

Among Bonard's early customers had been Aaron Gold, a struggling merchant who sold gently used table linens, nicked china plates, and recycled household items to the overworked, under appreciated housewives in the neighborhood. Gold hired Bonard to make deliveries and to avoid, at all costs, being intercepted by husbands who had laid down the law that their wives were not to spend a dime of their hard-earned money on items as frivolous as lace tablecloths.

Soon Gold and Company was attracting so many customers the owner moved it from a greengrocer's stall to a storefront in the heart of Baltimore. Bonard followed his employer to the city and was promptly promoted from delivery boy to packager, then to salesman, and after he finished night classes at Baltimore College with a degree in accounting, was given the job of keeping Gold's books.

Bonard's talent was obvious. He could make money from money. And as soon as he'd saved enough of it, he took on four more clients and hung out his own shingle.

Now, the oddly handsome man stood in front of Ida, head erect, a cardboard box in his hand, looking nothing like the long-haired delivery boy he had been years ago, but exactly like the mature wealthy suitor he was. As CEO and chairman of the board of Wilson Investments, Bonard wheeled and dealt with the movers and shakers in Washington business circles. Since the recent announcement of his candidacy for a seat in the United States House of Representatives, he had been caught up in the necessary grind of raising campaign funds. So far, his election treasury was twice as rich as his opponent's, while his personal fortune, as reported in *Black Enterprise* magazine, was edging close to three million dollars.

Greeting Ida, the smile of elation on his lips was matched by the spring in his step. He entered her sweet-smelling apartment and took a deep breath. He loved the atmosphere Ida created—soft music playing in the background, the spicy aroma of potpourri wafted from someplace out of sight.

Bonard closed the door, reached out to his fiancée, and took her in his arms. He pressed his full lips over hers, kissing her urgently and thoroughly as if he had thirsted for the taste of her all day.

"I've missed you," he whispered against her perfumed neck, running his palms down to her firm buttocks. He cupped her round bottom with both of his hands.

Ida pulled gently away, her gaze riveted on the cardboard box he held in one hand.

"What's this?" she asked.

"A surprise," Bonard laughingly answered, balancing the parcel on one open palm.

Ida took him by the wrist, pulled him into the candlelit living room, and perched anxiously on the edge of her black-and-white satin-striped sofa, patting the space next to her. "Sit, please. Don't keep me in suspense."

Bonard held the box above his head, grinning teasingly. "And what do I get for my efforts?"

She leaned closer, then half rose from her seat and put her hand on his thigh, trailing her fingers up to his groin. With little effort she began to slowly lower the zipper on his trousers.

In a throaty voice, she promised, "Whatever you want. Any way you want it." Then she pushed her hand inside his pants and let it rest there until he removed it, squeezing her fingers almost painfully hard.

"God, that's torture, baby," Bonard moaned, slipping down to sit at her side. "Three days is too damn long to be away from you." He kissed her again, his tongue darting past her teeth to taste her minty fresh mouth. "Happy engagement," he whispered, pulling back, putting the box on her lap.

Ida glanced at him with a flutter of her dark lashes, then turned her attention to the plain brown box. She tore the tape from the opening, tossed the shredded packing material onto the floor, then gasped aloud as she wrapped her hands around a ruby-colored candlestick that was nestled among folds of tissue paper.

Holding it up to the lamplight, she examined the design at the base and the top, a raised pattern of eight-pointed stars with hollow centers. When the light filtered through the unusual glass, Ida gasped again with delight. "Oh, Bonard. How beautiful!"

"I thought you'd like it."

"Is this the reason for your mystery trip? Where in the world did you *find* it?"

"Oh, I have my sources." He leaned back to watch her as he explained. "Soddy Glass may be rare, but once I put out the word that I was looking for a specific piece, along with an offer that couldn't be resisted, I was pretty sure I'd find what I wanted."

"Was it . . . terribly expensive?" she asked in a breathy voice, peering at him through half closed eyes.

Piercing Ida with a sizzling look of satisfaction, he replied, *"Terribly."*

Ida pulled her shoulders up to her ears, squirming in delight at the thought of how much money Bonard must have spent. Before rising from the sofa, she gave Bonard another kiss, then stepped in front of him, running her little finger over the satiny glass as she studied the primitive design.

"Did you see your stepsister yet?" Bonard asked.

Ida stopped in front of a tall lighted display case and unlocked it before answering. "Kiana? Oh. No. Her plans changed, or something. She's still in Houston, I guess." She moved aside an iridescent Tiffany bud vase to place her newest acquisition next to its twin.

"Too bad," Bonard said. "I was looking forward to meeting her."

"Maybe some other time," Ida casually replied, turning quickly to face her fiancé. She grinned at Bonard. "I never dreamed the mate to my lonely candleholder even existed. How much do you think a *pair* of Soddy Glass candlesticks are worth?"

"Thousands. Maybe priceless. Who knows?" Bonard said teasingly, then added in a serious tone, "But you'd better take them to Kresta's and get them appraised. I'll need to add them to the insurance policy."

Ida's eyes flitted in appreciation over Bonard's face, then she leaned over and kissed him tenderly, stroking his cheek. "This is the best present I ever received."

Bonard chuckled, nipping the end of Ida's nose with a light kiss. "I'm glad you're happy, baby."

Ida began to unbutton Bonard's silky white shirt. "I can't tell you how happy I am, so why don't you relax and let me show you?"

Chapter Seven

KIANA turned on her side, squinted at the clock, then groaned. Ten o'clock. After lying awake most of the night, considering her limited options, she had overslept, though why she had set the alarm for 7:00 A.M., she did not know. She had nothing to do all day but think, and worry, and try to salvage her research plans.

A wash of uneasiness surfaced. She sat up in bed and rubbed her eyes. For some reason she felt trapped, boxed in, as if someone were plotting against her. How had her carefully laid plans gotten so far off track? So quickly? And now it appeared as if she would have to start from the beginning—but one thing was certain, she was not giving up.

Shivering, though the room was pleasantly warm, Kiana pulled her knees to her chest and lowered her chin atop the soft blanket to think about what her next step should be. The museum would surely refund her money, but when? American Express had refused to reinstate her account so she had no credit reserve, and she wasn't desperate enough to ask Ida for money. Damn! Without enough credit on her Visa card she couldn't even rent a car, *if* she were brave enough to go it alone.

"Face it, girl. You need Rex Tandy," she told herself, a mixture of stirring anticipation and dread closing in. Rex probably knew shortcuts to find what she was searching for, and he knew the back roads of Tennessee as well as he did the network of streets and alleys of Washington, D.C. Without a guide she would be dismally handicapped.

Kiana tilted her head back and shut her eyes. Somewhere in the wild and rugged Smoky Mountains, beneath layers of rotted leaves, tree limbs, and crumbling mud brick houses, lay the forgotten story she was determined to re-create—with or without Rex Tandy's help. But he *would* help her, she could sense it, she just needed to come up with a very good plan.

Kiana threw the covers back, went into the bathroom, and ran the cold water tap full blast. After splashing a good deal of it on her face, she thirstily downed two glasses, then returned to the bedroom, and grabbed the phone. In rapid succession, she made two phone calls. The first was to the Visa hot line to confirm that she had enough credit to charge a one-way ticket to Centerville, Pennsylvania. The second call was to *Black Culture Watch* magazine. She prayed the office was open on Saturdays. A receptionist answered on the fourth ring.

"Rex Tandy, please," Kiana said breathlessly.

"One moment, I'll see if he's in," the receptionist said.

When his rich voice came through the line, Kiana stifled her anxiousness by placing one hand to her stomach. "Hello, Rex, this is Kiana."

"I recognize the voice," Rex said in a level, satisfied tone.

"You don't sound very surprised to hear from me."

"Well, yes . . . and no. I mean, I was planning to call you later today, but this is a pleasant surprise."

Kiana smiled, confidence gathering as she eased toward her request. "It was nice of you to take me sightseeing yesterday. I had a nice time."

"Then how about a repeat?"

"I don't think I'm up for seeing any more monuments, but I would be up for lunch." Kiana pressed her lips together, then plunged ahead. "Do you have plans?"

"Lunch? Well, sure. I'd like that."

A smile touched Kiana's lips. "Good. Can you meet me in the hotel lobby at eleven-thirty?"

"I'll be there," Rex said.

"See you then," Kiana replied, throwing back her head in relief. It was going to work out, she could feel it. Glancing at her watch, she knew she didn't have much time to draft her proposal, and it damn well had to be convincing.

Forty-five minutes later, Kiana sat on a squishy floral sofa in the hotel lobby, partially hidden by an enameled Chinese jardiniere sprouting a burst of lush green ferns. She held the latest edition of *Black Culture Watch* magazine in her hands. After flipping through the pages, she came to the article by Rex Tandy she had been looking for. Eyes riveted to the page, Kiana absorbed each word of the article: *Brothers Pulling Together for Change*—a feature story about a group of professional black men in the suburbs of Philadelphia who had started a weekend outing program to get inner-city male youths to visit farms and sites of historical interest outside the city. Traveling in an overhauled, bright red bus, the group took day trips every Saturday, providing the boys with an opportunity to see a world they did not know existed.

One of Rex's photos was magnificent in its captured spontaneity and vibrant colors. It was of three young boys smiling as they gobbled down fresh strawberries they had picked from the vines themselves. Another showed two youths grinning broadly into the camera, sitting atop horses, as proud as if they had scaled a mountain. There were other candid shots of the group eating barbecue, fishing in a flat blue lake, and at museums gazing at paintings by African-American artists.

Kiana was impressed, not only with Rex Tandy's photography, but the story he had told. The magazine slipped to her lap. The impact of Rex's talent sank in. He was a tender, intelligent photojournalist with the ability to inform and cause change.

Well, Kiana thought, looking up to see the author himself dashing between parked cars, this is the man for the job.

Rex dodged a taxi, then raced across the street. Kiana smiled, waiting, watching. He was dressed in black khakis, and a black Howard University T-shirt hugged his hard, flat stomach. He carried the same rumpled Armani jacket he had worn yesterday, holding it with one finger over his shoulder. He wore the same scuffed boots on his feet. On his head he had a baseball cap with REDSKINS on the front. To Kiana, he looked like a carefree college student on his way to class. After pushing through the revolving door, he waved, then came directly over to her.

"You're prompt," Kiana remarked, breaking the startled silence that sprang up when Rex sat down on the sofa.

"I try to be," he replied, pulling off his cap. He ran his fingers over his short curly hair.

Kiana rolled the magazine into a tube, but not before Rex saw it.

"Enjoying the magazine?"

"I just bought it," she hedged, not ready to tell him what she thought of his story. "I don't see it often in Houston. It's been awhile since I've read it."

"You ought to subscribe," he prompted. "I can get you a discount subscription."

"I'll bet you can." Kiana smiled and stuck the magazine into her large leather purse, then twined her fingers through the wood and cocoa bead necklace resting on her tan cotton blouse. "Where are we going to eat?" she asked.

"What do you feel like?"

"I'm pretty easy. As long as the food is good and the noise level is low. I'd like to have a decent conversation, you know?"

"Sounds serious," Rex said.

"Well, I'd like your opinion on something."

"No problem. Follow me."

"How much time do you have?" Kiana asked, rising from the sofa, picking up her Mysha-printed bomber jacket.

"Don't worry," Rex said. "I'm free all afternoon. My time is yours." He pulled on his cap with a tug.

"How nice," Kiana murmured, stepping around a suitcase to walk in front of Rex. As she pushed through the door, she hoped she didn't have a panty line showing because she sure could feel his eyes on her hips.

It turned out to be a Jeep Eagle, not a car, that Rex was driving. Kiana put on her sunglasses and settled back while he inched his way through a snarl of street repairs. A flush of contentment began to smooth out her worries, and she felt optimistic for the first time in days. Her initial take on Rex was right—traveling with him for an extended period of time would not be difficult at all.

After riding along listening to the radio for about fifteen minutes, Rex pulled to the curb in front of a small cafe.

"How does Brazilian food sound?" he asked, guiding his Jeep into a parking space.

The ruffled white curtains edging the cafe's windows and the geranium-filled clay pots on either side of the door made the place look as if it had been plucked from a side street in Rio de Janiero and plopped down in the middle of the city.

"Cafe Flora," Kiana read the name of the restaurant aloud. "Lovely." She waited in her seat until Rex came around to open her door.

Holding onto Kiana's wrist, Rex helped her step down from the Jeep. She saw blatant admiration in his eyes as he examined her boldly printed jacket, the twisted silver earrings brushing her cheeks, and her cascade of perfectly braided hair.

Stepping back, Kiana allowed Rex to pull open the carved, nail-studded door and she preceded him into the quaint square room. A huge wrought-iron chandelier that resembled a gigantic wagon wheel held candle-point lightbulbs above the room. Their soft glow tinged the white linen table cloths a muted shade of gold, highlighting bouquets of yellow daffodils in the center of each table. On bright green lacquered chairs with high ladder backs customers sat engrossed in low conversation or animated chatter. On the walls were giant hand-painted flowers, similar to magnolias, or maybe water lilies, which were painted in vivid hues of pink, purple, and red.

The woman who greeted them and escorted them to their table wore a three-tiered flowered skirt, a blouse with a Carmen Miranda neckline, and flat leather sandals that laced around her ankles. Her softly accented voice transported Kiana across a continent as she took their orders, recommending the chilled Chablis while they waited for their food.

"How did you get started giving tours?" Kiana asked.

Rex stretched his feet out beneath the table, unfolding his muscular frame. "My first assignment at *Black Culture Watch* was to accompany a group of women on a tour of restored plantations in the South. I was writing a story about the resurgence of interest people have in documenting their roots. It was a racially mixed group, and all of the participants were fascinated by the big houses, the antique furnishings, the flower gardens—all the usual things associated with the Old South. The tour director gave us anecdotal information about life before the civil war but . . ."

"But?" Kiana picked up on his sentence. "I can feel it coming."

"Yeah. The blacks on the trip kept asking me to take them behind the scenes of plantation life."

"I'm not surprised," Kiana commented.

"Right. They wanted to see the places of refuge and gathering spots where fugitive slaves had hidden. They wanted a glimpse of life outside the quarters and the big house kitchens. So I poked around and uncovered some fascinating stories about runaways— flight to freedom narratives, the fugitive life—stories the tour director couldn't give them."

"I know that's right." Kiana sighed. "In my research I've come across many intriguing tales about flight on the Underground Railroad."

"Yeah, those narratives about the years before Emancipation when the Underground Railroad flourished contain important information about slave life in America." Rex let his glance linger on Kiana as he lifted his glass to his lips.

"I think it's the story of the slaves' struggle to live free that attracts many people to read about and study slavery," Kiana agreed. "They are certainly curious and appalled by what they learn of the degradation blacks suffered in bondage, but I am more interested in the tenacity and courage our ancestors had."

The waitress placed their plates of steaming food before them. Kiana pierced a fried plantain with her fork, then popped it into her mouth. "Wonderful," she murmured.

Rex tasted his peppered chicken and nodded. "Good choice."

"Please go on," Kiana said. "I want to know more about your tours."

"Well, after my experience with that first group, I continued to work at *Black Culture Watch* doing personal, testimonial kinds of profiles. A few months later, one of the ladies who had been on the plantation tour wrote a letter to Ed Marshall, my publisher, asking him to consider doing a story to document the routes that the slaves took as they traveled the Underground Railroad. She suggested that the magazine sponsor a tour to raise money to support black genealogical research organizations. Ed loved the idea and ran with it."

Kiana nodded in approval as she ate.

"I was the designated tour guide and escorted the first group in 1990. I've made seven trips since then."

"I gather the Smithsonian heard about you and . . ."

"You got it, they offered me a contract to be on call as a guide. It's sporadic, but fun. Each trip is definitely an adventure."

"How would someone find information about a runaway slave who never made it to freedom?" Kiana asked, her voice more intense than she'd planned. "A slave who may have been killed— probably lynched for trying to escape?"

Rex pursed his lips thoughtfully. "Of course, documentation is scarce but not impossible to pull together. I spend a lot of time at the Library of Congress and I access many of the depositories of black history around the country. Through county records, family letters and papers, old newspapers, advertising handbills, anything printed. . . . Census records . . . I ferret out names. I'm sure you know the routine. Then I try to re-create the slave's life, going back to the plantation to re-create the route a slave might have taken when running away, though many just walked off the land, following the North Star, unsure where they would wind up." Rex watched Kiana intently, then leaned forward over his plate. "Do I detect a personal slant to that question?"

Kiana studied his face. "Yes. I want to take your tour, but I can't wait until August. There is some information I *must* find. Soon."

Rex tossed his napkin atop his plate, before pouring them each another glass of wine. "You've got my attention, Kiana. Tell me what's on your mind?"

Kiana stared across the crowded restaurant as if sorting through a very complicated issue. "The information I am looking for is personal, but I plan to use some of it to support my dissertation."

"*A Study of the Nineteenth-Century Black Artists' Struggle for Economic Compensation—A Reparative Approach.* Right?"

"I'm surprised you remembered."

Rex shrugged. "I found it very intriguing." His curiosity lit up his liquid brown eyes. "Care to elaborate? What's on your mind?"

Kiana sipped her wine, then set the glass down, twirling the tall crystal goblet as she began to tell him what she had seen at the auction in Houston. "And Soddy Russell was said to have come from a place called Magnolia Crossing, Tennessee," she finished. "Do you know where that is?"

"Never heard of it. You sure it's in Tennessee?"

"My grandmother says so." Kiana squared her shoulders and boldly asked Rex, "Will you take me there?"

Rex scratched his head. "Whew! I don't know. Where do you plan on starting?"

"How about Nashville? That's where our tour was going to begin. And I have the information on the antique dealer in Nashville. If he has access to originals I want to know where he got them, and if he's dealing in reproductions who's making them? Somebody is capitalizing on my family's heritage and making a lot of money."

"It's worth tracing," Rex agreed. "Could be quite exciting."

"Right. And if I can find the county where the plantation was, there may be records, local histories, some documentation of my great-great-grandparents' presence. Hopefully, I'll uncover enough information to prove my family's ownership to Soddy Russell's glass patterns—even if he created them while enslaved, they belong to his descendants, not to the family who owned him or the factory where he worked."

Rex shrugged skeptically. "That's expecting a lot."

Kiana gave him a bold, challenging stare. "Will you help me?"

Rex waited only a second before responding. "It's a chancy proposition at best. Believe me, going on a trip with you is a pleasant thought, but I'm way past deadline on a story I'm doing. Besides," he stalled, then blurted out, "I have expenses. Time is money, as they say."

"Yes, I understand." Kiana put her elbows on the table and leaned forward. "What is your fee?"

A low breath slipped from Rex's lips. "Gee, I don't know. I've never been a personal escort. I guess it would be about the same as what the museum pays me if I were taking a group."

"Which is?"

"A thousand a week," Rex replied. When she frowned in disappointment, he quickly added, "That includes everything."

Kiana grumbled, "You're that expensive?"

"Yeah," he grinned, offering no apology.

Undaunted, Kiana urged, "Think we can make a deal?"

Rex burst into laughter. "You don't give up, do you? What's your deal?"

"If you go with me and at your own expense, and I prove someone is illegally profiting from my great-great-grandfather's art, I will give *Black Culture Watch* the exclusive rights to serialize parts of my story. You could run it before the book is even finished." She waited for his reaction.

"Well . . ." Rex began, definitely turning the idea around. "What if you discover there are no reproductions . . . that nobody's ripping your family off? Maybe Soddy Russell left scads of his glass behind and it's scattered all over the country."

"If that's true, where's it been for all these years? Why is it just now hitting the market? Commanding such high prices?" Kiana's eyes gleamed. "Don't you think that's a story?"

"Could be," Rex admitted. "An example of how one African-American family lost . . . or perhaps found . . . a legacy that was rightfully theirs." Rubbing his forehead, he thought. "Your grandmother, Soddy Russell's granddaughter, is still alive, right?"

"Yes. She's ninety-one years old. Still lives on the land that Soddy Russell homesteaded after the Civil War, not very far from the original site of Porter Glass Works. She'd cooperate. I know she would."

"Does she know about these 'new found' pieces that are surfacing?"

"I doubt it, but she soon will. I'll be in Centerville tomorrow and I plan to talk with her." Kiana pressed her fingertips to her lips, waiting, her eyes riveted to Rex's face. "What do you think?"

"I think it could be a fabulous story!"

"Yes!" Kiana tilted her head back in joy.

"But," Rex cautioned. "The decision is not mine to make. You'll have to sell it to Ed Marshall, my editor."

"Is he in his office now?"

Rex checked his watch. "Probably. He usually comes in for a few hours on weekends." Rex handed the waitress the money for the check.

"Let's go." Kiana pulled on her jacket, silently praying that Ed Marshall would be as impressed with her idea as Rex Tandy had been.

Chapter Eight

KIANA shifted uncomfortably, thankful that Rex had had the foresight to warn her about Ed's brusque manner. From the look on the publisher's dark brown face, Kiana could tell that her proposal had not struck a positive chord. Holding her breath, she watched as Ed ran a slim hand over his salt-and-pepper beard, then squinted one eye into a slit. He tilted back in his swivel chair, assessing Kiana suspiciously before he spoke.

"You say you're related to an African princess?" he probed. "You're Soddy Russell's great-great-granddaughter? Where've you been all this time?"

There was a time when Kiana would have taken great offense at the way in which she had just been addressed, but today, instead of letting her temper flare, she forced a calm note into her reply.

"I've been in Houston, Texas, teaching high school history. Leading a normal life."

"Hmm," Ed murmured, suddenly thumping his chair back on all four legs. "What proof do you have that you're related to Soddy Russell?"

His pointed question grated on Kiana's sense of trust and she frowned briefly, then tossed back. "Proof? I know who I am. Who my ancestors were. I don't carry my family tree around in my purse, but if you want records, I can get them." She silently chastised herself for not at least having her mother's journal with her, though she doubted it would convince this man that her story had any merit.

Ed swept Kiana with the annoyed eye of a parent about to punish a naughty child. He swiveled back and forth, gazing out the floor-to-ceiling window behind his desk as he toyed with a silver pen in his hand. Cutting his eyes to Rex, he said, "I'd like to support you on this, Rex—financially and professionally. On the surface, I admit the whole thing sounds intriguing—definitely a way to put a personal face on the issue of reparations."

"Right! That's how I see it," Rex agreed, glancing quickly toward Kiana.

"But . . . there are an awful lot of holes," Ed hedged. He looked at Kiana. "Have you talked to this Marvin Watts, the dealer in Nashville who sold the glass to the auctioneer?"

"No, not yet," Kiana had to admit. "I've called his shop several times but never got an answer. I want to go down there and meet him personally, talk to him face-to-face."

"How much checking has been done to find this place . . . Magnolia Crossing?"

"Not a lot, yet," Rex volunteered.

Kiana felt her face begin to burn. Perhaps she had acted impulsively.

The room was silent, except for the tick of a small crystal clock sitting atop Ed's desk. She decided his perplexed expression was encouraging. At least she had gotten his attention.

Ed finally spoke to Rex. "This is not a good time for you to take off. I need you here." He turned to Kiana. "Miss Sheridan, I want to do the story. Your project does have merit and it could be quite compelling, but I can't spare Rex right now."

"If you're worried about the piece on the Sharps and Treps, it's almost finished," Rex told his boss.

"I needed it on my desk yesterday," Ed said.

"Tomorrow," Rex stated flatly. "Seven a.m. Not a second later."

"Fine," Ed replied. "When it's ready for press, we'll start on this trip to Tennessee." He rested his chin on his tented fingers. "In the meantime, Miss Sheridan, pull all of your research notes and family records together for Rex. He'll have to do this one as quickly as possible."

Rex stood. "Thanks." He headed to the door, letting Kiana pass into the corridor first.

In Rex's office Kiana sat with one arm across the back of the navy blue chair in front of his desk. "Well, looks like I've got some work to do, but isn't it great? He wants to do it."

"I figured Ed would grab this one. It's a fascinating story, Kiana. With photos and family testimony, it might be just the type of piece to push *Black Culture Watch*'s circulation sky high. Put it up there with *Ebony, Essence, American Visions.*"

"I know, but first we have to find the source of the legacy."

"Oh, we will," Rex said with confidence. "Believe me, we will."

"Ed won't stall on this, will he?"

"No. Staff is short, but don't worry, he'll come through. Just be patient. Tomorrow, as soon as I deliver my gang story, he'll be in here hashing over details for the trip." Rex fell silent and fiddled with a paper clip for a moment, then tossed it onto the calendar blotter on his desk. "So, what are your plans now?" His voice was suddenly much softer, lower.

"I think I'll leave tomorrow morning."

"To visit your grandmother?"

"Right. I'd like to get an early flight to Pittsburgh. I'll have to rent a car and drive from there to Centerville."

"Let me take you to the airport?" Rex asked tentatively, as if he were afraid to hear her answer.

"That's okay. I can take a cab," she replied quickly, louder than she had expected. "Sounds like you're going to be pretty busy."

"Please?" Rex pressed. "I can drop my story by the office, then swing by and pick you up. I'd like to see you once more before you leave."

She was secretly thrilled by his request but answered casually, "Sure, why not?"

Rex picked up a pad and pencil from his desk. "Here's my number at home. Call me later and let me know what time your flight leaves. I should be back from my rendezvous with the boys in the hood by ten." He handed it to her.

"All right," Kiana said, slipping it into her purse.

"I'll be waiting by the phone. You'd *better* call," Rex said playfully.

She smiled, then turned serious. "Oh, I'll call. Don't worry." She leaned closer, one hand on his desk. "Aren't you afraid of meeting with those gangs? And aren't the Treps supposed to be responsible for the rape and stabbing of a ten-year-old-girl? I heard about that on the news in Houston." A flicker of concern pulled her brows together. "Sounds dangerous."

"To be honest, I'm lucky I got an interview set up at all. It hasn't been easy getting to them," Rex told her. "They go underground when things get hot on the streets. They just disappear. It's hard to gain any ground, that's why this story has been so difficult to finish. And we've received three bomb threats here at the office."

"Bombs? God, Rex, that's scary."

"It's disgusting, that's what it is, and Ed is fed up with evacuating this place every time one of those punks decides to hassle us. When I suggested doing the story, I warned Ed that the magazine might take some heat." He glanced away, then back at Kiana. "Goes with the territory, I guess."

"Watch out," Kiana replied. "You might wind up being the next target."

Rex shook his head. "Nobody's after me. I'm meeting with Willi-Man Monty, the head of the Treps. He's promised to interpret some graffiti on the wall behind Corona High. A double shooting took place there last week. Hopefully, some of the Sharps will meet us there—their leader has made overtures of a limited truce. Maybe they're getting tired of the craziness. Who knows? Anyway, I hope to have a shot of the two gang leaders at the wall, initiating peace as the closing photo in the series."

The confidence with which Rex spoke about his project was impressive. Kiana could immediately see how seriously professional he was about his work. He was the right man to do her story. "I enjoyed your piece in *Black Culture Watch* about the Philadelphia men's group."

"Thanks," Rex said.

"What's your angle on the gang story?" Kiana asked.

"I want to demystify gangs. The media leads people to believe that gangs are secret societies hell-bent on destruction and violence, when sadly, most of the boys, and girls, in them have been abused, neglected, have very little love in their lives. No home training, so to speak. They're desperate for something or someone to give them a sense of belonging, and not surprisingly, they find it by joining a gang. I don't deny that many have criminal records and ought to be considered dangerous, but most aren't the monsters people believe them to be."

"I'm sure that's true," Kiana murmured. She'd been branded a radical and a troublemaker enough times to understand how easy it was for people to slap labels on anyone whose behavior might be outside their experience or expectations. "But," she cautioned Rex, "getting too involved could still be risky." Kiana remembered the training the teachers at Robinson High had been required to take in order to identify gang apparel and markings.

"Relax. I know I have to be careful, remember? We have a project to do." Shifting in his chair, he rubbed his hand on his thigh as if he were suddenly uneasy, unsure about what to say or how to say it. "You know, Kiana," he began, "I feel real comfortable with you. I think the research trip is going to work out fine."

"Same here," Kiana admitted, glad he had said it first. "I'm anxious to get started." Since their sightseeing outing along the Mall, she'd thought of little else.

"I guess we ought to discuss the thrust of the story. You know . . . the guts of the piece?"

Kiana nodded.

"You're going to link your findings to reparations, right?" Rex clarified.

"Exactly," Kiana replied.

"That's heavy," Rex commented. "We ran an article on reparations a while back, right after Reagan signed off on the legislation to compensate the Japanese-Americans who had been held in detention camps during World War Two."

"Precisely," Kiana said, "and I realize that it initiated a storm at the door of Congress."

"Yeah," Rex said. "House Bill Forty was introduced by Congressman Conyers." He paused, then asked, "I take it you totally support reparations?" Rex gazed thoughtfully at her. "I need to know your position on the issue to make the story credible."

"Of course I support reparations," Kiana replied, tensing as they eased into the controversial subject. "It's a matter that must be fully explored."

"Explored is one thing. Actively advocating it is another. I'm just trying to get a fix on where you stand, that's all. Dialogue is good. Action is another thing."

"In my opinion," Kiana stated firmly, "there's been too much talk, far too long. What's needed is concrete evidence, documentation to support some legal challenges. Slaves were responsible for many creations . . . artistic as well as practical. That's the position I want made clear. The work and creativity of the slaves made the lives of their masters more enjoyable . . . and at times more economically enriched. There was little to no compensation for them. Now we are due compensation for that."

Rex tilted his head to one side, but said nothing.

"Okay. So, my mission may be personal," Kiana admitted, "but it's a start . . . a reason to bring more attention to another facet of ignored contributions. Are you familiar with N'COBRA?"

Rex thought about the acronym for a second. "National Coalition of Blacks for Reparations in America. Right?"

"Very good," Kiana said. "Have you ever attended a rally? Talked to a member?"

Rex shrugged. "I must admit, I've never thought about getting involved."

Waving her hand, Kiana assured him, "Don't look so guilty. You're not alone. Most of us have been slow to admit that there ought to be some type of redress for the three centuries of slave labor, degradation, and second-class citizenship that has obviously affected the future of our race."

Clearing his throat, Rex smiled. "I'm convinced." He got up and walked over to a large corkboard covering one wall. On it was a map of the United States. It was covered with red stars and blue lines highlighting several routes. "You must have been a very good teacher. You state your case very well."

Kiana followed Rex across the room. "Are these your tour routes?"

"Yep. My strategic planning center."

"Do all of your tours follow the trail north through the Smoky Mountains?" Kiana asked.

"No, but the passage from central Tennessee, through Virginia, into Washington, D.C. and Pennsylvania is very popular. Being closest in proximity, it was the first one I documented and traveled over with a group."

"And the others?"

"During slavery, there were four major land routes, or arteries leading North. I've tried to re-create them on that map. Farthest west, the slaves would come up from Louisiana, cross Mississippi and Tennessee, until they got to Kentucky, where they would split off to the east or west, heading into Illinois or Ohio to reach the Canadian border. I follow the route through Ohio."

Kiana pushed a slender braid from her forehead. "And the other escape routes?"

"Out of Georgia slaves often headed toward the coast and stowed away on ships carrying cargo along the eastern seaboard to places like New York, Connecticut, Massachusetts. It's also been documented that many slaves slipped out of the States by crossing south through Florida to set off on boats hoping to find refuge in Cuba or the Bahamas."

Rex walked around Kiana and leaned against his desk, his tall, lanky form relaxed. He eyed her curiously. "Getting back to what you said . . . that you feel comfortable with me." He pressed his lips together, then plunged ahead. "I've got to ask."

"What?" Kiana laughed under her breath.

"Is there a husband, boyfriend, or a significant other waiting for you back in Houston?"

Now she laughed aloud. "Not by a long shot." Shaking her head she explained, "For the first time in years I am what you might call footloose and fancy free. This research trip is my own liberating experience."

Rex smiled broadly. "I didn't mean to give you the wrong impression . . . but," he lifted his chin, assuming a more professional stance, "I'm single, too, and basically unattached. I was just wondering . . ."

"It's okay," Kiana said, adding, "I was wondering, too."

Chapter Nine

THE snake-black streets sheened bright with a drizzle of rain. Like corridors of poverty, they were littered with trash that had spilled out of rusted garbage cans, wine bottles crumbling in the cement curbs, and homeless men huddled in groups on every corner, quarts of malt liquor pressed to their lips. The buildings facing Euclid Street, abandoned shells of a prosperous past, loomed as decaying testimony to the loss of dignity the neighborhood had suffered in the past fifteen years.

Rex slowed to a crawl as he passed Currie's Meat Market, now a windowless shelter for stray dogs and cats. Five years ago the owner, Ruben Currie, had been gunned down at his meat counter while serving a crowd of customers. The police report on the evening news had identified the robbers as young boys in masks who had gotten away with only forty dollars in cash. The killers probably still lived in the area, and roamed the maze of alleys and vacant buildings where so many lost souls smoked crack cocaine and sniffed glue to dull the reality around them.

Rex had come to Currie's Meat Market many times to fill his mother's weekly order; one pound of ground beef, four pork chops, and a thick slice of Virginia cured ham, and of course any bones decent enough to produce a pot of soup. That had been Carlotta Tandy's standing order for as many years as Ruben Currie had been in business, and every Saturday morning until Rex graduated from high school, he had bicycled over to the smelly little market the size of a walk-in closet, zipping through the familiar streets, waving at folks he thought of as family.

Rex had felt very grown-up to be trusted with such a mission and always returned home safely with the change from the five dollar bill his father had pulled from his worn leather wallet. A quiet hardworking man, Alvin Tandy made sure his family had meat on the table, and had never missed a day of work at the neighborhood post office where he unloaded and cleaned the shiny mail trucks until one day two years ago when he was attacked at his front door as he put his key into the lock. Tandy never recovered from his injuries and now lived on disability retirement in his war zone of a neighborhood.

Carlotta and Alvin Tandy had settled in Columbia Heights in 1942 when the neighborhood had been a friendly enclave of hard-working black folks who wanted no more than to live in peace and raise their children to be productive citizens. That was years before the emergence of street gangs and renters who descended on the neighborhood to displace the home owners. Now, advanced in years, with a rebellious son to contend with, Rex's parents were trapped at the site of their beginning, as isolated as if they inhabited foreign soil. Rex only wished they would pull up stakes and leave.

Feelings of apprehension crowded Rex as he rode down the slick wet streets. Not a day or night went by when he didn't worry that he'd get that dreaded call from the police informing him that some harm had come to his family. It had happened to many of his childhood friends and for some reason he was beginning to sense that his luck was running out.

He turned onto 11th Street and stopped at the light. He glanced to his left, peering across the darkened football stadium that stretched out behind Corona High. A misty rain had begun to fall again and a blinking neon sign at the Kwik Stop Shop on the other side of the street cast a melange of bright colors on the hood of his Jeep.

Rex rolled down the rain-splattered window to get his bearings, frowning as he tried to find the wall where Willi-Man had said to meet him. Realizing he was on the wrong corner, Rex rolled the window back up, went to the next light and made a right turn, then drove to the graffiti-laced wall where the Treps and the Sharps had left their marks.

He turned off the engine and sat watching, waiting, disappointed that Willi-Man was not on time. He didn't want to spend any more time than necessary camped out at the corner of Florida and Thirteenth.

Rex reached to turn on the radio, but stopped when the sing-song cadence of a hip-hop rapper boomed from the store that was directly in his line of vision across the street.

Hand in midair, Rex looked at two young men who were heading his way, trying to discern if either might be Willi-Man. Both were dressed totally in black and had caps twisted sideways on their heads. One was tall and thin, the other stocky and broad shouldered. Bantering to the music, oblivious to everything around them, they sauntered down the street with their boom box blaring "The Day the Niggaz Took Over."

Rex had only seen Willi-Man once, and then the gangster had been wearing a bandana—tied handkerchief style low on his forehead—and dark wraparound glasses over his eyes. Rex watched the youths closely, finally deciding that neither was his prospective interviewee. He shrugged, slumped down in his seat, but kept the boys in sight, making up his mind to wait ten more minutes, then get out of the neighborhood and finish the story without the last interview.

Suddenly the music stopped and the young men halted their swaggering pace when they got to a tree at the edge of the sidewalk. Within seconds, two shadowy figures emerged from a black sedan parked several yards from the corner and strode quickly toward the youths. In the yellow glow of the street lamp, Rex could easily see that the well-dressed strangers were white men in a hurry to take care of their business and get out of the hood. He'd seen this scenario dozens of times.

Rex sat up higher, instinctively grabbing his camcorder to record the flagrant transaction. Rex focused on the knot of men exchanging cash for small plastic bags. Suddenly, another young man raced across the street and shouldered his way into the cluster that was huddled in muted conversation.

Rex zoomed in, focusing first on the faces of the white men, then panning to the three black youths.

"Oh, God!" he spat out, yanking the camera from his face, taking in a gulp of a breath. Lionel was the late arrival. He was standing under the streetlight with a stupid grin on his face watching the transaction as if he had arranged it himself.

Rex stared incredulously at his brother. His hands trembled so much he could hardly hold the camera to refit the lens to his eye, worried that a bust could go down at any moment. Rex's throat constricted with worry. Cop cars with sirens blaring and colored lights flashing could streak onto the scene and surround them in a heartbeat. Or worse, a car could come careening around the corner, bullets flying from its windows, and obliterate the gathering within seconds.

Why Lionel so casually associated with petty thugs and brash lowlifes like those now dealing on the corner mystified Rex, but what was more disturbing and terrifying was the obvious fact that Lionel didn't give a damn about the consequences of his involvement with one of the most notorious gangs in the district. Rex prayed that the generation gap between them was not so god-awful wide and unbridgeable that he'd lost his brother forever to the streets.

As negotiations proceeded under the scraggly tree, Rex continued to film, finding it curious, though a bit calming to see that Lionel did nothing but observe the transaction. He never handled the money or drugs. Lionel didn't use drugs, Rex knew, because his brother was dedicated to boxing, body building, and staying rock-hard fit. He'd never pollute his body like that. Plus all the boxers in the program at the gym were tested on a regular basis. So why did Lionel have to push his way into this little bit of dirty business tonight? To prove how tough he was? To show he was connected? To reassure himself that his place in the Sharps was so solid he didn't have to deal, he could just hang around and observe?

Why hadn't the love of his family been enough? Rex wondered. What was it that Lionel needed so badly that he had to turn to the gang and stretch his luck to a wire-taut limit to garner a sense of pride?

Rex wanted to block out the horrible scene playing out across the street, but he didn't dare stop filming. With the camera back in place, he recorded it all until the cash had changed hands, the small packets of drugs had been tucked into pockets, and the gathering had broken up. The white men headed back to their car, Lionel loped across the street toward the Kwick Stop Shop, and the other two youths continued on their way.

Nauseous with rage, Rex swung his video camera down onto the passenger seat and yanked out the film. He stuffed it inside his jacket, then reloaded the camera with a blank cassette tape. Crouching down, he knew he had to wait until the area cleared before daring to make a move.

Rex sat stiffly, listening to the muffled sounds of footsteps on the pavement. He pressed his chin painfully hard against the cool surface of his video camera, lips clamped shut, praying he hadn't been seen.

A harsh rap on the window jolted him upright. Rex turned, startled to find himself face-to-face with the two young drug peddlers. Their noses were squashed against the rain-spotted glass of the driver's side window and their intense eyes pierced the dark interior of Rex's Jeep. He jerked back, mouth open, eyes wide in fear.

He shrugged and smiled his innocence, in hopes that they would go away. But they didn't leave. They didn't even flinch, but kept staring into Rex's Jeep, their eyes moving from his face to his expensive photo equipment and back up.

Rex swallowed dryly, resolving to stonewall the situation, but the tall one pulled out a gun and held it to the window.

"Open up!" he demanded, waving the pistol. "Get your ass out. Now!"

Blood rushed to Rex's head making him so dizzy he felt as if he were sinking under water, weighted down with cement blocks, yet he managed to open the door while his mind clicked off his options—he could talk to them, let them know he was from the hood, that he'd grown up two blocks away. Maybe they'd take his camera and leave. He only had about thirty dollars in his wallet and worried that it would not satisfy their demands.

"Gimme yo watch. Yo wallet," the stocky one demanded, as the tall one yanked Rex out of the Jeep and jammed a gun into his chest.

Without a word, Rex obeyed, his mind still ticking. "Hey," he started, sliding back to the street vernacular he knew as well as any gangster drifting through Columbia Heights. "Man, you ain't gotta do this shit. I was just chillin', waitin' on Willi-Man. You know. Got a little business to take care of."

"Shut up," the one with the gun shouted, slapping Rex across the face. "Ain't no more business goin' down in this dry-ass place tonight. If you lived here you'd know the streets is wired. What you doin' here? Huh?" He slapped Rex again, harder this time. "What you lookin' for?"

Rex's mind continued to click. Wired? Dry? The word was out, the brothers were sniffing for cops. Willi-Man sure as hell wasn't going to show his face tonight.

Rex rubbed the side of his face, wiping sticky blood from his fingers on his jeans. "Shit, man, you ain't gotta do this. What you want, huh? The camera? The Jeep?" Rex stepped back, throwing up his hands in surrender. "You got it, bro. Whatever. Take the shit. I don't want no trouble." He continued to back away.

The stocky youth lunged forward, grabbing Rex by the front of his jacket, throwing him to the sidewalk. The taller of the two jumped down on top of Rex, straddling him like a cowboy riding bronco, brandishing his gun—a long barreled piece of gleaming metal. He twirled it as if he were swinging a lasso.

"Ain't no cause to shoot me!" Rex yelled. "I told you, I'm waitin' for Willie-Man. He's gonna be pissed when he finds out about this," he added, recognizing the kerchiefs around the youths' necks as the colors of the Sharps.

"Yeah, sure," the one standing grunted as he dove inside Rex's Jeep and grabbed his video camera. "What makes you think I care if Willi-Man gets pissed off?"

Rex refused to be silenced. "He guaranteed me protection. It's a big deal . . ."

"Shut up," the boy atop Rex yelled, raising his hand as if to strike him again.

"Hey! I got it!" The youth who had plunged head first into

the Jeep stripped the film cassette from the camera. "This dude must think he's in Hollywood or sumthin'. Got the nerve to be filmin' out here."

The youth atop Rex glanced over his shoulder and, in a flash, Rex rolled away. He heard the crash of his photo equipment being smashed on the ground and his stomach curled into knots. In the flicker of a second, he looked across the street, searching the lighted sidewalk for help. He saw Willi-Man Monty standing under the neon sign at the Kwick Stop Shop, his expressionless eyes as blank as still water, and standing in the shadowed alleyway between the store and a vacant building was Lionel.

"Help! Help me!" Rex screamed, but Willi-Man just smiled in a sinister way, and Lionel edged back into the shadows. Rex screamed again, then doubled up in pain when his assailant belted him in the soft place below his ribs. Rex jerked his knees to his chest. The boy struck him again on his back, his side, and the top of his head. Falling forward, Rex felt his arm split open as it scraped the damp pavement. A fiery pain shot through his head, down both legs, consuming his body in a white-hot flash.

Knowing it was crazy to keep fighting, Rex resisted no more, crunching his body into a fetal position, pretending to be unconscious. Lying very still, he fought the urge to be sick on the pavement.

Immediately, the boy atop him got up. Rex eased one eye open just enough to see the gangsters divide up his cash, then stuff his credit cards and watch into the camera bag.

The tall one turned and glanced down, catching Rex watching. Grinning, he leveled his gun.

Rex squeezed his eyes shut.

A loud crack rang out and Rex pulled his body into a tighter ball as an explosion roared in his ears. He winced, certain he'd been shot, though he was so traumatized with fear he was numb. Lying on the wet cement he felt the rapid thump of his pulse in his neck and heard the muffled sounds of sneakers pounding the sidewalk. Then all was silent, except for the sound of his own ragged breath pumping up from his lungs and the wail of an ambulance in the distance.

Chapter Ten

THE alley parking spot assigned to AfroTreasures was blocked by a teetering stack of flattened cardboard boxes, two metal trash cans bursting with refuse, and an overturned wooden packing crate with the name WATTS ANTIQUES, NASHVILLE, TN emblazoned in large purple letters on its side. Beneath the cracked cement overhang extending above the alley entrance stood the owner of the minuscule curiosity shop, Frida Winer, a withered brown woman with a slender brown cigarette stuck between her lips, and a faraway look on her face. When she saw Ida's silver Mercedes approaching, she grinned, waving her arm to signal her visitor to pull into her neighbor's parking space.

A knot of young boys sauntered down the alley toward Ida. She stiffened, sorry she'd come to Meridian Park on a Sunday. During the week it was usually pretty quiet and no troublemakers were hanging around. During the middle of the day she could get in and out—take care of her business—without worry that she might be seen.

The youths were carrying large green trash bags in their hands. Their eyes were downcast as they scoured the alley for aluminum cans. When Ida stepped out of her luxury car, she stepped directly on a smashed Coors beer can, then angrily kicked it into the middle of the alley. Adjusting her oversized sunglasses more tightly to her nose, she lifted her chin and kept walking.

The clatter of the rolling can stopped the youths in their tracks. Two of them lunged for it, the oldest and tallest one got it.

Shaking her head in disgust, Ida signaled to Frida with a wave of her hand, in a hurry to get inside. She hated coming to Sixteenth Street and until recently had managed to avoid the area during the entire time she'd worked in D.C. But if Ida wanted to do business with Frida Winer there was only one way—she had to come to her.

The Jamaican woman could find whatever anybody wanted—at a price, of course. No questions asked. No explanations given. Ida's decision to use Frida's shop as the pass-through point for her shipments from Nashville had worked out beautifully, so she put up with Frida's quirky superstitions and made the trip to her shop.

"So, Missy Ida," the rail-thin woman crooned in a lazy accent. "You are on time, as usual. Welcome." She flicked the glowing red tip off her half-smoked cigarette, spit on the end, then stowed the butt in the handkerchief she had wadded in her palm. "Come een. Come een," she greeted, stepping back to let Ida pass.

Inside, Ida gave her eyes a few minutes to adjust. Once her vision had returned, she settled her gaze on the cluttered counter-tops and dusty boxes stowed around the musty space. Very little had changed since her first visit seven months ago.

Frida's flair for the exotic set the tone in her shop, which legitimately specialized in tropical decorative items: colorful paper birds in gilded cages, a riotous jumble of skirts, blouses, bolts of cloth, and pillows, which were beaded, feathered, sequined, or plastered with decorative patterns in brilliant rhinestones. The least gaudy object in the room was Frida herself, who always wore a black scarf tied over her thick springy hair, no jewelry, and never any makeup.

Ida walked to the curtained doorway that separated the shop from the tiny back room where Frida lived. She yanked back the curtain and peered inside. Turning back to Frida, she asked, "We are alone, aren't we?"

"But of course, Missy Ida," Frida assured, rocking back and forth on her heels. "All alone. Just you and me . . . and," she reached beneath the counter and pulled out a box, "this most important delivery for you from Mr. Watts."

Ida grabbed the box from Frida, who offered her a penknife to break the seal. With deliberate care, Ida pried loose the sealing tape around the edges, then cut down the center of the heavy cardboard. After pushing away the fluff of packing straw, she lifted out a massive double-handled tureen, its ornate fitted lid, and a gently curved ladle that was at least twelve inches long. Ida examined each scroll and star on the pale pink glass with the eye of a jeweler making an appraisal.

"Very nice," she murmured, setting the pieces down, her heart thundering with anticipation. This would bring a very good price and was so authentic looking, she briefly considered holding it back to add to her own collection. But Ida only wanted the real thing in her collection, and besides, her contact in Los Angeles was desperate for the tureen—a well-known TV talk show host had agreed to pay five thousand for it. Ida calculated her commission as she stroked the heavy glass, turning it over to examine the bottom.

"You like?" Frida interrupted her thoughts.

"Very much," Ida replied in a raw whisper. She was as charged up and excited as when Bonard presented her with some equally stunning work of art. Ida knew Bonard's love for her was deep and real, but what he loved with an almost equal passion was the feeling of power he got when he gave her something rare and expensive. He had bundles of money, more than he'd ever need, and for the first time in his life he had someone to spend it on. In Ida's mind, Bonard was the lucky one. If buying and presenting her with fabulous gifts brought him so much pleasure, why should she deny him? Keeping him happy was her personal mission.

She rationalized that Bonard's expenditures were no more than investments. Without hesitation he would dump money on the stock market, invest it in Treasury Bills, CDs, annuities, trust funds, and real estate. So what was a couple of hundred thousand dollars invested in art and antiques? For the woman he was about to marry? His refusal to consider a prenuptial agreement, which Ida had slyly raised first, meant she would soon share his fortune as an equal partner and she was counting the days until then.

"And the rest of the shipment?" Ida asked.

"In the back. Come with me," Frida said, coming around from behind the counter. She picked up a sign that said "Closed" and hung it in the front window, then pulled down the wrinkled curtain she used to cover the door.

Ida's eyebrows lifted as she watched Frida close up her shop. "A good shipment, this time?" she prompted.

"Very good, Missy Ida. Extraordinary."

Ida opened her purse and handed Frida an envelope. "Here's the list of contacts and what they need. How soon can you get this stuff distributed?"

"Soon. Very soon," Frida said, opening the envelope.

"When?" Ida snapped, not satisfied by her contact's easygoing attitude.

Frida held out her hand again.

Eyes on Frida, Ida reached back into her handbag and pulled out a wad of cash with a rubber band around it. Frida took it, caressed it, then stuffed it into the deep pocket of her black skirt. "You worry too much, Missy Ida. Just leave everything to me."

As soon as Kiana awakened, her thoughts flew back to Rex. A frown settled between her eyebrows and an apprehensive feeling fluttered inside her chest. What had happened to him? On Saturday night at precisely ten-thirty she had dialed his number, only to be greeted by his answering machine. No one had picked up when she had called back half an hour later, or at nine-thirty the next morning when she had left a message with her grandmother's address and phone number, checked out of the hotel, and taken a cab to the airport.

During the flight into Pittsburgh Kiana had been so upset she had not been able to read, so she'd slept—anything to keep her imagination from running wild. And now another day had passed and she still hadn't heard from him.

Had she misjudged Rex Tandy, been too quick to place her trust in him? Was he going to turn out to be like all the others—nothing but a big disappointment? Kiana turned on her stomach and buried her face in her pillow.

What is it with me? she worried, furious for having been sucked in again. Either my intuitive powers are completely out of whack or I am subconsciously setting out to punish myself. The painful press of tears held in check burned the backs of her eyelids. Well, I can do this alone, she decided, I just need to adjust my plan.

Sitting up, she surveyed the familiar room. A hint of daybreak was already glowing behind the filmy lace curtains her grandmother had hung in every room of the house. The old-fashioned windows seemed taller and wider than Kiana remembered, and a smile touched her lips as she recalled how she and Ida had played beneath their low sills, pretending that the big portals—usually flung open to the leafy tangle of giant oaks outside—were the entrances to castles where princesses lived.

Kiana looked up at the delicate folds of batiste gathered above her head, her mind drifting back to the winter afternoon so long ago when she and her mother had fitted the ancient four-poster bed with its new quilted skirt and gently ruffled canopy. A twinge of loneliness shivered through her, initiating a familiar sense of longing that she'd not felt for many years.

Since going to live in Houston, Kiana had been back to Centerville only two times, and now she prayed this visit would not deteriorate into a miserable trek through the past. Deciding to come back had been difficult, but if she wanted any help from her grandmother this was the only way to get it. Perhaps some near-forgotten event from Hester's youth or a snippet of conversation she had overheard as a child would push Kiana closer to solving the mystery of her roots her mother had left unfinished.

Kiana pulled the thick comforter over her shoulders in an attempt to ward off the summer chill that had settled over the room during the night. She looked around. The armless side chair with its rose-patterned needlepoint seat still sat by the bonnet-top highboy as it had for years. The twin Tiffany-style lamps that her mother had purchased in New Orleans when Kiana was about eight years old remained on the ancient mahogany serpentine chest of drawers, their stained glass shades dripping pink and purple fringe.

It was comforting to be in the old house again, despite the obvious changes that had occurred in everyone's life, including her own. Her parents were dead, Ida was settled into her new life in Washington, and Hester, according to Flo—her longtime friend and housekeeper—was not in as much control of her mental faculties as she desperately pretended to be.

Kiana had arrived very late, long after Hester had retired for the evening. When faithful, indispensable Flo had opened the door, Kiana had immediately sensed that she'd better not expect too much. While they munched on sticky cinnamon buns and drank mint tea, Flo told Kiana that Hester was struggling to hold onto the present, but often slipped into her own special world where no one could reach her for weeks at a time.

Some days Hester refused to eat a single bite of food or arise from her bed, let alone get dressed and come downstairs. During those times, Flo would wait on Hester around the clock as if she were a child. Then suddenly the spell would pass and Hester would perk up, put on one of her starched Lady Fair housedresses, her sturdy Old Main Trotters, and strut downstairs to resume whatever activity she had been involved in before suddenly taking to her bed.

Now the house was quiet. Flo had not yet awakened, and Hester was still asleep in her grand old bedroom, which was more like a sitting room-sewing room-studio. Kiana remembered her grandmother sitting by the window painting landscapes or puttering around with clay, making little fat dogs and long-tailed cats that she painted in vibrant colors to give to the children in the area.

Outside, a robin twittered noisily. Kiana threw off the comforter, hurriedly bathed, then dressed in blue jeans, a fleece sweatshirt, and her new rubber-soled boots. She crept down the creaky stairs, one hand clutching the polished banister, the other firmly wrapped around her mother's book. After a quick sip of orange juice, Kiana went out the back door, closing it quietly behind her, and headed up the hill at the back of the house.

The early-morning sun bathed the bronze-colored headstones with a yellow splash of light, reflecting off the marble in brilliant jewel-like rays. Kiana loved the look of the cemetery as dawn broke over the hills in the distance. The dark green forests became brighter, less ominous, and the countryside looked as if it had been plucked from Norman Rockwell's vision of rural America. She inhaled the pungent country air, its fragrance reminding her of a time when she had had no more on her mind than picking a bouquet of flowers for her mother, or gathering wild dandelions for her grandmother to brew into a clear white wine.

A still green pond lay flat and undisturbed in a grove of spreading elms. Kiana couldn't help thinking of her stepfather, Douglas, and the hot afternoon he had spent there one August while struggling to teach his girls how to swim. Kiana had caught on quickly, and done very well. Ida, who hated having water in her eyes and ears as much as she hated sharing her father's time with Kiana, had refused to cooperate and whined all afternoon. Kiana could still see the hurt and disappointment on her stepfather's face when Ida had jumped out of the pond and run off in a huff.

She still thinks everything should be easy for her, Kiana thought as she walked into a small patch of land that was surrounded by a spiked iron fence.

The tender grass gave way beneath her feet, and she could hear the sound of her own muffled footsteps in the early-morning quiet. Reverently, she walked past several tall granite and marble markers with family names inscribed on them: Soddy Russell. Lucy Russell. Thompson Lemuel, Hester's husband, though she no longer used his name, and at the center of the burial ground Kiana's mother and stepfather's double headstone. She ran her index finger over the names. *Douglas and Louise Sheridan, 1929–1973.* Tears bordered the rim of Kiana's eyes, and she could not help but wish that her natural father might have been buried there, too, but he was interred in his native California, so far away that Kiana often thought he might never have been real.

Louise and Douglas Sheridan had been born in the same year and had died together. Their lives had been as intertwined in life as in death, revolving around their commitment to the World Outreach Mission. They had traveled into Ghana, Togo, Benin, and Nigeria to distribute educational and medical supplies to the missionaries who were trying to improve the quality of life in some of the more remote villages. Sadly, their much needed work, and their lives, had ended when their chartered four-engine 707 crashed shortly after takeoff in the jungles of Nigeria.

Kiana missed them terribly—surprisingly more than during her childhood when she had accepted the absence of her globe-trotting parents with trusting, hopeful innocence. Kiana's most vivid memories were of the stoic good-byes she and Ida had had to give them—forcing smiles, waving frantically, wishing each departure would be the last, and each homecoming would be permanent.

Though proud of the good deeds her mother was doing for less fortunate children on the other side of the world, Kiana had been intensely jealous and secretly plagued by an ever-present loneliness. Ironically, death had served as the awful catalyst to bring her mother back to her permanently—only to be buried on the land that had been in the Russell family since 1871.

Aching with an inner pain, Kiana went to sit on a stone bench at the base of a flowering beech tree, drinking in the quiet surroundings. She opened the book that had survived the deadly plane crash, regarding it as the miracle it was. She had been reading it slowly, forcing herself not to devour in one sitting all that was left of her mother's words. But suddenly curious, Kiana decided to turn to the last page. A puzzled gasp escaped her lips as she stared at several intricately drawn symbols etched in blue ink at the top of the page.

My God, Kiana thought. These are exactly like the markings on the vases at the auction—scrolls and stars, the dog chasing his tail, the tight spirals set between diagonal stripes, and the flat oval fish. Kiana studied the drawings, her heart beating increasingly faster as she looked at her mother's sketches. I wonder what happened to all the Soddy Glass Grandmother used to keep locked inside the old curio cabinet in the dining room, Kiana thought as she turned back to where she had left off in the story. The second section of the book was titled: 1852—ADI'S JOURNEY.

"Ijoma's daughter," Kiana whispered, feeling again as if she were floating back in time, being pulled along by the scented breeze that had unexpectedly slithered down from the hills beyond the ridge of walnut trees that separated their land from their neighbor's. Silently she began to read.

Adi followed the tall man across the hard dirt road. He walked fast, as if he were in a great hurry to get rid of her, but Adi suspected his desire to put some distance between himself and the dark craggy forest they'd just come through was what truly propelled him up the winding trail.

The journey north had been a frightful experience, forcing Adi to cling to the sides of the rickety wagon as it had clattered over the rough narrow trails that wound in a convoluted maze of gray and green high above and away from the Georgia border. When the man had no longer been able to squeeze his low-sided cart through another narrow pass, he abandoned it, continuing on foot until reaching the clearing they now scurried across.

Adi had never been so far north, though she had made the trip from Dalton to McCaysville once. Now she was finally going to see what kind of people lived on the other side of the foggy peaks in the distance.

The hard-packed soil under Adi's toes felt strange—cold and unyielding—not at all like the soft red clay of Georgia, which by June was already nice and warm. The air was cool, and she inhaled, as if drinking from a spring, thinking at least the summers in this place the man had called Tennessee might be easier to bear than the scorchers she'd suffered through in Dalton. She shuddered to think how brutally cold the winters would probably be.

Adi hurried to keep up, her eyes darting fearfully from one shaggy white oak to another, frightened by the strange trees that were crowded thickly along the ridges and layers of outcropping hills rimming the highest mountains. Behind her, the forest created a solid barrier of prickly overgrowth that seemed to shut the mountaintop off from the rest of the world.

The sky above Adi was leaden and gray, hung with a misty veil of fog that drifted down low and curled about her ankles. The sun was partially hidden, as it had been all morning, but as she trotted along the mottled path she caught glimpses of a yellow glow illuminating the forest up ahead.

How strange, she thought, anxious to see more clearly. Running excitedly forward, she found herself almost even with the man, but when he scowled back at her Adi abruptly slowed her pace, contenting herself to walk in his shadow until they broke into the circle of light.

At the upper rim of the mountain, they stopped and gazed down into a big open valley. Like the stitches in a patchwork quilt, huge estates were laid out with arrow-straight lines of trees dividing one man's property from the other. Far to the east was a magnificent house, much more grand than the other plantations in the valley, and peopled with twice as many slaves.

Young green corn rippled in waves all across the valley floor, and she could see the slaves in the fields, their hoes pressed to the ground as they chopped and prodded the soil around each waving stalk. Several men in straw hats were riding their horses up and down the rows, hollering, threatening, pushing the men and women to get on with tending the master's crop.

Adi blinked, licking her dry, chapped lips. Never had she viewed so much open land, and never from such a height. Suddenly, she was frightened about meeting her new master and missus and wondered how she was ever going to adjust to living in such a closed-off place. During the journey she had put the eventual encounter out of her mind but now here she was at the end of the trail. Maybe the people who lived in this valley would treat her like the Dabneys had, but it was going to be awful hard to settle in without her mother's soothing voice to tell her what to do, how to act, and what to expect from these strangers.

They started down the steep incline. Adi hung back behind the man, staring at the huge structure before her—a two-story house made of white painted timber. It sat at the end of a winding path that was lined with thick bushy trees and a variety of brightly colored flowering shrubs. A double row of pillars fronted the house creating a wide carriage pass that was paved with bright red bricks set into pristine white mortar. The pillars at the entrance appeared to be *very* tall, maybe too tall, Adi decided, thinking that the man who had built that house must have been trying to sneak into heaven—force his way into the beautiful place where Adi's mother now rested. She shook her head, amazed, but not totally surprised that a white man would try such a thing.

Behind the big house, beyond the white fence railings that separated the work areas from the main house, she could see the kitchen, the smokehouse, the barns and outbuildings, and two clusters of slave quarters—one for the field Negroes and another, set apart, for the house slaves—but really all the same. They were just like back in Georgia—square wooden cabins with one window and a mud-stick chimney bunched together, facing one another, lined up in front of a narrow dusty road.

The closer Adi got to the imposing structure, the more nervous she became. They passed a tall wooden sign, and she slowed her pace to try to decipher the letters that had been carefully painted on a weathered pine plaque. MAGNOLIA CROSSING. That's what it said, she decided, grateful to the traveling preacher who had risked his life to teach her and the other Dabney slaves how to read a little. But she wondered why the plantation would have such a name—she hadn't seen a magnolia tree for miles—not since they crossed out of the mountain pass hours ago.

They neared the house. Adi swept it with a critical eye, from its steep wood shingled roof, to the tall chimneys jutting out of it, to the rows of white-curtained windows along its upper balcony. She was certain she could see someone at the window just above the entryway.

In Georgia none of the slaves had ever been allowed on the front lawn of the big house, yet the man who was now stomping over an expanse of freshly mowed grass did not act as if he planned to take her around to the back of the house. When they got to the wide stone steps that led straight up to the massive front door, the man started to mount them. Adi stopped, eyes to the ground.

The man turned. "Come on, gal," he said sternly, his tone firm, yet not unkind.

Adi didn't move. She had never heard a command quite like that and she felt confused, afraid to obey his order. Was this some trick to see if she would do as he said so he could whip her for his amusement? No, she'd better not chance it, she decided, remaining rooted at the foot of the steps.

"Dust your feet off on the grass, gal, and come on here," the man said, an impatient ring to his words.

Still Adi didn't move.

The man stepped down and stood above her, his elongated shadow consuming her small brown body. "There's nothing to fear. Not here. You oughta be grateful you been sold to Daniel DeRossette. Come on, now. I ain't got all day."

Adi stepped off the stone walkway into the patch of cool green at the foot of the wide stairs, rubbed her feet lightly—she sure didn't want to pick up any stain—and started up the stairs. Maybe in Tennessee, she would be permitted to live *inside* the big house, do the same kind of work her mother had done for the Dabneys back in Dalton, but she was certain she'd never enter that front door.

With a small hand, Adi wiped the front of the striped cotton dress the man had given her to put on. It was wrinkled, but not made of patched slave cloth as her only other dress had been. Maybe the mistress would not frown at her for daring to appear on her front steps.

At the man's loud knock, both of the polished double doors swung open simultaneously to reveal a dark-skinned woman dressed completely in white. Her skin shone with a healthy, youthful glow though Adi could see that the hair escaping her white head-wrap was streaked with threads of gray. The lady was thin, elegant, almost queenly in her posture, but there was absolutely no expression on her face. The impression she made was quietly stunning, as if she were the mistress of the house.

The man surprised Adi when he took off his stovepipe hat. She couldn't help grinning when he almost bowed. He had obviously been taken by surprise.

"Yes?" The woman's inquiry was low, like an unintentional whisper.

"This gal is . . . well, I'm delivering her to Mr. DeRossette." The man pulled a rolled paper from the pocket of his long coat. The woman took it. "I'm Wally Cudahey, from the Pettigrew Exchange over in Dalton. Mr. DeRossette said he wanted a nigra gal about this age, one who seemed kinda smart." He coughed, looked nervously down at Adi, then back up at the woman. "This was the best we could find. Hope she's what he wants."

"Wait here," the woman said calmly as she eased the doors nearly shut.

Suddenly Adi felt hot, as if the same fever that had gripped her last winter had returned. Alarmed at such a thought, she hoped it was not the case, for what in the world would she do without her dear mother to bathe her feverish skin and sit beside her—crooning those songs in a language Adi had never understood while her fingers fluttered like mating hummingbirds over the half-finished basket in her lap? A tug of sadness clenched her stomach and she prayed she would not start crying, but after twelve hours in the back of a wagon with nothing to eat since yesterday morning, was it any wonder she feared she might pass out, maybe even die before the lady decided whether or not to take her in?

Through the crack in the door, Adi could see into the spacious entry hall. The lady in white entered an open door off the foyer, then returned with a brown packet in her hand. Adi quickly averted her eyes as the servant drew closer.

"Here is your money, Mr. Cudahey." She handed him the packet and waited as the man counted the bills.

"My thanks to Mr. DeRossette," he said, replacing his silk hat on his head. With a nod, he turned and headed down the steps leaving Adi alone at the doorway.

The woman put four fingers under Adi's chin and lifted her face to see her better. "What's your name?"

"Adiaga. Adiaga Kante. But my mother always called me Adi."

Chapter Eleven

THE woman in white narrowed her small eyes until they resembled hard black beads. "How old are you, child?"

"Twelve," Adi said in her most grown-up voice, pulling her thin shoulders up around her ears, stiffening under the woman's terrifying scrutiny.

"Well, you sure don't look it," the woman grumbled. Sighing, she lightened her voice. "All right. You go on around back and pump some water in the bucket. You wash off good, you hear?"

Adi looked down at her dusty feet and legs, then nodded. "Yes, ma'am."

The woman stepped back from the door. "I'll be around shortly to fix your hair."

On the deep shady breezeway that connected the cookhouse to the main house, Adi let the woman coif and dress her in a white cotton skirt and midriff similar to her own. A white cap with a ruffled edge was pulled snugly over her freshly plaited hair. Adi grimaced but said nothing as her widespread toes were forced into shoes so hard and stiff they cut painfully into the sides of her feet. Finally, the woman looked Adi over with a critical eye, then motioned for her to follow her into the house.

Strutting like a mother duck leading her duckling to the pond, the woman moved swiftly through the cavernous dining room, past a room where the walls were lined with books, through a salon with a grand piano sitting on an Oriental rug, into a dim narrow hallway off the marbled foyer. At the end of the corridor, the woman stopped before a low door and knocked. A man's voice told her to enter.

Ducking her head slightly, the woman pushed the door open and descended two steps. The sun flooded the room with a splash of bright light. Adi felt as if she had been slapped in the face, and stopped at the door, one hand to her eyes to shield herself from the dazzling display of colors that burst before her in a wall of jewel-like puzzles. Mouth agape, she stared, unable to follow the woman inside.

"Marcela," the man said. "Who do we have here?"

Marcela turned around, frowning to see Adi still at the door, one small brown hand to her face. "Come in, girl," she ordered firmly.

Adi descended the two steps, advancing into a room set with a bank of arched stained-glass windows and gray-blue walls lined with imposing glass cases. Inside the cases were vases, pitchers, plates and bowls—goblets, compotes, jugs and tumblers of every imaginable size and color. It seemed to Adi that there must have been a thousand glass objects in just as many colors blazing in the small room that also contained a fancy gilded desk, two side chairs, a long pine table, and a fireplace fronted by an intricately designed iron grate in which a small fire burned.

"Mr. DeRossette," Marcela began. "This is Adiaga Kante. But she prefers to be called Adi."

Mr. DeRossette laid down the lapis fountain pen he had been writing with and got up, circling the gilded desk. It was piled high with an assortment of papers and dark green ledgers. He walked gracefully, in a way that made him appear to be floating, and his pale blond hair cascaded over his shoulders like a tumble of golden straw. He was small mouthed, with a decidedly narrow face and when he looped his slender fingers into the thin silver belt encircling his trim waist and tugged at his brocade vest, Adi thought him the image of a pale ghostly prince. He ran his tongue over even white teeth as he assessed his latest purchase.

Marcela motioned for Adi to come closer. She timidly approached her new master.

"Welcome to Magnolia Crossing, Adi," Mr. DeRossette said. He peered down the length of his aquiline nose as if using it to measure the distance between them.

Adi glanced up quickly, then lowered her head, expecting to feel a crack atop her skull for having had the audacity to look her master in the eye. But the sight of him had startled her—all that flowing blond hair, which she thought he should have at least tied back from his face with a ribbon, and that waxy skin upset her. Why, he was the most curious sight she'd ever seen, but then she had never been so far North either. Were all the white men in Tennessee like him? she wondered. She boldly sneaked another look, then riveted her eyes on the floor.

Daniel DeRossette watched Adi with an air of detached superiority, not so much as master to slave but as if he had a secret he delighted in keeping from her. There was a hint of a smile on his thin lips and his blue eyes were as steady and clear as a summer sky after a storm.

"I said welcome, Adi."

Adi's heart pounded fast and she stood rigidly still, shocked by the manner in which he had addressed her. Had he said welcome? Never had she heard a white man use such a greeting with a slave, and she worried again that she might be caught up in some horrible trick that would make her the object of a terrible joke.

She opened her mouth to respond, then clamped her lips together defiantly. An insolent burn crept into her cheeks as she decided, then and there, not to respond in a prompt cheerful manner as every master expected his slaves to do.

Welcome to what? she wondered. What did this new master expect her to say? That she was glad to have been wrenched from the only home she had ever known as soon as her mother had been buried? That she was happy to be sent up into the mountains, then down into a valley to a place where nobody would ever find her? She missed the old plantation and suddenly wanted nothing more than to go back. The Dabneys hadn't been so bad, at least they had never whipped her, and Adi had understood the routine—the boundaries imposed on the cycle of her days. Now she would have to learn everything all over again and the thought was absolutely frightening.

Adi began to worry. She was miles away from her mother's grave and the only place she had ever called home. She was far from the stone bench under the sumac trees where her mother had faithfully come every day at the noon hour to share an apple, a scrap of fatty ham, or whatever food she had pilfered from the Dabneys' kitchen.

During the short time they would have together, Adi would watch her mother absently though skillfully weave complicated designs into her baskets while telling Adi stories about the Kante clan and her life in Bwerani. Adi knew all about the Wangara, the old servant Tabansi, and the brave young man called Sekou, her father. But by the time the sun was shining fully into their faces, the midday bell would ring, and her mother would have to stop telling her stories and scurry back inside the big house, to be locked in until the next day.

"Welcome, Adi," Mr. DeRossette repeated, an inquisitive gleam warming his ice-blue eyes.

Adi only nodded.

"Speak up, girl," Marcela hissed.

Adi looked the servant straight in the eye, trying to decide if Marcela were friend or foe. Fearfully, she pulled her quivering bottom lip between her teeth and decided to say nothing.

"Leave us, Marcela," DeRossette said, taking his watch from his vest pocket. "Come back for her in half an hour."

Marcela sniffed, apparently affronted, and gathered her full white skirt in one hand as she swept toward the door. Turning around for one last glance, she pierced Adi with a look that was chilling, then opened the door and left.

Adi's heart beat rapidly against her breast. What was going to happen now? She fixed her gaze on the shimmering reflection of an amber fluted bowl set against the stained-glass window. She silently counted the yellow silk roses that it held.

"Do you like all of these pretty things?" DeRossette asked, opening both arms wide, sweeping the room with an expansive gesture. He turned slowly, making a complete circle, his caressing gaze flitting from one brilliant creation to another.

Adi tentatively raised her head and looked around, enthralled by the ceiling-high cases filled with delicate glass objects.

DeRossette picked up a heavy iron ring hung with keys and went to the glass case nearest the door. He opened it, took out a rose-colored pitcher that had a gracefully curved spout and a fanciful ripple of scalloped ridges surrounding the footed base. He ran his hands lovingly over the pink swell of the vessel, then turned to Adi.

"Come here."

She cautiously approached him. He held the pitcher out to her. "Take it," he said.

"Oh, no, Master," she protested, speaking for the first time. She took a step back. "I couldn't. I'd break it, sure."

DeRossette tilted his blond head back and gave off a trilling giggle, the kind of merry squeak that Adi had often heard coming from the porch when the two Dabney girls were playing with their rag dolls. Her new master's laugh didn't sound like a man's laugh to her, and in fact he looked rather young, but not young enough, Adi concluded, to have such a high-pitched voice.

"No you won't break it. I promise," he said, forcing the glass into her hands. "Lovely, isn't it?"

"Yes, Master."

"It was made by my father more than fifty years ago, and it's your responsibility now, Adi." He left her holding the pitcher and went back to his desk. He sat down, leaned back in his chair, and held up the ring of keys. "All of this is yours to take care of."

She stared at him in confusion.

"It's your job, Adi, to make every piece of glass in this room sparkle. You are to unpack and wash new pieces when they arrive. Others must be carefully packed in sawdust to be shipped to the East."

Adi looked around her, feeling overwhelmed. "Everyday, Master?"

"Yes. Everyday. By the time you get to the last piece, the first will all be dusty again or a new shipment from England will have arrived." With a shrug of his shoulders and a knowing smile, he dropped the keys in the middle of his desk and watched for Adi's response.

Daniel DeRossette was very pleased with the girl Mr. Cudahey had delivered. A very busy man, DeRossette had little time and no stomach for standing around with other plantation owners while they bid and haggled over the price of a slave. He'd avoided what he termed the "unpleasant experience of trading in flesh" by using the Pettigrew Exchange to arrange the purchases of all fifty-seven of his slaves. He made a mental note to draft a letter of thanks to Pettigrew for doing such an excellent job of selecting just the type of nigra he would have picked himself. Adi seemed perfect. Her hands were small enough to get inside the narrowest pieces in his collection, and the man, Cudahey, had said she was smart.

The only son of Edward DeRossette—a celebrated English glassmaker who once held a royal commission—Daniel was content to be referred to as a Southern gentleman planter, though his heart was still tied to the family glass factory.

In 1797, Edward DeRossette and his brother, Alfonse, had pooled the meager wages they received from working as lackeys and chimney sweeps and started their own glass factory. With the help of an impoverished Venetian artist whom they met on the streets of Manchester, they created and produced a stunning line of glass, which owed its brilliance to the addition of lead, and its vibrant ruby color to the infusion of gold.

Their pieces were cast in the pattern mold method, blown into a contraption similar to a waffle iron, then cooled to create the gently scalloped edges and shell-like swirls around the rims and pedestals of each piece. In this manner, they produced an extensive assortment of plates, bowls, cups and saucers, creamers, sugars, compotes, and tumblers. The eye-catching pattern caused quite a stir in the factory town of Manchester, and Edward came up with the bright idea of offering it to the royal court as its official glassware.

King George III quickly embraced the work of the DeRossette brothers and offered DeRossette Glass Company a royal commission for one thousand pieces in a variety of colors.

Production moved ahead full speed, with chemists called in from France and Italy to help create the colors brought about from just the right amount of iron for yellow, manganese for pink, copper for deep greens and blues, and, of course, the gold dust to make the favored ruby-red hue that Edward DeRossette considered most royal.

Elated at having been chosen to fulfill such a lucrative royal commission, the brothers exhausted all their financial resources and lines of credit in order to pay for the chemists, the raw materials, the new workers to be hired, and the expansion of their tiny factory. Three new furnaces also had to be added.

It took three years to complete the royal order, but by then, the queen had tired of waiting and turned her eye on a fancy French design. She easily persuaded King George to cancel the old contract, leaving DeRossette Glass financially ruined with a huge inventory, which the king decreed could not be sold in England.

The brothers were devastated. Their future seemed doomed, until a merchant from America walked past the factory and saw the royal pieces gathering dust in the window. He stopped to inquire about purchasing several place settings to sell in his shop back in Boston.

The idea of exporting the languishing line of glass to America was born and Edward promptly sent his son, Daniel, to New York to find buyers for their wares. By promoting it as tableware fit for royalty, Daniel soon lined up more orders than the factory could readily supply. Within a matter of months, DeRossette Glass was back in full production, exporting the line it called Queensware to upscale brokers of pricey shops that were strung along the eastern seaboard from Baltimore to Boston.

Daniel, who scorned life in bustling cities like Philadelphia and New York, bought one thousand acres of fertile land near the Cumberland Plateau, fifty-seven slaves, and all the machinery, bricks, and lumber needed to create his gracious plantation. He settled in on his property to live the life of a cultured Southern gentleman, raising corn to support his comfortable lifestyle, while traveling back and forth to New England, taking orders from merchants who could not get enough of his family's elegant glass.

Now Daniel's face seemed to grow even narrower as he turned a questioning eye on Adi and asked, "Can you write your letters?"

Again Adi feared to make any response. What did he want her to say? That against the orders of Mistress and Master Dabney, she had gone to the creek bank and listened to the traveling preacher as he had repeated the alphabet over and over? That she had once stolen a stub of a pencil from little Fannie Dabney's desk to practice her letters late at night in front of the fire while her mother called out the words? Oh no, he'd never get her to admit to that.

"Well?" he pressed for an answer, his manner brusque. "I specifically asked for a smart nigra," DeRossette said as if talking to someone else. "Can you write your letters or not?"

Adi remained firm in her refusal to admit to what she knew could only bring her a beating with the strap.

DeRossette threw his arms down flat on the desk and scowled darkly at Adi, all kindness vanishing from his white pinched face. "Dammit, answer me! Or I'll have you whipped. If you don't know your letters, out you go!" He motioned jerkily toward the windows. "I didn't pay good money for a stupid nigra!"

Terrified of being cast out into the hinterlands of the strange mountain top, Adi finally nodded, murmuring lowly, "A few letters, sir. Only a few."

DeRossette smiled broadly now, and the pale flesh on his cheeks folded inward, elongating his delicate face. "Good. Marcela will teach you more, because you're not only to clean the glass, but keep an inventory, too."

Lifting her head, Adi stared, confused.

"A ledger, girl. A record of what I have here."

"Oh, yes, Master," she murmured, shocked to hear such words. Why, in Georgia a white man could be lynched like a Negro—or at least drummed out of town—for saying such dangerous things. Certainly all the white men in Tennessee weren't like her new master, were they?

Adi cupped her small fingers around the heavy pitcher and let the smooth glass settle into the palm of her hand. It felt solid, comforting in an odd sort of way, and she guessed she could do as she was asked. It sure beat picking cotton or slopping hogs and Mr. DeRossette at least *could* smile.

He held out a pair of white cotton gloves to her and she crossed the room to take them. When she extended one hand, the pitcher slid from beneath her fingers like chicken fat over a hot iron griddle and splintered with a crack on the hard polished floor.

"Oh!" Adi gasped, horrified. The vessel lay in shards at her feet.

DeRossette jumped up, fled around his desk, both hands at his throat, his white cheeks stained purple with rage.

Adi fell to her knees, grabbing at the broken glass that shimmered like a shower of rubies.

"That's right, Adi," DeRossette said in a shockingly surly voice. He sounded like a growling dog, gearing up for an attack. He deliberately placed his small kid boot over the back of Adi's hand and pressed down until she heard the sound of glass cracking under her flesh and felt a sharp pain in the center of her palm. "Stay down there on your knees, you little pickininny! That's right! You clean that up!"

Grimacing, Adi fought back her tears, but did not cry out as he pressed harder and harder, grinding his heel down like a mallet against her fingers until she felt the splintered glass cutting deeply into her skin. Blood oozed from beneath DeRossette's boot, mingling with the glittering red glass.

"You clean every bit of it up!" he shouted.

She tried to move her hand but it was no use, he had pinned it to the floor.

"I could whip you within an inch of your life . . . or hang you for breaking that pitcher. It's been in my family for over fifty years. A priceless, irreplaceable heirloom."

Confused, she froze, not daring to move for fear that he would come down on her with the fireplace poker or whatever heavy object he could get his hands on.

The chime of the tall case clock next to the door filled a terrifying silence.

Suddenly DeRossette removed his foot, giggling in a nervous trill as he spoke in an eerily calm voice. "But *this* time I will forgive you, Adi." He bent down and peered at her, his curtain of blond hair cascading over his upside-down face.

Adi chewed the inside of her cheek. This man was mad! Possessed! What in God's name was he talking about. Forgive her?

"But only *this* time," he said, straightening up, tossing his silken mane from his face, sniffing loudly as he wiped his brow with a ruffled bit of lace.

She held her breath.

DeRossette stepped away, his footsteps a mere whisper of a shuffle as he headed toward the door.

Adi watched his shadow stretch out in a thin silhouette on the gleaming yellow pine floor. "But if it ever happens again," he said, the giggle completely gone from his voice, "you will feel *more* than the bite of the strap on your back." He put his slender hand on the doorknob. "Do you understand what I am saying?"

Shrinking into herself, not daring to even half raise her eyes, Adi shifted on her knees, then nodded. "Yes, Master," she answered lowly, wishing the floor would open up and take her away from this strange man whose changing moods she didn't understand.

DeRossette mounted the two low steps and left the room, quietly closing the door behind him, leaving Adi on her knees.

Tears broke loose and spilled from her sad brown eyes as she slowly raised her head and stared miserably at the massive carved door. A pulsing fear burned in her chest. All she wanted to do was go back to Georgia, back to the kind of people she understood. Thumbing away a tear, she wondered why God had taken away her mother and left her all alone in the world?

Chapter Twelve

"KIANA!"

With a snap, Kiana jerked upright and looked around, blinking her eyes against the intrusive glare of sunlight.

"Kiana! Kiana!" Flo was standing at the back door waving her arm in the air. Her big red-and-white apron flapped in the wind. "Better come in. Breakfast is on."

Shading her eyes with one hand, Kiana called back, "I'll be right there."

"Hurry. Hester's already down."

Kiana lowered her hand from the side of her face, then stared at the spot of blood in the center of her palm. How odd, she thought, rubbing at the patch of red, wondering how she had managed to cut herself. She slammed the book shut, feeling edgy, anxious to talk to Hester, and hurried down the hill into the kitchen where she washed the blood off her hand, then went straight into the dining room.

In the high-ceiling room where her father had sat at the head of the table, her mother to his left, her grandmother facing him, Kiana greeted Hester Russell with a generous hug and a kiss on her softly wrinkled cheek.

"Good morning, Grandma," Kiana said, relieved that Hester

had finally come out of her room. She had been beginning to worry that her visit might be for naught.

"It's good of you to come see me," Hester said, taking one of Kiana's hands in hers, patting it. "Too long, child. You've stayed away too long."

Hester's silver-white hair shimmered like a fluffy cloud of iridescent cotton around an oval-shaped face the color of vanilla wafers. She carried her ninety-one years with grace and beauty, having managed to maintain the elegance of an almost Victorian lifestyle that most of her contemporaries had long ago abandoned. She called it the gentlewoman's way of living, which she and her husband had created and enjoyed during their forty-seven years of marriage.

Thompson Lemuel, who married Hester Russell in 1922, the day after he graduated from Antioch College, had been madly in love with his eighteen-year-old bride, and willing to devote every moment he was not bent over some merchants' thick ledgers to her whims, desires, and fancies. When he went off to Fisk University to pursue an advanced degree in economics, he took his young wife to the bustling center of black culture and there, in Nashville, in the protective, sheltered enclave of good manners and breeding, provided Hester with the opportunity to find out who she was.

In the university setting, Hester found an exciting circle of women like herself—intelligent, brave, wanting only the best for their families, and for the first time she made friends. She soon adopted the ways of the middle-class faculty, paying careful attention to the minute details of their structured lives, reproducing their table settings, interiors, and ways of dress with a zeal that delighted her husband.

As time permitted, the handsome couple would take the train to New York, Washington, Boston, or Philadelphia to see how the rest of the world lived. Hester loved traveling and shopping, and was happiest when wearing the latest fashions, and always surrounded herself with pretty things. She certainly could not afford to buy what she wanted from the shops on pricey avenues where the wealthy people shopped, so she often ferreted her precious finds from secondhand stores or from discarded furniture stacked in the alleys of better neighborhoods.

It took Thompson Lemuel four years to complete his master's degree, then he and Hester returned to Pennsylvania where he took a job with the Federal Bureau of Labor and Standards and even taught economics at the University of Pittsburgh. They built a house on the family land where Hester had been born and transformed it into a Victorian showplace with hydrangeas spilling out of vases, lace dripping off of tabletops, mums and tulips sprouting in the gardens, and muted images of hand-painted landscapes set in silver frames bunched atop every table.

The upstairs rooms had white plaster picture moldings all around, which Hester promptly and brazenly painted a deep shade of pink to compliment the cabbage rose-patterned wallpaper she hung on every wall. Her home became a Victorian jewel with high ceilings, heart of pine floors, huge doors with etched glass transoms, and a fireplace in every room.

Thompson Lemuel enjoyed a long, distinguished career and a comfortable, compatible life with Hester. He was awarded citations, ribbons, and plaques of honor for his work, garnering accolades from both the black-and-white press. Throughout the country his name was well-known, his reputation highly respected, and he became a sought-after speaker at meetings and conventions all across the country until the cancerous lump that had been slowly growing inside his chest sent him to bed in exhaustion.

After Thompson's death in 1969, Hester grieved publicly for exactly thirty days, then put her mourning clothes at the back of her closet, pulled on the most colorful of her imported lace dresses, and shocked the genteel black folk in the tightly knit social circle of Centerville by changing her last name back to Russell—her mother's name—the same name she had carried as a child. Though proud to have been Thompson Lemuel's wife, she was even prouder to be known as Soddy Russell's granddaughter.

Now Hester adjusted her silver-framed bifocals on her high-bridged nose and looked her granddaughter up and down. "My, my. You are prettier than the last time I saw you. A little thin, though." She shook her head in admonishment. "I hope you're hungry."

"Famished," Kiana replied, slipping down onto the soft velvet seat of the polished cherry chair, still puzzled by the small cut in the center of her palm. Had she been so absorbed in her mother's rendition of Adi's life that she had gripped the book too tightly? Cut herself with her own fingernails? Whatever the case, she could hardly pull her thoughts from what she had read and was anxious to get back to it.

The table was set with Hester's pink-and-white Lenox china plates, heavy sterling silver flatware, and thin china teacups that were as translucent as wafer-thin paper. Four miniature Waterford jam pots filled with a variety of homemade jellies were clustered next to a bushy bouquet of garden lilacs that was set in the center of the table in a heavy old-fashioned crock. Linen napkins, monogrammed with the letter R, were rolled and stuffed into worn silver napkin rings at each place setting.

Flo drifted in with a steaming platter of ham and a basket of her cinnamon rolls, which she plunked down with a smile in front of Hester, then disappeared back into the kitchen.

Kiana could tell from the grin on Flo's face that she, too, was relieved and happy to see Hester in good form—at the table, dressed in her starched floral dress, looking as if time had whipped her back to 1950 when she had been at the pinnacle of health and happiness.

Kiana unfolded her napkin and spread it over her lap. "You look great, Grandma."

Hester made a little shaking motion with two fingers. "Old age is not pleasant, Kiana."

Kiana laughed softly as she poured tea into her cup.

"So, I hear from Ida that you have left that dangerous city and are moving to Tennessee."

Kiana's hand froze on the warm handle of the teapot. She slowly set the heavy silver pot down, then picked up a wedge of lemon. "You spoke to Ida?" she asked, wondering why.

"Oh, yes," Hester remarked with a little jolt, blinking, as if the memory of her conversation with Ida was beginning to clear. "She telephoned yesterday . . . no, not yesterday." Hester buttered a roll as she thought. "Must have been . . . oh my. I can't remember. But not so long ago. Such a good girl, Ida. You know, she finds the time to visit me the first Monday of every month. Never misses. Never."

Kiana swallowed her tea with an uncomfortable gulp. "Every month?"

"Never fails," Hester replied. "Sometimes I think if it weren't for her visits, I'd completely lose the track of time."

Kiana bristled. That liar, she thought, telling me she hadn't seen Grandmother for months. Why did she have to lie?

"I don't hear from you often enough," Hester complained, hurrying to add, "but I'm glad you've come home."

"Did Ida tell you she's engaged?"

"Yes. Yes. Sounds like a fine young man." Hester pierced a slice of ham with her fork. "Now what was his name?"

"Bonard," Kiana supplied. "Bonard Wilson?"

Hester nodded. "Yes, that's it. But don't get off the subject, Kiana. What are you going to do?"

Kiana was shaken by the thought that Ida was so cozy with Hester, but knew she had no one to blame but herself. She should have made the effort to stay in touch. "I'm finishing my Ph.D, Grandmother."

Hester lifted one small shoulder, shrugging off Kiana's remark as if it were a piece of lint to be brushed away. "Well, Ida told me you quit your teaching position and gave up your apartment. If you're not working, how in the world are you going to live? What do you plan to do with yourself, child?"

"I'm just taking time off to finish my degree. I got a grant from the Urban Women's Coalition. The money is not in yet, but eventually I'll have enough to live on, for a while," Kiana said, hoping her current financial situation would not continue to deteriorate.

"Ida said something about that, but I couldn't get it straight." Hester waved at Flo through the dining-room door. "This ham is delicious, Flo. I know it's too salty and I really should not eat it, but . . ." She took another bite. "Delicious." She turned her attention back to Kiana. "I am proud of your ambitious approach to your studies, dear, but quitting a perfectly good job? I can't condone that."

"I had to in order to be free to do my research."

"So. Where are you off to and what are you looking for?"

"I am going to Tennessee," Kiana said, cautiously watching for Hester's reaction. "To Magnolia Crossing, I hope."

Hester's thumb and forefinger locked on her teacup and she lowered it into its saucer, looking as if she'd felt the kiss of a ghost on her neck. "Where?"

"You know, Grandma. Magnolia Crossing. Where Great-great-grandfather was born."

"What *are* you thinking about, child?" Hester's soft cheeks folded into crepey lines as she pursed her lips and waited for Kiana's answer.

"My dissertation topic is on black artists of the nineteenth century. So I want to include our family . . . the story of Soddy Russell."

"What?" Hester managed, a tremor in her voice. "What about Soddy Russell?" Her glasses magnified the trepidation filling her eyes. Hester crushed her napkin to her stomach and stared at Kiana, waiting for a reply.

Kiana hedged, avoiding Hester's probing stare by toying with the food on her plate.

"What are you trying to do?" Hester repeated hoarsely.

Kiana glanced up, meeting Hester's inquisitive expression. "I'm writing about reparations."

"Reparations?"

"Yes . . . you know, the compensation African-Americans should get for the losses suffered as a result of slavery. I will reference the biographies of talented black artists . . . including Great-great-grandfather's as examples of how black artists suffered economically and never benefited from their work. Legacies were lost, even stolen."

"What in God's name are you talking about, Kiana?" The skin at the base of Hester's throat corded with pulsing veins. She frowned, narrowing the space between her thinning gray brows and dashed her napkin down onto her plate. In a voice like hammered steel, she said, "*Nothing* has ever been stolen from this family. Nothing. Don't you dare go inferring that I want . . . or need . . . a government handout! Not after all your grandfather accomplished during his lifetime. Reparations!" She spat the word at her plate. "How could you associate yourself with such a cause? How?

It's no more than another way for lazy Negroes to shift the blame for their failure to make something of themselves. Food stamps, welfare . . . now reparations!" Hester clenched her teeth in anger.

Kiana jerked back, shocked by Hester's unexpected outburst. "Please, Grandma, you don't understand. I am not setting out to paint the Russells as a greedy, angry black family hell-bent on getting a check from the government. I know better than that."

"Then keep our family name out of whatever you are writing. Nothing's ever going to come of that mess. I want no part of whatever it is you are doing."

"But, Grandmother," Kiana rushed on, determined not to alienate Hester, "something is happening and you need to know about it."

As Hester sat rigidly listening, Kiana told her about the glassware she had seen on the auction block in Houston, of the prices they had brought, and of her plan to uncover the truth about the source of it.

Hester tapped her spoon nervously on the side of her cup as she stirred her strong herbal tea. "Kiana. I apologize for raising my voice. It was not called for. I understand and appreciate what you want to do, but there's no point." Her voice, no longer tinged with anger, nevertheless had a dismissive ring. "That old stuff Soddy made cannot be what you saw selling for thousands of dollars." She sniffed. "When those people from the museum called and asked me to lend them my vase, I told the man that I didn't see what all the fuss was about. Art! Those pieces of glass were nothing but little whimsies the boss man let my grandfather make to pass the time at the end of the day. He just fiddled around the factory while he was cleaning up after the white men who worked there went home. Nothing to be making such a fuss about." She grunted under her breath. "Now I wish I'd never lent that vase to the museum. It's all a big mistake."

"Mistake? Oh, you're wrong. The recognition Great-great-grandfather received in that exhibit has placed his work alongside other important artists. Where it should be! It made me see how much our family took his talent for granted. By the way, what happened to all the pieces you used to have?"

Hester glanced across the room to the empty cabinet and

shrugged. "Lord only knows. I think I gave all that stuff away over the years. I don't recollect now. So long ago."

"While he was alive, Great-great-grandfather got no recognition or compensation for his work. Did he?"

"Times were very different, Kiana. Let it go."

"Why? If reproductions, or his original works, can be sold at such high prices, something is going on. I've got to know more."

"Impossible, child," Hester threw back. "You'll find no records to prove a thing. He was not so long out of slavery when he worked at that glass factory. But that's the way he was treated . . . as a slave, not an artist. There's not going to be any records. Soddy Russell was paid a dollar a day to clean up after the white men, not to create silly designs. And now you say folks are paying high prices for that stuff." She snorted in disgust.

"Exactly! Don't you see? His designs should have been patented. Papers might have been filed. I believe there are records somewhere and I'm going to find them," Kiana adamantly declared.

"Let it go," Hester repeated sharply. "Going down into the hills of Tennessee, digging around. Don't do it. Please. Don't stir things up. No good can possibly come of it. Besides, I told your mother and I'm telling you—I don't believe there ever was a place called Magnolia Crossing."

"But I believe there was," Kiana protested.

"No, no," Hester protested. "Soddy made that up to throw slave hunters off his track once he made it to freedom. He lost his wife, Adi, on the road trying to make it North and he knew the bounty hunters were determined to get him, too. He had a baby —Lucy, my mother—to care for and he wasn't about to let it slip where he'd run from because he'd be hauled right back to slavery. So why would he tell folks the truth?"

Kiana's shoulders drooped with each word from Hester's mouth. Maybe depending on Hester's support had not been such a good idea.

Hester went on. "My mother tried to find out what happened to Adi. Your mother was searching, too." Hester stopped suddenly, hugging her arms about her waist as if trying to hold her emotions in check. "And both . . ." she hesitated, looking warily at Kiana, then said in a whisper, "both died trying to find that cursed Magnolia Crossing."

Kiana's mouth opened slightly in surprise. "That's not true!"

"Oh, yes, it is," Hester replied flatly. "And if you go poking around, asking questions, talking this reparations mess, something awful is going to happen to you, too."

"What about Mother's research? Her story?" Kiana asked, deciding to press Hester a little harder since she was obviously extremely alert today.

"That old book?" Hester cut Kiana off. "Louise made most of that up. Nonsense. Fantasy! That's all that is."

"Did you ever read it?" Kiana asked.

Hester shook her head.

"Then how can you call it nonsense?"

"Because she told me she was making up the parts she had no information about . . . so what good is it?"

Refusing to be put off, Kiana said, "I plan to study it . . . use it as a guide. Mother may not have had all the facts, but I have a feeling she was close to the truth."

Hester patted her fluff of silver hair as if trying to put herself back together. "You go down to Tennessee talking reparations . . . snooping around and you'll be sorry. You might even end up in jail. Things have not changed so much, my dear."

"Uncovering our history might be worth going to jail for."

"And I can see you haven't changed, either." Hester folded her wrinkled fingers into clawlike fists, as if to gird herself for what she had to say. "When you were in high school, in college—every time the telephone rang I was terrified that it would be the police telling me you'd been arrested again. All that protesting and carrying on you used to do took years off my life, Kiana."

"I never meant to worry you," Kiana said. "I just can't stand by and let injustice prevail. In any type of situation."

Hester grunted in dismay. "Well, I see now that you didn't come home just to see me, did you? What do you really want?"

Kiana pushed her chair back from the table, angling it to face her grandmother, praying she had not alienated the only person who could help her now. "I want you to tell me everything you remember your grandfather ever said about Magnolia Crossing. And as much as you remember about him."

Pulling into herself as if to hold onto the past, Hester shrank back in her seat, then calmly poured herself another cup of tea. "There's not much to tell. He was a lonely man. Didn't like strangers. Kept to himself. Died when I was a girl. And I have to say it's a good thing all this whoop-de-do about his work didn't happen until after his death. He'd never have wanted it. Never."

"That may be true, but I have to do this, Grandma. I had hoped you would help me."

"You're going to do this with or without my blessing?"

"Yes," Kiana said firmly.

"Well . . ." Hester said as she rose, picking up her teacup and saucer. She pushed her chair up to the table. "I can't talk about it today. Maybe tomorrow. Will you help me back up to my room?"

Chapter Thirteen

REX had barely awakened when Ed Marshall pushed through the door.

Ed stroked his pointed goatee as he approached the hospital bed. "God, Rex. Glad to see you've finally come around."

"What time is it?"

Ed checked his watch. "Eight-thirty—*a.m.*"

Rex squinted in confusion.

"You slept yesterday away. How are you feeling?"

"Groggy."

"What do you remember about what happened?"

"Not a hell of a lot," Rex said.

"Well, the police drilled me about who you were and if you really worked for the magazine. They were out there tracking a drug deal when you were attacked. They're convinced you must have seen something." Ed paused, then asked directly, "Did you?"

"Nope. Not a thing," Rex said flatly. "Wasted my time . . . Willi-Man never showed." His words were controlled but his insides quivered. Had the police discovered his videotape of the drug deal? It would place Lionel smack in the middle of the action.

Ed came closer, concerned. "The cops told me they've been undercover in that area for months, trying to make a case on some midlevel government workers who are doing dope at the main post office. Didn't see anything out of the ordinary, huh?"

"Naw," Rex replied.

"I tried to explain to the officers that you had nothing to do with anything, but I didn't get the impression they believed me. You can bet they'll be in here real soon asking you a lot of questions."

Rex tried to sit up, then fell back, relieved that Lionel hadn't actually handled anything. "God, my head," he moaned.

"A slight concussion, I was told," Ed informed him.

"I feel like hell, Ed. I remember being dragged from the Jeep. There were two guys. They beat on me like a punching bag. There was a gun. I remember the sound of the shot."

"Don't worry. They missed you," Ed filled in.

"Scared the hell out of me more than anything else," Rex muttered.

"Other than a giant headache and a few bruises, you ought to be fine."

Rex groaned, but pushed himself upright, letting Ed adjust his pillows. "So? What's the deal with the story, now? What do you want to do?"

Ed rubbed his chin with his thumb. "Your smashed camera and a roll of blank film were deposited at the front door of *Black Culture Watch* sometime during the night."

"Really?" Rex squirmed.

"Yeah, along with a note to me that you'd better stay out of Columbia Heights and I'd better kill your story or somebody was going to be hurt. More seriously this time."

"Damn!" Rex struggled to sit up, then ran his fingers over his matted hair. "Those punks!"

"Listen, Rex, this could get ugly. Maybe you'd better pull back," Ed said. "I've got a magazine to get out, but I'm not going to have you looking over your shoulder every time you leave the office."

"So?" Rex said.

"So, I think you ought to get out of town. Lay low. Go and do the Soddy Russell piece."

"You serious?"

"Sure. But I want it done fast. Got that? This is not a vacation, Tandy. As soon as you're released, drop by the office and we'll work out the details."

"Great," Rex said, pulling the stiff white sheet up to his chest. He slid down onto his back, and gave Ed a thumbs-up gesture. "Thanks. You will not be sorry."

When Ed left, Rex eased over to his side and his thoughts flew back to Kiana. He had promised to take her to the airport. Damn. She must be pissed. He wondered what she thought of him and what she had decided to do. He reached for the telephone, but a pain shot through the base of his skull forcing him back onto his pillow. He lay still for a moment, then his eyes closed and he drifted back to sleep.

With his black Malcom X cap in his hand, Lionel eased into the dim room. He frowned at the smell of antiseptics and sterility. Stopping just inside the doorway, he rested his head against the jamb and let out a long tired sigh, almost afraid to approach the form lying on the bed draped in a tent of white sheets. A pang of guilt sliced through him for not having done a thing to save his brother from Willi-Man's boys. He could have covered Rex's back and gotten away with it, too. But he'd been scared the gang might turn on him or worse, throw him out, so he'd let the attack go down, acting as if Rex were not his brother. The sound of voices paging doctors filtered in from the hallway and Lionel cleared his throat loudly to alert Rex that he was there.

From his narrow chrome-railed hospital bed, Rex lifted his head, craning his neck forward in an attempt to see who this visitor was, hoping it was not his mom or dad. They'd be hysterical if they knew what had happened.

"Lionel," Rex whispered, his dry throat hardly able to release the word.

"Hello, Rex. How you doin'?"

"I feel like I just crossed the Sahara Desert—bare-headed with an empty canteen. My head hurts like hell." He pushed himself up on stiff arms. "Any water in this place?"

Lionel came to the bedside, poured a half glass of water from the stainless steel pitcher, and handed it to Rex. "The doc said you gonna live."

A confusing mix of gratitude and annoyance swept over Rex as he watched Lionel's face. He loved his brother very much, but Rex's tender emotions were suddenly colored by a desire to punch him out. Rex balled his fists beneath the sheet, ready to launch a verbal dressing-down, but bit his tongue and waited. What good would more words do? Looking at Lionel, Rex didn't see a confused young man. He saw a plump brown baby he had diapered, and fed, and carried around the neighborhood on his shoulders, proudly showing him off to every person he passed. When had that innocent bubbly child transformed into the angry stranger who stood before him now?

Rex reached over and switched on the lamp on the nightstand.

Glancing over his shoulder, as if he expected the law to come in behind him, Lionel moved closer to the bed. He summoned up a half smile, that Rex did not return. "Man, I'm glad you're okay," Lionel started, obviously ill at ease.

"Could be worse, I guess," Rex replied. "Pretty bruised up and some surface cuts on my arm. Other than that, I'm going to be okay."

"Good, good." Lionel averted his gaze, his mouth turned down. "I told you not to go out there with that camera, man. I warned you, bro. Don't say I didn't."

Rex saw the beginnings of tears sheening Lionel's eyes and realized how hard it must have been for his brother to come. "Yes. You warned me. You did." Rex reached up and tugged on Lionel's jacket. "Come on. Sit down."

Lionel slumped on the edge of the bed, his gaze riveted to the floor.

"I don't blame you, Lionel. Not for this," Rex said. "But I saw you there. Got it on tape."

Lionel nodded glumly.

"And you saw me, too, didn't you?" Rex asked. "You stood by and watched me get beaten. How could you be so cold?"

"Wasn't nothin' I could do. I *warned* you, man. You shoulda listened!"

"How would you feel if you were standing downstairs right

now identifying my body in the hospital morgue instead of talking to me here?" Rex asked.

Lionel hunched his shoulders in a dismissive shrug. "Hey, man. But you ain't dead."

"But I could have been killed! Think about it, Lionel. You could be making funeral arrangements right now!"

Tears spilled over Lionel's cheeks. He angrily brushed them away with a swat. "Wasn't nothin' I could do. I already told you. What's it gonna look like . . . me runnin' across the street trying to stop what I told you was gonna go down? Be a death sentence for me, man. I'da been history."

"Yeah," Rex pressed on, hoping to get his brother's attention. "You could be in jail right now, or worse—Mom, Dad, and I could be burying *you*. Is that what you want? Is that where you're headed?"

"Ah, man. Get real. Ain't nothin' gonna happen to me!"

"Oh! So you're some kind of superman? Huh? Bullets bounce right off of you?"

"I know my way 'round out there. I can take care of myself."

Rex winced as he tried to lean forward, as if getting closer or talking more loudly would make the slightest difference. "Don't try to make yourself believe that, Lionel. It's not true. You better listen to me. You've got to stop running away from who you are. Cut the tough-guy bullshit and get off the streets! Please . . . not for me or Mom or Dad . . . for *yourself*. Register for summer school. Get something on your mind besides hanging with the Sharps."

Lionel opened his mouth, gulped in air, then fastened tearful eyes on his brother. "Get real. It ain't so easy."

"It's not that hard! Try." Rex unflinchingly held Lionel's defiant gaze. "I'll help you."

After twirling his hat around nervously in his hands, Lionel whispered, "You gonna tell the police what you saw?"

The fright in Lionel's face cut to the core of Rex's love for his brother. "I haven't decided, yet," he hedged, wanting to hear what Lionel had to say.

"Don't sing to the pigs, man. You hear me? It'll only make things worse . . . a whole lot worse for both of us. I didn't do nothin'. You *know* that."

With a droop of his shoulders, Rex absorbed Lionel's plea, knowing he had to make some sense of the situation. "Lionel? I don't want to be the one to send you to jail."

"Yeah. So, don't be showin' no cops that tape, you hear?"

"If I keep my mouth shut, maybe even disappear for a while until this mess cools down . . . will you clean up your act? Get out of the gang? Go on to summer school and straighten up?"

Lionel fidgeted with the black hat in his hands, squirming on the edge of the bed. "You wouldn't say nothin'?"

"That's right," Rex answered.

Lionel sniffed suspiciously, turned his head to the side, then looked back at Rex. "Sure, man. I'll do it."

"Summer school? No more running with the Sharps? You mean it, brother?" Rex pressed. "You're not just saying this to get me off your case, are you?"

Lionel shook his head. "Naw. I guess I gotta make a few changes."

"Promise?"

"Yeah, man. I promise," Lionel reluctantly agreed.

Rex plunged ahead with his plan. "I want you to go home. Tell Mom and Dad that I'm taking a tour group out for the Smithsonian, okay?"

"Sure."

"Tell them I'll call in from the road. Lionel? You got that?" Rex grabbed Lionel's sleeve.

"No problem. I hear you, bro. No problem," Lionel said.

"Good," Rex said firmly. "Because I *will* be calling. You hear me? I'm going to be checking on you."

With a grunt of understanding, Lionel stood. Hitching up his low-slung pants, he strutted to the door in that rolling gait that infuriated Rex, but he stopped halfway across the room, returned to Rex's bed, and leaned down to hug his brother to his cold leather jacket. "Later, man," he whispered. Then like a shadow flickering over the wall, he turned and disappeared.

Chapter Fourteen

IDA glanced approvingly at the number of people filling her spacious apartment. The group assembled included men and women, blacks and whites, prominent Latinos from the local business community, and a group representing the Asian import/export industry. All had braved the evening rush hour traffic and a pounding rainstorm to attend Bonard's first big fund-raiser. There were entrepreneurs, politicians, corporate types, financiers—a variety of backers who were pledging their support to Bonard to promote his conservative position on the gritty issues facing the nation.

In Ida's lovely apartment, thirty of the most influential Republicans in the city nibbled smoked oysters and sipped white wine while tossing around election strategies they hoped would ensure the election of their candidate.

These were money people with clout, power, and influence. They willingly put their names on Bonard Wilson's list because they found him intelligent, politically and financially astute, and brave enough to be openly critical of Arthur Rilan, the incumbent who had been accused of placing every dime of government money he could into the hands of his cronies—a tightly knit group of men and women who managed an astonishing number of community-based programs which, so far, had done little to improve the quality of life of the constituents in the district.

Bonard's background of poverty, escape from the projects, and eventual rise in the world of high finance, made him a compelling candidate. He had caused quite a stir when he changed his party allegiance from Democrat to Republican, though he maintained a moderately aggressive position on the issues of welfare reform and affirmative action.

Accused of taking a middle-of-the-road position in order not to alienate the black movers and shakers, whose vote was actively courted by all African-American candidates, Bonard did not let such name-calling bother him. His strategy was simple: he kept the traditional African-American cultural and social organizations like the NAACP, Urban League, National Organization of Women, and PUSH from bad-mouthing him too loudly—even getting the leaders to reluctantly forgive him for deserting the Democratic party—by donating huge amounts of cash to their tightly stretched budgets. From the looks of the turnout, Ida felt certain that Bonard's chances of winning were excellent.

She poured herself another glass of Chardonnay, one eye steadied on society columnist Glenda Vine. The reporter had been especially blunt with her personal questions, pumping Ida about her childhood, her educational background, and details of how Ida and Bonard had first met.

Ida had kept cool, answering as politely and forthrightly as possible, but she remained unconvinced that the nosy gossip-monger was through digging around in her past. Thank God Kiana is not here, Ida thought, turning her attention to Nicky Malone, a well-respected dealer in African art.

A flush of pleasure rose to her cheeks as she raked Malone with smug appraisal. The snooty art dealer had been absolutely stunned by Ida's extensive collection. Her treasured pieces of Soddy Glass, which were arranged by color inside a lighted curio cabinet, had stopped him in his tracks. Mouth agape, he had critically, lovingly, examined each piece, her matched Soddy Glass candlesticks nearly bringing tears to his eyes. Malone had practically begged her to unlock the case, then held them up to the light, inspecting them with an expert's eye.

Few people knew how to distinguish authentic Soddy Glass from professional imitations, but the secret method had been passed to Ida by Grandma Hester many years ago. The old woman had told her young granddaughter to hold a plate over the light of a beeswax candle. When Ida had done as instructed, a flat oval fish with tiny pointed teeth had emerged like a faint shimmering shadow on the bottom of the plate. Ida had laughed with delight, telling her grandmother that the fish looked like it was swimming in its own little pond of glass.

Ida knew another reason why that day remained so clearly imprinted in her mind. It had been the same day her father and stepmother had departed on what would be their final trip to Africa. Grandma Hester had been trying to amuse Ida, to distract her from missing her father too much. Two weeks later her father and Kiana's mother had come home in polished mahogany caskets.

Ida felt her resentment toward Kiana building, as it always did when such unpleasant memories came back. Louise Sheridan had seduced her father, married him, then drawn him away from his daughter. If it had not been for Louise and her crazy missionary zeal, he never would have died.

Ida shivered, her memories dissolving as she realized that Bonard was telling his guests the story of her familial connection to the nineteenth-century artist, Soddy Russell. It was a story he loved to tell.

As the well-heeled attendees gathered closer, Ida tuned her fiancé out, concentrating on the time frame left on her plan to push the demand for Soddy Glass so high that the eventual sale of her growing collection would make her four times as wealthy as any of the snobs sitting in her living room nibbling her hors d'oeuvres.

There were not many original pieces the quality of hers still floating around on the general market. Ida knew her collection, which she'd managed to slip piece by piece from Hester's china cabinet, was larger and of a better variety than the collection at the National African-American Museum.

Ida felt no guilt about taking Hester's Soddy Glass. Hester didn't know the value of what she had and if Ida hadn't taken it, the senile woman would have probably given it away to strangers. But, Ida worried, Kiana was more than likely poking around now, trying to find out where it was.

A sense of triumph shot through Ida at the thought of out-smarting Kiana. The girl might be close to having a Ph.D. but she was no match for Ida's inventive mind.

Ida was elated that her partnership with Marvin Watts was turning out to be a very lucrative arrangement. When she had lent him her personal collection to copy and had seen how flawless and well crafted his work had been, she'd checked him out thoroughly. It hadn't taken long to uncover a little detail she decided to use to entice him into partnership. He was well respected, talented, and firmly connected to the world of antique glass in a way that would make his endorsement sterling, but he also had a blot on his record that he had worked very hard to keep in his past.

Fifteen years ago, Marvin Watts had served six months in a federal prison for mail fraud when a mail order collectible company he had started went bust and he had been unable to make good on a fifty-thousand-dollar check. Just the type of man she needed for the job.

It was actually fun, easing Watts's reproductions into selected markets, but how the glass Kiana saw in Houston had come to auction, Ida didn't know. Watts had some explaining to do. If he'd deliberately cheated her out of one dime of her share on that deal, she'd personally make sure he never fashioned another piece of glass as long as he lived. She had no problem dealing with people who broke her trust.

Artists! Ha! A temperamental lot they were, she thought. Watts was a slow, tedious man, who took far too long to create each new piece. Ida had hoped to move more quickly with her plan, but when she'd fussed at him to make him more productive, he had balked, deliberately seeming to move even slower. If Marvin Watts were not the master of his craft, she would have dumped him long ago. But he had the skill she needed, and the ability to keep his mouth firmly shut. No one except Frida could connect her with Watts, and if she could just keep the supply flowing for a few weeks longer, and if Kiana didn't botch things up, she'd be able to sell her burgeoning collection, take the cash, and finally kiss Bering & Overton good-bye.

Through half-closed eyes, Ida focused on Bonard. Her ears burned as she listened to his loud, vulgar boasting. Now and then a twinge of embarrassment flared as she realized how easily he had been fooled. If only he knew that each piece of Soddy Glass he bought from Frida Winer only fattened Ida's bank account. Well, *he* was the financial expert, she thought. He ought to pay more attention to the source of his investment instead of the fire she lit in his pants.

You stupid, love-starved fool, she mused, watching him puff up his chest as he proudly informed his guests of the rarity and investment potential Soddy Glass held, and how much of it he had already purchased for his bride-to-be. If you only knew what you were spending your money on, Ida thought calmly studying Bonard while he quoted price comparisons between Soddy Glass, Tiffany, and Steuben.

Everyone murmured in appreciation, then crowded around Ida, delighted to have such a near-celebrity in their ranks. Ida grinned, chatting with ease about her interest in art, demonstrating an extensive, perceptive understanding of the market, not only as a collector but as a very astute investor.

Immediately Ida sensed a shift in everyone's demeanor—a heightened respect of Bonard's choice for a mate. Ida didn't doubt for a minute that the "oos and ahhs" coming from all around her would translate into bigger checks, more enthusiastic support, and an easier acceptance into their tight little social circle where she planned to become a regular. And if she understood the hunger fueling every one of her guests as well as she thought she did, the demand for and price of Soddy Glass had already increased threefold.

Ida took a sip of wine, told Cora to refill the plate of miniature crab-stuffed pastry on the sideboard, then crossed the room to chat with Alicia Dufur, a business writer for the *Washington Post*.

The gathering broke up about midnight and after saying good-bye to the last of her guests, Ida went to the kitchen and told Cora to leave the rest of the cleanup until morning. As soon as Cora departed, Ida sank down on her satin sofa, extending her arms to Bonard.

Gazing down at his fiancée, he said, "It was a smash, wasn't it?"

"Perfect," Ida agreed.

"With this type of support, nothing will stop me."

"I think you're right," Ida replied, shifting aside to make room for Bonard to sit next to her.

He placed his arm along the back of the sofa and loosened his tie. "Come here," he commanded playfully, pulling Ida to him, kissing her in a slow, thoughtful way. "You were quite the topic of conversation. I think I can now safely move you to the asset column of my balance sheet," he jokingly told her, nibbling at her red pouty lips.

"Ah, ha! The truth," Ida countered in an equally light manner. "You're marrying me for my family's legacy so the rich white folks in the world of art will embrace and respect you for your good taste in . . ."

"Women," he slyly finished. "You, my dear, are a stunning example of beauty, sophistication, culture, and class." He began kissing her ear, flicking his tongue over her perfumed lobe.

Ida shifted slightly, trying to disengage his tongue from her ear without appearing too repulsed. If there was one thing that unnerved her, it was Bonard's tendency to roam over her body with his thick pink tongue. Kisses she could tolerate, but the licking sometimes got to be too much.

Bonard eased back. "After the election, we are going to be very busy," he said. "And very visible. We'll be entertaining often, Ida, and I am proud that our home will properly reflect your good taste in art . . . and my ability to acquire it."

Bonard got up from the sofa and approached the glass curio case. He opened it and took out a tall amber-colored pitcher with raised hollow-center stars around the rim and the handle. Staring at it he asked Ida, "Are you sure your grandmother doesn't still have the cups that match this piece? Having the entire set would be such a coup."

Ida went to stand next to Bonard. "I doubt it. The last time I was back in Centerville, I checked again. Looked everywhere. Nothing is left. I have everything she had."

Bonard replaced the pitcher in the cabinet and pulled Ida to him, turning her around so that her back was against his chest. He circled his arms around her waist. "If matching cups exist for that pitcher, I'll find them. Would you like that?" he asked, nuzzling her neck.

"But you're spending so much money," Ida replied in mock protest, placing her hands over his at her waist, her mind whirling as she calculated exactly how much money he had already handed over to Marvin Watts. Leaning back, she allowed her buttocks to press against his groin, then tilted her head onto his shoulder. She heard a long whisper of a breath slip from between Bonard's lips, then he began kissing her ear again.

"Don't worry about the expense," he whispered between kisses. "I just want to make you happy."

"I *am* happy," Ida purred. Slightly turning her head, she asked, "How does it feel? Having money to do what you want, buy whatever you please? It must make you feel very . . . powerful."

"It does," Bonard acknowledged, squeezing her tighter. "I've worked hard to stay ahead in a white boy's world, and believe me, Ida, I never plan to worry about money again. The money men come to *me* now because I've proven to them that I know how to invest and it's working." He slicked the side of Ida's neck with his tongue. "And as soon as you are Mrs. Bonard Wilson, you will know that feeling of power, too."

Ida turned fully in the circle of Bonard's arms, and planted a kiss on his forehead. If only you knew the truth, Ida thought, you'd see just how much power I already have.

Chapter Fifteen

HESTER didn't come out of her bedroom the rest of that day or the next. Kiana and Flo checked on her regularly, read to her when she was awake, and generally tried to pull her out of her wandering state. They met with little success. It was as if Hester had withdrawn to a world peopled by her friends and family who had already passed into the place she called "the better life."

She carried on running conversations with her deceased husband and her daughter, and even with the old preacher who had married her to Thompson. She flatly refused to eat, but did sip herbal tea and tried to keep her appearance up by demanding that Flo paint her fingernails and make up her face. Flo, who was used to these spells, knew exactly how to handle it and with a smile and a lilt to her voice, assured Kiana that nothing was wrong.

Kiana was worried, but not alarmed about Hester's condition. The elderly woman had moments when she didn't know Kiana, then she'd be cheerful and talkative, happy to see her. The lucid periods didn't last very long, and Flo cautioned Kiana to be patient, caring, attentive. Hester would snap out of it. She always did.

On the third evening, before retiring, Kiana entered Hester's room with a pot of herbal tea on a heavy silver tray. Hester's bright eyes glistened. She sat up and immediately gave an order to Kiana.

"Open the bottom drawer of the highboy," she said, her voice as strong as it had been when Kiana was growing up.

Kiana did as she was asked, gripping the shiny brass fitting on the bottom drawer to pull it open.

"See that purple velvet book? Take it out."

Kiana lifted the old-fashioned photo album from the cedar-lined drawer and cradled it in both hands.

"Bring it to me," Hester said, motioning that Kiana put it next to her on the bedside table.

Angling it so that Hester could see the pages, Kiana sat on the edge of the bed.

"Didn't you say something about wanting to know about Soddy Russell?" Hester quipped.

Kiana smiled. Hester had picked up their conversation exactly where they'd left off. She seemed lucid, enthusiastic, and anxious to talk. Gingerly, Kiana opened the worn velvet picture album that had stiff pasteboard pages with cutouts holding faded photos. She vaguely remembered seeing the album as a child but had completely forgotten about it.

Using an arthritic hand to carefully page through the book, Hester finally placed her little finger on a single photo of a young woman who was standing next to a fence. She had a hoe in one hand, a straw hat on her head. Kiana could not remember ever seeing that photo.

"And this is?" Kiana prompted.

"My mother, Lucy—your great-grandmother. She came out of slavery with Grandfather . . . but she was only a babe in his arms at that time, too young to know what was happening to her."

"Did she talk about her childhood? The early years after Great-great grandfather settled here?"

Hester made a little shrug. "Momma didn't talk much. Didn't pass anything to me."

Kiana was tempted to ask Hester more about her own childhood, but was hesitant. Kiana's mother had cautioned her and Ida years ago to avoid the touchy subject. But as a girl, Kiana had listened carefully to the family whispers and had eventually managed to patch the truth together—Hester was a child of rape. No one knew who had fathered her, and that was why she had always used the last name Russell. And why, Kiana always suspected, her grandmother avoided the past and hated to discuss anything about their family history.

Before Kiana could ask another question, Hester flew ahead with her story. "All I ever heard Momma talk about was returning South to try to find her mother. Every day, she'd go about her chores, taking care of me and Grandfather, but at the end of each day when we knelt together to say our prayers, she always ended with a promise to Adi that she'd come back for her . . . find out where she was living—or buried, whichever was the case."

"What did your grandfather say about that?"

"Oh, Soddy grieved for his wife, but he was convinced she was dead. The years passed, and when I was about seven, he left me with Flo's family up the road and took off with Lucy, trying to get back to Magnolia Crossing, his old master's house. They had a terrible time. Everything was still torn up from the war, roads destroyed, landmarks gone. He and Lucy wandered for days, asking questions. They were chased off property lots of times and once the sheriff held them in jail for three days for disturbing the white folks by being too familiar."

"Did they find any clues about what happened to Adi?"

"Nothing. Never turned up a trace of Adi. Didn't even find the old plantation, either. So they came on back home to Centerville, looking like they'd just been released from some wartime prison camp, and resigned themselves to never finding Adi. Momma did tell me that while they were on the road, thieves stole Grandfather's shoes off his feet, and he walked the last hundred miles home barefoot, leaving a trail of blood from Morgantown to Centerville."

"Did Lucy ever talk about where they went? Which roads they took? Anything about the route?"

"She fell seriously ill not long after she got home. Her mind was never the same. She talked a lot about hills. She said the hills had been too steep for her and Grandfather to climb and they were covered with thorny bushes and strange trees. I always believed they got turned around and never made it as far as Kentucky."

Kiana shook her head as she gazed at the picture of Lucy. "When did she die?"

"I was eight years old. It was terrible, losing her. You see, my mother lost her mind trying to find Magnolia Crossing and when she came back home she just gave up. For the rest of his life, at least as far as I can remember, Grandfather never mentioned the word Tennessee again." Hester slammed the book shut and shook her finger at Kiana. "I want you to leave it alone, Kiana. Let the past stay where it is. It's not such a glorious story, you see."

Kiana opened her mouth to protest, but the telephone rang. Flo had gone to visit a neighbor, so Kiana hurried from the room to answer it. Telephone calls to Hester's house were few and far between and rarely did anyone call so late.

"Hello. This is the Russell residence," Kiana said.

"I was hoping it would be."

"Rex?" Kiana stuttered, unable to believe her ears.

"Glad you recognized my voice," he said. "Makes me feel better already."

The sound of his voice on the other end of the line flooded her with relief. "Where are you? What is going on?"

"I'm at home. Packing," he said, a hint of laughter in his voice. "God, I'm glad I caught you."

"Caught me?" Kiana replied.

"Yes. Before you took off by yourself."

"You must have been reading my thoughts. What happened to you? I called and called."

"It's a long story, I assure you. I ran into a little trouble when I went to meet with Willi-Man."

"Trouble? Oh," Kiana groaned, holding her breath as she listened to Rex explain how he had been attacked. "How awful! You've been in the hospital since then?"

"Yep. Got myself released this morning."

"How do you feel?"

"A hell of a lot better than I did yesterday. In fact I feel better than I have in a long time."

"Did you file a complaint with the police?"

"All finished. The police came to see me in the hospital. I gave them all the information I could. Kind of sketchy. I really couldn't see the guys very well. It was dark."

"That's awful, Rex. I hope they catch those thugs. You could have been killed."

"Sure, but I wasn't."

Kiana's pulse was racing. He had been very lucky, and he hadn't run out on her. "You said you're packing?"

"Mmm-hmm."

"Why? Where are you going?"

"That's up to you," he replied. "My story on the Treps and the Sharps is on hold. Ed thinks we'd better let things cool down. So, he's given me the go-ahead to take you to Tennessee and start on your search. And I must say I agree with him. I'll feel a lot safer once I'm out of D.C."

"That's great news!" she replied, anxious to get started, yet concerned about her financial situation. The delayed grant and recent cancellation of her American Express card were beginning to put a damper on her enthusiasm. "What about my refund? I might have to wait for it to come through before I take off."

"Don't worry about that," Rex told her. "I'll pick up the check from the Smithsonian and bring it along."

"Well . . ." she drew out her response, thinking, then stated with confidence, "Let's go!" Her spirits had recovered quickly and she felt relieved that her first take on Rex had not been wrong. She *could* trust him and he wasn't going to back out of their deal. He wouldn't let her down. "I was praying you'd come through," she admitted.

"Did you get much help from your grandmother?"

"We've talked several times," Kiana said, going on to summarize what Hester had told her. "She's in better shape today, but maybe I expected too much."

"She's . . . how old, again?"

"Ninety-one."

"Maybe she's told you all she can right now. But, don't be discouraged. We can make quite a bit of headway with what we have."

"Oh, I'm not discouraged," Kiana hurried to add. "I've been reading more of my mother's book, and even though Grandmother discounts it as fantasy, it feels so real to me. I have a sense it's going to be very helpful."

"Good," Rex said. "Let's get started."

"Where do we go from here?" Kiana asked.

"Well, I think we'd better start in Nashville as originally planned. We'll track down that antiques broker, then visit the courthouse and check any land or state census records you haven't already covered. From Nashville, we'll probably head to Knoxville, then down to Chattanooga. We need to dig around to see if there is any mention of a plantation or settlement called Magnolia Crossing. I feel certain it was not a town, and as you know many plantations were destroyed during the war."

"Yeah, it could be difficult," Kiana replied. "So where do we hook up?"

"There's a United flight from Pittsburgh to Nashville that leaves at eight tomorrow morning. Think you can make it?"

"No problem," she told Rex, not even balking at the ungodly hour she'd have to get up. "I'll meet you at the Nashville airport."

Chapter Sixteen

KIANA pressed the button above her head, sending a single beam of yellow light into the darkened space of her window seat. The plane was half empty and since no one was seated beside her, she spread out, placing her black sweater, a straw hamper of sandwiches Flo had insisted she take along, and her coach cabin bag onto the adjoining seat.

It was good to finally be on her way. She'd faxed a copy of her itinerary to Ida, along with a note about Hester's fragile condition. Kiana had no doubt that Ida would be checking in very soon, though why she was playing the dutiful granddaughter, Kiana didn't know.

Kiana unzipped her flight bag and took out her mother's book.

As soon as the plane leveled off, she flipped through the pages she had already read, and stopped at a new part titled, THE RIVER, 1856. Kiana kicked off her shoes, tucked one foot beneath her hip, and settled in to read.

Ofia threw back her head and screamed, her grieving wail shooting out of the slave quarters like a whizzing arrow sprung from its bow. The eerie howl sent chills of sorrow rippling over Adi's folded arms, and she pulled her coarse cotton shawl more tightly across her chest, rising on tiptoes to see over the shrubs that divided the big house from the plot of land that was the burial ground for the slaves.

Adi yearned to join those comforting Ofia, but feared Marcela might be watching, and might make good on her threat to tell Master Daniel if she ventured one more time into the field slaves' quarters.

Adi's status as a house slave kept her physically separated from those who labored in the outbuildings and the fields, but did not prevent her from feeling their pain. How could Marcela expect her to shut her eyes and ears to the sorrows of those who slopped the hogs, sowed the fields, and hoed the skunk weed from between the rows of corn, when not too long ago Adi had been the one chopping cotton while her mother polished silver and scrubbed floors under the watchful eye of Mrs. Dabney? Marcela's chatter about how much easier it was to bear the sorrow of bondage because she didn't have to labor in the sun, didn't make much sense to Adi, and she knew it was not true.

Adi glanced back at the big house and frowned. It was not yet dark but Marcela had already begun lighting the downstairs lamps. Master Daniel must be in the library reading his newspapers, Adi thought, knowing that her master devoured no less than ten different papers a week—papers from the North and the South, from big cities and tiny townships. She wondered what it was he read about and what was happening in those faraway places she would never get to see.

Another yellow glow erupted in the front parlor, and Adi calculated that she had only a few minutes more to stand at the fence before Marcela would come looking for her.

Turning her eyes back on the funereal gathering, Adi saw Ofia push away the restraining hands of two women who were trying to prevent her from throwing herself into the tiny grave where her first-born child lay still and cold in his miniature white pine coffin.

Clustered at the edge of the hole in the ground were all fifty-seven of Daniel DeRossette's field slaves. They stood with heads bowed, listening as a gnarled, white-haired man, whom Adi recognized as Rusty, the oldest slave on the place, spoke a few words of prayer.

As soon as the final send-off was finished, two muscular young men began tossing dirt onto the wooden casket while others initiated a mournful tune that hung in the twilight like a swollen teardrop. In the soulful melody, the slaves thanked God for the blessing the child had been and praised Him for liberating the innocent boy from a life of shackles and misery. The little boy would find happiness, they sang, on the other side of glory, beyond this mortal place of toil and hardship.

After so many slave funerals at Magnolia Crossing, Adi knew the words by heart, and also knew the song would continue long into the night, drawing her into the pulsing anguish of her brothers and sisters in bondage.

She sighed, remembering the last burial a few weeks ago—also a child. Adi had heard that the little girl, who had been in the fields with her mother sowing seed behind the plow, had been kicked in the head by a cantankerous mule. Adi calculated that Master Daniel had lost five slave children this month to accidents, illness, disease—what many called the fever of bondage.

Blinking back tears, Adi listened to the swell of music as it filled the fragrant evening air. It rose from the floor of the valley, over the mountaintops in the distance, and floated off into places in the heavens where Adi believed the children must have gone to rest.

"He's free, now." A voice from beneath the low-hanging fronds of a weeping willow tree on the other side of the fence jolted Adi.

She spun around, peering toward the spot. There, watching her was Price, one of Master Daniel's wagon drivers. He was standing with his raggedy black hat in his hands.

"Yes," she agreed softly. "The child's gone to peace."

The newest slave on the DeRossette plantation came two steps closer. Adi stiffened, her eyes boldly fastened on his partially shaded face, not fearing him, but intrigued by his audacity. In speaking to her, in coming so near the big house, Price had violated Master Daniel's rule that the only slaves permitted to pass information across the fence were the little boys especially selected to approach the house slaves with messages from the field.

"Hard on a mother. Burying a child," Price said.

"Yes, it's a pity," Adi agreed, grasping the opportunity to talk with the man she had been secretly watching from the big house for weeks. "But maybe laying him to rest is not as hard as watching him be sold away," she added.

Price nodded, lifting his eyes toward the mourners again.

Adi assessed the man who had protested adopting his master's last name, defying Daniel DeRossette's order that all his slaves use the surname, DeRossette. The rumor from the quarters was that upon his arrival at Magnolia Crossing two months ago, Price had told DeRossette that he'd rather die than call himself by a white man's name and had given himself the name Price because of the high prices he brought each time he went onto the auction block. Eleven times he claimed, his last owner being a tobacco farmer somewhere in North Carolina. From the first day Price had set foot on the place, Adi had become as aware of his presence as his obvious interest in her.

Now that she was approaching seventeen, Adi knew that Master Daniel would soon pair her off with a man, most likely by the end of the year. She had been worrying about that quite a bit, and since Price appeared young, though Adi calculated that he must be at least twenty because of all the masters he bragged he had lived under and all the places he said he had been, he was easy to look at—not handsome, but clean and plain, like a polished piece of ebony. He was tall and thick, with muscled arms that strained at the sleeves of his tattered cotton shirt and he had a set of square shoulders he held proudly erect, in contrast to the submissive demeanor of many of the other slaves.

The first time Adi had seen Price he was strutting through the field slaves' quarters like a rooster circling the henhouse. She had tensed with fear, guessing Price to be dangerously rebellious, but when she saw how gently he treated the children and how patiently he assisted the elderly slaves who could no longer fetch wood or water or patch their cabins by themselves, she rethought her opinion of him. And he obviously had Master Daniel's trust because she had seen Price drive off alone in the wagon many times, heading toward the mountains in the east.

If Master Daniel gives me any say, Adi thought, I'll tell him I'd be willing to go live with Price, because I might fare a lot worse if I don't speak up.

"Miss Ofia's sure heartbroken over this," Price said.

"I know. The boy was only about six months old," Adi replied. "And such a pretty child, too. A good baby. Rarely cried. Nobody had an inkling he was so sick. Just had a little cough. Marcela sent some chicken bones down to Ofia only yesterday, hoping a little broth might pull him out. When I heard this morning that the child had died, I was shocked, shocked and saddened."

"Everyone was," Price agreed. "But what kind of life would he have had if he'd lived?"

Adi paused, tilting her head to the side, letting herself get used to the level tone of his voice. Impressed by his words and manner of expressing himself, she wondered how he had learned to speak so well and if, perhaps, he knew how to read and write.

Price went on. "The boy would never be free. He'd grow up under the yoke . . . like a mule in a harness. Maybe God's got better plans for him."

"You think death is better than life?"

"Could be," Price answered. "I know there're better places to be than here. Maybe heaven's one of 'em."

"Master Daniel's not so hard to please," Adi countered. "He's never whipped one of us, and him being a single man makes it a bit easier than if there was a mistress dogging my tracks all day. But, Lord, Marcela can press me sorely."

Price grinned. "I don't figure you to be one to let anybody press you too hard."

Adi squinted, trying to see Price's expression better. "Why do you say that?" she asked. Had he been watching her more closely than she thought? Had he been talking to Marcela about her?

"No particular reason," Price hedged. "I've just got a sense you can take care of yourself, that's all."

"You been watchin' me?" she asked, hoping it were true.

"Can't say as I have time to stand around watching anybody." Price dodged her question, sending her a smile as bright as a moonbeam.

Neither spoke for a moment, then Adi summoned the courage to ask Price what had been on her mind since his arrival. "What do you know about life in other places?" Certainly, he seemed to be the most worldly slave on Master Daniel's place.

Price eased nearer the fence. Adi stepped closer. He glanced up at the big house, then told her, "Plenty. More than I could tell you right now."

Adi's heart raced, and she cast her glance to the freshly cut lawn while nervously rubbing the grass with the toe of her boot. "Maybe you could tell me . . . some other time?"

"May be," he started, then stopped when he heard a window being raised. Lights appeared in the rear rooms along the upper balcony and Price quickly stepped back into the shadows.

Adi looked up to see Marcela passing the curtained windows, and prayed the housekeeper would not lean over the sill and start hollering for her to come in. Turning back, she smiled at Price, deciding to press her luck a few minutes longer. "Tell me, what kinds of things do you know about?"

"I know how free black men live," he said confidentially, drawing back his solid shoulders.

"Have you ever talked to one?" she asked, shocked that he dared to admit it. Associating with free Negroes was strictly prohibited and Adi had heard about the lashing given a slave on a neighboring plantation for speaking to a free Negro on the road. The overseer had chased the stranger out of the valley, then hauled the slave back to his master who had wielded the whip himself, giving the man twenty lashes. Afterward his neck had been collared with an iron ring hung with bells so his movements could always be tracked. Adi believed the man still wore that shameful burden on his shoulders to this day.

"Yeah," Price admitted. "I've talked to free Negroes. Those what made it across the river."

"What river?"

"The big river. The Tennessee. It runs right into the mountains where the freed men told me it's easy to slip into the woods and make your way North." Price put on his hat. "I never been that far east, but I make regular trips to the mill up by the foot of the ridge. If you want, I'll take you along since you never been no place." He flicked the brim of his black hat with his index finger, then added, "That is if you can get Master Daniel to give you a pass."

Adi's heart thundered in her ears, and she grasped Price's challenge as if it were a silver dollar. "When?"

"Next time I go."

Clasping her hands tightly she contemplated the idea of going off with Price. She had not been off the plantation since her arrival with the exchange man four years ago. Some of the DeRossette slaves were allowed to visit blood relatives on the neighboring plantations, or deliver building supplies, food, or tools to the white planters who needed help. A few were even hired out to planters as far away as Memphis, and at Easter and Christmas Master Daniel let many of his slaves go to the creek bank and listen to the Negro preacher—as long as a white minister was present. But none of that was the same as getting a pass to go across the valley. She had never had a reason to go anywhere.

"Oh, I'll get a pass," Adi brashly promised, her excitement ebbing as Price backed away. She wanted him to stay longer, tell her more, but she knew he'd better leave. "Master Daniel never fusses much at me. I think he'd let me go to the mill . . . as long as I'm back before dark."

"Try," Price urged, tipping his head. "Try, Adi. I'd like you to go with me." He smiled good night, then disappeared into the darkening shadows that had quickly settled over the grounds.

Adi gathered up her full white skirt with both hands and dashed up the hill toward the house. To see the river! To ride in a wagon with Price!

Her thoughts churned. How would Master Daniel react if she asked him to give her to Price? When might be the best time to approach him? Still unable to predict his changing moods, she worried that her timing had to be just right.

Daniel DeRossette could be pleasant, smiling, and easy to serve one day, then turn sour and edgy the next, though Adi calculated that he was usually in pretty good spirits during the days right before he left on one of his regular trips to the East. There, she knew, he sold the vases and bowls and compotes she so carefully packed in sawdust and straw. He was due to leave again in two days, and it would be another month before he got back. She didn't want to wait that long to make her wishes known.

The next morning Adi rapped softly on the door of her master's study and waited, feeling as if she were about to make her appearance before the Lord on judgment day.

After giving her permission to enter, DeRossette, never lifting his eyes from the newspaper on his desk, asked, "What is it?"

"Master Daniel. If you've plans to pair me with one of the men, I wanted to ask you if it might be with the new wagon driver."

DeRossette's head snapped up and a puzzled squint wrinkled his face. "Price?"

"Yes, Master."

"Why, Adi, I hadn't given any thought to mating you, but when the time comes I'll remember what you said." He picked up his paper and continued reading. "You may go," he muttered.

Adi didn't move.

"I said I'll think on it, Adi," he said curtly, waving his fingers in a quick flutter, pulling his newspaper back before his eyes.

When she didn't leave, he crushed his paper in his lap and glared at her. "Is there something else?"

"Yes, Master," she replied, swallowing to still the foreboding anxiety rushing into her throat.

With an irritated sigh, he asked, "What?"

"I . . ."

"Yes?"

"I was wondering if you might give me a pass to go over to the Sorrell place to visit Miss Ruby tomorrow. Marcela's needing more soap berry and Miss Ruby's got a real good supply."

DeRossette opened the center drawer of his gilded desk, took out a flat stiff card, wrote a few lines, then handed the pass to her in a distracted flourish. "You may leave now," he said, dismissing her firmly.

Adi accepted the precious paper with a quaking hand and stuffed it into her apron pocket, quickly retreating from the room.

At daybreak, Adi stood by the front parlor windows watching her master's carriage sweep down the tree-lined road as he set off for Boston to take more orders from the merchants who were anxious for his wares. A flutter started up in her stomach as she worried over how to send word to Price. Now that she had her pass, he'd have to make good on his offer to take her to the mill.

Chapter Seventeen

THE next morning, Marcela shook Adi awake at the crack of dawn. It had rained heavily during the night, but Adi could see out the window that the spring day was coming on clear and the sky had been washed a pale pink.

"What is it?" Adi asked, surprised to find Marcela standing over her sleeping pallet. She sat up, trying not to awaken the three other young house slaves who shared her tiny cabin. Adi looked groggily into Marcela's stern face.

"I hear you want to see Miss Ruby?" Marcela declared, propping both hands at her hips, glaring down at Adi. "I have plenty of soap berry. Why did you tell Master Daniel I needed more?"

Unsure about what to say, Adi blinked her eyes more fully open, fearful she had been found out.

"I didn't see any in the wash house. Even the lye soap is getting low."

"Hmph," Marcela grunted. "Well, go on then. The wagon driver sent word he'd take you over."

"He did?" Adi pushed her hair back from her brow and began tying a white kerchief around her head, forcing herself to remain calm. So, Marcela was suspicious. Damn. She'd have to be sure to scour the trail to the mill for the fleshy berries and bring some back to the old witch!

"Get up," Marcela ordered. "Price is waiting at the east gate near the barn. He's leaving in fifteen minutes."

Adi jumped to her feet and began pulling on her clothes.

Marcela raked Adi with disapproving eyes. "I don't take kindly to Master Daniel letting you off the place. You better be back by noon, or I'll send Tom looking for you."

Incredulous, but certain that Marcela would sic the brutal white overseer after her, Adi tried to clarify the situation. "I know I have chores that need to be done today before . . ."

"I guess they'll have to wait," Marcela interrupted sharply. "Since you made this arrangement with Master Daniel, go on. But you get back here as fast as you can and I expect your work to be done before sundown." Marcela turned abruptly, then vanished through the door.

Adi shook her head. Marcela was a whole lot like Master Daniel—as unpredictable and finicky as an old lame mare. At times she was tolerable, almost friendly, but mostly she was unapproachable. And if the house work was not done to her expectations, she'd get as angry as a hornet driven out of its nest. And she hated when anyone else had the favor of Daniel DeRossette. Sometimes Adi thought Marcela wished she were the lady of the house.

By the time Adi made it to the east gate Price was sitting in his wagon ready to go. The bed of the clumsy high-sided cart was piled with pieces of timber to be ground at the mill into a load of sawdust. Price smiled and nodded at Adi, helping her climb up.

"Got word you talked Master Daniel out of a pass."

"Yes," Adi said breathlessly, "but he thinks I'm to visit Miss Ruby over on the Sorrell place."

Price clucked his tongue in mock admonishment and gave her a sly smile.

"So," Adi said, "I must come back with soap berries or Marcela will have my hide."

"No problem," Price chuckled. "I think I know where a Wild China tree or two is giving off berries about now." He pulled his hat down low over his eyes and settled into his seat.

They were about to shove off when Ofia, the slave woman who had lost her son, stepped from behind the barn, a big straw basket in her hand.

"Ofia!" Adi cried out, surprised by the haggard figure standing in the dirt road. Ofia's hair was matted with bits of hay, her scrawny legs were still dusty from the prior day's work in the fields, and her eyes were red-rimmed and swollen as if she had not stopped crying since the night her child was buried. "I'm sorry about your boy."

Ofia blinked rapidly, jerking her head up and down sharply, then drew Adi in with an imploring expression. "Thank you kindly, Adi." She extended the basket to Adi. "Take dis, please," she said. "You gonna need it."

Thinking there might be food inside, Adi took the hamper from Ofia, but it was not heavy at all and she wondered if Ofia wanted her to gather some cabbage palm or yellow root for her along the way. But before she could question Ofia, the woman had disappeared.

"How odd," Adi remarked to Price, setting the empty basket atop the load of wood.

Price shrugged and picked up the reins.

"How far is the river?" she asked, relieved to be getting started.

"Not so far," Price said. "Beyond Walden Ridge over there to the east, about an hour this side of Possum Creek. Once we get to those red gums over there we gotta cut through the woods, then on the other side is the river."

Adi chuckled. "It's got a odd-sounding name doesn't it?"

"The Sequatchie River, just like the county," he replied, taking his eyes off the road to solemnly gauge Adi's remark. "Named by the Indians . . . used to be a lot of 'em in this area." He shook his head. "You got a lot to learn, don't you, Adi?"

She grinned, astonished at how comfortable she felt with a man she really didn't know. "Guess I do."

"Well," Price began, his gaze settled on her face, "I'm glad to be the one to teach you."

Adi folded her arms about her waist and squeezed tightly, glowing inwardly at her good luck. To be alone with Price! After today she'd know for certain if he, indeed, was the man she wanted to live with, and she prayed Master Daniel would grant her request very soon. She liked the casual way Price said her name, as if he really knew her and seemed glad to have her along. "Seems like I've been shut off for so long. Nobody tells me a thing," Adi said.

"Don't you 'insiders' hear all the news when Master Daniel and the men from 'round here crowd up in the big house and talk? I figgered you and Marcela heard everything." He slapped the reins on the bristly backs of the mules. "Might be wise to listen, Adi. Pay close attention, even if you don't understand what they're saying. Might be a time when you do."

Adi pensively turned Price's advice over in her mind as the wagon rumbled away from the property.

With one foot propped on the high rail at the front of the wagon, Price remained with his hat pulled low to shade his eyes from the rising sun, and stared off down the road.

"Marcela mostly serves Master Daniel and his friends," she said finally. "Sometimes, she asks me to help . . . maybe clear away the dishes, poke up the fire, but mainly I stay shut up in that room cleaning and packing all that fancy glass."

"So I hear," Price said. He leaned forward. The mules were stepping lively now so he let the reins fall slack between his knees. "Guess I'd go kind of crazy if I had to stay inside all the time." He looked to the side of the road and took a deep breath. "When Master Daniel bought me, he knew I wouldn't be good for nothing 'cept driving wagons. That's all I ever did. But if I ever get to freedom, I swear I'll never sit behind the rear end of a white man's mule again." He laughed aloud, tilting his face to the sun.

Adi said nothing, intermittently glancing at Price then back to the road. From beneath her lowered lashes, she noticed how high up he sat in his seat, how straight his back and shoulders were, how strong and solid he seemed. He was strangely calm and confident, as if he had made this trip so many times he knew the route by heart. And how easily Price had said the word freedom, as if it truly were a possibility. To her the word was frightening, threatening, and she could not envision a place where black men and women could walk around and do as they pleased in the faces of white folks. Even if there were such a place, would she or Price, slaves all their lives, ever come to know anything about it?

The morning hours drifted past as they made their way eastward. The sun inched its way high into the sky. Adi delighted in

Price's willingness to talk and she was amazed at how much he knew about the various trees and plants—which were edible, which might be used to make potions to heal or even kill a man. He said that traveling through strange territory was easy if a man knew how to read the moss on the tree trunks, the bend in the branches, the sun, the moon, and most of all the stars. He said these were the markers provided by nature to guide a runaway slave through forests, swamps, mountains, and into freedom.

Adi hung on Price's every word, straining to see what he pointed out, asking questions about unusual foliage, understanding why her first impression of him had been correct: he was smart, curious, and driven by an inner will to grasp as much control over his life as he possibly could in spite of being enslaved. He'd do just fine in freedom, she thought. He would thrive like a wilted plant suddenly splashed with water, and she knew Price was the man she wanted to stay with, for the rest of her life—if he'd have her.

After a while, Price began humming to himself, then lifted his voice in song as he prodded the ornery mules up the path. Adi dared to let herself relax, putting Magnolia Crossing, Master Daniel, and Marcela out of her mind. Price's rich smooth voice sank over her like honey spread on a hot biscuit and she wanted the morning to go on forever, to be at Price's side for longer than one day.

Soon the trail narrowed and they came to a split where the road divided. Price directed the mules from the main road into a craggy patch of forest where hemlocks and red gum trees tangled their branches with thick vines, their trailing limbs slashing the brilliant sunlight in half. Ferns nearly as high as the big wagon wheels sprouted among the tree trunks, and the deeper Price drove into the thicket, the denser the foliage became, until Adi felt afraid for the first time since climbing into the wagon.

Silently reassuring herself that Price knew where he was going and would not do any harm to her, she asked no questions. Surely this was no more than a shortcut to the river, but as the sunlight dimmed and the overhanging tree limbs reached closer to the earth, she sensed Price had penetrated the wilderness for another reason.

The forest around them became a living, pulsing cave. They

crept along, Price reassuring Adi with a glance or a nod, letting her know he understood her uneasiness, but he put a finger to his lips, indicating she must be quiet.

Eyes wide, Adi nodded, glancing back across her shoulder to the tiny patch of sunlight that had become a mere pinpoint of light behind them. She shuddered. Anything could happen in this strange, isolated place. They could be attacked by bounty hunters and disappear—never to be found. But looking over at Price she steeled her mind against such thoughts. He seemed very much in control as he guided the mules forward with deliberate urgency, his bottom lip tucked between his teeth.

The huge wagon wheels made little noise as they rolled over a path padded with many seasons of fallen leaves, pine needles, and rotten vegetation. Adi swallowed dryly, tensing her hands into fists in her lap while Price clucked at the mules and pressed onward, driving the wagon beneath the heavy limbs of a giant chestnut tree where he gently reined to a stop.

Adi pulled in a long breath through her nose and held it in her lungs, attempting to still the trembling she felt quickening in her body. Sitting there rigidly, she tried to imagine why they were there and what Price planned to do.

Suddenly footsteps crackled on the floor of the forest. Adi jerked around with a gasp. A shiver of fear crept up her back as she watched a pale-skinned man emerge from behind a huge pal-metto tree twenty feet into the woods. She stared in horror. He looked like an apparition, his snow-white skin was more fragile and translucent than that of Master Daniel's. He was dressed in the rough work clothes of a man who made a living with his hands, and his coarse cotton pants were stuffed into heavy black boots that were laced to his knees. He wore a broad-brimmed gray hat on his head that cast a shadow over the top half of his face. The stranger's dress was not at all like that of the whites who worked the land in the valley, though he was obviously dressed in white man's clothes. There was a foreign look about him and Adi wondered if he might have come from the land Master Daniel called home—England, he had told her more than once. He had pictures sitting on his desk in his study of his father and uncle in front of their glass factory in Manchester wearing very similar clothing.

As the man walked, dark blond hair that hung to his shoulders floated in wisps about his face. The shape of his head, and the arrogant flare of his nose were so much like Master Daniel's that Adi could not keep from staring in disbelief. But his eyes were sad, oddly piercing, and he looked like a man who had suffered a great deal. Raising his chin, the stranger boldly advanced closer, a determined set to his jaw.

Adi clutched Price's arm. He put a reassuring hand over hers, frowning her into silence, shaking his head quickly so she immediately understood that the meeting had been prearranged, the man could be trusted.

Adi pressed her lips into a firm line, but her eyes were wide open, taking in the startling figure before her, who definitely looked like an older, paler, less refined version of Daniel De-Rossette. She wondered if this man could possibly be a brother, or a cousin, some shadowy link to Master Daniel's past who had been ripped from his life long ago. For she had certainly never seen him at Magnolia Crossing.

Price jumped down from the wagon, circled it, and began pulling off pieces of wood.

The man came straight toward Adi, looked into her face, then reached into the open wagon bed and took the basket Ofia had pressed into Adi's hands that morning. Unable to keep her curiosity at bay, Adi turned around to see what he would do next.

Price set aside three big pieces of wood, reached beneath the remaining timber and tugged out a big wooden box. The slats had been loosely nailed together and there were gaps between the boards. The crate was so heavy the man had to help Price lift it out and set it on the ground. With a metal bar, Price pried the lid open and Adi leaned over to see what was inside.

Stifling a scream, she jumped down, pushing herself roughly between the two men.

"That's Ofia's baby!" she cried out, shoving Price away as he tried to push her back. "What are you doing with that baby's body?"

Price grabbed her, circling her waist with one arm, clamping the other hand over her mouth.

"Shh," he hissed. "Shh!"

Adi struggled to get free, watching in horror as the man took the body out of the box and set it in the big basket.

Horrified, confused, she flashed questioning eyes at Price. He only glared at her, but when the stranger picked up the basket and started away, Price stopped him with a touch on his arm. Letting go of Adi, he saw that she had calmed, so he took her hand in his, guiding her fingers to the soft brown skin of the baby boy's cheek.

Adi pulled back her hand in shock. The skin was warm! The boy was alive! But she had seen him buried three days ago. How had this happened? What did it mean?

She stepped back, her hand on her chest, heaving in horror, her frightened eyes boring a hole in the stranger's back as he disappeared through the trees with the baby. The sound of his footsteps were no more than a gentle swish of scattering leaves, like the brush of the wind feathering the tops of the trees.

Price did not look at Adi as he replaced the timber where the slatted box had been hidden, and Adi dared not ask a single question during the rest of the journey to the river.

Chapter Eighteen

DURING the balmy spring of 1856, Daniel DeRossette's slaves continued their elaborate funeral ruse, burying racoons and rabbits in the pitiful graves, mourning loudly, while slipping their children out of bondage. Adi and Price made six more journeys to the palmetto tree in the forest, delivering six more black babies into the hands of the elusive figure Price would only refer to as the conductor.

Soon fugitives from the lower South began appearing at Magnolia Crossing, telling stories of their desperate flight through swamps, rivers, and valleys with mounted men and hound dogs tracking them all the way. They said they stopped at Magnolia Crossing because DeRossette's plantation had acquired the reputation of a place where the master was often away and there was no eagle-eyed mistress on the property—only a stern Negress named Marcela who managed the house slaves and made decisions for the household as if it were hers, but who never set foot into the field slave quarters.

Word of the freedom workers who ran the Underground Railroad in Ohio, Pennsylvania, New York, and other free states soon flashed through the valley, instilling both hope and fear. There were clandestine meetings in the woods where men called abolitionists spoke in protest of slavery, urging Negroes to follow them

North out of slavery. In flagrant violation of the Fugitive Slave Act of 1850, they were willing to help runaways allude their captors by hiding them in cellars, haystacks, attics, and barns during the day —then passing them on to the next conductor under the cover of darkness.

Abolitionist newspapers and public speakers like Frederick Douglas and William Lloyd Garrison condemned the institution of slavery, and fought the attempts of slave owners to recover their property, often spiriting the slaves safely into Canada.

In her most dangerous move, at Price's request, Adi stole pen and paper from her master's desk and forged passes for two runaways who had made it as far east as Possum Creek but had been stuck beneath the bridge for three days. With quaking fingers, Adi had gripped the quill and written what Price had told her to, terrified that her letters were too crudely fashioned to ever be taken as Daniel DeRossette's fancy script.

For the rest of the year, Adi and Price continued to make trips to the forest whenever they could get away and the weather permitted. Each trip back to the woods tested Adi's courage, but she willingly took the risk, sitting bravely in the wagon next to Price, her thoughts riveted on the innocent, slumbering babies secreted beneath the timber. Her mind stayed clouded with worry, her insides knotted in icy fear. The elixir of molasses and opium fed to the babies kept them quiet during the journey, but Adi couldn't help worrying that something might go wrong, especially if they were stopped. Price remained stoically calm, talking very little as he passed through the valley at a slow, deliberate pace, determined to keep the white men patrolling the roads from becoming suspicious.

When stopped and questioned about their destination, Adi and Price would show their passes, identifying themselves as slaves of Daniel DeRossette. Reluctantly, the red-faced men would wave them on, grumbling about DeRossette's lenient practice of letting his niggers traipse all over the valley as if they had the right to come and go as they pleased. It was clear that Daniel DeRossette commanded little respect from his neighboring landowners and was considered a very reluctant master at best. The men's words of criticism settled at the back of Adi's mind.

Master Daniel *was* much more concerned with books, music, drinking fine wine, and his collection of beautiful glass than the long-standing traditions and local laws used by farmers to control their human chattel. High-strung and a bit frail, DeRossette preferred to spend his mornings reading newspapers in his study to riding over his land cracking a whip and shouting orders. Such mundane tasks he left to Tom, the ruthless overseer who slept in his boots and stayed in his saddle from sunup to sundown, driving the slaves to work hard for their master. But Adi had witnessed DeRossette's darker side, and she had never broken another piece of glass since the day of her arrival. She still carried a scar in the middle of her hand.

Along the road, in addition to the patrollers, there were cruel, rangy bounty hunters roaming the heavily wooded lowlands that butted up against the mountains. With packs of well-trained bloodhounds at their sides they pounced on any black man, woman, or child caught on the roads, declaring him or her to be a runaway. If free papers were produced to prove otherwise, they could be dismissed as inconsequential—or destroyed—leaving the Negro at the mercy of his captor.

On a late afternoon in May of 1857, Price pulled the wagon to a stop beside the same towering palmetto tree where he always met the conductor. When the man appeared, Adi stiffened. Though she knew he could be trusted, she never got used to seeing him come out from where he hid behind the trees.

Today, Adi noticed again how sad the man's eyes were. Without speaking, Price jumped down, uncovered the small crate holding a sleeping baby, and quickly made the transfer. The man hurried away once more, never saying a word, never acknowledging Adi's presence. He simply vanished, his precious cargo tucked under his arm.

Half rising from her seat, Adi watched him disappear, tears welling in her eyes. "Who do you think he is?" she asked Price, breaking her long honored vow not to ask questions.

Price clucked to the mules, turned the wagon around, and started back toward the entrance to the forest. "Don't rightly know," he answered, leaving Adi feeling ashamed for even asking.

Twisting around in her seat, hoping to catch one more glimpse of the conductor, she told Price, "I think he's related to Master Daniel."

"Shut your mouth!" Price admonished sharply. "Talk like that could cause a heap of trouble. I told you not to ask questions."

"But," Adi insisted, "he must be. It's not by chance that he shows up here, looking practically like Master Daniel's twin. You know how to find him, don't you, Price? Tell me. Who is he, really? Where is he from and where is he headed?"

Price stared across the swayed backs of the dirty brown mules, a slight downward curve pulling at the corners of his mouth. "Knowing too much can be real dangerous, Adi. But," he slapped the reins, quickening the mules' lethargic pace, "you strike me as mighty brave, and . . . pretty darn smart."

"I can't help it, Price, I have to know more. Please."

He remained quiet for a moment, then nodded, as if reassuring himself before going on. "You knowing how to write has helped greatly. Maybe you do need to know a little more . . . but it's a mighty dangerous business, this freedom work."

"I don't care," Adi said. "I'm already in it. You *pulled* me in it and you can trust me. Tell me all you know."

"Can't do that," Price hedged, "but I can tell you that the conductor comes from very far away. Miles beyond the tallest mountain. He'll lay low until sundown, then he'll give the baby a little more of that sleeping water to keep it quiet. When it's dark, he'll strike out, pressing north till he reaches the next station."

"How far away is that?" she asked.

"Could be ten, twenty miles upriver."

"How does he know who to trust?"

"Oh, he knows. His eyes and ears are tuned for signals—burning lights, a basket of corn by the side of a gate, a sheet on a clothesline, even the color of a handkerchief tied around a white man's neck might take on meaning for him. There's signs all along the way . . . and folks to give him a hand."

"But the babies," Adi asked, her heart and mind filled with worry over each infant she'd helped put in the conductor's hands. To her, each child safely smuggled into freedom was like a shiny new star in the sky. For a year now, she had been making little drawings of birds, or fish, or long-tailed dogs—the intricate tribal designs she had learned from her mother—to tuck into the bottom of each basket. Adi hoped that the people who received the sleeping infants at the end of the line might recognize the symbols as coming from their homeland. Even Price agreed it was a nice thing to do.

"Don't worry 'bout them," Price answered. "Those babies pass from one conductor to another, on and on, until they land on the doorstep of some angel—man or woman, black or white—who will deliver the child into the arms of an auntee, a cousin, a momma or daddy who ran off from slavery and is now free."

Encouraged by Price's willingness to talk, she asked, "How do runaways find their way? The woods are thick, the mountain passes are steep. It's pitch black out here at night."

"Just follow the Star," Price said cheerfully.

"Which one?"

Price laughed aloud, his eyes flicking over Adi in a mixture of surprise and pride. "Looks like I got some more teaching to do," he told her, propping his foot on the wagon rail. "Can you find the Dipper in the sky?"

"Yes."

"All right then. The two stars opposite the handle in the bowl of the Dipper are called Pointers—they point directly to the North Star. It's the brightest star in the sky." He hunched forward, pressing his lips together. "Tonight oughta be clear. Look out and see if you can find it."

Adi found it comforting to be with Price in spite of the danger they faced on every trip and Marcela's grumbling about the frequency of her absences from the big house. Adi told Marcela she was either going to see Miss Ruby, with whom she convinced Marcela she had struck up quite a friendship, or to the mill with Price to get more packing sawdust for Master Daniel's glass.

"Ever think about striking out yourself?" Adi let the question slip out, hoping Price would not get mad.

"I been wanting to go North since the day I learned there truly was a place where black men could live free," he replied, shocking Adi with his candid answer. "Oh, yes, Adi. I'll be leaving here one day."

The urgency beneath Price's words was alarming. Would he

be so cruel as to disappear one day, leaving her behind? "How will you know when to go?"

"Things are changing, Adi. Slavery's about run its course. Though the law says a master can track his slave into a free state and bring him back, it's getting a lot more difficult to do it. Too many free Negroes roaming the roads, helping to hide the runaways. It's more than the white folks down here are gonna tolerate, and you can bet they're not gonna give up without a fight. Looks like war is brewing . . . only thing left for the South to do. They gonna fight to stop those Northerners from interfering with their rights. Trouble's coming, and it's not far off."

"Is it true that once you cross the river you're free?"

Price smiled. "Depends on which river. The Ohio maybe. The Tennessee, no. Heading east from here, there are terrible mountains and rivers to pass over before you get to Pennsylvania."

"Have you been high up in the mountains?" She pointed skyward to the misty gray Smokies in the distance. "As far as that ridge of pines?"

"No," Price admitted, "but I'd chance it." He raised his face to the sky as if he were facing tomorrow. "One day you're gonna look around, and I'll be gone . . . just like that . . . gone. And Master Daniel won't ever get me back. But for now, if I can keep this wagon rolling, I'm content to wait. I'll know when it's time to go."

Price's confession was not surprising, but Adi was devastated at the selfishness of his reply. He would leave her! Without a second thought! Tears threatened to shatter her uncertain resolve.

During their trips together she had come to trust him, admire him, yet remained somewhat frightened of the effect he was having on her. When she was with Price, it was difficult to concentrate on anything but his nearness, and her heart thumped unmercifully against her breast. What she wanted—almost as much as freedom—was to be Price's wife. His *real* wife in a place where they could make a home. Master Daniel still hadn't given her an answer and there was nothing she could do but wait.

Today, Adi and Price proceeded straightaway to the mill, where Price unloaded the timber and took on a load of sawdust. Starting back, Adi noticed that they were taking the long way home, skirting the southern leg of the river. She worried that they might not make it back before sundown. She might get a scolding from Marcela, but Price stood to be severely reprimanded by Tom, the overseer, who was always threatening to hire Price out to old man Sorrell on the western side of the valley.

When Price pulled to a stop in a shady grove of hemlock, Adi felt her pulse quicken. A warm flush inched onto her face. "We'll be late," she said hoarsely, unable to hide the anxiety in her voice.

Price coolly scrutinized Adi, then blurted out, "If I leave Magnolia Crossing will you come with me?"

A flicker of apprehension burned quickly, then faded. Adi twisted her trembling hands into hard fists in her lap. "Run away to freedom?" she whispered, as if saying the words too loudly might bring the patrollers crashing into the grove.

Price nodded stiffly.

Shaken by the invitation she had been praying might come, she panicked at the realization of what Price was asking of her. Adi shifted to face him more fully. "But you said . . ." she started.

He reached over and gently placed two fingers on her sleeve. "I know. I said I've been waiting for the right time to strike out, but maybe what I've been waiting for is you." He lowered his eyes to the floor of the wagon. "Would you think on it?" he asked.

Adi turned her hand palm up, letting Price's work-roughened fingers close over hers. "I don't have to think about it, Price. If you leave Magnolia Crossing, I'm leaving with you."

Adi edged nearer, closing the gap between them on the hard wagon seat. Price put his arm around her shoulder, letting her settle her head beneath his chin. They sat silently, watching a covey of ducks skim across the deep green pond.

In his arms Adi felt safe, but more than that, she felt important. Price valued her for who she was, while Master Daniel, who did compliment her from time to time on her ability to clean and neatly pack his fancy pieces of glass or wash a shipment of opalescent vases, only valued her ability to serve. Price had trusted her enough to include her in his freedom work, and now she would be a part of his future in freedom. It was time to take the chance.

"It will be dangerous," he warned. "The mountains are the most difficult route to take. You must be prepared for a hard trip

. . . sleeping in caves or a thick stand of brush. Eating berries or tubers we can find in the forest. And . . . we might *not* make it."

Adi reached up and put her fingers to his lips. "Shh," she murmured. "No reason to say that. We will get to freedom. Together. And when we do," she laughed in spite of the seriousness of her decision, "the first thing we're going to do is find the conductor and have us a celebration. A real party. In a real house of our own."

Price's somber expression dissolved, and he chuckled in satisfaction, tracing the planes of Adi's soft brown cheeks with a loving eye. "I promise you, Adi. If we make it to freedom I will build you a house and I won't rest until I find the conductor and get him to come for a proper visit."

Adi felt proud and embarrassed at the same time. All this talk about a life that she could call her own—a life out of slavery—was making her light-headed, and she quivered as a rush of hope quickly erased her anxiety.

Price cupped her chin between his hands, urging her lips toward his. "We're going to get away from all these evil people and live a peaceful life, Adi. Even if we have to leave this country."

"Where would we go, then?" Adi asked.

"A place called Canada. Beyond a great lake at the edge of the country. Many are crossing over and if we have to go there to be treated like human beings then that's what we'll do," Price vowed. He slowly lowered his lips to Adi's, sealing his promise with a gentle kiss. Pulling away, he started to speak, then hesitated, as if giving her time to consider his decision.

"I'd be proud to go with you, no matter how far," Adi replied softly, wrapping her arms around Price's broad shoulders, gathering him closer. Propelled by desires that had been smoldering for nearly a year, she brashly kissed him back, silently rejoicing in the revelation that he wanted her as much as she wanted him!

A moan of satisfaction escaped Price's lips as his hands roamed down Adi's back to her waist. He caressed her with such urgency he nearly squeezed Adi's breath from her lungs, yet she clung to him with no doubt in her mind that together they would build a future in the North.

With a gentle nudge, he pulled away, then slipped down from the wagon to hold out his hand to her. Adi lowered her eyes, taking

Price's hand, following him to a soft grassy knoll shaded by a vibrant canopy of pale green leaves that hung from the limbs of the sycamore trees. They sank down on the grass, lying side by side to watch the afternoon sun begin to ease behind the tall pine trees ridging the valley.

Soon chilling winds blew down from the mountains, encircling the grove, but never touching the lovers. Treasuring the precious moments they had so brazenly stolen from their master, they remained enveloped in each other's arms long after gray shadows had darkened the trail back to Magnolia Crossing. In excited whispers, they dreamed, planning their escape, exchanging the meager details they knew about themselves in an attempt to weave together some semblance of their ancestries.

Adi told Price that her mother had been a princess from Bwerani and that the pictures she placed inside the babies' baskets had been taught to her by her mother.

Price told Adi that he knew nothing of his parents, having been sold as an infant to a cotton farmer in Georgia, then to a tobacco planter in North Carolina. He'd been passed from owner to owner during his life, never remaining in one place long enough to call it home.

Resting contentedly in Price's protective arms, Adi blocked out the ugliness of the world into which she had been born, willing her thoughts and attention to the man whose solid frame was firmly molded to hers. When Price eased over her on the cool green grass, Adi smiled, welcoming the soft carpet beneath her, anxious to exchange her innocence and childish dreams for the daring challenge of womanhood.

Chapter Nineteen

IT was far into the evening when Adi and Price got back to Magnolia Crossing. Adi was worried that Tom had already checked the cabins and had most likely informed Master Daniel of their absence. Price shrugged her worry off, confident that Marcela would not tell their master and he could take care of himself. He kissed Adi softly, holding onto her tightly for a long time before he finally let go.

Adi found Marcela waiting for her inside the rear fence, arms crossed over her bony chest, her bottom lip pooched out in anger. Marcela's tongue-lashing immediately rolled from her mouth, and continued while Adi ran ahead of her up the path. Once inside the big house, Marcela raged on for nearly an hour as they went from room to room tending the lamps.

"You've put every one of us on the place in danger," Marcela said, shaking a dark finger, glaring angrily at Adi. "I thought you had better sense. You took a dreadful liberty, staying away so long. It's dark! Dark! So thoughtless, so selfish of you. You just made your last trip to the mill, young lady."

Undaunted by Marcela's threat, Adi summoned up the courage she would not have had that morning. After committing herself to the man she loved, she suddenly felt grown up enough to defend herself. "I can get a pass from Master Daniel whenever I want," she shouted. "I don't need your permission to go to the mill. You are not my master!"

Marcela's hand shot out and with a crack she slapped Adi across the left cheek. "You stupid little fool. What makes you think that callous wagon driver will ever sit up in a wagon again, let alone hold a rein after Tom has dealt with him?"

"Dealt with Price?" Adi asked, her anger instantly gone. "What's that mean?"

"It means your wagon driver is going under the lash. At high noon tomorrow." The words came out in a hiss. Marcela turned from Adi and began fussing with the lace cloth on the massive dining-room table. Her long, thin fingers tugged at the delicate fabric, her eyes still flashed with anger.

Visibly shaken, Adi whispered, "Master Daniel told Tom to whip Price?"

"Yes," Marcela said sharply. "And it's only because I convinced Master Daniel that Price kept you away from here for his own nasty pleasure, that you are being spared the whip yourself."

"How could you say that? Price didn't force me to—" Adi started.

"Shut up, Adi! That's the fool in you talking. You can still be dragged out there to the whipping tree, too."

"But Master Daniel's never had a whipping here. He's not that . . . cruel."

"Don't you believe that!" Marcela spat out. "He's no different from any other white man in this valley, and to him, Price is no better than a ornery mule. Master Daniel can damn well do as he pleases with him . . . and with you, too, young lady. It would serve you well not to forget it." She yanked a wilted day lily from the vase of flowers in the center of the table and crushed it between two fingers.

Adi glared at Marcela, her mind spinning. A lashing! At Magnolia Crossing? Surely Marcela was bluffing, trying to scare her into staying away from Price. Master Daniel had never put a slave under the whip as long as she'd been there. Why would he start now?

"Price is the kindest, most gentle man," Adi protested. "You had no right to tell Master Daniel I was taken advantage of. It's not true, Marcela." Adi shook her head, frowning, a ridge of lines marring her smooth forehead. She was deeply disappointed in the woman she had tried so hard to please. "I love Price. I stayed with him of my own free will."

Marcela's head snapped up and she pierced Adi with an incredulous look. "Free will! Child, are you crazy? What kind of nonsense has that man put into your head? You have no free will, understand? I lied for you because you're too young to see what a mess you got yourself in. But don't think I'll do it again. You stay away from Price, away from the quarters, 'cause all hell is about to break loose."

Throughout that evening Adi drifted through the house checking the lamps, drawing the curtains, nodding absently at Marcela whenever she barked an order, but as soon as her chores were completed to Marcela's satisfaction, she retreated to the cookhouse to sit by the single window facing the quarters, searching the black night for a light to appear in Price's cabin. Silently, she implored him to be strong, not to let this turn of affairs force him to flee without her.

The next morning Adi was busy polishing a tall gilt-edged urn that had recently arrived from Manchester. She was about to set it next to its mate on the fireplace mantel when Master Daniel entered his study. He went over to the open crate and began rummaging around in the tumble of sawdust and straw, whistling a tune she didn't recognize. To Adi, DeRossette seemed oddly buoyant considering he was about to hold the first public whipping of one of his slaves.

A mass of jitters, her heart thundering in her chest, she made up her mind to plead Price's case. "Master Daniel," she started, her hands firmly gripping the fragile urn, "it wasn't the wagon driver's fault I got back so late from the mill yesterday."

"Oh?" he said, twirling gracefully to face her, blond eyebrows raised on his pale smooth forehead. He picked up a translucent green wineglass from the newly arrived shipment, tossed his straight blond hair to the side and lifted his chin, holding the glass to the sun, spinning it around to create dazzling prisms of reflected light. "Is that so? What do you have to say for yourself?"

Adi girded herself to speak, keeping her eyes lowered on the urn in her hands. "Well, Master Daniel," she said, praying she'd correctly assessed his mood, hoping the arrival of the new shipment from England had put him in good spirits, though she never could be sure. "I was the one at fault. I asked Price to stop the wagon so I could hunt for yellow root. I wandered so far, the time just passed on by."

"Well," he said rather blithely, "that's too bad, but don't bother explaining it to me, Adi. I instructed Marcela to deal with you." He picked up another glass. "I gather she expressed my deep displeasure that you would take advantage of my permission for you to have a pass now and then. I was greatly disappointed. I thought I could trust you."

"Oh, but you can, Master Daniel. I promise never to be late again."

DeRossette's eyes glinted in a malicious taunt. "I know you won't be . . . because you're not to go off with Price again. You understand? No more passes. You are to remain here with Marcela, inside . . . so you can fill your idle mind with more substantial thoughts than rolling in the hay with one of my niggers."

Adi froze, her stiff fingers clutching the neck of the urn. "Nothing like that happened, Master Daniel," she lied, horrified to hear him refer to their wondrous union in such vulgar terms.

"Be that as it may," DeRossette said, "Price must be punished for taking liberties with *my* property."

"Then it's true?" Adi asked. "There is going to be a whipping?"

DeRossette circled his red leather wing chair, then flung himself down into its luxurious seat, stretching his feet out in front of him. He scrutinized the gold buckles on his boots. "I take it Marcela told you that?"

"Yes."

"Oh, my. I threatened as much in a moment of rage. But I've told Tom there can't be a whipping today, or any other day." He shuddered in disgust.

A wave of relief charged through Adi. "And Price?"

DeRossette got up, walked to the window and looked out,

watching the wagons rolling out in the fields. "I can see now that Price is, indeed, a troublemaker. Too damn arrogant to keep on the place. As a matter of fact, I've decided to sell him."

Horrified, Adi sucked in her breath. She watched DeRossette warily as he paced back and forth in front of the window casting nervous glances outside. "Yes, it's time to make some changes around here." He stopped, giving Adi a taut, forced smile. "Leave me, child." He waved his hand toward the door. "Go and tell Marcela to pack my valise. I'm going to Nashville for a few days to make inquiries. I'm sure I can get a good offer for Price while I'm there."

"Yes, Master Daniel," Adi murmured, her words forced from a throat constricted with fear. With unsteady hands she placed the gleaming urn on the mantel, then hurriedly left the room. Taking the wide carpeted stairs two at a time, she flew up the wide staircase, where she found Marcela straightening the pillows on Master Daniel's four-poster bed.

Within moments of DeRossette's departure from the valley, Adi rushed out of the big house, over the fence, down the path to Price's cabin. Flinging the door open, she found him sitting on a wooden stool, a broken harness in his hands. At the sight of her, Price dropped the harness on the floor and quickly stood, his massive frame consuming nearly all the space in the dismal shack. Adi looked up at Price, noticing that his head was close to touching the raw wooden beams that supported the rickety loft he'd constructed at the top of the cabin. For the first time, she saw fear in his eyes and it frightened her more than anything else. He shook his head slowly as if warning her not to come closer.

Adi slammed the door shut with a crack. Striding across the dirt floor, she stood in front of Price, hesitating only long enough to caress his face with her velvet brown eyes before boldly throwing her arms around his neck.

He stood stiffly, arms dangling at his sides, making no move to embrace her.

Undaunted, Adi laid her head on his chest, silently vowing not to back down. She shuddered in relief when the tension in Price's body eased and his arms inched up to encircle her. Adi snuggled closer, giving herself over to the unbearable pleasure of being close to Price again. Desire swept through her veins like wildfire, and when his hand moved haltingly to caress the top of her head, she realized that this was the first time he had seen her hair freed of its white cotton wrap. She held very still letting him stroke her unbound plaits that rippled like spun cotton past her shoulders. Filled with an urgent tenderness that was both terrifying and calming, she held Price tightly and closed her eyes.

"Why did you come here?" he murmured against her hair.

Adi leaned back to look at Price, her mind whirling with the fear of losing him. "I came to warn you."

Price pushed her to arm's length and searched her face.

"Master Daniel said he plans to sell you."

Releasing her, Price strode to the far side of the room. "When did he say this?"

"This morning. He came into the study while I was cleaning."

"And why would Master Daniel be discussing me with you?" Price demanded in a surly voice.

Shaken by his tone, Adi trembled. Did she dare tell him that she had initiated the discussion with her stupid attempt to clear him of blame? She licked her lips. "It just . . . came up," she hedged. "He was talking about change. Said he . . . he was beginning to think you are too dangerous to keep around and he was going to make inquiries about selling you."

Price continued to pace the tiny room. "Where is he now?"

"On his way to Nashville. I helped Marcela pack his valise. He took clothes enough to last two weeks or so. I think he'll be gone for some time. What should we do?"

"Nothing," he told Adi, walking toward her, reaching out to guide her once more into his arms. "Master Daniel thinks he's pretty smart, but he'll not bait me into running. Not tonight. You can be sure old Tom is primed and waiting for me to try. No, I won't fall into that trap."

"Please," Adi pressed, "let's go now, while Master Daniel is away."

"No, not now," he said. "Tom will be watching the quarters all night. Sitting up there in that cracker box shed, his gun trained down on me. He's seen you, I know, so you must be careful. Go back to the house and go about your business as usual. I'll get word to you, but don't come here again." He gazed into her eyes, silently begging her to understand. "Will you do that, Adi? Stay away?"

Adi answered him with a kiss, the taste of him leaving her breathless.

Price traced the lines on her brow with a rough finger. "Don't frown, please. A face as pretty as yours should never be wrinkled in worry."

Pulling back, Adi let a half smile crinkle the corners of her lips, but inside she was filled with terror. She and Price had to escape! And as perilous and frightening as the journey might be, she knew they would survive because loving Price had already flung her into a world where the heavy yoke of slavery no longer numbed her soul or cast its ugly shadow on her future.

Chapter Twenty

DANIEL DeRossette made no move to sell Price, in fact nothing changed at Magnolia Crossing. Spring folded into summer and life on the huge plantation rolled along in its regular cycle with the slaves tending crops, slaughtering hogs, watching the weather for summer storms, anticipating a bountiful harvest.

Adi kept her promise to Price and stayed away from his cabin, though occasionally they were able to slip away into the woods to be together. She also caught glimpses of him from the big house windows now and then and it took all her courage to keep from rushing to him. Sheltered by Marcela, watched suspiciously by her master, Adi felt trapped, and her hope of reaching freedom slowly dimmed.

By mid–July Adi knew she was carrying Price's child, and once again, the prospect of escaping Magnolia Crossing became an obsession. She sent word to Ofia, hoping she would find Price and let him know about her condition, but the news came back that Price had been hired out to the Sorrell plantation for the duration of the harvest and would not be back to Magnolia Crossing until late fall.

In early November there was a rap on Adi's cabin wall. She went out to find Price standing before her, eyes dark and brooding, his chest heaving. He had run the thirty miles from old man Sorrell's farm near Whitwell straight to Magnolia Crossing. He enveloped her, smothering her with a trembling eagerness. "I wanted my child born in freedom," he told her. "But we'll have to stay put through winter, now."

The gentle sound of his voice and the warmth of his body against hers did little to calm Adi's fears. "Master Daniel is furious," she said, her voice tight with uncertainty. "He curses me, then scowls at me, treating me like a contagious animal he'd rather not have around. And Marcela! She's unbearably mean . . . working me so hard, I fear for our child. Oh, Price, how will I . . ." She broke off, sobbing against his chest.

"You hush, now," Price crooned, smoothing the back of her rough cotton dress. "Time will take care of that." He lowered his face to look into her eyes, then kissed her softly. "Master Daniel might rant and rage and carry on for a spell. Probably gonna try to sell me for sure once the harvest is finished. But you can count on one thing."

"What?" Adi asked, snuggling her head once more to his shoulder.

"I won't be sold. I'd rather die than be sold away from you and my child."

"Don't say that," Adi sobbed, her slight body shaking uncontrollably.

Price tried to calm her with gentle strokes to her back, but she squirmed away, then lashed out. "How can you say you'd rather die!" Sobs racked her, doubling her over.

"Don't you cry," Price pleaded. "I won't be sold away from you. And I'm not gonna let anything happen to you." Price put both hands on her shoulders and pushed her back. Hesitantly, he placed a hand on the swell of Adi's abdomen, gazing down upon the unseen life growing inside the woman he loved. Adi put her hand over his.

Price went on. "Master Daniel hasn't turned you out on the roads and he won't sell you in your condition." Eased by her silence, he said in a firm, strong voice, "As soon as the birthing is over, we're leavin'."

Adi reached for Price, but he shook his head, forcing their inevitable separation. "No," he whispered. "You go on back inside, now. Take care of yourself. Ofia will get word to me when you are strong enough to travel, then we'll make our break for freedom." Inclining his head in a gentlemanly nod, he smiled.

Adi's heart sang with joy, but an ominous lump of fear was settled painfully in her throat. When Price turned and slipped back into the black night, Adi remained staring after him, tears running down her cheeks.

On February 16, 1859 Lucy was born at the first light of dawn. Twenty-four hours later, Adi heard a tapping on her cabin wall, got up, and slipped out to find Ofia standing with her thin arms wrapped around her chest. She jerked her head several times toward the northern side of the big house.

"Price?" Adi hissed. "Is it time?"

Ofia nodded vigorously, then stepped closer. "Get yo child. Follow me." Ofia looked at Adi without hiding her envy. The moonlight softened the haggard woman's weathered face and, in the shadowy light, Adi thought Ofia looked beautiful, as she might have looked years ago before the burden of slavery had drained the beauty from her face.

It was time to go. Adi was leaving Magnolia Crossing forever. Easing back inside her cabin, she wrapped Lucy in several layers of homespun, then covered her with a frayed patch quilt. She spread out a small piece of slave cloth on the dirt floor. Atop it she laid a half loaf of bread, a piece of paper, and a nearly dried bottle of ink that she had taken from her master's study. Next to it she put a bladder of water and a handful of the sleeping root she'd gotten from Miss Ruby months ago in preparation for this moment.

Quickly, Adi pulled up the three corners of the cloth and tied them in a tight knot. She tucked her bundle into the quilt next to her infant and stole away into the night.

Following Ofia closely, Adi raced across the moonlit grass, frightened to be heading toward her master, back toward the place she was so desperate to escape. Ofia yanked open the cellar door and pointed down into the musty hole.

"Down dere. Go!"

Adi went in first, stopping at the foot of the rotting steps while

Ofia lit a stub of a candle. When the darkness brightened into half light, Adi could see that she was standing in a large oval area, from which radiated eight different passageways. The cellar was stuffed with crates and boxes and tools Master Daniel had put down there for safekeeping. Ofia pointed to the tunnel to the north.

"Run, child. Run," she said breathlessly, pressing the candle into Adi's hands.

Without saying good-bye, Adi fled, gasping for air as she pressed deeper into a tunnel so narrow her shoulders brushed its sides. After a short distance, the tunnel emerged into a high vaulted cave. A pool of water lay in front of her, and on the walls, a trickle of early runoff from the mountain snows was dripping into the black pool.

Adi held the candle high, steadying herself as she stepped onto a natural bridge created by limestone ledges jutting over the lagoon. Fearful of falling into the water, she took her time crossing.

Once on the other side, she reentered the narrow tunnel at a faster pace. It seemed as if she had been traveling for hours when suddenly the land beneath her feet rose in a steep inclination and she started her assent from the catacombs.

Emerging into the pitch-black forest, she found herself standing on the valley rim. Adi turned around and gazed down. She easily located the big house, its sheening whitewashed fence and silvery pillars glowing in the full moonlight, its slumbering image filling Adi with a surge of unexpected memories.

She fought hard to keep from crying. The tears brimming her eyes were tears brought on by fear—the fear of leaving all that was familiar to enter a dangerous new land. Adi shook her head. No time to worry about that now. She had to keep running, find Price.

The black forest was wide awake, filled with the evening songs of crickets, cicadas, and croaking tree frogs. She quickly cut into the tangled thicket, ducking under branches, pressing her baby girl to her chest, praying she was heading in the right direction. Looking up, she saw the North Star and felt better. Price had assured her if she kept her eye on it, she would never be lost.

Up ahead was a cave in the mountains where she had created the forged passes for the fugitives who'd been hiding under the bridge. If Price were waiting for her, that's where he'd be.

Walking faster, she pushed on, her feet sinking into the soft valley rim, her boots filling with water when she sloshed across a silver thread of a spring. With her feet already soaking wet, and not even off DeRossette's property, it was suddenly very clear to Adi just how long and dreadful the trek was going to be. After squeezing through a tangle of vines that were draped between two giant white oaks, she abruptly came face-to-face with Price.

A startled cry flew from her lips.

Price threw a protective arm around Adi and immediately fell into step beside her, not breaking her frantic stride. Together they moved quickly, half running, determined to put as much distance as possible between themselves and their master. They continued at a breathtaking pace for nearly an hour, then Adi stumbled, crumpling to the ground. Price said nothing. He merely reached down, took his daughter, helped Adi to her feet, and urged her forward. Not daring to rest, he gave her his support by putting an arm about her waist, almost lifting her from the ground. Their pace did not slow until they left the thicket and burst into a small clearing near the cave. Moonlight illuminated its wide black entrance, and a white man crouched down beside it.

Adi stared in disbelief. It was the conductor! His hair caught the brunt of the moonbeams and shined like a handful of silver. His face was as somber and white as she remembered, and his clothing remained the same. Adi hung back behind Price at the edge of the clearing, unsure if they should enter the circle of light.

The conductor motioned them over. "You are here. Good."

Startled to hear the man speak for the first time, Adi jumped, but Price steadied her, holding fast onto her arm, giving it a reassuring squeeze.

She crossed the clearing behind Price, and the three of them entered the cave to huddle on the floor next to a sputtering lamp that created a yellow circle of light.

"Did you bring paper and ink?" he asked.

Reaching inside the baby's quilt, Adi took out the bundle and opened it on the ground. "I could only get one sheet," she apologized.

The conductor took it from her, pulled a sharpened feather

from his pocket and dipped it into the ink bottle. "What's your name?" he asked Adi.

"Adiaga Kante."

"That won't do," he told her bluntly. "From now on you are Ada Kent." He hastily wrote her new name on the pass, signed it, blew it dry, then folded the paper and handed it back to Adi. She stuffed it in the bundle, then retied it.

Turning to Price, the conductor raised his shoulders in a shrug. "I can get you across the Tennessee River without a pass, but after that we'll have to be very careful. There's a steep climb through the Unaka . . . the mountains are dangerous, it's rugged country, but we should not be stopped. Once we get through I will pass you to another conductor."

"Where?" Adi asked, ignoring Price's frown. If she was going to make her run for freedom, she wanted to know as much as possible about where they were headed. They might get separated. Lost.

"On the other side of the river, beyond the mountains is an Indian camp at the foot of a gorge where you will be able to hide for a while. You may be there several days before someone comes to take you farther. I must leave you there and move on. Crossing into Virginia is very dangerous now." He stood, brushing bits of leaves from his pants legs.

"Thank you," Adi whispered.

Price helped her to her feet. "Yes, we truly thank you."

"Let's go," the man said. "It's late. We have a lot of ground to cover before daybreak." Noticing Adi's tense face, the man comforted her. "Please don't be afraid."

Adi stared at the pale stranger, unable to say a word. It was real! She had a pass. She was traveling with a white man who was willing to protect her and her baby. Freedom was coming and she was paralyzed with joy. What would she find on the other side of the mountains? Would it be as wonderful as she hoped? Or maybe it was all a lie and this man would lead them to nothing . . . nothing but more trouble and sorrow.

"It's all right, Ada," the man said, using her new name with ease. "Do not be afraid. You must trust me. Follow me carefully and do as I say."

Adi took a deep breath. "Yes. But, please, tell me who you are. One day I want to find you and thank you proper for helping me and my family get to freedom."

With a slight bow, the man took off his gray, broad-brimmed hat. "I apologize, ma'am, for not introducing myself. My name is Soddy Russell."

Kiana's eyes gripped the brittle page in shock. Stunned, she blinked, turning the book over to see if there were more pages to be read. There were not. Her heart pounded. Blood raced to her head making her dizzy. There was an ugly scrawl extending from the last word, down the page in a scraggly blue line. It must have been made by a jolt to her mother's hand. Did this page contain the last words her mother had written? Was it at that moment that the plane had exploded? Kiana pressed her quaking hands to her stomach in shock, as a chill rushed over her arms. Suddenly, her mouth felt as dry as sandpaper. What was Louise Sheridan about to write?

Kiana didn't know what to think or what this revelation meant, but one thing was certain—she was going to find out.

Chapter Twenty-one

IDA hung up the receiver and leaned against the smudged glass door of the telephone booth. A cattish smile touched her lips, though a vague foreboding quivered through her mind. Watts had better do exactly as she'd ordered, but at least it was out of her hands. All she had to do was wait.

With a disapproving glance she watched two women with rollers in their hair and house shoes on their feet shuffle past the customer service area. They chatted intently, leaning heavily against the handle bars of their shopping carts, while a voice on the PA system announced that the Blue Light Sale on K Mart shoes would end in exactly five minutes. God, she thought, who would buy a pair of shoes in this place!

Shaking her head in disbelief, Ida turned away and walked toward the ladies' room, anxious to get out of the discount store, but not sorry she'd ducked inside to place her call. Phone records could be traced and she sure didn't want any calls to Marvin Watts to ever show up on her phone records—at home, from her office, or on the mobile unit in her car.

At the sink, she splashed cold water over her wrists, then ripped a paper towel from the metal dispenser. Ida slowly dried her hands, beginning to feel more calm, more at ease with her decision. If Watts's contact delivered on his promise, Ida could move forward much more quickly, and without the nagging fear that Kiana's snooping around was going to royally foul things up.

Ida pulled her sunglasses over her eyes and headed toward the front of the store. Glancing up, she checked the time on a yellow plastic clock above the doorway. It was already twelve-thirty. She quickened her pace to a near jog, exiting through the double glass doors, hurrying across the black asphalt parking lot.

In her car, she turned the air-conditioning on full blast, then snatched up the mobile phone. The planning meeting on the Techni-Trak account was set to begin at one o'clock, and if she was not there to lead the meeting, she knew Bill Lewis would jump at the chance to take her place.

"Not on your life," she muttered under her breath as she rapidly pressed the buttons to dial the private number to her office, hoping her secretary, Sandy, had not tied up the line.

Rex crossed the parking lot in front of Kiana and opened the back hatch of the cherry red Blazer. Reaching inside, he began shoving his gear around to make room for her large bag.

"Good Lord," Kiana exclaimed. "Is all that yours?"

"Ours. We have to be prepared. Don't know what we might run into."

Kiana leaned into the vehicle. Her shoulder brushed against Rex's and she looked at him briefly, then quickly turned away, somewhat startled that she'd caught his eye.

"Let me have your bag," he said quickly, bending to take it out of her hand, lowering his head so that Kiana could not see his face.

She hastily let go, watching Rex closely as he stowed the suitcase inside. He had greeted her at the gate with a warm smile and a firm handshake, but Kiana had sensed he was nervous. Floundering, unsure of what to say, she felt his disquiet and it stirred old feelings of fear and insecurity of her own. How much longer, she wondered, would they be able to dance around this sudden, yet obvious attraction?

"Okay," she said, anxious to clear her mind of her rank speculation that his feelings were equal to hers, "what do we have here?" She surveyed the contents of the Blazer. "You brought your laptop, I see." She held up her oversized handbag. "I'm a yellow legal pad and pen girl, myself. That is until I get ready for the final draft. Then I can get on the computer." She turned her attention back to the pile of items in the vehicle. "Photo equipment, a tent, sleeping bag, camp stove . . . a Coleman lantern?" Curious, she picked up and examined a pair of brown Wellington boots and a bright orange hunter's jacket. "You brought all this stuff from D.C.?"

"Yep," Rex said, adjusting Kiana's luggage to fit it into the crowded baggage area. "I'm used to lugging my gear around. We *could* rent most of this here in Nashville, but why spend the money? I've found it's always easier, and less expensive, if I bring my own stuff. If we don't use it, that's fine. But . . ." He playfully raised an eyebrow.

"You must have been a Boy Scout," Kiana interrupted, impressed by Rex's forethought and down-to-earth approach. He was charming, bright, and as eager to get to the heart of her family legacy as she was. That alone made him unbelievably attractive to her.

"Mmm, mmm," he murmured, a mirthful lilt in his voice. "An Eagle Scout at that."

Kiana stepped back from the vehicle and brushed her hands together, then propped them at her waist. "Guess I'm in good hands, then," she replied.

Rex straightened up, leaned against the open hatchway, and crossed his arms atop his multipocketed vest. "Very good hands. I guarantee."

The moment was taut with an undertone of promise that gnawed at Kiana's resolve. The tiny voice in her head, which she had ignored so many times in the past, was warning her, again, to be careful. But when she handed Rex her other bag, and his hand deliberately closed over hers, she let it linger there for a moment before pulling away.

From the sidewalk opposite the parking lot, a man dressed in faded khakis and a black windbreaker watched Kiana and Rex through powerful binoculars. He was glad that Marvin Watts's description had been accurate this time, because he'd vowed never to work for

Watts again after that job in Memphis got so botched up. But he needed the money and this job sounded easy—at least no guns were involved. He continued his surveillance of Kiana and Rex, grinding his back teeth together as he watched. When they got into the Blazer, he hurriedly opened the door of his battered white van, and with one eye trained into his rearview mirror, he started the engine, determined not to let them slip away.

Kiana and Rex headed directly to Watts Antiques to question the owner about the source of the glass Kiana had seen at the auction in Houston. Rex swung off Woodmont onto Twelfth, then went up to Blakemore Avenue.

"Should be in this block," he said, almost to himself.

Kiana checked the address she had scribbled on a piece of paper after looking it up in a phone directory. "Let's hope he keeps some kind of records of his acquisitions," she said, glancing around. "There it is. Go left."

Rex turned.

"Watts Antiques. See it? Across the street from that red sign next to the Ace Hardware."

Rex nodded, cut to the right and parked. "After what you told me was in your mother's book, I can't wait to hear what this guy has to say."

"Me, too. But I'm beginning to think that maybe Grandmother was right," Kiana said glumly.

"About what?"

"My mother's book. She called it a bunch of nonsense."

"Had she read it?"

"No."

Rex squinted into the afternoon sun, considering Kiana's comment. "Then I wouldn't be too quick to dismiss what you've got. From the way you described your mother, it's apparent she took her research very seriously."

"Oh, she did," Kiana agreed. "She was very committed to her project. Mother had a degree in education, taught fifth grade for years. She had planned to return to school for her master's, but when my real father died, she gave up that dream. She was always reading, studying, educating herself. Her work for the

World Outreach Mission inspired her to start digging into her own past and that's when she got caught up in genealogical research. It was a hobby, but it certainly influenced me. My decision to pursue a degree in history and go for this Ph.D. was very much motivated by her unfinished dream. I'd like to . . . kind of make up for what she wasn't able to do."

Rex turned off the engine and set the emergency brake. "That's admirable." He gave Kiana an appreciative look, then said in a low voice, "You're really special, you know that?"

Kiana felt a warm glow in the center of her chest. She lowered her eyes and studied her hands. "Oh, I'm not so special. Just very curious. When something strikes me as interesting, unusual, or mysterious, I have to know more and I don't let go very easily."

"I can see that," Rex said. "We'll get to the truth about your great-great-grandfather, and it could be that your mother's story is much closer to the truth than *some* folks want to believe."

The sidewalk outside Watts Antiques was crowded with samples of antique furniture. In the shade of a red-and-white-striped canvas awning were Shaker chairs, pine chests, an assortment of dark mahogany and cherry spool pieces, and a set of six armless Victorian side chairs upholstered in dark plum velvet.

Kiana lifted a tag or two as she squeezed through the jumble of items, grimacing at the prices. Marvin Watts not only knew exactly what he had, but had overpriced his pieces terribly.

"We're not talking trash and treasure here," she remarked.

Rex lifted his camera to his face and shot the outside of the building. "Stand over there," he told Kiana, motioning toward a table near the entryway where an antique Victrola sat next to a stack of leather-bound books.

Kiana moved toward the table and posed with one hand resting on the big fluted horn of the antique record player. "Our first photo to document the search?"

"Right," Rex said, clicking away. He stepped back and photographed the sign above the doorway in a close-up shot, then put the lens cover back on his camera. He held it loosely in his hand as they pushed through the wood and glass door.

Kiana looked around, eyebrows raised, as soon as they got inside the door. The owner had put yellow plastic over all the windows to prevent the sunlight from fading his treasures, but the sunscreens made the room seem small and almost sinister. Several women and one man were browsing in the cluttered, musty room.

"This is high-class stuff," Kiana whispered to Rex. "I doubt he'll be very eager to discuss his sources with us."

As soon as the words were out, a man emerged from the back of the shop and stood watching them. He was wearing a green short-sleeved shirt and his arms had the pallor of someone who never spent time outdoors. His graying hair was rumpled and wiry, giving him a distracted look. From the corner of his mouth dangled a burning cigarette, but he quickly stubbed it out in an overflowing ashtray beside the cash register.

"No pictures inside," the man sternly admonished Rex.

"Oh. Sure. No problem," Rex replied, shrugging. He left Kiana standing next to a table of pewter plates and strode over to the man behind the counter. "Hello. I'm Rex Tandy."

"Hello. Marvin Watts. The owner."

The two men shook hands.

Kiana stared at Rex in surprise. Well! He certainly had taken charge. She bristled at his rude dismissal, firmly clenching her teeth as she made her way across the room. Maybe she'd better remind Rex Tandy just whose story this was and who had initiated this trip. She stepped up beside Rex, and put her hands, palms down, on the glass case. He shifted aside to make room for Kiana at the small counter.

"Good afternoon," Kiana said in a strong voice, already sensing a reluctance on Watts's part to open up. "I'm Kiana Sheridan. Rex Tandy is my . . . assistant."

"Oh?" Watts answered, not offering his hand. His narrowed eyes locked on Kiana's and he remained perfectly still.

Kiana stared back, suddenly feeling very uncomfortable.

"Anything in particular you two looking for?" Watts's inquiry was stiff and not welcoming. He folded his arms on his chest as if waiting for an explanation.

"Yes," Kiana said, determined to conduct the interview. She might need Rex Tandy to guide her around, but she certainly didn't need him to talk for her! "As a matter of fact, there is. I'm interested in acquiring some pieces of decorative glass that I saw at an auction in Houston." Kiana physically maneuvered herself more fully into Mr. Watts's line of vision. "I was told they came from this shop and I'd like to see what else you have."

Rex set his camera on the glass counter and stepped back in an obvious gesture to let Kiana have control of the situation.

"What did it look like?" Watts asked dully, no spark of interest at all.

Kiana hauled her mother's book from her bag and opened it. She pointed to the sketches on the back page. "The vases had designs similar to these. Various colors, but most of the pieces might have been amber."

"Hmm," Watts stalled. "Maybe. Yes. I did have some glass similar to that in the shop. A few months back." He paused, offering no more information.

Kiana opened her mouth to ask another question, but a customer who needed help stepped up. "Excuse me, Marvin. I'm interested in that steeple clock. New Haven, isn't it?"

"Yes, Mrs. Ouster. Circa 1890. Works, too."

"Really?"

"Yes. Let me show you how to get the pendulum going." He stepped away, then turned. "Excuse me," he said, leaving Kiana and Rex standing at the counter.

With their back to Watts, Kiana murmured to Rex, "He sure is edgy."

"Kind of vague," Rex agreed, picking up a copy of *Antiques Today* from a pile of magazines stacked on the floor beside the counter. He thumbed through it as they waited. "You know, I hate to say this but maybe he doesn't know much."

"Not know the source? Please," Kiana said under her breath.

"Dealers often buy antiques in huge lots without knowing exactly where each piece came from."

Kiana didn't buy that. "I think this man knows more than he wants to admit to us. He's holding back. It's obvious."

"Maybe," Rex murmured, still paging through the magazine. When he came to a dog-eared page, he stopped. "Look at this." He slid the magazine across the counter under Kiana's gaze.

She rapidly devoured the familiar article that had been written about the exhibit that had included the vase by Soddy Russell, which her grandmother had donated to the museum. "Yes. This is the right place. Watts knows what Soddy Glass is and has read this story, too."

"So, why's he's acting so cold? What's he trying to hide?" Rex whispered into Kiana's ear, just as Watts came back.

Kiana boldly picked up the magazine and held it in front of her face. "How odd," she said, lowering it, then spinning it around so Watts could see the article. "This is exactly what we were talking about. Have you read this?"

Watts scratched the gray hair at his right temple, glanced up at Rex, then back down. "No." He scanned the page. "But it looks like the glass. I don't remember much about that purchase. Not much at all. This is a funny business, you know. People come in all the time with stuff they want to get rid of. Some of it's trash, some is worth buying. I get ten or twelve inquiries a day."

Kiana frowned and bit her lip to keep a flippant retort from flying off the tip of her tongue. This man is a weasel, she thought, then pressed him, "Where did you get the Soddy Glass?"

Watts finally began to talk. "At first I thought the lady's pieces might be Queensware," he began, "which has similar lines, but not the same patterns. I thought it was unusual and I knew I could move it, so I offered her a price. She agreed. That was about it."

"And the dealer in Houston?" Kiana prompted.

He shrugged. "She came in two days later, looking around. Said she was on vacation . . . saw the glass, wanted all of it, so I sold her the whole lot."

"How many pieces?" Rex asked.

"Oh, three wooden boxes full. Maybe thirty pieces in all."

Kiana closed the magazine, and leaned closer to Mr. Watts. "Where does the woman who brought in the glass live? Do you have her name? Could you tell me?"

Watts's grin faded. "No, I can't. Even if I had her name it would be confidential anyway. Sorry. One of the conditions of my purchases is that I never reveal my sources."

"Can you describe the woman?" Kiana asked. At this point she'd take anything she could get.

"Elderly," Watts volunteered.

"White?" Rex asked.

"No. Black. Light-complexioned, though. She had silver gray hair. Small woman. Very fragile looking, but rather attractive."

"Was she alone?" Kiana asked.

"Oh, I don't remember," Watts said.

Suddenly the woman who had been interested in the clock approached the counter again.

"You want the clock, Mrs. Ouster?" Watts asked, edging toward her, away from Kiana and Rex.

"No," the woman replied quickly, stopping Watts in his tracks. "But I couldn't help overhear what you were talking about . . . that glass that looked like Queensware. I remember it, Marvin. Remember? I was in here the day the lady brought it in."

Watts's pale face turned pink, and he rubbed his hands together. "You were?"

Kiana turned around quickly and extended her hand to the lady. "My name is Kiana Sheridan and I'd really appreciate anything you can tell me. I'm tracing some family heirlooms."

"Well," Mrs. Ouster started, briskly shaking Kiana's hand. "I'm glad to help. I'm a regular in here. I shop for clocks, mainly. I have two hundred fifty-three in my collection, but I'm always looking for something new."

Kiana smiled in understanding. "You said you remember the woman?"

"Clearly," Mrs. Ouster said. "She wasn't alone. She had a driver . . . like a chauffeur . . . it was so interesting. She sat in the back seat. He was a black man. Middle aged. Graying. Very polite and helpful. I remember him because he was so agreeable to driving around to the back to unload the crates. Marvin, remember how crowded it was that day?"

Watts tilted his head in a noncommittal gesture, obviously unhappy with the conversation.

"What kind of car were they in?" Rex wanted to know.

"Interesting you should ask that." A faint smile came to Mrs. Ouster's lips. "A 1955 Pontiac Star Chief. Red and white."

Rex lifted an eyebrow, whistling lowly in appreciation. "A real classic, huh?"

"Vintage! My grandfather had a car just like it," Mrs. Ouster ran on. "I doubt the old lady has any idea how valuable that car is either. Shiny. Clean. Looks like it must have the day it was driven off the showroom floor."

"And probably has fewer than fifty thousand miles on it, too," Kiana added, trying to keep the woman in a talkative mood.

"Probably." Mrs. Ouster chuckled. "A car like that you don't see everyday. Gleamed like a brand new penny."

"You think the lady and her driver were from around here?" Kiana pointedly asked, steering the woman back to their discussion.

"I couldn't say," she replied. "Acted like it, but I don't know. I didn't get the idea that she had come from too far away." She craned her neck toward Watts who was standing tight-lipped, listening. "Don't you think she acted strangely, Marvin?"

He lifted his shoulders nonchalantly. "I don't ask too many questions. It was clear to me that the old lady wanted to get rid of the glass and get back on the road. I've learned over the years not to pry. When people come to the point where they are willing . . . or have to . . . part with family heirlooms, it can be quite an emotional experience. I try to keep my transactions as businesslike as possible."

Rex jumped in. "Did you hear her refer to her driver by name?"

Mr. Watts shook his head, "No."

Mrs. Ouster did likewise. "No. Not really. He just unloaded the boxes."

"Did you pay her by check?" Rex asked.

"No," Watts said. "I paid for the glass in cash . . . she insisted on cash. Then they left."

Rex pulled out his wallet and handed the man his card. "We're doing some genealogical tracing, and Miss Sheridan believes the glass may have come from her family's estate in east Tennessee. Magnolia Crossing. Ever heard of it?"

"No, can't say as I have." Mr. Watts tucked Rex's card in his shirt pocket, picked up the magazine and closed it, dismissing his visitors.

Mrs. Ouster, who had warmed to Kiana, seemed happy to chatter on. "You know another reason I remember that sale so well?"

"Why," Kiana answered.

"Because the glass was packed in the most unusual crates.

Three old wooden boxes. Had the letters PGW in fancy script on all four sides. I mean they were *old*. I told Major Moore about them and he called me back that same day . . . gloating . . . he'd snapped them up. I knew he would. How much did he pay for those old things, Marvin?"

"A hundred dollars, I think."

"Each?" Kiana asked.

Watts nodded.

"Who is Major Moore?" she pressed.

"You must not be from around here," Mrs. Ouster said. "The major is our local expert on the Civil War. Quite an authority. He said he thought those crates might have been used by the Union to ship ammunition into Tennessee."

"How can I get in touch with the major?" Kiana asked.

"Oh, he's in the phone book. Major Sterling Moore," Mrs. Ouster volunteered. "But just go on over. He lives in the red brick house at the corner of Tatum and Lang."

Kiana scribbled the street names in her small notebook.

"The major is quite a character," Mrs. Ouster continued. "He'll talk your ears off, I promise."

Chapter Twenty-two

REX snapped on his seat belt and put the key into the ignition. He struggled to keep his temper from flaring while realizing he'd just been relegated to the position of assistant on his own tour. He was so upset he dared not speak. Wasn't he supposed to be in charge, asking the questions, deciding where to go? Kiana obviously had other plans. Hell, she might as well have come by herself and hired a cabbie to drive her around.

Something cautioned him not to say anything. Not just yet, though he was very tempted to go ahead and clear the air. Kiana was capable of conducting research, he knew, and she had every right to be fully involved, but he hadn't expected her to annoy him quite so much. Pressing his foot down on the accelerator, Rex revved the engine loudly.

Kiana opened the notebook and studied the street names.

Rex stared straight ahead through the windshield, his face expressionless. "Well? Where to now, Miss Daisy?" he grumbled. "What were those cross streets, again?"

"What?" Kiana frowned, puzzled by the sarcasm in Rex's tone.

"You've got the address. Which direction?"

Kiana stared at him while she fastened her seat belt. "Whoa. What's this about?"

"What's what about?" Rex answered coolly.

"This attitude I hear in your voice?"

"No attitude. I was just asking for directions, that's all. I'm at your disposal." Rex sat steely rigid, staring ahead, determined not to look at her.

"Directions?" Kiana tossed back. "Hey, I don't know this city. You're the one who does."

Now Rex faced Kiana. His breath was held tight in his chest as he curtly responded. "Right. So tell me where we're headed so we can get going!"

Kiana slowly handed Rex the address.

Rex glanced at it, then handed it back to Kiana. "It's pretty far out. Near Hickory," he said, his voice sounding contrite.

"Look," Kiana began, not wanting the tension between them to grow worse. "It's almost three. Why don't we go to the hotel, check in, and get something to eat. Maybe it's time for a strategy session. Before this discussion goes any further, we'd better clarify a few things. And a full stomach might help both of us."

Rex put his sunglasses over his eyes, settling into his seat. "Yeah," he said. "I think that's a very good idea."

After checking into the Ramada Inn downtown, Kiana and Rex put their bags in their rooms, which were side by side on the seventh floor, then took the elevator down to the restaurant. They were promptly seated and waited on in the near-empty room, and once the waitress departed, feelings of remorse crept over Kiana.

Since leaving the antique shop, she had sensed Rex's annoyance with her growing. He was much more distant than he'd been only hours ago when he'd met her at the airport. Perhaps she should have let him do more of the talking—the last thing she wanted was a rift between them that would severely hamper the search, and it looked as if they were heading in that direction unless they set some ground rules—fast. Her tangled thoughts raced.

"Rex," she began. "I certainly hope you are not having second thoughts about this trip."

He took a sip of water, put the glass down carefully, a pensive look on his face. "As a matter of fact, I am," he finally said.

Kiana's stomach tightened. "What should we do to straighten this out?"

"You mean you don't know?"

"No," she said quickly. Though she had a pretty good idea what he was going to suggest, she wanted to hear him say it. "Tell me."

With an awkward jerk of his shoulders, he lifted his chin. "I thought you understood that *Black Culture Watch* is underwriting this trip and I am on an assignment for my magazine."

"I know that," Kiana replied.

"Then it ought to be clear. I have a story to write, an editor to report to . . . and I have certain questions to ask, specific information to gather. Both of us can't be in charge. I've got to be in control in order to make the story work. You'll have to let me do a lot more of the questioning."

Kiana stiffened, but didn't remark.

"And to be honest with you, Kiana," Rex continued, "I can see that you'll have a problem with that."

Kiana cleared her throat. "Oh? The fact that I am working on a Ph.D. doesn't count? You think I don't know how to ask the right questions, conduct research?"

"I didn't say that," he countered.

"You might as well have." Kiana averted her eyes, glaring out the window at the people passing by the restaurant.

"I don't think that's fair, Kiana. I never meant to imply that you couldn't participate, it's just better for me to take the lead."

She jerked back to look at Rex, seething. "*You* may be on assignment for *Black Culture Watch*, but it's *my* story you are going to tell, and without my cooperation you have nothing. I've got the information that will guide us, so I have to be involved. I've got specific questions I need answers to also."

"I understand that," Rex said, "but if you're going to undermine me . . . if you *must* be in charge, it won't work. You might as well find someone else to drive you around or forget it and go back home."

Kiana glared at him, almost choking with reproach, yet she was shaken by the truth of his words. She needed him, he needed her, and despite their rocky start neither was going to abandon the project. It was definitely time for compromise. "Okay," Kiana said, anger ebbing from her face. "Let's make a deal."

"You're good at that, aren't you?" Rex sat in stony silence, waiting.

Kiana ignored his remark. "We'll make a workable plan that will clearly outline who does what and when."

Rex rolled his eyes.

"No, hear me out," Kiana rushed to say. "In some instances you'll take the lead, in others I will be in charge. Sometimes we will split up and work independently."

"Like?" Rex wanted to know.

"Tomorrow, why don't you go to the courthouse and search land records while I dig around in the public library and the Tennessee Historical Society's archives. This way we can cover more ground, in half the time. And stay out of each other's way. What do you think?"

"Probably best," Rex conceded.

"Great. Now do you want to question the major? That is if he agrees to talk."

Rex shrugged.

"Fine, you do it," Kiana said, "because we can't turn this trip into a power play, Rex. We've both got too much at stake."

Rex drew in a long breath. "I'm glad to hear you say that." His voice was firm, yet tinged with relief. "You'd better believe Ed expects regular progress reports, and I'd hate to tell him he's wasted his money because we can't decide who's going to be in charge."

Kiana nodded, forcing a stiff smile to her lips. "That'd be embarrassing, wouldn't it?" She tilted her head back and extended her hand. "Truce?"

Rex squinted suspiciously, then grinned. Accepting her hand, he repeated softly, "Truce."

His easy answer initiated a vague, sensuous flutter deep inside Kiana, immediately dissolving her irritation with him. She disengaged her hand from his. "Fine. Let's get down to business." Reaching into her purse, she took out the notebook.

"If he's listed, I think I'd better call first," Rex volunteered. "In spite of what the lady said, the major may not welcome us with open arms."

"I think you're right. You want to call Major Moore and see if he's willing to talk to us while I order?"

"Yes, ma'am," Rex replied in a clipped, brisk manner. "I'll take a cheeseburger and fries. Diet Coke." Raising one hand above his brow, he gave her a mock salute.

Kiana reached out and playfully swatted at Rex. "Don't rub it in."

He saluted again.

"Come on now, stop it. This is serious. This Major Moore may be exactly the contact we need to get this thing rolling."

"Let's hope so," he said, taking a quarter from his pocket. "If we hurry we might be able to get out there and back before dark, and if we're really lucky, he's already traced those wooden crates back to our mystery lady."

During the short ride to Major Moore's house, Kiana re-thought the conversation she and Rex had over lunch. She understood how he must feel. On his regular tours he could be in charge, but this was different. He couldn't make all the decisions, she was going to be totally involved. This trip was the most important one she would ever make and no way was he going to hold her back. It meant too much to her.

Kiana looked wearily out the window. Rex definitely had a stubborn streak, but, she had to admit, she did, too. Kiana sneaked a glance at Rex. The two of them had much more in common than she had originally thought. As they rounded the corner of Tatum and Forest, Kiana forced herself to relax, convinced that she and Rex were destined to take this trip together.

The major's house was a neat colonial brick at the end of a quiet shady street. When they had pulled up the driveway, Rex cut the engine and faced Kiana.

"This is it," he said.

Kiana looked the place over, alarmed to see one of those black stable boy statues with a lantern in its hand positioned at the end of the driveway. "You said Major Moore sounded okay about talking to us?"

"Yeah. Okay . . . not really enthusiastic. Seemed more curious than anything else."

"All right." Kiana took in a deep breath. "Let's hit it."

A man dressed in a multicolored plaid flannel shirt and denim pants, which were held up by suspenders that looked as if they'd been cut from a Confederate flag, emerged onto his shady front porch. A big dog followed him out the door, across the porch. The man stood behind a white wicker chair, his hands on the back of it as he studied his visitors.

Kiana and Rex exchanged worried glances, then got out, walking side by side up the driveway. The man eyed them curiously, then descended the short flight of steps, and started across the lawn.

"Hello," he said coolly, greeting them with less than enthusiastic handshakes. His playful, nosy golden retriever licked at Kiana's shoes while introductions were made. "Y'all come on inside. Let's see what we got here."

Kiana nudged Rex. So far, so good.

Major Moore led his guests through the front of his house toward a sunny yellow kitchen at the rear. Along the way, Kiana and Rex had time to look at the walls, which were covered from floor to ceiling with an astonishing collection of Civil War memorabilia. There were faded photos of battlegrounds, oil paintings of historic plantations, portraits of pale Southern belles wearing hooped skirts with wide straw bonnets on their heads. There were Currier & Ives etchings, pale watercolors, and vibrant oil renderings of mounted soldiers, Confederate generals Jackson and Lee, along with a huge mural-like painting of the Battle of Gettysburg by renowned Civil War artist, Mort Kunstler.

"Quite impressive," Kiana told the major, her eyes riveted on a faded rendering of General Lee and his staff.

"I've got four times this much in storage," Moore replied as he headed into the kitchen. There, Kiana noticed a tall bookcase with deep-set shelves on which were piled all types of Confederate articles—enough miniature flags, counterfeit Confederate money, muskets, bayonets, munitions, and cannon balls to stock a tourist shop at a Tennessee truck stop.

Once settled at an oval pine table, Kiana sat quietly looking around while Rex explained in more detail who Soddy Russell was and what they were searching for.

Major Moore said little, but nodded from time to time, then excused himself and went down the steps to his basement. When he returned he had one of the old wooden crates in his arms. "This what you want to see?" he asked, setting it on the table in front of Rex and Kiana.

They examined the dark wood carefully. It was obvious that the wooden box had been stored inside, out of the weather, because it was in excellent condition for its age.

Major Moore appraised his visitors with a curious eye. "I was able to trace the crates. That fancy PGW on the sides is the symbol for the old Porter Glass Works near Centerville, Pennsylvania."

Kiana flashed a smile at Rex. "Great!"

"So," Moore went on. "Looks like your great-great-grandfather's glass coulda been what was in those crates. You say he worked there?"

"Yes," Kiana said.

"Hmm," Moore hedged. "And you say he was from Magnolia Crossing, huh. Owned by the DeRossette family? That's what you're looking for?"

Kiana spoke for the first time. "Yes. And," she eyed Rex before going on, "I'd like to talk to anyone who may have recently acquired glass with designs similar to this." She reached into her bag and pulled out her mother's book, showing Moore the sketches inside.

Major Moore studied the drawings. "Marvin Watts says the old lady had glass like that in these crates?"

"Yes," Rex replied, giving Kiana a smile, grateful she had brought along the book.

"I've got a book you need to look at," Moore said. He got up and disappeared into an adjoining room, returning with a faded red book in his hand. "Ever seen this?" he asked Kiana, holding the heavy tome with its cover toward her. Its cloth binding was dusty and frayed, a testament to its owner's use.

"*The Tennessee Tracers*," she read the title. "No. I've never heard of this book," she replied, reaching out to take it from the major.

"Well, it's old, but very useful. The Tennessee Tracers are one of the earliest genealogical groups around here. They put this together about twenty years ago. It lists the people—professionals and amateurs—who were doing family tracing back then. Kinda sketchy, but it does have one black lady in it." He took the book from Kiana, checked the table of contents, then turned to a page in the middle of the book. Pulling a pair of bifocals out of his flannel shirt pocket, he hooked them over his ears. "Let's see," Moore murmured, reading silently for a moment. "Here she is."

He laid the book down, turning it toward Rex and Kiana, who both shifted their chairs to read what was on the page. Moore went on. "I've never heard of a town or a plantation called Magnolia Crossing, but the name DeRossette rang a bell as soon as you said it on the phone, young man. You see there?" He tapped his pudgy finger on the page, indicating a photo of an elderly black woman sitting amid a stack of papers and books. "This here is Daisy Hudson. She used to be involved with the Tennessee Tracers, and when we were working on this book, I spoke to Daisy several times . . . you know, exchanging information on the phone. Quite an interesting lady, she was, but I never met her. She was about the only black genealogist I knew of at the time this book was put together." He leaned over the open pages. "She was old when that picture was taken, so it could be she's dead by now. I don't know."

Rex eagerly scanned the article. "Kiana! It says here that her maiden name was deRossette. Spelled with a lower case 'd,' but maybe . . ."

"Yep," Moore murmured. "That's what I remembered as soon as you said the name. It's such a fancy French name, but I remember Daisy making a point to tell me her family name had Italian origins."

Rex began rapidly copying the information about Daisy from the book while Kiana hunched closer to read. "Maybe a different version of DeRossette?" she noted.

"Sure could be," Moore agreed. "This says she lives in Bedford County, south of Shelbyville. At the end of the Duck River. Might be pretty hard to get to her, so I wouldn't strike out without trying to contact her first. Might be she's no longer alive, but somebody in her family could be willing to search her records for you."

Kiana reached down and petted the major's retriever who had settled on the floor at her side. "Thanks a million, Major Moore," she said. "This is very helpful. I appreciate you taking the time to talk with us."

"Right," Rex agreed, "but would you mind doing me a favor?"

Kiana glared at Rex. Don't push the man, she thought. He's gone out of his way to be pleasantly helpful.

"Well." Moore looked puzzled, a hint of irritation rising for the first time. "What is it?"

"If you get any information about the whereabouts of the lady who had those Porter Glass Works crates will you let us know?"

"I . . . I guess I could, but how would I contact you?"

Now Rex consulted Kiana. "What do you think? We're going to be moving around."

Kiana stood up, pushing her chair to the table. "We'll be here in Nashville for a few days. At the Ramada downtown. Just call and leave us a message, or we'll check back with you. Would you mind, Mr. Moore? Especially if you get a definite lead?"

"I don't mind," he said after a few seconds of thought. "But I doubt I'll learn any more about where those crates came from."

Kiana quickly wrote her name on a piece of paper torn from a Ramada Inn notepad and handed it to Major Moore.

Chapter Twenty-three

ON Thursday morning, Ida boarded a 7:00 A.M. flight on American Airlines to Pittsburgh. After securing her rental car at the airport, she drove directly to Centerville and surprised Hester by showing up at the back door of the farmhouse with a dozen white roses in her arms.

"Why, Ida," Hester said, carefully arranging the flowers in a tall, double-handled urn, "I wasn't expecting to see you again so soon."

"It's a very busy time at the office, Grandmother, but you know I can always find time to come home for a visit."

"I know you do, and I appreciate it, Ida. I do. I've been rather distracted . . . since Kiana left."

"Left? You mean she's already gone?" Ida asked, forcing surprise into her voice.

"Oh, yes. Kiana left on . . . let me see." Hester put four fingers to her forehead. "Tuesday! Yes. It was Tuesday. I remember because Flo makes her smothered chicken every Tuesday and I had so wanted Kiana to stay for dinner, but she left that morning. Early."

"How selfish of her," Ida commented. "That little sneak. She told me she'd be here for at least a week and it was her idea that I come out while she was here. I had hoped to catch her. It's been a long time since we've both been in this house at the same time."

"That would have been lovely, wouldn't it? Both of my girls here together. Like old times."

"She could have telephoned me and let me know she wasn't going to be here," Ida grumbled.

"Kiana is an adventurer," Hester defended. "I guess she's a dreamer." Hester clipped the stem of a rose as she talked. "So bright. So focused. Just like her mother."

Ida flinched at the comparison. "I gather Kiana told you what she's doing? What she's looking for?"

Hester set the scissors down and scowled as if she'd just remembered how disturbing Kiana's news had been. "Oh, my. Yes. And I warned her not to go."

"I did, too," Ida said, watching Hester very closely. "I told her she was making a big mistake and she ought to let those old stories stay in the past."

Hester picked the scissors up again, waving them as she spoke. "You are right, my dear." She stopped, went over to Ida, and put her hand on her arm. "But you most always are. I don't know what I'd do without you. You're such a comfort." She went back to her task, picked up a rose, and tore off the lower leaves. "I couldn't love you more if you were my own flesh and blood. I just wish Kiana could be more like you."

The Ramada Inn's parking lot was jammed with cars when Rex and Kiana pulled in. After circling for a few minutes, they got lucky and Rex snagged a good space directly in front of the entrance to The High Note, the hotel nightclub. It appeared to be a very popular watering hole.

Kiana watched a young couple walk under the bright fluorescent sign and enter the club. The pulsing sound of a live band jamming inside drifted out.

Rex turned off the headlights and faced Kiana. "Well, we made some headway at the library today, don't you think?"

"So far, so good," Kiana answered. "Those old Confederate maps will be helpful. Too bad the archivist didn't mention them earlier." Kiana rubbed the back of her neck, trying to ease the cramps that bending over books for eight hours straight had brought on. "Tomorrow I plan to go over those maps with a magnifying glass. If there ever was a Magnolia Crossing, I'll find it."

"Daisy Hudson should get her certified letter tomorrow," Rex said. "Cross your fingers and pray that she calls . . . if she's still alive."

"Yeah," Kiana agreed, "but unless we are able to identify the woman who sold Watts the glass, we may never get to the source. That's what I really want . . . to find out whether or not the pieces she had were originals or reproductions." Kiana slipped her handbag over her arm.

"Exactly," Rex said. "And I have a feeling that Major Moore will start doing some digging of his own, now that we've stirred his curiosity. You think he's not interested? Don't believe it. People who are avid collectors and who love to dig up information about the past are usually happy to help others out. Makes them look like experts, and feel that all that scattering of knowledge they've picked up along the way is finally being put to some use."

"You could be right," Kiana said, stifling a yawn, glad that the long day was coming to an end. "I'm fading."

"Yeah, it's been a day."

Kiana put her hand on the door handle as if to get out. "See you in the morning. What time you want to get started?"

"As early as possible," Rex said, stopping her exit with a gentle touch on the arm.

Kiana looked at him in the dark interior of the car. Shadows played over his rugged features and she realized how easily they had worked together today, and it was difficult to believe that only the day before yesterday she had been ready to strangle him. So far, their agreement seemed to be working fine, and she was relieved that Rex remained as enthusiastic about the project as she was. She glanced down at his hand on her arm, then up into his questioning brown eyes.

"How about a drink?" he asked. "Wine? Coffee? Whatever you want. The High Note seems to be a pretty hot spot. Want to go in?"

Though flattered that he'd asked, Kiana's internal warning clicked in, bringing back the conflicting emotions that Rex always seemed to stir in her. She gave him a wary look. "I don't think so. Like you said, it's been a long day. I'm a little tired."

Rex would not be put off so easily. "We don't have to stay long . . . but I'd like to talk a little more. We can plan our strategy for tomorrow. We've got a lot of ground to cover before we pull out of Nashville. If we hear from Daisy and decide to head toward Shelbyville, we won't go to Knoxville as originally planned."

"Well," Kiana hedged, her vow to keep things professional uppermost in her mind. "Maybe we ought to make some decisions."

"We deserve to relax for a while."

Kiana opened her mouth, then closed it, giving Rex a genuine smile. His eagerness warmed her right through and she faltered for words to turn him down. Pressing her shoulders to the soft seat cushion, she stared uncertainly out the windshield, fixing her gaze on the blue note blinking jauntily over the club's entrance. It was clear that they were going to be joined at the hip for the next few weeks, so why be wary of entering a nightclub with Rex? After all, she was about to tear off across the country with him. But he was so attractive, Kiana knew she'd have to be careful. Now was not the time to get personally involved or lose focus of their mission.

Kiana's worried thoughts were shattered when Rex suddenly got out, circled the Blazer, and pulled her door open. "Come on, Kiana. Do the rest of your thinking inside, okay? It's silly to sit out here any longer."

She gritted her teeth. Just when she was about to forgive him his controlling manner, here he was making decisions for her again. But instead of getting on her high horse and snapping back at Rex, Kiana gave him her sweetest smile, jumped out of the car, and fell into step beside him.

Threading through the noisy crowd toward a table near the band, Kiana's spirits were immediately buoyed. The pulsating music drove away her fatigue and she started humming along with the saxophone player. It did feel good to be in a club again, and she suddenly realized how long it had been since she'd been dancing.

Rex ordered a beer. Kiana ordered a decaf coffee and they sat in comfortable silence for a few minutes watching the band and the couples jamming on the dance floor. When their drinks arrived, Rex spoke first.

"I am still puzzled by what your mother wrote about Soddy Russell. It's been on my mind all day. Did you ever hear anyone in your family say that your great-great-grandfather was white?"

"Never!" Kiana said. "I told you . . . I was in shock when I read that."

"I take it no photos exist of him?"

"No, but if he had been white, I'm certain I would have known it . . . somehow."

Rex swept Kiana with a critical eye. "But what about Lucy . . . your great-grandmother? According to your mother's book, Lucy was the child of Price, the slave. So where's the connection to Russell?"

"Confusing, isn't it?"

"Sure is. Something's missing," Rex said.

"A whole lot more than I thought," Kiana agreed. She sat back from the small round table, an expression of dismay clouding her face. "And there must be a connection between Porter Glass Works and Queensware, don't you think?"

"Yep," Rex agreed. "If the DeRossette family in England exported Queensware to the States, and Soddy Russell's glass, which had similar lines was made at Porter Glass Works, the two could definitely be intertwined in some way."

"And Mother wrote that Soddy Russell looked a lot like Daniel DeRossette. Brothers? Cousins? Could I be related to the DeRossettes?"

In a thoughtful tone, Rex offered his opinion. "A family that split somewhere along the line? A black side. A white side. That's very common."

"I know. It's also very possible, but why did my grandmother lead me and Ida to believe that Soddy Russell was black?"

"Shame. Pride. A mixture of both. And remember the designs he used on his glass, Kiana. What white man during those times would use African tribal symbols on his works?"

Kiana slumped in obvious exasperation. "I don't know, Rex. This is much more complicated than I thought it would be. I hope you're not beginning to have doubts about me . . . my family legacy."

With an air of relaxed self-assurance, Rex shook his head. "No. And don't you go getting discouraged on me. It's too early in the game."

"Oh, I'm not. Really," she quickly answered. "Just perplexed."

"What we have to do is follow one lead at a time to its conclusion, see what we have, not get distracted or waste our time."

Trying to remain optimistic, Kiana asked, "What's the next step? Which lead?"

"Daisy deRossette Hudson. We must talk to her. The letter was sent overnight, certified mail return receipt requested. We'll be around here for a few more days following the paper trail in the courthouse and the library. Hopefully, Daisy will contact us. If we don't hear from her, at least a notice that the letter was undeliverable will let us know she's not there."

"And?" Kiana prodded.

"We're going to scour every antique shop in the area . . . find the mystery lady in the red-and-white Pontiac Star Chief. She must be local. Doesn't make sense for an elderly woman who is eager to dispose of family heirlooms to travel too far away from home to do it."

"But why do you think she wanted to remain anonymous?"

"Maybe some family feud . . . you know how greedy family members can be. Aunts, uncles, sisters, or cousins often turn incredibly ugly when it comes to getting their hands on the family jewels, silver, things like that. The lady must want to avoid a row within her family, and I'll bet Watts Antiques was not the only place she dumped some of her stuff. I have a few good contacts here in Nashville. We'll call on them tomorrow."

"You sound like a detective." Kiana laughed, sipping her coffee.

"That's not a bad way to put it. Genealogical and historical research is like sleuthing . . . not much more than logically and methodically exploring each lead until some scrap of information turns up to shove you in a better direction. My adage remains, 'follow the land' because that's where black folks have been recorded—in the land and property transactions of white people."

Kiana drained her coffee cup and pushed it to the center of the table.

"It's beginning to feel as if I'm trying to resurrect ancestors who don't want to be found!"

"We'll find them."

Kiana shook a finger. "Be careful about making a statement like that. I'll hold you to it." Struck by his optimistic attitude, Kiana's second thoughts about socializing with Rex dissolved and she relaxed as they conversed. "You know, I think I'd like—" she began.

"To dance?" Rex jumped into the middle of her sentence.

Kiana laughed. "Well, I was going to say I might like a glass of wine, but a dance sounds even better."

The band eased into a soulful ballad by Anita Baker. Rex held up a hand. "This song okay?"

"Fine," Kiana replied, knowing she'd do much better on a slow song than a frantically paced hip-hop number.

They walked to the center of the dance floor and Rex took her in his arms.

"I'm excited about doing this story, Kiana," he said as they slowly rocked back and forth. At her questioning look he added, "Really. I'm intrigued by the whole thing, especially since you've filled me in on what your mother wrote. It's going to make a dramatic piece, and . . ." he stopped short.

"And?" Kiana prompted, head to one side waiting for him to finish his sentence.

"And," Rex hesitated, "I hope . . . maybe we can work together again. You know, collaborate on another historical, genealogical, type of article."

His statement took Kiana by surprise, though she could tell he was sincere. "Maybe," she replied thoughtfully, liking the idea. Rex pulled her a little closer, his chest brushing hers. Kiana swallowed hard, but didn't move away. Each time their bodies touched, she felt a spark of attraction and when he spun her into a graceful slide and moved across the dance floor she was lost to everything except the feel of him in her arms.

"Kiana?"

"Yes?"

"I think we were meant to do this together. I've been waiting a long time for a story like this to come along . . . and . . . someone like you to do it with. I want everything to work out exactly as we planned."

The music swelled to a stirring crescendo, then came to an end. Kiana stepped back, studying Rex in the dim blue light, not letting go of his hand. It had been exactly one week since she'd met him, and she couldn't deny her pleasure at being alone with him on the road. It certainly beat being paired with an aging scholarly type, for whom she might have had respect, but not this physical attraction that refused to go away.

Kiana had no reply to Rex's comment, yet she knew any move he might make to get closer to her would be very difficult to repel, even if it began to get serious. He could be irritating and exasperating when he ordered her around, but every word that came from his mouth stirred her like a gentle wind drifting from a tropical shore.

Rooted in front of him in the middle of the dance floor, Kiana waited until the band gently segued into a tune by Luther Vandross. Without a word from Rex, she slipped easily back into his arms and was lost, once more, in the music. She hummed along with the band, following his lead, unable to resist the imperceptible pull that eventually had her flush against his chest. She was tempted to lay her head on his shoulder, but fought the urge, keeping her neck stiff, her face only inches from his.

"You speak as if you believe our meeting was predestined. That perhaps none of this has happened by chance?" Kiana grasped the opportunity to try to alleviate some of the electricity sparking between them.

"To be truthful," Rex started, his fingers now on her shoulder, inching toward the soft curve of her neck, "I consider myself lucky. I love the work I do, and meeting someone as beautiful and smart as you confirms my belief that if I keep my options open, all kinds of good things will come my way."

"Good attitude to have," Kiana commented, her skin burning under his touch while her heart struggled to remain cool. She liked what he had said, but hoped his words were not standard lines he used on other women who happened to cross his path.

With parted lips, he hooked her with a delightful grin. "When I met you, Kiana, I have to admit that I thought of little else but seeing you again. I could not get you out of my mind." He slid his thumb along the edge of the collar on her jacket, observing her with soulful tenderness.

Kiana felt as if he had caressed her, and a deep, unfamiliar longing slipped gently into place. Relaxing her rigid shoulders, she acknowledged the delicious heaviness that was gathering between her legs. Running her tongue over her lips, she moved in tandem with him, absorbing the electricity in his touch.

She'd been under so much stress in her chaotic relationship with Stanley that her emotions had been dulled for months. But now, as her defenses weakened and her professional resolve softened, she felt compelled to explore this stirring attraction. Primed for change, Kiana knew she was treading shaky ground again, but Rex Tandy was too good to ignore.

Boldly, she confessed, "I can't deny that I thought of you, too." Flickering dots of light bounced off the faceted crystal ball above the dance floor, reflecting scattered images of the couples who were crowded together in the tiny space between the tables and the stage. Kiana watched the lights sheen Rex's eyes with an almost hypnotic sparkle. "I am terribly ashamed of how I acted in the antique shop. You must have thought me rather childish."

Rex leaned back slightly, his thumb brushing the soft hollow place at her throat. "Childish?" He chuckled. "No, not at all. Maybe a little eager . . ."

Unable to deny the truth of what he'd said, Kiana gave Rex a one-sided smile, then said, "That's probably true."

"Surely," Rex went on, "you know that I respect you. You're capable, extremely confident in yourself . . . a rather wonderful combination, I think."

Kiana lowered her lashes, thinking. So, he thought of her as wonderful, yet he was quite an enigma himself. Knowing precisely what she was about to initiate, she told him, "You're not exactly the average brother on the street, Rex. If you know what I mean."

He laughed aloud, his pleasure in her observation emerging. "There are those who would differ with you, I'm afraid. My life is really rather ordinary."

"Please," Kiana said, "don't be so modest. How ordinary is it to earn a living traveling through the country taking pictures, experiencing the joy of unveiling long lost historical facts? Traveling back roads . . ."

"With a beautiful woman," he slipped in, bending to place his lips only inches from her face. "Under primitive circumstances, sometimes."

Kiana let out a silent gasp, taking in the faint woodsy smell of his aftershave, resisting an urge to change the subject. "And how exactly do you define primitive?" she teased, taking up his suggestive banter. God, she had never felt this relaxed, this drawn to any man.

Rex placed one hand beneath her chin, tilting her face up to his. "At times we may have to sleep on the ground in my tent. It's a very small tent for two, and we'll have to wash in cold water, at outside pumps . . . cook over an open fire."

Kiana almost melted from his nearness, her composure rapidly fading. Swallowing, she asked, "How cold does it get in the Smoky Mountains in June?" She quivered as his fingertips slid to the underside of her jaw. Slowly Rex drew her lips toward his.

"Cold enough for you to be glad that my sleeping bag is also big enough for two," Rex said, impulsively capturing Kiana's lips with his.

The deep moan that swept through Kiana was lost as she surrendered her lips to his. With a clarity never experienced before, she absorbed his tender overture, her body vibrating under his. With his heart beating intimately against hers, she abandoned all attempts at remaining aloof, dissolving in the pleasure of his kiss. It was a dangerous stage she knew she was setting, yet Kiana tossed aside her concerns and kissed Rex back with equal urgency, aroused beyond expectation.

Rex's touch gently laced a trail of heat from her neck, across her shoulder, down her spine to stop at the firm flare of her jean-clad hips. With both hands he pulled her firmly, yet tenderly, flush against his body.

Kiana responded as if she were hypnotized, circling Rex's neck with her arms, anchoring her clasped hands at his back. It was impossible to lift her lips from his. A delicious shiver threaded down her legs, weakening her so much she tightened her grip. Trembling, she savored the flicker of his tongue over hers, and opened her mouth wider to accept the completeness of his kiss. The sheer pleasure of it dispersed the disturbing residual of every ill-fated relationship of her past. When their kiss had run its natural course, they separated slightly and gazed in astonishment at each other—unable, or unwilling, to move from their embrace.

"Well!" Rex breathed, shaking his head as if to clear it of the impact of their encounter. "I must admit I've been wanting to do that since I first saw you at the museum." He put a hand at her waist and escorted her back to their table.

Taking her seat, Kiana smoothed her hair with a jittery hand, feeling shaken, though not unpleasantly so. "We'd better not let that happen again," she said in a husky voice, ashamed of her eager response. He must think I'm desperate, she chastised herself.

Looking away, she felt Rex staring at the side of her face. She lifted a hand to get the waitress's attention, anxious to get back to her room and sort her feelings out. Her breasts burned from the press of his chest against hers, and her lips remained stained with his taste. Turning back, she told Rex, "I can't deny that I enjoyed the kiss, but we'd better keep things cool . . . on a professional level, okay? We can't afford to get too distracted." She willed herself to remain detached and calm, but when he eased one hand over hers, she shuddered, then threaded her fingers through his and held on tightly as she studied his face.

"You're right," he murmured, skin glowing bronze under the candlelight emanating from the hurricane lamp in the center of the table. "From now on we'll behave like business partners. I promise. No more unexpected advances. We have a job to do."

"Fine," Kiana answered, stirred by the sultry tone in his voice, not at all convinced that he meant a word of what he said. His magnetic presence and the way he massaged the back of her hand with his thumb affirmed Kiana's suspicions that Rex Tandy had no intention whatsoever of keeping his promise.

Chapter Twenty-four

KIANA slowly moved her index finger down the page, carefully reading each name in the ledger: Denfort, Depis, Derle, Devereaux—every name, it seemed, except DeRossette. She slammed the dusty book shut and shoved it to the center of the table, then leaned back in her chair, lifting her chin toward the paintings of angels and clouds that were splashed in muted colors on the ceiling of the library archives. She turned her options over in her mind.

Yesterday she'd shut herself up in the musty basement of the courthouse to search probate records, estate settlements, wills, circuit court records, newspaper clippings, and every land transaction recorded between 1797 and 1900. She hadn't found a single reference to Magnolia Crossing or Daniel DeRossette.

Today she'd been cloistered in the library archives since 8:00 A.M. and her luck so far had not been much better. She had found information on Queensware glass, but not the man who had imported it.

With hands folded atop her head, Kiana contemplated her next move. At two o'clock she would meet Rex at the Tennessee Historical Society where he'd gone to dig through family histories and personal journals written by pioneers and early settlers in the state.

After lunch they were going to tour Belle Meade, the restored plantation south of Nashville that was owned and operated by the Association for the Preservation of Tennessee Antiquities. Mary Miller, one of the docents there, was purported to be an expert in nineteenth-century glass. Kiana hoped the woman might know of people in the area who were avid collectors and might have recently purchased pieces of Soddy Glass.

Tomorrow afternoon, they were scheduled to leave Nashville and head toward Knoxville. In the eastern part of the state, they planned to zero in on specific county and regional depositories to continue the search.

Kiana pulled another tome closer and read the faded title—*Tennessee Artisans 1850–1900.* Again, she scanned the index for any familiar names, and seeing none, quickly closed the book. With her chin in her hands, she sat thinking about her mother's efforts many years ago. Where had Louise Sheridan gone to uncover her roots? How had she pried the information she wrote about from the deep secret crevices of the past?

Unexpectedly, Kiana's thoughts drifted to Rex—back to the kiss he had so boldly placed on her lips. She shivered, drawing her arms close to her body as the image of her and Rex swaying together to the music came back. The feel of him brushing against her, and the reality of his sensuous mouth covering hers revved her emotions into high gear again. The thought of meeting him in just a few minutes brought a smile to her lips. Though two days had passed since their dance floor encounter, the memory was as vividly clear and erotically charged as if Rex were still holding her in his arms.

Since that night, Rex had been discreetly silent about the kiss, but it kept replaying itself before Kiana's eyes like a video rewinding in her head. And now, every time their hands or arms touched, she felt as if she'd been shocked.

Rex was much more handsome, talented, and professionally focused than any man Kiana had ever dated. She thought of Douglas Sheridan, her stepfather—the man who had captured, then healed her mother's broken heart, and realized that he'd been much like Rex. Douglas Sheridan had been an avid historian, an amateur photographer, a researcher who had been brave and committed enough to devote his life to traveling the globe with the woman he loved. Was it sheer luck that Kiana should meet a man with the same sharp energy and affable nature that Douglas Sheridan had possessed? Or was it what Rex had said—that their meeting had been predestined? He still could be brash, even irritatingly smug, but Kiana realized now that his bossy nature was only a result of his eagerness to do his job. And he was very good at it. Kiana only wished the trail they were following would become clearer, and very soon.

Kiana sensed that Rex was waiting for her to make the next move and act on his teasing invitation. But the thought of initiating a romantic relationship was frightening. What if she moved too soon, made a mess of things again, and ruined what potential there was for a more solid relationship later? No, she did not want to take that chance. Her demeanor had to remain strictly platonic. But, she reminded herself, it's going to be damn near impossible to keep that front up. Her mind raced forward to the rest of the trip and she knew that more than one challenge lay ahead.

Kiana picked up several books, then put them down. A young woman who worked in the archives, who had pulled the books for Kiana, approached the table with a new stack of books in her hands. Kiana glanced up.

"Find what you were looking for?" she asked, pushing a long strand of blond hair from one eye.

"I did have a little luck, but I didn't find the family name I'd hoped to come across." Kiana explained in more detail what she was looking for.

The clerk nodded. "From what you told me, you'll probably have good luck in the library in Chattanooga. And . . . are you familiar with the Chattanooga Regional History Museum? They have a large collection of photographs and records of families who settled in that area."

"Oh, yes," Kiana said. "I've already placed a call to the archivist there. He's checking now."

"Good." The clerk paused, then added, "What about the Houston Museum? On High Street?"

"I'm not familiar with that," Kiana replied.

"Chattanooga is my hometown," the girl said. "I love to go to that museum whenever I get home. Give it a try. The director is Joe Dawson, and he has assembled an interesting collection. Furniture, textiles, ceramics . . . and the Queensware glass collection is one of the . . ."

"Queensware glass?" Kiana stopped her.

"Sure. It's quite an extraordinary exhibit. I've been through it several times. Mainly decorative pieces from the eighteenth through the twentieth centuries. Quite impressive."

"How interesting," Kiana said. "Do you have the address?"

"Right here," the clerk responded cheerfully, handing Kiana a threefold leaflet. "This is from the Tennessee Tour Guide Book. Joe Dawson will be glad to help you, I'm sure. He's quite an expert in regional and ethnic art."

Kiana took the pamphlet and stuck it in her bag.

"And I thought you might want to take a look at this book," the young lady said, handing Kiana a slim green volume with gold lettering on the front. "It was written in 1915. You might find something helpful in it."

Kiana took the book and read the title—*An Old Man's History of Sequatchie County*. "Thanks," she murmured.

"No problem," the girl said, starting back to her desk.

Kiana slipped down lower in her seat, stretched her feet out before her, and opened the self-published memoir. She examined the table of contents, her eyes drifting lazily over the listings. Then she riffled a few pages, skimming the entries that were rambling vignettes of a man's childhood memories of growing up in the valley along Walden Ridge. Kiana bit her lip as she ploughed through the dull writing, and was about to dismiss the book as another dead end when a word caught her eye. She gripped the pages tightly, devouring the shocking entry.

"My God! I don't believe this." Kiana bolted ramrod straight in her chair, then turned around, and frantically searched the now-empty room for the librarian. "Miss!" Kiana hissed across the room.

The blond woman came from behind the stacks and looked at Kiana. "Yes?"

Kiana started across the carpet, book clutched in her hand. "Miss! Do you have a photocopy machine?"

Over a late lunch, Kiana and Rex filled each other in on the results of their day of research.

"I discovered that Queensware," Kiana started, "was very popular glass . . . but not like the Depression glass of the late eighteenth, early nineteenth century. The DeRossette Glass Company in England exported quite a bit of it to America, but it never became truly affordable. Not many families had the money to buy it."

"Who sold it? How was it distributed?" Rex asked.

Kiana clenched her jaw in thought. "That's the zinger. All the books I came across referred to shops in Boston, New York, and Philadelphia as receiving and selling Queensware. Not one mention of any distribution through merchants in the South. The clerk did suggest we visit a museum in Chattanooga that has an extensive collection of Queensware."

Rex took a swallow of iced tea. "You did better than me. I'm afraid I came up empty."

"Wait," Kiana said excitedly. "I'm not through."

"Oh, there's more." Rex looked at her in curious approval.

"Lots," she said, pulling out a sheaf of photocopied pages. "After researching glass, I had asked the librarian to pull any books that focused on the antislavery movement in eastern Tennessee to see if I might find references to the plantation Magnolia Crossing or slaves who had fled the area."

"That's a real stretch," Rex said, widening his eyes.

Kiana frowned at the not-so-subtle criticism, determined to show him she knew what she was doing. God, at times he could be impossible. He might be drop-dead handsome and a good tour guide, but his subtle superiority still irritated the hell out of her.

Before this little adventure is over, she vowed, I'll show Rex Tandy how dangerous it can be to underestimate a sister with a mission.

Squaring her shoulders, she told Rex about *An Old Man's History of Sequatchie County*.

"That's north of Chattanooga," Rex interrupted.

"I *know*. I checked the map," Kiana tossed back lightly, really trying not to sound annoyed. "Anyway, the book was written by a man whose grandfather had been an abolitionist. It kind of rambled, but . . ." She took a bite of her club sandwich, then swallowed. "Listen to this:

" 'Underground Railroad sympathizers in Sequatchie County were harshly dealt with when discovered. Many whites were drummed out of the county due to their antislavery views. The route out of Tennessee into the Appalachian Mountains was reputed to have been one of the most dangerous but most frequently used avenues of escape for runaways, especially during the years immediately preceding the Civil War. Hundreds of slaves from West Tennessee and the lower south passed through the Sequatchie Valley on their way north. Whites and free blacks who participated in abolitionist activities did so under the threat of death. At a plantation in the northern tip of the county, the owner posted a notice of reward offering one hundred dollars a piece for the return of two of his escaped slaves—a young dark-skinned girl of seventeen with a newborn child, and' . . . get this, Kiana pointed out . . . 'his wagon driver, a black man thought to be about age twenty-one.' "

Rex hunched forward. "That description could apply to lots of slaves."

"Probably," Kiana grudgingly agreed, "but there's more. Listen. 'The planter, who signed his notice of reward, D. DeRossette, went so far as to offer a matching one hundred dollars for the deliverance to his plantation, Magnolia Crossing, any man, woman, or child—black or white—who helped his slaves escape.' "

"God! Kiana, that's it!"

"Right. I think I've got something here!"

Rex excitedly reached across the table and grabbed her hand, sandwich and all. "Sequatchie County is where the plantation was. That's our target."

Grinning hugely, Kiana tossed her braids from her shoulders, unable to resist saying, "And you were worried about my ability to help push this search along?"

Rex groaned. "Please. I apologize for anything stupid I ever said. Congratulations on your discovery."

"I was lucky," Kiana corrected.

"Maybe," Rex admitted. "But for whatever reason, you've found a major key to this search."

"I was beginning to wonder how in the world my mother had managed to come up with her story, but it exists, Rex. It really does! It's been locked away in books, and ledgers, and old folks' minds. If only her papers hadn't burned in the crash, I wouldn't be going through this now."

"But she left you enough of a trail to finish her journey."

Kiana toyed with her glass of iced tea, then said lowly, "I know. And it's rather eerie. What if my mother, during her research, had come across this same book?" Kiana shuddered. "It's an odd feeling. She very well could have held that memoir in her hands . . . become as excited as I am now."

"It's possible," Rex said.

Kiana finished her tea, then pushed the plate with the rest of her sandwich away. "I'm too excited to eat. Are we still leaving Nashville tomorrow?"

"Sure are," Rex answered. "Early. I'd like to make it to Chattanooga by noon. We can check out the museum you mentioned, then go up to Sequatchie County and track down whatever we can on the DeRossettes who lived there. Cross your fingers."

Kiana nodded, pulling her bag over her arm. "You know how to get to Belle Meade, right?"

"Absolutely," Rex replied. "That's where my career as a tour guide actually got its start."

Chapter Twenty-five

"THE docent I spoke with yesterday sounded very willing to talk with us," Rex told Kiana as he checked his rearview mirror, then changed lanes. "I don't know how much help she will be, but the more people who know about our search, the better. We never know where a lead will come from. It's like a chain reaction. Your discovery is a great breakthrough, but . . . all we have is a county, Kiana."

"And the first mention of Magnolia Crossing. It *was* a plantation!" Heat rose in her chest as she thought about walking the grounds where the plantation had been, the same ground Adi and Price would have walked. Please let some remnants of it remain, she mused as they headed south on West End to Belle Meade Avenue, then followed the signs to the restored plantation. In the parking area, he stopped behind a rusted-out van that was very badly dented in the rear.

Kiana looked across the grand expanse of meticulously tended grounds and took in the perfection of the restored plantation. "So, this is where the angry sisters pressed you for *their* history, right?"

"Exactly," Rex replied, exiting the car. Kiana jumped out. Together, they left the parking area and headed toward the main house.

"Belle Meade is an important historical site," Rex said, "don't get me wrong. It's an excellent example of a working plantation in the mid–1850s."

"Must have required a lot of slaves to keep it going," Kiana muttered, hurrying past a group of tourists who had just emerged from a big Greyhound bus.

A docent dressed in period costume introduced herself as Mary Marks, and invited Kiana and Rex to join the tour she was about to escort through the pillared mansion and the restored outbuildings on the property.

Mary told the visitors the story of the origins of Belle Meade, which were centered around the construction of a log cabin known as Dunham's Station that had been built in 1807. Kiana was swept back in time as she listened to the docent describe life in antebellum days; mint juleps on the veranda, parties on the lawn, carriage rides, and horse shows, all described without one reference to slavery. Kiana deliberately kept her eyes averted from Rex's as they listened to Mary's version of life at Belle Meade.

"Belle Meade was brought to world recognition as a thoroughbred stud farm by Confederate cavalry officer, General W. H. Jackson, after his marriage to the daughter of the creator of Belle Meade, William Harding. Now Belle Meade is fully restored with outbuildings and interiors refurbished in period detail. It remains an accurate reflection of the sumptuous elegance of nineteenth-century life in the South."

They toured the 1790 log cabin, the 1820 Smokehouse, the 1884 Creamery, and an 1890 Carriage House that sheltered one of the largest collections of antique carriages in the South.

Kiana tried to envision the place with slaves all around—in the fields, at the huge fireplaces tending pigs roasting on spits, at the looms spinning cotton, in the elegantly appointed rooms in the mansion polishing silver, lighting lamps, putting food on the great dining-room table that looked as if it could seat fifty guests.

This is how Magnolia Crossing might have looked, she thought, her blood still racing with the excitement of her discovery that morning. The words *Magnolia Crossing* had leapt from the page of the old book, as if they had been lingering there, just waiting for her to set them free. And how many other men in eastern Tennessee shared such an elegant name as D. DeRossette?

How many would have posted a reward for slaves with descriptions matching the people described by her mother? None, Kiana assured herself. Louise Sheridan's story was not fantasy at all.

Mary Marks continued her remarks about the plantation's history. "As early as 1816, Belle Meade was known as a famous stud farm because of the thoroughbreds bred here. Construction on the original mansion was begun in 1853, interrupted by the Civil War, and in 1864 the place was riddled with bullet holes during a skirmish between Rebel and Union forces. This plantation used to be a fifty-four-hundred-acre spread. Over the years it's dwindled down to about thirty, yet it stands as an example of life as it was more than one hundred fifty years ago."

"It is a lovely place," Kiana conceded to Rex as they walked a brick path through the garden. "So serene and orderly, almost idyllic. But I have to echo what the outspoken ladies asked you . . . where is the evidence that black folks were the ones who kept all of this afloat?"

Rex grimaced, then said, "Hey. You're asking me? Talk to the Preservation Society."

Kiana lifted one hand, palm up. "If this is all that tourists see, they'll never fully understand how much slave labor was necessary to create and maintain this lavish way of life." Visiting Belle Meade only underlined for her how landowners enjoyed a lifestyle that was completely out of reach of slaves . . . and poor whites. Blacks endured brutal, dehumanizing living conditions while plantation masters and their families basked complacently in splendiferous comfort. "Say what you want, but some type of reparations are long overdue," Kiana added, her tone impatient, and there was a quivering timbre in her voice.

A young white couple in the tour group who were standing nearby had apparently overheard Kiana's words. "You make a very valid point," the woman said.

Kiana smiled appreciatively.

The woman's husband jerked her by the arm and pulled her toward the next bed of roses.

Rex gave Kiana a wan smile, then said, "I agree with the lady, you do have a point, but don't get on your soap box now."

"I am not on a soap box," Kiana replied tersely. "It's just the truth."

The tour came to an end and Mary Marks remained behind to speak to Kiana and Rex. "I can't say that I know of anyone who has recently sold or acquired a collection of Soddy Glass. That's not surprising, of course. It's so rare."

"Very," Kiana replied. "However, a lady in this area sold quite a few pieces to Marvin Watts. Watts Antiques. Do you know him?"

Mary's face lit up. "Of course. He's been in business for years. He helped the association track down several mirrors and an 1820 sideboard that had originally belonged at Belle Meade."

"I thought perhaps you had heard of the glass transaction."

"No," Mary said slowly, "but I wish I had known about it." She sighed with envy. "If you ever see another piece give me a call. I'd be very interested in acquiring an item or two . . . for the historical society collection, of course." She handed Kiana her card, then hurried off to begin the next tour.

By late afternoon, Kiana and Rex were on the freeway heading back to the hotel. Their inquiries of the dealers in White Way Antiques Mall had not been productive. They'd uncovered no new clues from their stops at three other antique shops along West End Avenue. During the ride back to town, Kiana and Rex made plans to head on toward Chattanooga early the next day.

"We've got to find the lady who brought the PGW crates to Marvin Watts," Kiana said as she watched traffic thicken on the freeway. They had been gone all day and were now caught in rush-hour traffic. "That's the vital link!" she went on, talking more to herself than Rex. "Was the glass the old lady sold to Marvin Watts originals or reproductions? And how did it come into her posses-sion? Does she have more?" Kiana clenched her teeth as she tried to sort out the jumble of clues she'd come across so far. Resolving the identity of the mysterious lady was important, but also weigh-ing heavily on her mind was the challenge of proving whether Soddy Russell was black or white.

"Do you think we should check with Major Moore before we leave town?" Kiana asked.

"Why?" Rex replied. "He said he'd leave a message at the hotel if anything turned up. Better not push. If he finds out who the mystery lady is, I think he'll let us know."

Kiana lifted her eyebrows skeptically, not at all as convinced as Rex seemed to be that the major was on their side.

They rode along without speaking for a while, inching through the traffic on Route 265. When a break occurred, Rex sped up, then glanced into his rearview mirror. He swung into the far left lane and skimmed along at a faster pace.

"That's odd," Rex muttered under his breath. Frowning, he leaned closer to the mirror.

"What's wrong?" Kiana asked.

"That white van. I swear it was parked next to me at the historical society this morning and I saw it, again, in the parking lot at Belle Meade this afternoon. There it is again, right behind us."

Kiana turned around in her seat and looked out the back window. She squinted at the rusted van behind them, unable to see the driver very well through the dark tinted windshield. "Probably a tourist." She turned back around and focused on Rex. "Who'd want to follow you? This city has a lot of sightseers poking around just like we are."

"I don't know," Rex said. "But there's one way to find out." He stepped down hard on the gas pedal and sped up, speeding dangerously close to the concrete barrier that divided the freeway into north and southbound traffic.

Kiana looked over her shoulder, surprised to see the van speeding up, too. It rushed forward, staying on their tail. "It's coming up pretty close behind us," she warned Rex.

He suddenly changed lanes, weaving to the right, then back to the left, to settle once again in the inside lane.

The van stayed to the right, but pulled alongside.

Rex took his eyes from the road and quickly glanced over, past Kiana toward the driver of the van.

"God!" he said in disgust. "I don't believe it. He's laughing."

"Let's get out of here," Kiana said.

The van slowed, then dodged behind the Blazer again and charged up so closely, Kiana braced herself for an impact.

"He's covering me like white on rice," Rex said in alarm. "What the devil's going on?"

"He'd better hope you don't slam on the brakes," Kiana muttered, tensing. The traffic ahead was beginning to back up as motorists fought their way toward town. She turned in her seat to see what was happening. The van was close, but all she could make out was an image of the driver, who was wearing wraparound sunglasses and a black windbreaker type of jacket.

"Maybe he thinks you're somebody he knows," she offered.

Rex increased his speed, then had to abruptly slow down when the brake lights of the car in front of him flashed bright red. "Jesus!" He jolted to a screeching halt. The white van thundered to a stop only inches behind them. "I don't know what his problem is, but I have a bad feeling about this."

Kiana studied Rex's profile. "Are you thinking about the threat you got in D.C.?"

Rex nodded. "Who knows?"

"I doubt Willi-Man Monty's boys have tracked you to Nashville."

Rex shrugged. "Anything is possible. I told you my brother said I was marked."

Now Kiana squinted with concern as she noticed the white van pulling alongside them again. She saw the man laugh, then jerk the steering wheel. "Rex. You're right. This guy is—"

"God!" Rex screamed, swerving to the left as the van bumped into the passenger side door.

Kiana was thrown against Rex. There was a loud squealing sound as cars behind them slammed on their brakes to avoid being involved in the clear makings of an accident.

Kiana righted herself, her seat belt taut. Her heart was pounding and her mouth had gone dry.

Rex struggled to keep control of the Blazer. "You all right?" he called over to Kiana.

"Yes. But try to get away from him. He's trying to run us off the road." She glanced out the window, then stiffened. "Rex!" Kiana screamed.

The van slammed into the Blazer again.

"Hold on!" Rex yelled. "Close your eyes!" He whipped the wheel to the left and rumbled onto the shoulder, speeding ahead of the long lines of traffic, scraping the concrete divider as he went.

"There's no place to go but over the side and I'm not going!" He whooshed past cars and a big oil tanker truck, then cut to the right and skimmed past a pickup truck and dodged into a narrow opening in the next lane. He maneuvered the Blazer across three lanes of traffic through horns blasting in outrage and careened down the exit ramp.

Looking back, Kiana saw that the white van was trapped in traffic. Both she and Rex let out long sighs of relief at the same time.

"That was strange," he said.

"Strange? Bizarre is more like it. We almost got *killed*," Kiana fumed, pressing a fist to her mouth as she continued to watch the van. It whizzed past the exit and entered the flow of traffic in the middle lane. "No plates," she said. "Rex, that van has no license plates! That's scary."

"Very," he agreed grimly.

The Blazer thumped over a speed bump, jolting Kiana as she turned around. Rex made a right turn and pulled into the parking lot adjacent to the hotel. With trembling hands, Kiana unbuckled her seat belt, then scanned the area carefully before she opened the door.

Chapter Twenty-six

"MISS Sheridan?"

Ida raised her eyes from the magazine and set it aside. "Yes?"

"Mr. Anthony will see you now."

Ida got up from the floral-patterned love seat and followed the secretary into Dale Anthony's richly appointed office. It had been a year since Ida had visited the longtime family retainer who was only ten years younger than her grandmother. The lawyer who had been taking care of Sheridan family matters for nearly a half century, stood and extended his hand as Ida crossed the room.

"Good to see you, Ida." He blinked his shiny brown eyes rapidly as he shook her hand.

"Thanks for squeezing me in," she replied.

He laughed. "I'm not so busy anymore that I have much trouble seeing whomever needs me now. So, what is it you want to talk about, Ida?"

Ida opened her leather portfolio and removed a sheaf of papers. "I just returned from Centerville. I had a nice long visit with Hester."

"And how is she?"

Ida crossed her legs as she settled into a chair opposite Dale Anthony. "Frankly, I think she's slipping away," Ida began. "She has good days, bad days. Sometimes she knows me, other times she is in her own world."

"That's sad," Anthony replied, "but not unexpected, considering her age."

"While I was there, she was in very low spirits, and wanted to make some changes in her will." Ida handed the papers to the lawyer. "She was adamant about me bringing these directly to you. She thinks she's slipping away from us, Dale, and I could not get her to change her mind."

"Let me see what we have here," he murmured as he accepted the papers from Ida.

The room was silent as he looked them over. When he spoke, Ida lifted her brows. "These are pretty drastic changes, Ida. What made Hester decide to appoint you executrix of her estate and take Kiana completely out of her will? Has something happened that I should know about?"

Ida uncrossed her legs and sat more erect. "Hester realizes, as I always have, that Kiana is not stable enough to handle the details of managing her estate."

"Not stable? What do you mean?"

"She's disappeared. Kiana quit her job in Houston. Moved out of her apartment. No one knows where she's gone."

"That doesn't sound like the Kiana I know, although it's been a long time since I've talked to her. She always struck me as very levelheaded. Very responsible."

"Well, that's the impression she likes to give everyone, but really, Mr. Anthony, Kiana has a very impulsive personality. Hester was so upset when she learned that Kiana had left her job and taken off without telling a soul where she was going, she had a very bad turn. She was in bed for nearly a week. She's so disappointed that her only flesh and blood would treat her so shabbily. I tried to smooth things over, make excuses for Kiana, but it did no good. She wants nothing to do with Kiana now. She's adamant. She wants these changes made."

Dale Anthony sat back in his chair. "Fine, but before I draw up the papers, I must talk to Hester."

"I'm sure she'd be glad to hear from you," Ida said calmly.

Dale Anthony put his arms on the desk and looked at Ida's flat, unreadable eyes. "I am beginning to think that a power of attorney might be warranted, but I'll need a doctor's assessment of Hester's mental state."

"I think that's a good idea," Ida agreed. "Why don't you go ahead and make the necessary arrangements?"

At the front desk, Kiana and Rex stopped to check for messages. She slumped against the counter in exhaustion, worried that Rex was taking the gang threat much too casually. The possibility that one of the Sharps or the Treps had pursued him to Tennessee didn't seem so farfetched to her.

She sneaked a glance at Rex. He was still visibly shaken, but not as tense as he'd been only moments earlier. What impact was this incident going to have on the future of their project? she wondered, realizing how little she really knew about Rex's past. If thugs were really out to do him harm, he ought to contact the police. But when she'd made the suggestion that he go to the authorities, he'd flatly said no way.

The clerk interrupted her thoughts. "Yes, Miss Sheridan, there is a message for you."

Kiana took the pink slip from the young man and read it. "Bingo!" she said to Rex. "Daisy Hudson. She got my letter this afternoon and wants to talk to me. Left her phone number!"

"Very good!" Rex said enthusiastically, his mood improving. They hurried across the lobby to the elevators. "Major Moore's lead did come through, after all."

They stepped out of the elevator and walked toward their rooms. Rex slowed his pace, drawing slightly nearer to her. "I know you believe the trouble on the freeway was deliberate, but . . ."

"But what, Rex?" Kiana started. "That nut pointed his van straight at us. He was laughing."

Rex sighed. "Yeah, but I can't imagine that the driver has anything to do with the story I was writing for *Black Culture Watch*. If any of those punks had wanted to get to me, they could have done it while I was in Washington. Why go to the trouble to track me down here?"

"I don't know, but we'd better not let down our guard. I'm a nervous wreck. That was scary."

"Let me make it up to you," Rex said. "Want to meet downstairs for a drink? Dinner? Or we could go check out a restaurant in the city. There is great barbecue at Uncle Bud's over on Stewart Ferry's Pike. Or we could go listen to some jazz."

Kiana raised her shoulders in a lighthearted shrug. Turning to Rex, she told him, "Thanks, but I think I'll stay in tonight. Maybe just order room service. Besides," she added, "you aren't obligated to entertain me."

"I don't feel obligated," he said, his feelings clearly hurt. "I thought you might like company for dinner, that's all."

"I know. I know," Kiana tried to take the edge off her refusal. "Barbecue sounds very tempting, but I'm pooped. Really." She adjusted her grip on her heavy leather bag. "I'm going to call Daisy Hudson, take a long, hot shower, then get packed."

"Sure." Rex backed off. "I understand." At Kiana's doorway, they paused. "I checked the map," he said, "but I couldn't find Rural Route Seventy-seven. If Daisy Hudson agrees to see us, ask her for directions to her house. Some of the back roads in that area look like no more than gravel strips. Might be a bumpy ride. I'd like to be on the road as soon as we settle on repairs of the Blazer with Hertz. We'll have to drive straight to Shelbyville and go south from there to her house, then hopefully, get into Chattanooga before dark."

"How long of a drive to Shelbyville?" Kiana asked.

"With no detours, probably a couple of hours."

"Sounds good to me," Kiana said, putting her key card in the security lock. "I'll buzz you after I talk to Daisy." She opened the door and went inside.

Rex remained standing in the hallway feeling deflated, wondering why Kiana was so damned standoffish. All he'd suggested was going out for dinner. What was eating her?

Was it the kiss? Well, she sure hadn't resisted, in fact she had kissed him back. So why was she working overtime trying to make out like it had been a big deal? He didn't need a hassle like that —what kind of guys had she dated who had rattled her faith in men?

Rex was not used to being treated as if he were a threat. Women usually swarmed all over him and he could count on one hand the number of times he'd been spurned this bluntly. Unless Kiana thawed her icy personality, she'd never have a decent relationship with anyone, especially not with him.

Entering his room, Rex shoved Kiana to the back of his mind, deciding he would go check out the action in the city alone, have a good time, listen to some music, though he knew he ought to get busy planning and outlining the story he'd promised his editor. But instead of clicking on his electronic notebook, he opened his suitcase and shook out a fresh shirt and a pair of dark brown slacks. The last thing he needed to do was sit around his room with Kiana right next door and listen to her every movement.

He pressed the remote control to the TV, then kept punching the channel button until he came to CNN, paying little attention to the headline news as he moved about the room. He felt restless and annoyed—not only because Kiana seemed determined to keep him at arm's length, but because he knew Willi-Man Monty was brash enough to have sent his punks to Nashville to find him—to punish him for filming in his territory. Thank God Rex had had the forethought to leave the film in his wall safe at home, but he couldn't get the thing off his mind. And what was Lionel up to, he wondered, praying his brother had kept his word and was out of the gang, going to school.

"I'd better check in," Rex decided, reaching for the phone, dialing the number to his parents' house. Quickly his perplexed ruminations were interrupted by his father's voice booming over the line.

"Hello!"

"Dad, it's Rex."

"Rex! Thank God. You finally decided to call. Where are you? Why'd you leave town without telling anybody?"

"Didn't Lionel give you my message?"

"Lionel's at the police station right now."

"*What?*" Rex lowered his head into his hands.

"Yeah, he was arrested today."

Well it's finally happened, Rex thought, listening to his father's anxious breathing. The pause on the line was alarming. "What's going on?" Rex demanded. "I take it he never registered for summer school?"

"Hell, no," Mr. Tandy replied. "And he's got big problems now. The police came by this afternoon and hauled Lionel to the station for questioning."

"About what?"

"They say he was seen selling drugs, but they won't tell us who the eyewitness was. Some undercover sting, they say. They want Lionel to give up the names of the guys he's been running with. There was a drug bust in the neighborhood. The police are trying to identify gang members who they think are supplying drugs to some government workers. They've been asking everybody on the street a lot of questions. Of course, I can't tell them a thing. Once I come inside this house, I don't want to know what's going on outside."

"Does he have a lawyer?"

"Not yet, but if they keep him he'll have to use a court lawyer. Maybe he could get out on bail, but who's got money for all that? It's a mess, son, a real mess."

"So, the police say Lionel's been doing drug deals?" Rex groaned. He had the videotape. Lionel hadn't actually been involved in the transaction, but he'd been there—a definite party to the deal.

"Yeah," Mr. Tandy said. "The police handcuffed Lionel, dragged him off, and shoved him into the squad car like a common criminal." The old man's voice cracked with shame. "It was awful. Awful."

"How's Mom?" Rex wanted to know.

"Taken to her bed. Can't get her to say a thing. All she does is cry. We've seen this coming, Rex. It was just a matter of time."

Rex's thoughts whirled. The thought of his baby brother sitting behind bars was devastating, but he wasn't going to bail him out. Not just yet. Maybe this was just what Lionel needed to scare him into straightening up.

"Can you come home, son?" Mr. Tandy asked.

Rex opened his mouth to reply, then clamped his jaw shut, biting his tongue to keep from saying yes. Why hadn't Lionel listened to him? To his parents? And now why should Rex throw away his opportunity to write what might be the most important story of his career to rush home and bail Lionel out of a situation he had warned him was coming.

Rex splayed his fingers across his face and took a deep breath. "Not right now, Dad. But I'll keep in touch. Don't worry. We can get through this. After Lionel's seen the judge, we'll decide what to do."

"If you come home and talk to Lionel, he'll listen to you, Rex."

"I don't think so, Dad. He never has."

"All he has to do to clear this up is give the police the names of the guys who are dealing drugs right outside my front door. He knows who they are!"

And I do, too, Rex bitterly reminded himself.

"Your mother can't go through much more."

"Do you need money?" Rex asked.

"I hate to say it, but things are tight."

"Don't worry about, it, Dad," Rex said. "Let me know what the judge says about bail, then I'll do what I can."

"Thanks, son," his father whispered in tired resignation.

"I'll call you tomorrow," Rex promised, before gently hanging up the phone.

For the next fifteen minutes, Rex sat staring at the dark red carpet, trying to block the image of his baby brother in a cell, but the image kept pushing itself to the surface. Swallowing back tears, Rex fought the urge to break down and cry.

What good will crying do? he thought angrily. Lionel made the decision to run with his street buddies rather than keep his promise. Some time in jail might shock him into understanding why his family cared. Every effort Rex and his parents had made to keep him out of a situation exactly like this had failed, and now he'd have to face the consequences.

Running his hands through his hair, Rex worried. Where did *his* responsibilities lie? With the police—who were charged with stemming the runaway crime that was destroying the lives of young men in Columbia Heights, or with his brother, the one person he had believed he could save?

Rex slammed his fist into the mattress. What the hell was he supposed to do? "I *can't* desert Kiana now," he muttered. "Not when we're so close to finding the truth." With a tired shove, he got up, went into the bathroom, and turned on the shower. As he waited for the rushing water to get warm, he made up his mind to wait until bail had been set, then he'd tell Lionel's lawyer about the videotape. Once it was turned over to the attorney, it would be out of Rex's hands. His brother's future would be his own responsibility as it had been all along.

He showered, then began to dress—anything to keep from thinking about the pain his parents must be in.

From the room adjoining, he could hear the muffled sound of Kiana's voice as she spoke on the phone.

"Yes. This is Kiana Sheridan calling from Nashville. I had a message that you called this afternoon."

"Oh, my, yes," Daisy replied in a much more sprightly voice than Kiana had imagined the elderly woman would have.

"Thank you for getting in touch with me," Kiana began. "As I stated in my letter, Major Moore here in Nashville suggested I contact you. I'd appreciate any information you might have about descendants, or land owned by the DeRossettes." Kiana went on to tell Daisy about her discoveries so far.

Daisy chuckled aloud. "Well, my maiden name is deRossette, small d, you know? Different spelling."

"Yes," Kiana said.

"But I admit, I have come across some DeRossettes in my genealogical research. English people . . . from Manchester, I think. Long ago there were plenty of DeRossettes not far from here, but it seems over the years the name has fallen out of the records."

"Were they in the area over near Walden Ridge, Sequatchie County?" Kiana held her breath as she waited for Daisy's reply, which came after a long, agonizing pause.

"Yes . . . I believe so. I've seen that name in census records for that county. I'd have to dig through my papers to be sure, but I *know* that name because it kept popping up when I was researching my own family."

"Are you related to the DeRossettes of Magnolia Crossing at all?"

"Nope," Daisy replied with assurance. "Sorry. My heritage

stems back to an Italian man named Luigi Rosette who settled up around Crossville . . . northeast of here in Cumberland County. He owned several vineyards, worked his slaves to make some of the best wine produced in Tennessee. You know they're still producing wine over there. Blue Ridge Blush, it's called, but you can only buy it in Cumberland and Putnam counties."

"That *is* interesting," Kiana replied politely, not wanting to cut the old woman off but she had to stay on track. "I'm curious about the DeRossettes you discovered while researching your family . . . were they black or white?"

"Well, some black, some white, but I focus my genealogical research on my race, but you know how mixed up everyone really is."

"Oh, sure," Kiana said distractedly, her mind whizzing forward with each word Daisy uttered. "If the original DeRossettes were white, their slaves would have called themselves by their master's last name, right?"

"Probably. That was common practice before the Civil War, but after emancipation, many ex-slaves took on brand new names. Just made up who they wanted to be."

Kiana nodded, her theory beginning to take shape. "So the blacks you uncovered in your research could very well have been the descendants of the slaves owned by the DeRossette family?"

"Oh, sure." She laughed in a kind of playful whooping sound. "I can't think of any other reason for black folks to be carrying around such a fancy name."

Kiana's heart pounded. She wanted to see this woman's research. "Would it be possible, Miss Hudson, for me and my . . . uh . . . assistant to visit you? We're heading to Chattanooga tomorrow morning. I don't want to impose, but I'd love to take a look at the documents you have referring to the presence of DeRossettes in Sequatchie County."

"No problem at all, child. I'd be happy to show you what I have," Daisy cheerfully replied. "I need a little time to get everything together. You just call me when you get into Lewisburg and I'll tell you how to get here."

After hanging up the phone, Kiana immediately rang Rex's room, informing him of what Daisy had said.

"Thank Major Moore for that lead," he said enthusiastically, then reminded her, "We'd better be at the rental place as soon as they open and see what they want to do about the Blazer door, then get on the road before the traffic is too heavy." He paused, then asked again, "Why don't you have dinner with me? We can plan our interview with Daisy Hudson. Plot the route together."

Kiana was very tempted to say yes, and almost did, but stopped short of committing herself when memories of their kiss brought a vague sense of unease. As much as she would prefer eating barbecue with Rex to nibbling a burger and fries on a tray in her room, she didn't dare open herself to such temptation again. Running around doing research was one thing. Dinner and drinks and intimate conversation outside the hotel suddenly seemed a little scary—a repeat of what happened the other night could not occur again.

"No. I don't think I'm up to going out. Thanks for asking."

"Okay," Rex replied, a forced lightness to his words. "But I think I will go out for a while. See what's happening. Nashville's got some pretty lively spots. Lots of good music in this city."

"I'm sure there is," Kiana agreed, with a spasm of regret. "Have a good time," she managed.

"See you at checkout, then," Rex said lightly. "Six o'clock?"

"Right," Kiana answered, closing her eyes, taking a deep breath, fighting an image of Rex out on the town, laughing and slow dancing with some strange woman in his arms.

A hot shower, a double cheeseburger with fries, and a Susan Hayward tearjerker did relax Kiana but did little to keep her thoughts from wandering back to Rex. After the movie, she dozed off, then snapped awake about midnight. She turned the blank TV screen off, but couldn't get back to sleep.

As she lay with her eyes forcibly closed, her imagination began to get the best of her. Sitting up, she listened for sounds of movement next door, then gave in to her curiosity and rang Rex's room, ready to hang up if he answered. But she got no answer, and wound up feeling worse—humiliated that she'd fallen so low as to check on him, and furious at him for still being out. More angry at herself than Rex, Kiana jerked the covers over her shoulder and promptly fell back to sleep.

Loud voices and the sound of doors slamming somewhere in the hallway jolted Kiana awake again. She peered at the glowing face of the digital clock. It was one-fifteen. Half groaning, knowing she'd probably never be able to get back to sleep, she tossed back the sheet and went to the bathroom for a glass of water. On the way back to bed, she couldn't resist going to the window. The cherry red Blazer was in the parking lot. Rex must be in his room.

At the window, she watched the bright lights of cars whizzing along the freeway just beyond the feeder road, then froze when she saw a battered white van streak off the exit ramp and pull into the parking lot. It stopped beside their Blazer. It was the same van that had smashed into them on the freeway. A man dressed completely in black got out. Kiana was certain it was the man she'd seen through the passenger window earlier that evening.

What was going on? she wondered, moving closer to the window.

The man strode confidently to the Blazer, pulled a knife from his hip pocket, then bent down next to the left rear tire.

Kiana gasped aloud.

With strong methodical thrusts the man began slashing, his arm going up and down like a lever on a mechanical toy.

"Stop!" Kiana involuntarily yelled, pounding on the window. "Stop!" She raced to Rex's door and banged loudly on it. "Rex! Rex!" She beat even harder. "There's a man in the . . ."

The door swung open. "Hey! Kiana! What's up? You okay?" Rex was standing in the doorway, bare-chested, in faded jeans, sleepily rubbing his eyes. "What's going on?"

For a moment, she couldn't answer, then blurted out, "Over here. Look!" She grabbed Rex by the hand and nearly dragged him to the window, where he saw the man move from the rear to the front of the vehicle and start attacking another tire.

Rex got closer and pounded the window. "That's him! The man who was following us on the freeway! Jesus! He's destroying the car. Oh, hell." Rex snatched up the phone. "Hello? Hotel security. Fast." He eyed Kiana apprehensively as he waited. "Yes. Rex Tandy Room 715. There's a man in the hotel parking lot slashing my tires. Yes. Yes. From my window. A red Blazer! Right now."

Rex dropped the phone, whirled around, went into his room, and grabbed a T-shirt. He yanked it over his head, then raced across Kiana's room. "Lock the door. Stay put! I'm gonna kill that crazy bastard!"

From her window, Kiana watched the man move from one tire to another, methodically slashing each one. When he was finished, he looked around, then jumped into his van and took off. Within seconds, the hotel security guard and Rex raced onto the parking lot and headed toward the Blazer. They stopped and looked around, but the man was gone.

From her perch at the window, Kiana could see the white van rumbling like a ghostly shadow down the deserted feeder road. She watched it until it careened around a curve and disappeared into the black shadow of the underpass at the next intersection.

Kiana was still sitting with her fist pressed to her lips when Rex came into her room. She jerked around, stunned by the worried frown immobilizing Rex's features.

"He got away." His voice was thick with disappointment.

"I know," Kiana replied.

"My God. What is going on?" he whispered, moving to stand at her side. "Someone is after me . . ." He stopped and looked down at Kiana. "Or you."

Kiana stood, her lips parted in surprise. "Me? Who? Why?"

"I wish I knew," Rex said, easing an arm around Kiana's waist. He pulled her to his chest, then lowered his lashes as he gazed into her eyes. "I don't know who is trying to frighten me or you, but believe me I'm going to find out." He put his other arm around her shoulder and urged her toward him. Kiana didn't pull away. "I hadn't wanted to mention this," Rex went on, "but I had a call from my father last night. I think you ought to know. My brother is in jail." He explained what had happened.

"Are you going home?" Kiana asked, her sympathy for Rex not nearly as strong as her apprehension about being left alone in Nashville.

"I had thought about it, but not now," Rex promised. "I can't leave you. Not with some nutcase tracking us, and truthfully, there's little I can do for Lionel. He'll have to deal with this on his own."

Kiana nodded numbly, feeling ashamed at her relief.

Rex brushed his hand over her braids and she rested her head on his shoulder. "Thanks for not bailing out on me," Kiana murmured. "But I know your family needs you."

"So do you, Kiana," Rex replied in low, soothing tones. "I won't let anything happen to you. I promise."

When he stroked the swell of her cheek, then eased his hand beneath her chin, she looked up, but did not flinch. When he lowered his mouth toward hers, she rose on tiptoes to kiss him fully on the lips. Kiana clung to Rex's solid shoulders, momentarily setting her fears aside as she finally gave herself totally to the electrifying thrill of being in Rex Tandy's arms.

Chapter Twenty-seven

IDA'S high heels tapped sharply on the slick marble floor. With her chin lifted haughtily, she crossed the foyer to her office, nodded curtly to Sandy, her secretary, then strode past the middle-aged woman who was deeply involved in what Ida suspected was another one of her numerous personal phone calls.

I ought to fire her right now, Ida fumed, but her attention was too keenly focused on the vicious attack Bill Lewis had made on her during the regular Monday morning sales meeting to divert any energy toward dealing with Sandy. Pressing one hand flat against the door, Ida flung it open and entered her lavishly decorated office.

She surveyed her attractive surroundings in calm approval. Decorated in pale earth tones—tastefully and richly accessorized with choice pieces of art from her personal collection, it always had a calming influence. Ida's emotions shifted from seething anger to mild irritation in the space of just a few seconds, and her office became a welcome refuge from the chaotic turmoil of the Planning and Assessment Room down the hall where she'd just been royally insulted.

Ida spent no less than twelve to sixteen hours a day in her spacious office and loved being there. The bank of windows lining one wall and the panoramic view of Capitol Hill offered testimony to her position in the company as a savvy, fast-tracking vice-president who deserved much better treatment than she had just received. Ida balled her manicured nails into a hard fist and licked her bright red lips. She wanted to scream.

Bill Lewis had better remember who pried his ass off a metal stool in the sales rep bull pen and put him in a leather chair on the thirty-first floor, she silently fumed, still bristling over the as-inine remarks he'd made about her management of the Techni-Trak account. He might be director of new accounts now, but he had seriously overstepped his authority by challenging her decision to shoot the Techni-Trak ads on location in Hawaii. Who in the world would believe that the beaches off Florida could hold a candle to the white sands of Maui?

The disastrous exchange in the meeting had started out as a professionally restrained discussion, but had quickly deteriorated into a heated confrontation, forcing Ida to lose her composure. Just because Bill was from Palm Beach and knew the area well, was no reason for him to tout it as the perfect location for the photo shoot on *her* account.

Lewis is just trying to impress management with his snobby background, Ida calculated. Everyone in the room knew he had sketchy credentials for the job he now held and had been brought into the sales department of Bering & Overton only because his father spent tons of money with the firm to promote his nationwide chain of putt-putt golf courses.

Ida's colleagues had gasped in horror when Lewis had literally shredded her prospectus and flung it onto the table. When Harry Overton, her immediate superior, had grabbed Ida and physically forced her back into her seat, she'd lost control and impulsively tried to slap Bill Lewis's face. The meeting had disintegrated quickly—so badly, in fact, that it had been canceled until the next morning.

"If Bill Lewis thinks for one minute that I am going to bail out of this account or change the photo locations, he's out of his mind," Ida grumbled to herself. "He'd better not make one move to turn the Techni-Trak account over to someone else."

Ida went behind her desk and perched on the edge, folding her arms across the gold buttons on her Liz Claiborne jacket. She stared defiantly at the pointed spire of the Washington Monument in the distance while toying nervously with the heavy gold chain around her neck, struggling to regain control of her emotions.

"They can all go to hell," she grumbled. "I'm not going to take this crap much longer." Her mind zeroed in on her fast moving plan, which would result in the establishment of her own agency. She would derive a great deal of satisfaction from putting her two-faced boss and his prick of a partner out of business. She had a long roster of loyal clients who would gladly follow her when she left—enough to nearly bankrupt Bering & Overton. All she needed was enough capital to secure her space—facilities that would be custom built—first class, with real Persian rugs, suede couches, and priceless objets d'art all over the place.

Squinting into the sky, Ida saw a silver plane descending toward National Airport. If her plans stayed on track, she'd have the necessary capital in less than two weeks, and then she'd make her move and get out.

"Almost there," she whispered, a frisson of excitement shivering up her spine. "And when I leave this place, the first thing I'm going to do is slap Bill Lewis's face, then I'll take off for Europe."

Ida had never been to London, Paris, or Rome and if she planned to thrust her own creative team into the international arena, she'd better familiarize herself with the foreign competition. And what could be more fun than perusing the famous art museums and galleries of Europe with bundles of cash in her purse?

Ida relaxed, crossing her legs, grinning at the heady thought of putting everybody at Bering & Overton who had ever snubbed her into their places. Her vengeful ruminations were suddenly jolted from her mind when Sandy buzzed her on the intercom. Turning around, Ida leaned over a stack of photographs and folders atop her desk to press the blinking white light.

"Yes, Sandy?"

"Line two, Ida. Long distance from Nashville. Wouldn't say who it is but he assured me you'd take the call."

"Yes, I will," Ida said, snatching up the phone. "This is Ida Sheridan."

"You better get me the money you promised, then get down

here and take care of your baby sister yourself," Watts hissed in a threatening voice. "My contact completed his mission, and now he wants to be paid."

Ida sank into her beige leather chair and swiveled around, putting her back to her door. "What happened? Did he find Kiana?"

"Oh, yeah. He found her, okay. Right where you said she'd be."

"And?" Ida prompted, heat rising to her face. "He got to her?"

"Yeah! Twice. On the freeway and . . . the tires! Remember? The tires. Isn't that what you wanted? To frighten her enough to send her back home?"

"Sure," Ida replied. "So what happened?"

"You said she'd be alone."

Ida groaned. She had taken Kiana's word that she was going on alone after she'd learned the tour had been canceled. Ida gritted her teeth until her back fillings hurt. "Listen, Watts, you told me you could get someone who could scare Kiana into going back to Houston. All you needed was a little, shall we say, advance?"

"Yeah, and it probably woulda worked," Watts said, "if she had been the one driving."

Ida's mind was ticking furiously. Dealing with Kiana was one thing, but someone was with her? "Who's the driver?" Ida asked.

"A guy named Rex. They were together when they came into the shop."

"Damn!" Ida tossed back, furious. Things were much more complicated than she had planned. "You said you'd take care of it."

"Listen. I did what you asked, but I don't have time to fool with this anymore. You got me inta this mess and now you'd better get me out. I want the money wired down here today."

Blood drained from Ida's face, rushing into her stomach in a sickening wave. "Don't press me, Watts. And . . . I told you not to call me here. Where are you? I'll have to call you back. I can't talk about it now."

Watts gave up a derisive cackle. "Call me back? I don't think so. We're going to settle this now. The security at the hotel gave the police a description of my friend's van. They're looking for him. Doing time in the Nashville city jail doesn't sound very appealing to him, sweetheart. He wants his money so he can get out of town."

"Where is Kiana now?" Ida asked.

"Gone. Checked out this morning, according to my contact at the Ramada."

Ida pushed scattered papers aside on her desk until she came to the itinerary Kiana had faxed her. After Nashville, Knoxville. At least she had some time.

"Listen," Ida said, her voice stretched thin. "I'll bring the money to you, but I want to pick up the last shipment personally. Hold it until I get there." The phone was silent for several seconds, and Ida wondered what in the world had possessed her to trust Marvin Watts to get Kiana out of her way. "It's ready, isn't it?" Ida whispered loudly. "I want it packed and ready to go when I get there."

"When?"

"Tonight, you idiot. When do you think?"

"You gotta pay for it. Cash. Full price. No split."

"That will not be a problem. Just have it ready when I get there." She hunched over her desk, eyes glittering in rage, trying to find the words to put this little twerp in his place. "Listen, Watts. I gave you a thousand dollars to stop Kiana, remember?"

"That was a partial. I told you it'd cost two."

"Yeah, but it didn't work out," Ida reminded him. "She's gone, so what are you going to do, sue me?"

"No," Watts growled. "But, if you're smart you won't get on the bad side of my friend. He did his job. You owe him. Understand?"

Ida was so mad she started to hang up on Watts, but she put the phone back to her ear. "I'll be there before nine tonight. And, Watts, don't you ever threaten me again, understand? You are hardly in a position to throw your weight around, so don't even try it, hear? And after I pick up this last shipment, I want nothing else to do with you. Ever."

After slamming the phone back into its cradle, Ida pushed the button to the direct line to Harry Overton's office.

"Harry. Ida." She addressed her boss in a clipped, efficient manner.

"Listen, Ida," Harry said. "About this morning . . . I'm sorry you took Lewis's remarks personally. He didn't mean to get you upset." Harry Overton quickly rose to his colleague's defense.

"Sure," Ida coyly agreed. "I've calmed down considerably, Harry. I see now that Bill has a valid point. We could stretch the budget considerably on this campaign if we shoot in Palm Beach instead of Hawaii."

"Good." Overton breathed the word in rushed relief. "Glad you've come around. We'll have another go at it tomorrow morning. Fresh start, all right?"

"Well," Ida began, her mind sorting out the details. "I've been thinking. Maybe I'd *better* move on Lewis's suggestion and get down to Florida. Start scouting locations right away."

Harry chuckled approvingly. "I knew I could count on you to do what's in the best interest of the agency, Ida. Sure. Go ahead. When do you want to leave?"

"Immediately. This afternoon."

"Oh? Well, sure. Get after it. The Techni-Trak account is too lucrative to lose momentum now."

"Thanks, Harry," Ida said as she opened the bottom drawer of her desk and hurriedly removed her eelskin purse. "I'm on my way out the door now."

"Good. Have Sandy reserve you a car at the airport and a suite at the Fountainbleau, okay?"

"No!" Ida said curtly. "I'll take care of that myself. I have a good friend in Palm Beach. I think I'll stay with her."

"Okay. Check with me when you're settled then. Good luck."

"Thanks," Ida replied. "I'll be back in a few days . . . before you know it, and I think you're going to be very impressed with what I find."

She shot to her feet and rushed to her door, put her ear to it and listened for a moment, then quietly turned the lock. She went to the other side of the room, pushed aside a burnt-orange leather sofa, and moved a three-panel Oriental screen.

With a quick flick of two dials, she opened the walk-in closet that she had modified into a security safe. She pressed a button to illuminate the interior, then went to a shelf and pulled down a reinforced cardboard box. Opening it, she took out a .25-caliber gun and shoved it into her attaché case. Dropping to her knees, Ida tore the lid off another box and began sorting through thick bundles of papers that were covered with Louise Sheridan's old-fashioned script. Frantically, Ida tossed page after page of the research papers she'd taken long ago from her stepmother's desk to the floor until she came to what she was looking for.

"Dove Hollow," she read softly, her eyes roving nervously from one line to another. "Sequatchie Valley." Ida jammed the papers into her attaché case, mumbling words of vengeance. "This better be right. I have neither the patience nor the time to be fooling around with Kiana's crazy ass. I need to get in, get what belongs to me, and get out."

At her apartment, Ida snapped her suitcase shut and telephoned Cora, giving the maid the rest of the week off. Ida felt thankful, again, that she had had the foresight not to move on Bonard's suggestion that they live together. She was perfectly content with an absence of Bonard's personal imprint on the sanctity of her boudoir, and she sure as hell didn't need his robe behind her bathroom door or his slippers under her bed to remind her of how much he had invested in the place.

Bonard had been ready to merge households the morning after their first night of lovemaking, but she had gently guided him toward her way of thinking. Such a move would be a big waste of effort. And money, she had told him. If their relationship developed as they both felt it would, she convinced him they should wait and design exactly the type of house she'd always wanted and settle in once and for all.

She paused to think about the piece of real estate in Virginia less than an hour from the city she had had her eye on for months. As soon as she took care of this messy business in the hills of Tennessee, she planned to call Century Properties and close the deal.

Well at least I don't have to answer to Bonard now, Ida thought as she dialed the number to his answering service, then waited for Vera, the operator, to pick up her call.

"Yes, Vera. This is Ida. Fine. Fine. Please tell Bonard that Harry has decided to send me to Palm Beach to scout locations for the Techni-Trak ad. Yes. Right now. No. I don't know which hotel. I'll call him tonight and let him know."

With that piece of business settled, Ida called TWA, crossing her fingers that there might be a direct flight from Washington to Nashville departing within the hour. She sure as hell didn't want to get stuck overnight in St. Louis.

Chapter Twenty-eight

On Tuesday morning, the next leg of the journey was finally underway.

"I think that's it," Rex called to Kiana from the side of the Blazer. He flipped the lever back up and replaced the pump nozzle in its holder, then screwed the gas cap back into place. He tossed his keys through the open window onto the seat. "This is going to be a very long day."

"I know," Kiana replied, watching Rex as he headed inside to pay for the gas. She pressed her head against the headrest, taking in the pale orange strip of light spreading on the horizon through half-closed eyes. She was excited about getting on the road, but was still nervous and puzzled by what had happened. Though Rex had not wanted to get the police involved, the hotel security guard had done so.

The police had not been able to do much except warn Rex to be alert and careful, and as far as anyone knew the vandal who had attacked their vehicle was still at large. Now, Kiana glanced over her shoulder as if half expecting to see the white van parked nearby, waiting to trail them all the way to Chattanooga.

Kiana's heart sank as she remembered the punishing thump of the van as it had slammed against the passenger side of the Blazer. She'd felt violated and vulnerable then, just as she had when the tires had been slashed, just as she did now. Thank God, neither she nor Rex had been physically injured.

She'd awakened at three this morning, long before the hotel operator had rung through with her 5:00 A.M. wake-up call, and hadn't been able to get back to sleep. The past two days had been a high-pressured nightmare of answering questions, giving statements to the rental agency, and filling out forms. After a detailed inspection of the Blazer, the Hertz rep had agreed to settle the damage claim on Monday, leaving them stuck for the rest of the weekend. Finally the police reports were in and the vehicle replaced with another just like it. All she wanted to do was get out of Nashville and put the incident out of her mind, but that wasn't going to be easy.

She watched Rex coming back with two cups of coffee in his hands, and was struck anew at how supportive and protective of her he'd been throughout the horrible ordeal. He had problems of his own, and she knew he could have left her to go home and take care of them, but he hadn't. And he was trying so hard to make her feel safe. Though he still casually dismissed the possibility that the gangs were after him, Kiana knew he was worried. Whoever had attacked them was a dangerous man.

Rex stopped at the side of the car and handed Kiana a cup through the window. She took it, and sipped lightly, then frowned. She really hated the stuff, but she needed something to jolt her awake, to get her mind working, to force her spirits back on track. Kiana could not shake the bizarre reality that someone wanted to do her harm, and might still be very close on their trail.

Rex buckled his seat belt and started the engine. "Ready?" he said, tuning the radio to WLAC, grumbling when he heard the morning traffic report. Construction on Interstate 65 between Brentwood and Columbia was closed and traffic was being detoured onto U.S. 31.

"What's that mean for us?" Kiana asked, gingerly sipping the hot caramel-colored liquid. She juggled the state map with her free hand, trying to find the detour route as Rex zoomed down the highway.

"It means," he said dryly, "that in about two minutes we have to cut west and get off of Sixty-five to go south on a two-lane road for about forty or fifty miles. It's going to add about an hour to our trip."

"Ugh," Kiana replied, tracing the red line on the map with tired eyes. "That's not good."

"No, it's not."

"No way to get around it?"

"Not that I recall. I don't think there's a decent highway east of Sixty-five. We're trapped, I guess."

Kiana squinted at the network of red-and-black lines crisscrossing the area Rex had highlighted with yellow marker. "You're right." She tossed the map to her feet and slumped back. "Might as well relax and go with the flow."

Rex nodded, giving her a confident nod as he swung from 440 onto 65.

The sky was rapidly growing lighter, and Kiana stared at the crush of cars inching their way toward the detour. It was a glorious June morning—the kind of mild southern awakening that was gentle and fresh. Kiana looked out at the lush forest of pines banking the highway and tried to relax, but she was still too tense to let the beauty of the day pull her away from the nagging thought that this trip was beginning to have more twists and turns than either she or Rex had anticipated.

Glancing over at Rex, Kiana felt better. He was totally absorbed in the music on the radio while easily maneuvering through the tangle of morning traffic. He appeared unperturbed by the upcoming detour, and the thought crossed Kiana's mind that if she had to drive hundreds, or thousands, of miles escorting strangers across the country, she'd be on the verge of a nervous breakdown. But it was clear that Rex liked his job and was very good at it. He was confident, relaxed, yet focused—not easily distracted and not a complainer. Kiana hated drivers who spent most of their drive time cursing, or weaving in and out of traffic, trying to push themselves ahead of the pack. Kiana felt perfectly at ease with Rex at the wheel.

But he's got to be worried, she thought, wondering if there was going to be a delayed reaction. The attack had cost them two days of travel and it crossed Kiana's mind that Rex had not mentioned anything more about his brother. Certainly he must have called home to find out what was happening, but he seemed content to keep everything to himself.

Soon, they were crawling through a bottleneck where three lanes of traffic funneled into one. From her vantage point high above the cars, Kiana looked down, alarmed to see how the tall orange barrels were forcing the traffic into a very narrow opening. She watched drivers cutting each other off, jockeying to get ahead, and could almost hear the grumbling and cursing that must have been going on inside every car.

Kiana's attention was caught by a car that suddenly swerved dangerously close to theirs. "Rex! Watch out," she warned, then bolted ramrod straight in her seat. "There it is!"

"What?"

"The Fifty-five Pontiac. Red and white!"

"You're kidding," he said, slowing down to let the car pass in front of them. "Jesus! You're right." He pulled closer. "A black man is driving."

"A light-skinned old lady is in the back," Kiana finished, grabbing a pen and her notebook from her bag. "How many 1955 red-and-white Star Chiefs are cruising around Nashville with an odd couple like this?"

"None, I'd suspect," Rex agreed. "Quick. The plates. WHX 890," Rex told her, inching closer, trying to stay with the car. "What are all those decals on the rear window? Can you read them?"

Kiana scooted up closer to the windshield and squinted. "Cades Cove. Roaring Fork. Oconaluftee. Heintooga."

"Sites in the Smokies," Rex explained. "Maybe the lady lives close to the mountains."

"They must spend a lot of time there. Look at the decals! The bumper stickers!"

"You got all that down? As soon as I can get out of this mess and find a pay phone I'll call the license number in to a buddy of mine at the highway patrol in Virginia."

"He'll trace it?"

"Sure. For me. Paul Pinzer used to do freelance work for *Black Culture Watch*. He also worked for the *Washington Post* covering criminal stories. But he always wanted to be a member of the highway patrol. When he got accepted into the training academy, he quit the *Post* and went off to Virginia. Great guy. We collaborated on a few stories together. Stayed in touch. He'll do it."

Kiana could not tear her eyes off the car. Folding her arms on the dashboard, she watched curiously as the huge classic car inched through traffic. The strips of chrome running across the hood and around the body were as shiny as pieces of new silver. Its big white-walled tires were striped with red and they looked as clean as if they had just been mounted.

"It's a beauty," Kiana said. "I see why the lady in the antique shop remembered it." The traffic began to ease and Kiana didn't want to let the car get out of her sight. "Let's follow them. What do we have to lose? Talking to that old lady is much more important than getting to Daisy Hudson's house right away. She's not going anywhere."

"Right," Rex replied, attempting to maneuver forward, but the sudden appearance of a highway patrol car stopped him. Rex angled to a stop directly in front of the black-and-white patrol car. The officer got out, held up his right hand, and signaled all traffic to come to a stop.

"Damn! They made it through," Rex said.

Kiana gripped the armrest at her side and watched morosely as the big Pontiac rolled on down the highway.

Rex massaged the steering wheel in frustration, glowering at the patrolman who was beginning to let the buildup of cars in the opposite lane pass through first. "There they go," he sighed in disappointment, watching the two-toned car disappear around a curve in the distance.

Kiana wiped a nervous hand across her cheek, then sighed in resignation. "Well at least we've got the license number. We'll find them."

"I hope so," Rex replied, "because they could be halfway through the state of Alabama by the time we get through here."

Kiana sipped her now-cold coffee and tried to imagine where the mystery lady was headed and who she really was.

For the duration of their miserable creep down U.S. 31, Kiana occupied herself with reading about towns in eastern Tennessee in the Triple A Tour Book. The information she came across was fascinating, and she found herself wishing for a time to travel with Rex just for fun—without the pressure they were under.

When they came to the exit for Franklin, Rex decided to keep going because the exit ramp was jammed with motorists who had decided enough was enough. Kiana would have liked to have driven through the town that boasted possession of the first three-story building to be constructed in Tennessee—the 1823 Masonic Hall in the downtown historic district.

After checking the map, Rex decided to press on to Columbia before stopping. The drive was magically scenic and Kiana drank in the rolling green farmland, the bluegrass meadows, and wooded hills of Maury County. In peaceful appreciation, she surveyed the serene landscape, understanding how Rex had fallen in love with his job. To be paid to travel around and explore the remote jewel-like areas of the nation was an enviable position to be in.

"They have Mule Days in Columbia in early April," he told her as he guided the Blazer toward the center of town. "Folks say Columbia has the largest street mule market in the world. In the spring there are parades, races, shows. All kinds of wagons, decorated with flowers, are pulled by mules through the streets for days."

"James Polk's house is here, too," Kiana volunteered.

"Right. I've toured it. If we had more time, I'd take you over there."

"Maybe we can do it another time," Kiana said, her heart racing as Rex turned to give her a knowing look.

"Maybe we can," he said softly, reaching over to take her hand. "But," he went on, "right now I'd better call my friend Paul, and see if he can give me a lead on the couple in the Pontiac."

Rex drove slowly through the quiet town whose marker indicated a population of 28,600. A towering billboard gave Columbia the title of dairy and livestock center of the state. Built on the low limestone bluffs of the Duck River, the quaint town looked to Kiana like the nostalgic kind of place many people were proud to claim as home. An authentic piece of the American past, Kiana was thinking. But when Rex came to a stop in front of a rustic log cabin with a sign that read Bluegrass Cafe, she began to feel a little uneasy.

"We can grab a bite here and I'll call my buddy." Rex started to get out.

Kiana didn't move. "Ahh," she hedged. "You've been in here before? It's kind of . . . well . . ."

Rex exhaled loudly, leveling stern, fatherly eyes on Kiana. "Look. You've got to get ready for these sorts of places, Kiana. The people may stare at us and probably won't welcome us with slaps on the back, but we've got every right to eat here and use the facilities. Don't get so antsy."

"You didn't answer me. Have you been in here before?"

Rex stuffed his keys into his pocket. "No. But that's no reason to avoid the place. I've spent a lot of time in small towns like these. Never had a problem."

"So far," she cautioned.

"Don't worry," he replied.

"Okay," Kiana said, getting out, biting the inside of her cheek to keep from making a smart remark. She was not in the mood for a hassle and definitely didn't want any reason to cause friction between her and Rex when things were going so smoothly.

Once they were settled at a square table at the front of the cafe, a plump, efficient waitress smiled stiffly, patted her teased beehive hair-do and stared down at her customers. She clutched her menus to her uniformed bosom.

"Y'all must not be from 'round here," she said in a drawl as thick and syrupy as the honey in the decanter in the middle of the table.

Kiana jerked her head around. "Why do you say that?"

"Mule days is 'bout the only time we get folks like . . ."

"Like?" Kiana prompted, her voice cool, her heart quivering in her chest.

"Oh, I only meant," the waitress floundered, "this here's just a family-type place. Most strangers comin' through eat at Denny's up on the highway."

Rex glared a warning at Kiana.

"Well, I don't patronize Denny's," Kiana began in a sugar-sweet tone of her own. "You know they got sued by some black customers because they refused to serve them. A big discrimination case."

"Really?" The waitress fidgeted with the corner of a menu.

Kiana nodded. "You didn't know about that? The government fined them . . . quite a lot of money, I think."

The waitress pulled the menus off her chest and handed one to Kiana, then one to Rex. "That so?" she replied, licking the end of her pencil. "Well what you two gonna have?"

They ordered ham and cheese sandwiches and glasses of lemonade.

When Rex lowered the menu from his face, Kiana caught him grinning at her. "You sure are something else," he said, as the waitress snatched the menus and stalked off.

Kiana shrugged and turned her attention to a hanging basket of Swedish ivy that was suspended above their table.

Rex went to use the pay phone.

Kiana amused herself by reading a carved wooden plaque mounted above the front door. It said: DRINKING DOESN'T DROWN YOUR TROUBLES, IT SIMPLY IRRIGATES THEM. She smiled, glancing around the big open room that had a low rough-beamed ceiling, a worn wooden floor, white curtains at the windows, and about twenty-five tables covered with red-and-white-checkered table-cloths. A crying tune by Johnny Cash drifted from an old jukebox in the corner.

A pimply faced blond girl sitting with a young man wearing a straw cowboy hat shoved her menu over her face when Kiana looked at her. The bearded farmer at the next table hooked his thumbs into the straps of his blue coveralls and glared. When Kiana made eye contact with him and smiled, the farmer did not smile back. He scowled so deeply his thick gray brows furrowed together in a straight bushy line. Kiana quickly turned around.

Riveting her gaze on the huge magnolia outside the window, she hugged her arms to her body defensively. Why the hell had Rex wanted to come in here? Under these circumstances even Denny's looked good.

Rex hung up the phone and headed back to the table. Kiana's uneasiness faded when she saw the expression of satisfaction on Rex's face.

"Can he do it?"

Rex slipped into his seat, leaned back, then flipped back a page in the small notepad in his hand. "It's a done deal. Paul punched it right in and Bingo! We now know who our mystery lady is."

"Who?" Kiana said, jolting forward, hand outstretched as if trying to snatch the notepad from Rex. He laughingly held it high above his head.

"Hold on. Her name is Muriel Quinn. Eighty-three years old. African-American. Lives in Van Buren County. RR Forty-seven. Near the Rocky River."

"Where's that?" Kiana pulled the wrinkled road map from her bag and spread it over the table.

"North of Chattanooga. See McMinnville?"

"Yeah, I see it." She took her pen and circled the area. "West of Falls Creek Falls State Park."

Rex leaned over the map, following Kiana's finger as she traced the squiggly Rocky River. "Paul said RR Forty-seven is east of Riverview. Pretty rugged terrain where she's located. Might be difficult to get to her."

Kiana raised her eyes from the map, narrowing them as she spoke to Rex. "I don't care if we have to be helicoptered in. I'm going to have a face-to-face with Muriel Quinn."

Chapter Twenty-nine

BONARD wiped his forehead with his monogrammed handkerchief and turned Sandy's words over in his mind. When he'd spoken to Ida at eight o'clock Monday morning she had not mentioned anything about leaving town, especially about having to go to Palm Beach. Now, twenty-four hours later, he was determined to find out where Ida had gone.

"You must be mistaken," Bonard told the woman who made all of Ida's travel arrangements, answered her mail, paid her bills, and generally knew every move his fiancée made. "I don't mean to imply that you are lying, but this is very unusual, isn't it?"

"Yes. Extremely," Sandy replied, pulling back her shoulders, poking out her well-endowed chest. She was obviously annoyed that Ida had slipped away without letting her know. "She flew out of here yesterday morning in a real dither, let me tell you. I asked her what was going on but she just shook her head. Refused to answer my questions."

"What time was this?" Bonard wanted to know.

Sandy paused, then touched her cheek in thought. "Right after the staff meeting. Maybe about nine forty-five. Mr. Overton told me a few moments ago that Ida went to Palm Beach to scout locations for the Techni-Trak shoot."

"I thought the photos for that account were going to be shot

in Hawaii," Bonard said. He and Ida had discussed the possibility
of combining the business trip with an extended honeymoon, going
on to Hong Kong and Japan. "Apparently Mr. Overton and Ida
worked this out very quickly."

"I guess so!" Sandy complained. "Nobody knows where she's
staying."

"I want to speak to Overton," Bonard demanded.

"He's already left for the day. But don't worry. He said Ida
was going to call him when she got settled . . . I think at her friend's
house."

"What friend?" Bonard asked, furious to have to deal with this
clerk to get information about his fiancée. The embarrassment of
it was mortifying.

"I don't know. Some girlfriend, according to Mr. Overton."

Bonard's nostrils flared in irritation. To his knowledge, Ida
didn't have any girlfriends in Palm Beach. In fact, Ida didn't have
any girlfriends at all. Irritated by the fruitless conversation with
Sandy, he brusquely strode past her and pushed through Ida's
closed door. He crossed the room to her desk and flopped down
heavily in her chair. When he began rummaging through the papers on her desk, then opened the middle drawer, Sandy flew from
behind her computer and rushed toward Bonard. "I don't think
you'd better do that."

Bonard riveted the woman with an icy stare. "Miss Williams,"
he said in a level, matter-of-fact tone, "I don't really care what you
think."

He got up from behind the desk and slowly approached the
secretary, his steps steady and deliberate. In tandem, she advanced
backward with each move he made.

"I mean . . ." Sandy stammered, "Ida's so particular about who
comes in her office. She hates for anyone to touch her things."

"I *am* her fiancé, remember? Her husband-to-be." By the time
he was inches from Sandy's face, her back was to the door jamb.
With a squint of his dark angry eyes, he sent her flying out of the
room.

Bonard slammed the door shut and locked it, then he went
back to Ida's desk and examined her desk calendar. He scanned it
quickly to see if he could find any clues. Nothing. He yanked all

the drawers open and checked their contents, not surprised to see that the inside of her desk and her entire work space were as equally organized as the contents of her apartment.

He tossed scribbled notes aside, examined page after page of interoffice memos, and leafed through the folder marked Techni-Trak. He found nothing to indicate a location change to Florida —no notes about her planned photo shoot, no list of possible sites to scout, no names of agencies or the camera crew she was going to use.

Bonard slammed the bottom drawer shut and paced to the window. How could Ida have gone off like that without telling him? His heart raced at a sickening pace and he mopped rivulets of perspiration from the sides of his face. Sinking, again, into Ida's beige leather chair, Bonard twirled back and forth nervously, trying to think things through.

If Ida wasn't telling anyone about her plans, the account must be in trouble. He eased into what he imagined Ida's mind-set to be. She must be under pressure. Someone internally must be trying to beat her out of the account and she was being very careful about her records. Smart move, Bonard concluded, well aware of the lucrative nature of the Techni-Trak account. He also was more than familiar with how conniving and cutthroat jealous colleagues could be when it came to getting ahead. He had been warning Ida to watch out for that man Lewis who she had been grumbling about lately. It had been because of Bonard's friendship with the president of Techni-Trak that Ida had managed to snag the account for Bering & Overton in the first place.

Though worried, Bonard couldn't help grinning as he thought about Ida. She had developed quite a roster of high-powered clients, and Bonard was extremely pleased that she listened to him, was willing to learn from his experiences. She had picked up on many of the tactics he used to move ahead of the competition.

Bonard shot to his feet. She must have stashed her plans in a safe place. Away from the enemy within her camp. But where?

Bonard strode to the center of the room and turned slowly in a circle, scanning the room. Suddenly he went to the door and unlocked it; then he went back to the desk, and with a hard push buzzed Sandy on the intercom.

"Come in here, please," he said very politely.

Within seconds, Sandy timidly opened the door and stuck her head inside. "Yes?"

"Come here. Come here," he coaxed her closer.

When she was standing in front of him, he spoke to her calmly, with respect, as he did with his own secretary. "Does this office have a safe?"

Sandy stared numbly at Bonard, considering whether or not to answer. "Yes," she finally told him.

"Where?"

With a jerk of her head, Sandy indicated the screen standing behind the burnt-orange love seat.

"Do you have the combination?"

Sandy stood silently, perplexed.

Bonard shot to his feet. "Do you?" he yelled.

"No," Sandy said, then went on in a shaky voice, "but I think Ida keeps the combination on the back of the screen. I've seen her look at it before she opens the safe." Sandy backed away. "But I've never opened it. Never. I swear."

"I believe you," Bonard replied, circling the desk, heading to the screen. "Thank you. You may go now," he told Sandy.

Once he was alone, he shoved aside the love seat and pulled back the folding screen. He examined it carefully, then noticed numbers written in thin black marker along the bottom edge of the molding. He squatted down to read them, then stood and rotated the dial. Immediately the door popped open, and Bonard let out a gentle, satisfied chuckle.

Reaching inside, he pressed a button to illuminate the interior. The gasp of surprise that flew from his throat startled him enough to make him step back.

Lining the shelves, stacked in piles on the floor, crammed into corners, and encased in plastic were many of the expensive paintings, sculptures, wall hangings, and decorative objects he'd either given to Ida or allowed her to purchase when she was redecorating her apartment. On unsteady legs, he moved more fully into the safe, gingerly lifting and examining each and every piece. These were the originals, all right. So what was filling Ida's apartment? Reproductions? Of everything? Why?

A duplicate set of Ida's Soddy Glass collection was arranged neatly, by color, on an intricately scrolled wrought-iron stand at the far end of the small room. In the hazy gray light of the single fluorescent tube overhead, the priceless items shimmered like elegant ghosts.

Bonard noticed a flat gray suede case that was wedged between several silver items stacked on the floor under the last shelf of the étagère. He bent down and eased it from beneath a pile of oversized antique sterling silver picture frames he had personally picked out for Ida. She had wanted them to frame portraits of her grandmother and her father. They had cost twenty-five hundred dollars a piece, which had been a steal because the dealer had owed Bonard a favor.

A bitter rage welled inside Bonard. He remained frozen with shame, with disbelief. Disappointment coursed through his limbs and threatened to pull him to his knees as he surveyed the incredible bounty spread out before his eyes.

"Looks like Jean Lafitte's treasure cove," he muttered, almost afraid to look inside the heavy gray case. He flipped back the solid gold clasp with his thumbnail. Hesitating, he lifted the lid. Tears sprang to the brims of his eyes as he gazed down upon every ring, brooch, necklace, and bracelet he'd bought for Ida since the day they met.

He fingered the rubies, diamonds, pearls, and sapphires that he had had the finest jewelers create for him. They felt heavy, expensive—very real, and he faced the awful truth that what Ida had been wearing must be made of paste, and what she felt for him must be contempt.

Rex had calculated, from studying the map, that the drive from Columbia to Shelbyville might take forty minutes—an hour at most, but instead of heading south to Lewisberg, then north to Shelbyville, he had mistakenly decided to cut straight east, cross Interstate 65, then take his chances on the meandering roads that he hoped would lead him to Daisy Hudson's house.

The tedious drive was frustrating, but not nearly as disturbing as the news his father had given him. Before leaving Columbia he had checked in at home to learn that Lionel was remaining close-mouthed. When he had been brought before the judge, and had refused to talk even his court-appointed attorney was exasperated and threatening to drop him if he didn't cooperate. Lionel was still in jail, and had been formally charged as a material witness to a felony drug transaction. His bail had been set at fifty thousand dollars.

As much as Rex knew he ought to go home and give moral support to his parents, he couldn't leave Kiana. What would she do if after he took off, leaving her on her own, another attempt on her life occurred? He'd made a promise to stick with her through to the end of her search, and he had a story to write. He could not let her down and he doubted he could persuade her to put off her search until his personal problems were settled. Besides, Rex rationalized, if Lionel was refusing to talk to his attorney, what good would his going home do? Apparently Lionel would rather sit in jail than give up his buddies' names to the police. So let him, Rex decided, speeding down the dirt road, creating a whirlwind of dust in his wake.

"Over there!" Kiana broke into his thoughts. "Two big black stones on either side of the road. There they are, Rex. We're here!"

The rough split-log cottage sat nestled in a field of bluegrass that was dotted with patches of vibrant color. A stand of pink rhododendron created a lacy bridge from the wood-shingled roof to the shore of the river that curved like a blue-green ribbon beneath the limestone ledges rising behind the house. A fringe tree, its white feathery blooms bursting from its branches, draped its limbs above the bright red door. And all along the gravel walkway from the dirt road to the door, were clumps of brilliant yellow flowers that Kiana could not identify. They looked like inverted buttercups with bright orange dots on their backs.

Kiana and Rex mounted the whitewashed steps almost reverently, peering cautiously and curiously at the dark screen door as they approached the entrance. Once they were standing in the shady quiet of the gabled porch, a voice boomed loudly to them from inside.

"Come on in, the screen's not latched!" the voice called out.

Inside, Kiana and Rex found themselves standing in a square room with a vaulted ceiling, facing a withered woman in a wheelchair. She looked for all the world like a tiny walnut doll, but had the voice of a baseball umpire.

Kiana looked around. The small house vibrated with the colors, textures, shapes, and sounds of ancient objects that had been hammered, twisted, cast, and carved into a myriad of marvelous shapes. Brass pendants, charms, and intricately carved Nigerian ankle bracelets rested on crates and tables beside carved masks, ancestral stools, and a stack of ivory boxes that had yellowed with age. A bronze double-handled urn filled with black-eyed Susans sat on a low bench beneath an original oil painting that depicted three fugitive slaves fleeing through a dismal swamp, their bodies half submerged in water. The tarnished brass plaque at the bottom of the frame had the words "Freedom's Journey" inscribed on it. No artist's name was given.

There were books, maps, prints, and crumbling old ledgers stacked on every surface, piled beneath the windowsills, scattered over tables and chair seats. And sitting in the midst of her collection, her legs covered with a quilt that looked as if it had been pieced by mountain pioneers sat Daisy Hudson—a book on her lap, a corncob pipe in her hand, tendrils of smoke curling past her brown wrinkled face.

"Miss Sheridan?" she said, wheeling toward them. "I'm Daisy Hudson. Welcome."

Kiana's hand was shaken quite vigorously while introductions were quickly made. Daisy invited her guests to have a seat at a claw-footed table in front of a curved bay window that provided a commanding view of the Duck River. As her guests told her about their mission and what they had found so far, Daisy listened with enthusiastic interest. When Kiana finished explaining their project, Daisy prattled on in her amazing voice about her delight at hearing from Kiana. She was very excited about the search and was more than happy to help.

Narrowing her keen dark eyes, she began, "Pull your chairs up closer. Let's see what we got." She opened a book and flipped through the pages.

"I really appreciate you helping us," Rex said, scooting his rush-bottomed chair closer to the table.

"It's my pleasure," she replied. "This kind of tracing is what I love to do. And it's been a while since I've had something this interesting to tackle."

A veteran of the public school system, Daisy had retired twenty years ago at the age of fifty-five to devote herself to learning more about her own family while her mind and her eyes were still good enough to keep up with her feet and legs. She had been traveling and digging up genealogical information all her life, and in retirement she easily finished tracing her own family tree, then went on to unearth more interesting characters whom she would have liked to claim as her ancestors.

Now, with arthritis and glaucoma hampering her work, she was anxious to share her treasury of knowledge with friends, associates, and even strangers like Kiana and Rex, whom she hoped might benefit from the wealth of material she had collected over time.

"My pleasure," Daisy repeated. "Glad you thought to send me that letter. Sounds like you two got quite a challenge ahead."

Rex rubbed his chin. "As Kiana told you when she called, she was able to get some help on her family history from her grandmother, and has a story her mother had been working on before her death, but we're not sure how much of it is reliable . . . it appears to be highly fictionalized."

"Dramatized," Kiana clarified with a bit of a frown. It seemed real enough to her, and unless information surfaced to prove the story fiction, she had no reason to doubt what her mother had written. "But it does make interesting reading," she said, going on to give Daisy a summary of what her mother had written.

While Kiana talked, Daisy curved her dark lips around the yellow pipe stem, a knowing smile on her wrinkled brown face. She nodded now and then as if she'd heard it all before, and when Kiana finished, Daisy turned to Rex.

"I wouldn't be too quick to dismiss a thing this girl's said," she told him. "I've been scrounging up tales about dead folks for years, and I've come across some doozies . . . Lawd have mercy . . . true stories, that would curl an Indian's hair. Many a time I'd just close my eyes and try to imagine the carrying on that folks did and wonder how they survived it. There're books here"—she flung out her arm, pipe in hand, pointing from floor to ceiling—"with true stories in them that'll take your breath away. If I told them to you, you'd say I made them up."

"I imagine so," Rex conceded.

"From what I have managed to uncover," Kiana began, "all I know is that Daniel DeRossette settled in the northern part of the Sequatchie Valley west of the Tennessee River."

"Maybe near Walden Ridge," Rex added.

"Sounds about right. But that still leaves a lot of space to cover. Especially if no traces of the old plantation exist," Daisy said, slowly pursing her lips. "After I got your letter I started digging." She stopped and gave her visitors a mischievous grin. "My, this is so much fun! It's been ages since I've had any reason to get this excited about anything."

Rex and Kiana exchanged glances of relief as Daisy fussed with some ledgers on the table.

"I found two pieces of research I think might be helpful," she said. "As I told you, Kiana, I've come across the name DeRossette a few times in my research, and this is what I've got." She placed one hand on a stack of brittle pieces of paper lying on a nearby foot stool, then picked up the top one and handed it to Rex. "Read this."

He took the page from Daisy and read aloud. " 'Report to the Freedmen's Bureau for activities in Sequatchie, Hamilton, and Bradley counties, July 1863 from Jas. Hoag.—I have taken charge of the land set aside by the Union for Negro use and have attempted to organize the Negroes in order to protect them and see that they have the necessary food, shelter, and provisions to sustain themselves. Their number is high and increasing daily, making it difficult to complete the required census. To the best of my ability I have gathered this information in the three counties under my supervision and submit this report in the earnest belief that it represents the truest account possible.' "

Rex's eyes darted quickly over the report, then he continued reading. " 'There are no Negroes presently housed or working land at Magnolia Crossing . . .' "

"Magnolia Crossing!" Kiana interrupted. Her heart began to race. "Rex. This is important."

"Right," he said, then continued reading, fingers crossed. " 'I found the land there burned out. All crops were destroyed. I took into custody—Sam, dark-skinned male, age twenty-two. Wife of Sam, age twenty and girl child, three years of age, fair. Essie, mulatto girl, age twelve. Old Negro man, age estimated to be sixty-one.' "

Disappointment clouded Kiana's face. "They're listed mainly by sex, age, and skin color. Few names."

"True," Daisy agreed, "but keep reading, never know what might be there."

Rex continued, " 'Old Negro man, age undeterminable. Jacob, Negro male, large scar on left arm, age nineteen. Woman who appears sickly and without ability to speak. The Negroes here tell me her name is Ofia.' "

Kiana put a hand on Rex's arm and squeezed it. "Ofia," she whispered. "The one who helped Adi escape."

Rex nodded, then finished reading the document. " 'Brothers, Henry and Alex, ages eighteen and twenty-two—medium brown skin, of average height tell me they were not slaves at Magnolia Crossing, but belonged to Welton Gray on the neighboring plantation. Also here is a dark-skinned male, no teeth, thought to be about sixty, answers to the name Rusty . . .' "

"Rusty?" Kiana stopped him excitedly. "Mother referred to an old man named Rusty in her writings."

Daisy gave up a short, knowing chuckle. "Honey. In all my years of researching the black folks of Tennessee, how many old men named Rusty you think I've come across?"

Embarrassed by her premature leap to make a connection, Kiana answered, "Hundreds, I'd guess?"

"If not more," Daisy answered. "Any slave who was old and 'rusted out' got called Rusty back then, but I think this report verifies that the place existed at least in 1863. What's happened since then is the key. The plantation was apparently burned out when this report was written, so I doubt any traces of it are still around."

Rex finished reading the document, then handed it to Kiana, laying a hand of caution on her arm. "At least we now have an official—government—record of Magnolia Crossing's existence, and this supports the history you found in Nashville."

"Exactly," Daisy said, tapping ashes from her now cold pipe. "Never can tell what links up with what unless you keep searching. Like a puzzle, it is, our history, with so many pieces forever lost." Turning to Kiana, she said, "When you telephoned, I started going through all my trunks of material I'd used in the classroom. I've got so much stuff, I need to donate it to somebody. But who wants it? Really? You see, black folks don't always give up their family papers to the museums and libraries. Most information is sitting in trunks, in dining-room sideboards, or up in attics gathering dust, waiting for some family member who's curious or greedy enough to go through it. Well, me, I'm curious," she laughed, "and once you called, I knew I couldn't do much but I couldn't turn down the chance to do what I could."

"Oh, you've been very helpful," Kiana rushed to say.

Daisy lifted the black book that had been resting on her lap since the arrival of her visitors and offered it to Rex. "We're not finished, yet." She grinned. "I came across another piece of information I think may be of help. Lay this on the table, young man," she told Rex, "so the both of you can see what it is."

Rex took the oversized book and put it on the table. Daisy opened it, her gnarled, arthritic hands carefully separating the stiff black pages. Kiana turned her eyes away for a moment, absorbing the intriguing collection of objects and artifacts crammed into the room as she waited for Daisy to find her place. It was clear that Daisy Hudson had devoted her life and a good deal of money to amassing an eclectic assortment of historical materials to document the history of her race.

Rex shifted the big book to position it between Kiana and himself. Kiana leaned close to what appeared to be an old-fashioned scrapbook with yellowed clippings pasted to black construction paper pages. The glue had dried, wrinkling the edges and the corners of many of the articles, documents, and photos Daisy had pasted in the book over the years.

Daisy wheeled her chair flush to the table at Rex's side, looked past him over to Kiana, then took her pipe from her mouth. With the stem, she tapped lightly on a small rectangle clipping that looked as if it had been torn from a magazine or an historical publication. The article was entitled, "The Black Angel of the Hills."

"Read this," Daisy told Kiana. "I tore this out of a publication the black teachers of Chattanooga put together many, many years ago. I used it quite often in the classroom to teach my students about their heritage. I found this particular article so intriguing I cut it out. Lord knows I never thought it might mean a thing to anybody, but read it. Out loud, so I can hear it again. My eyes are so bad I can't read small type anymore. But you see if this doesn't make sense."

Kiana hunched nearer, glanced at Rex, then began to read.

" 'On a quiet street on the far west side of Chattanooga stands an unassuming two-story brick house that has quite a story behind it. The house is now a vacant, run-down shell—a place where rats and stray dogs reside. But many years ago the house at the corner of Douglas and Eighth was alive with the voices of children. It is believed that this is where Marcela DeRossette . . .' " Kiana froze. Her hand flew to her lips and she paused in shock until she felt calm enough to go on. " '. . . the woman historians often refer to as the Black Angel, provided food, clothing, shelter, and love for children who were orphaned, displaced, or lost during the tumultuous days immediately following the end of the Civil War. After emancipation, Marcela somehow acquired ownership of the narrow structure that once had two acres of land around it, and started bringing in children—black and white—who had no place to call home. Fortunately, or unfortunately, depending on who tells the story, the Freedman's Bureau, an agency charged by the government to round up and assist the pitiful ex-slaves who were wandering and starving on the roads, decided to take away all the Negro children Marcela had been caring for in her makeshift orphanage and place them in the protective custody of the bureau. Marcela was said to have been outraged and fought back with letters to the head of the Freedmen's Bureau, to Frederick Douglass, and even to President Lincoln. But her efforts failed and the black children she had rescued and cared for as if they had been her own flesh and blood were eventually taken away. Outraged and despondent, this woman—whom many considered a saint—stole away in the night a short time later, disappearing with the children who had been left in her orphanage. It is thought that Marcela De-Rossette headed north into the hills where she raised the white children in isolation, never to return to the city. No one knows exactly where she went or what happened to her and her band of white orphans, but the story has persisted over the years. Many little black children who survived the harsh years following Emancipation owed their lives to the protective wings of Marcela DeRossette, the Black Angel. Little is known of her origins, but she was said to have told people when she came to Chattanooga that she had escaped slavery by fleeing from a plantation called Magnolia Crossing in the Sequatchie Valley area, but no traces of such a place have ever been found. So the myth arose, of course, that perhaps she truly was an angel, sent to save the lost children of Chattanooga.' "

Kiana's mouth was so dry by the time she finished reading, she could not speak, but the look she gave Rex spoke volumes. As she glanced from him, to Daisy, then back at the article, a cold chill swept over her heart.

Chapter Thirty

DARK clouds rolled down from the north in a ragged curtain of gray, then burst open, dumping a torrent of rain into the valley. Kiana watched the dismal landscape slipping past. Her gaze flitted from the soggy woods to the fast-moving water that filled the ditches lining the road. It fell like water pouring over the side of a dam. She worried that the gravel path might wash out from beneath the wheels of the Blazer, leaving them stranded in the isolated woods.

Rex was silent, eyes focused on the ground as he held the steering wheel tightly. With quick twists and turns, he managed to maneuver around the ditches and avoid the eroding edges of the country road. The tangled thicket bordering the trail was no more than a blur of green behind a heavy veil of water.

Unable to decline Daisy's invitation to stay for dinner, they had gotten a late start toward Chattanooga, and for the past thirty minutes had not passed a single car on the desolate shortcut Daisy had sworn would take them directly to the highway.

They crept along at a snail's pace as the rain continued to pummel the roof of the car in a relentless steady clamor. The road was rapidly beginning to resemble a creek bed after a flood. As gravel flew from beneath the tires, Rex dog-legged, U-turned, and backtracked the trail that vaguely followed the convoluted Duck

River. The Blazer bumped from stretches of smooth black pavement onto narrow gravel roads, then back to dirt that had dissolved into mud.

Each move jolted Kiana's thoughts back to the Black Angel and the mystery that still remained. She was getting nearer to the land where her ancestors had once lived and she was anxious to get into Chattanooga to see if she could find the house where Marcela had once lived, then on to find Muriel Quinn.

They were climbing in elevation, but Kiana watched apprehensively as water continued to rise in the deep gullies, while the lowlands collected standing water. Above them, rain drained from the hills in fast-moving streams, coursing down the steep limestone ledges to spill across the road, then down into the river below.

When the threatening clouds blotted out almost all light, Rex flipped on the headlights and pressed forward, hunching close to the windshield in an attempt to see more clearly. He drove through the rapidly darkening woods in taut silence, his jaw clamped shut, the swishing of the windshield wipers and the pounding rain the only sounds in the car.

At a crossroads, Rex stopped and turned to Kiana. "Right or left?" he asked rather curtly.

Steeling herself for his 'I should never have listened to you' remark, Kiana snapped on the inside light to read Daisy's directions.

"Left," Kiana replied. "Look for a sign that says Normandy Dam, go south five miles, then we should see Highway Fifty-five. According to Daisy, Fifty-five will take us to Twenty-four . . . and on to Chattanooga."

Rex drew air in through his mouth, let it out, then shifted the Blazer into first gear. Head lowered, he stared icily out the windshield. "This was a big mistake," he grumbled, clearly expressing his annoyance with Kiana. "I told you we should have gone back the way we came. I have no idea where the hell we are!" He jiggled the defrost button, saw that it was no longer working, then in exasperation, took out his handkerchief and wiped at the cloudy vapor forming inside the windshield. After looking both ways, he stepped on the gas and pulled into the intersection.

Immediately the Blazer dipped low in the front, then spun off to the right.

"What the hell?" Rex cried out, rapidly spinning the steering wheel hand over hand, to the left. The rear of the vehicle slid around and they made a three-hundred-sixty-degree turn in the middle of the road. When the vehicle came to a stop, its front end was pointing skyward, its rear wheels hanging over the mountain ledge.

Rex gunned the engine, but the tires only whined in a high-pitched squeal as they raked the rocky hillside. A noisy spray of gravel kicked up and clattered against the underside of the car. Mud splashed over the rear windows.

"Rex!" Kiana screamed. The Blazer jerked, then tilted to one side. She clutched the armrest to keep herself upright and pressed her face to the window at her side. All she could see was streaks of silver rain cutting through the pitch-black night. "God! We've run off the road."

Rex tucked his lips between his teeth, narrowed his eyes, and jammed his foot down hard on the emergency brake pedal. The Blazer shuddered as if it had been rocked by a tremor, then shifted farther back onto its rear wheels, propelling the front end of the vehicle higher into the air.

"Rex. We're going over!" Kiana yelled, straining against the pull of gravity that flattened her to her seat.

"No, we're not," Rex vowed, unfastening his seat belt, unlocking the door on his side.

A vicious torrent of water ripped through the open door and soaked Kiana in a matter of seconds. Bits of gravel, dirt, and twigs pelted Kiana's face and the wind whipped her braids across her cheeks.

"Take my hand," Rex yelled above the howling wind as he leaned across the front seat.

Kiana stared blankly at him, unable to move. She cut her eyes to the right. On the passenger side of the Blazer there was only blackness, a sheer drop-off of about fifty feet. Again, she tried to move but her seat belt had slipped, trapping her left hand low against her thigh. When she attempted to yank it free, the shifting of her own weight and her fear of toppling over the cliff kept her pinned to her seat in shock. "I can't! Rex! I can't move."

Quickly, Rex scrambled back inside and eased down onto his stomach on the driver's seat. The Blazer rocked dangerously to one side, then the other, then settled back into place.

"Rex!" Kiana screamed, terrified. When she felt his hands fumbling with her seat belt, she squeezed her eyes shut, unable to look into his face. Suddenly, the strap across her waist popped loose. She groped blindly for his hand. Holding tightly, she let him drag her across the seat.

With a yank, Rex tore Kiana from the teetering vehicle.

The force of his tug propelled them both into a water-filled ditch at the base of the cliff. Kiana landed with a dull thud on her side. Instinctively, she opened both arms and wrapped them around Rex's waist. He collapsed with a muddy splash atop her.

Holding onto each other, breathing suspended, they listened to the grating sound of metal rubbing stone as the Blazer slipped more perilously toward the bottom of the gorge.

"Look!" Kiana screamed.

The headlights were still on and they could see that a big craggy tree branch was the only thing preventing the Blazer from going over the side.

Fragile limestone ledges broke apart. Rocks tumbled in a loud clatter down the side of the hill. Kiana flinched, tensing at the noise, expecting to see the Blazer disappear off the side of the mountain, but was surprised to see it held fast.

"Good Lord," Rex said, rising to his knees, shocked by what he could see.

A rumbling sound began on the rocky cliff above them. He looked up, then covered Kiana's head with his hand, pressing her forehead to his chest. Together they scooted back against the rocky wall, settling into a muddy ditch. Rex lost his hold on Kiana when water poured down on them like a frigid waterfall cascading into a frothy riverbed. Once the torrent had passed, he reached for her again, but his hands were too slippery to grab her. Another blast of rushing water careened down the hillside. When it slammed into them, Kiana screamed. Rex groped for her, but didn't make a connection before the rushing water swept Kiana away.

"Coffee. Black. And a ham and cheese on rye," Ida said, kicking her Louis Vuitton garment bag more fully under the table. Furtively, she scanned the faces of the customers sitting in the airport cafe. None were remotely familiar. She tried to relax, but as soon as the waitress had jotted down her order, Ida turned her chair more fully toward the window and scowled at the slashing rain that was pummeling the slate-gray tarmac.

The plane that should have been winging her from St. Louis to Nashville was still on the ground, and would remain there, the gate attendant had announced, until the weather cleared. Ida hated flying and especially hated being delayed, though she usually weathered such annoyances by hanging out in the private clubs, chatting with fellow first-class travelers.

Tonight, Ida had no choice but to remain where she was. Bumping into a business acquaintance or a colleague of Bonard's in the VIP Lounge might put a serious wrinkle in her plans.

When the waitress returned with her coffee and sandwich, Ida's stomach curled painfully. She took a quick sip of the coffee, but pushed the plate away. Checking her watch, she tried not to panic. It was already after seven. If the rain didn't let up within the hour, she'd be stuck in St. Louis all night.

Kiana had never slept outdoors in a tent, let alone help put one up in the middle of a driving rainstorm, but by the time Rex had pounded the last stake into the ground, and she had tied the last window flap into place, she was grateful to take refuge inside.

Miraculously, she was not hurt. The water had swept her into a grassy low spot where she'd suffered no more damage than a ruined pair of jeans and a bruise on her arm.

The Blazer remained stabilized halfway off the shoulder of the road, its rear wheels wedged into the rocky ledge. Rex had been able to open the back hatch and ease the camping gear and their bags from the rear, so at least they had shelter and a clean change of clothes.

Kiana sank down on the floor of the tent and wiped a grimy

hand over her face, slicking more mud across her cheeks than was already there. She looked through the pile of supplies Rex had shoved inside and found a big plastic jug of drinking water. Wetting the tail of her ruined cotton chambray shirt she dabbed at her face, the cool touch of the damp fabric soothing her nerves and the tiny cuts she'd suffered in the fall.

"You need soap," Rex quipped, sticking his head inside, then fully entering to sit down beside her. He was soggy and chilled, but not in bad spirits considering what they'd been through.

"Don't I know it," Kiana frowned, continuing to dab the mud that was beginning to dry like a mask on her face.

Rex unzipped his green duffel bag and took out a small white towel, wet it, then squeezed on a dab of liquid soap from a tube. "Let me," he said, turning up the shimmering light of the glowing Coleman lantern. He crouched on his knees above Kiana and reached out to take her chin in his hand.

Kiana pulled back stiffly, locking eyes with Rex for a fraction of a second, then let her body go limp. She was dirty, exhausted, and scared. There had been warning signs all along the road about bears, snakes, and wild boars in the woods. She didn't have a good feeling about the situation they were in, and if it had not been for the confidence she placed in Rex's camping experience, she doubted she'd ever be able to sleep.

How would they ever get out of this mess, she wondered, trying to relax as her body trembled beneath her rain-soaked clothes. With a weak smile, she thanked Rex and lifted her upturned face to him.

He dabbed at the mud, saying nothing.

"I won't get mad if you go ahead and blame me for this mess," Kiana muttered. Her cheeks burned hotly, as much from her shame at causing their mishap, as from the tingle of his gentle touch. "I should have listened to you. I'm sorry I insisted we follow Daisy's directions."

Rex still did not respond. He finished wiping her face, then reached for her suitcase and pulled it closer. "Better find something to change into. You'll get sick if you don't get out of those clothes."

Kiana nodded, so tired and ashamed of herself for being so

stubborn, she had no energy to protest. Besides, he was right. If she planned to get through this little adventure in one piece, she had better not get sick. She unzipped her suitcase and pulled out a heavy sweatshirt with matching pants.

Rex politely turned his back as she stripped off her mud-soaked clothes and wiggled her chilled, tired body into the sweatsuit.

"Perhaps I should have taken a different route," Rex finally said, keeping his back to her. "But I didn't. So in answer to your question . . . no . . . I don't blame you."

"That's a relief." She tugged her sweatshirt firmly over her hips, then told Rex, "You can turn around now." She looked at him, furrows of concern on her brow. "What are we going to do?"

"Now? Nothing." He grinned. "Get some sleep I guess."

"At times like this a cellular phone would come in handy," Kiana said.

Rex made a gesture in an offhand manner. "Maybe, but we'll be all right. When it's light, I'll walk out of here and get us some help. Hopefully a tow truck can get the Blazer out. I really don't think there's any damage."

"Let's hope not," Kiana said, tossing her muddy clothes into a pile in the corner of the tent. She sat back down on the Grand Teton sleeping bag that Rex had unzipped and spread over the floor. She furiously toweled her braided hair as she spoke. "You know, this is not half bad." She assessed her surroundings, resigned to the situation. The tent was roomy enough, cozy, warm, and dry. Not the Omni Princess by any means, but under the circumstances, it would do just fine.

"I can't believe you've never slept in a tent." Rex laughed, pulling his wet shirt over his head. Without a hint of embarrassment, he sat beside her, bare-chested, while rooting through his bag for a shirt.

Kiana stared at his bronze back, then reclined on her elbow to prop her chin on one hand. "I never was presented with an opportunity to go camping, and I guess it was not something I felt inclined to do on my own."

Rex looked down at her and smiled. "I like camping . . . sleeping in a tent. This is the life. Believe me. It's quiet in the woods. Peaceful, even when it's raining. I think it's a good idea to just disappear now and then, to be someplace where no one knows exactly where you are."

"You like hiding out?" Kiana asked.

"It's not hiding out," Rex said. "But I don't have Ed coming in and out of my office yelling about deadlines and rewrites. I may be in the woods, but I'm working, and I'm not under a lot of pressure. I can do things my way. It's great."

Rex was sitting quietly, cross-legged, in front of her and he toyed with the damp shirt still in his hands while looking at Kiana.

"I see," she replied, unable to keep her eyes from roaming the golden sheen of his shoulders. "Despite the mud bath I just took, I have to admit that I like it here, too. I've been itching to get out of the classroom and go off like this to do my research, but I never envisioned myself stuck in a tent in the middle of the mountains. I see why you love your work so much."

Rex took a dry T-shirt from his bag but did not put it on. "Where are you going when this is over? Back to Houston?"

Kiana tucked her bare feet under the front flap of the sleeping bag, and turned over on her back. Rex looked inquisitively down at her, and Kiana boldly captured his gaze. She gulped dryly, attempting to clear away the uneasiness that suddenly filled her. Being so close to Rex, under such intimate circumstances, was forcing her to deal with the strong attraction she had felt for him since the day he walked into her life.

"Houston?" she finally managed. "I don't think so. I left some painful memories back there and I have no reason or desire to go back and resurrect them."

"An old flame?" Rex prompted, then he hurried to say, "I don't mean to pry into your personal business, but you told me you were unattached. There's not any unfinished business back in Houston, is there?"

Kiana chuckled lowly, then lifted her chin toward the roof of the dark green tent. "No. Not at all. Thank God. I must admit that I did make some stupid choices when I was frantically searching for Mr. Right."

A smile of understanding touched his lips.

Kiana sat upright, pulled her knees to her chest, and tugged the arms of her sweatshirt down over her hands. With her head on her knees, she tucked her balled fists under her arms. Hugging herself, she went on. "I used to worry that I was being left behind. That time was running out. You know? Most of my friends and coworkers were married with two or three children, and during a desperate hour I panicked and hooked up with a guy named Stanley. A big mistake. I had to find out the hard way that it's infinitely better to be alone than to try to force a future from a relationship that has none."

In a gentle movement, Rex scooted closer. "Isn't everybody lonely at one time or another? Don't say you regret what you did." He placed a hand on her knee. "You acted on your instincts—"

"That's the trouble," Kiana broke in, her mind racing back to her pledge to steer clear of any involvement with Rex. "I have come to the conclusion that my instincts are extremely unreliable."

Rex lifted one eyebrow in question, a charming grin curving his lips. "If you want to talk about it, it's okay with me."

Kiana loosened the protective shield she had unknowingly put across her chest, and unfolded her arms. She relaxed, extending one hand to let it lay palm up on her thigh. "There's not much to say . . . I gave all I could to the relationship, but it wasn't meant to go anywhere."

"You mean . . . you didn't want to face it, but you were willing to settle for someone you didn't love in order to keep from being alone?" His gaze roamed from Kiana's face to her upturned palm. He moved his hand over hers and laced his fingers through hers.

At his touch, a tremor rippled up Kiana's arm. Relieved that Rex had made the first move, she wasn't sure that she wanted to discuss the disaster she'd made of her love life.

"You pegged it right," she finally admitted. "I was lonely. And afraid." Kiana sighed. "When I met Stanley I was desperate . . . an insecure mess. I guess I was aching to be with somebody. Anybody. So I latched onto a man I really didn't know."

"Happens to lots of us, Kiana. Lighten up. Don't be so hard on yourself."

Kiana tucked one leg beneath her hips, leaning up. Rex placed a folded blanket behind her, his reach extending over her shoulder. She focused on Rex's eyes, prolonging the moment.

"So, what about you?" she asked. "Have you ever felt like that?"

Rex pulled back, letting go of her hand. He threaded his fingers through his damp curls. "Insecure? Hungry for love? Sure." He turned to face her, gentle contemplative eyes meeting hers. With both palms flat on the tent floor on either side of Kiana, he formed a protective circle around her. "I've felt like that many times. But you're the first woman I've ever admitted it to."

Kiana studied Rex, recording the burnished sheen of his skin, and the smoldering warmth of his eyes. An intensity was building between them and her pulse thundered in anticipation.

"Then why are you telling me?" she asked, drinking in the perilous nearness of him, realizing that what she wanted was to move fully into his arms. But she held back, trapped by the consequences she knew such a move would bring. In a teasing voice, she masked her mounting anxiety. "Do you expect me to believe that you've never discussed this with any of your girlfriends?" She recklessly gave him a flirtatious smile. "Ever?"

He bent even nearer, his breath warm on her cheeks. "Well, I can't say never, but I don't really spend a lot of time talking to women about whether or not I'm feeling lonely. Sometimes I like being alone."

His maddening self-assurance stirred Kiana's blood, but instead of spurring her to make a defensive reply, she eased closer. He was so damn comfortable with himself, but maybe that was what made him so terribly attractive.

It occurred to Kiana that Rex might find it amusing to say things like that to get a rise out of her. Irritated, but unable to tear her eyes off Rex's smooth, muscled chest, she blinked, swallowing the flippant remark that burned on the tip of her tongue. In a flat voice, she stated, "It sounds like you're telling me that any worries you might have about loneliness can be cured if you find someone with whom you can get through the night?"

Rex moved, putting both hands on either side of Kiana's face, then eased her mouth toward his. With a whisper, his breath mingling with hers, he said, "I admit I've been with my share of ladies, Kiana. And I've been lonely now and then, but I don't let things like that get me down. It passes, like everything else, and I have always believed I'd come across the right person in time. All I had to do was wait." He boldly, teasingly feathered his lips across hers, then said, "I think I've finally found her."

The quiet expression on Rex's face delighted Kiana more than it frightened her. She listened as he continued.

"Now that I've met you, I know my search is over."

Kiana shied back, stung by the fire Rex was deliberately igniting. His nearness was both comforting and terrifying. She felt torn between rushing headlong into Rex's unspoken request and protecting her newly healed scars from being opened again.

Rex swept his palms along the curve of her neck, then kissed her fully and deeply. Kiana didn't have time to hesitate. She kissed him back, accepting the fiery pull of his lips, letting it sweep away her fears. As her fleeting resistance melted, her internal defenses rapidly crumbled, and the ever-present nagging inner voice finally left her alone.

Kiana clung to Rex and gently slipped down onto the sleeping bag. Her heavy sweatshirt rose up to reveal the silky skin of her abdomen. She tugged at the bulky fabric, trying to cover herself, but Rex interrupted her efforts with a gentle press of his hand, then slid it beneath her shirt. With a delicate touch, he stroked the smooth skin at her waist.

"Kiana?" he prompted.

"Hmm?" she murmured through compressed lips, her body afire, her veins swollen with desire.

"I have this disturbing feeling that we're going to make a very good team."

"Disturbing?" she threw back, then quickly realized he was laughing at her again. She playfully swatted at him. "Don't tease!"

Rex seemed pleased to have been able to get a rise from Kiana. Chuckling, he clarified. "I'm serious. If we can stop bossing each other around for a while, we might be able to make a go of it."

Kiana grinned, but held her breath tightly, afraid to reply.

Rex finished his sentence. ". . . and not just professionally, if you know what I mean?"

Exhaling nervously, she chewed her bottom lip. "I know what

you mean," she managed hoarsely, lowering her eyes. "I've been thinking about that, too." Caught up in her need to love and be loved, Kiana let Rex Tandy's words sink in. If she went all the way, this had to be her final commitment, her final passage, the end of a very rocky journey.

Kiana shifted in his arms, shuddering under his touch, feeling a delicious weakness flood her limbs. She felt hazy and heavy with longing.

This is not love on the rebound, she reassured herself, pulling him closer, tighter. The temperature had dropped during the storm and it was suddenly very cold in the tent, but Kiana was warmed by the thought that their mutual magnetism *could* blossom and mature if she dared open her heart to it.

Unwilling to break the magical moment, Kiana snuggled down on the sleeping bag, allowing Rex to ease his body over hers. He gathered her to him like a mother protecting an injured child, yet kissed her with a male urgency that jolted her body with the intensity of a tidal wave.

She placed her chin atop his soft damp curls and inhaled his intoxicating scent, shocked, yet reassured by her own eagerness to keep his hard-muscled body close to hers.

Rex rose up on his elbow, supporting his chin with one hand, reaching for hers with the other. She let him loosely hold her fingertips. He lifted dark eyes to hers, then with both hands, eased her sweatshirt over her head. Kiana didn't protest as he freed her full bare breasts.

Rex wrapped her with his arms, his kisses burning a trail of bliss from the soft spot beneath her chin, to the warm center between her breasts, to her hardened nipples, which strained like dark rubies against his lips. His touch tore through her body like wildfire.

Kiana drank in the beauty of his near-naked body like a magnolia suckling the faint evening dew and quivered against him, absorbing the drugging pressure of his rock-hard manhood pressed to her thigh.

Kiana let out a deep breath, looking down. "Rex, I . . . I am so attracted to you. But . . ."

"But?" he said in a husky voice, his hands curling over her

shoulders, gathering the soft folds of her braids into his fists. "But you want me to stop?"

Kiana felt her need for him surge like a thundering flash flood roaring through a rain-starved valley. "No," she whispered, feeling her pulse quicken as the word slipped out. "No, please, don't stop."

Rex pushed himself upward and recaptured her lips.

She opened her mouth wider, tasting and accepting his mutual quest, the prospect of total, mutual surrender, exciting her beyond expectation. Kiana could not help measuring the glow of her desire, that grew hotter by the second, against the melting resistance she had struggled to keep intact.

Her own insecurity about her judgment in men faded into the background as the enchantment of the moment took over. Enveloped in Rex's arms, all her negative thoughts evaporated, and she was flooded with a confidence she thought she had lost.

Rex gently urged Kiana under the warm thick flap of the sleeping bag, then settled in beside her, casually yet pointedly flinging his muscular, jean-clad leg over her thigh.

Kiana buried her face in the warm hollow created between them when his body had settled the length of hers.

With a muffled cry of pleasure, Kiana rejoiced in the virile scent of him, and the anticipation of complete surrender. She reached down to the front of his jeans and located with no difficulty the pull of his zipper.

She tugged urgently.

Rex curled his expansive fist over her hand and clasped her fingers in his, assessing her in the dim lantern light with a raw, hungry gaze.

Without waiting for him to say a word, Kiana answered the question he did not have to ask. "Yes, I'm sure," she said softly, feeling flushed with desire, yet oddly calmed by the sense of relief and empowerment spawned by her decision.

He made no reply, but closed his eyes and let a shuddering breath drain through his lips. The skin on his chest glowed wet with perspiration and Kiana trailed her fingers through the tangle of fine hair covering his corded stomach.

Smiling with the faintest hint of relief, Rex reached over her and slipped his hand into his nearby canvas bag.

Kiana was glad he was prepared to protect them both. She snuggled deep into the fluffy sleeping bag and opened her arms to Rex.

Rain thumped in a staccato beat on the roof of the tent, and rushing water swished through the forest in a steady hum, and the sounds in the forest lulled Kiana and Rex into an exquisite euphoria that lasted throughout the night.

Chapter Thirty-one

THE Houston Museum in Chattanooga was closed to the public until nine-thirty on Thursdays, but the director had agreed to bend the rules and let Kiana and Rex in at nine o'clock.

As they drove toward the center of town, it struck Kiana how easily she and Rex had already settled into the rhythm of their rapidly evolving relationship. After the tow truck had come to pull them out the day before, they had come straight to Chattanooga and checked into the Colonial Inn. This time they took a single room and had luxuriated together in a long hot shower. As the mud of the previous night slid away, so did all of Kiana's fears.

At the hotel, they'd made love again, and the same joyful stir that had engulfed her in the tent had surged back under much more civilized conditions.

In the woods, the sounds of yellow warblers twittering in the trees had jolted her into wakefulness. This morning it had been Rex whistling as he shaved. Though she'd been startled momentarily by Rex's cheerful presence, she soon relaxed and lay very still, thinking about what was happening.

The precious moments of their lovemaking came back to her in astonishing clarity. Every kiss, every caress, every touch of his skin to hers had been recalled and savored again. She had wanted him, he had wanted her, and together they had managed to discover the invisible connection that now bound them in a way that Kiana hoped might be strong and deep and secure enough to last for the rest of their lives.

She was free of disturbing afterthoughts, and had no reason to doubt her judgment. Their joining had been a natural expression of their mutual attraction—a testament to their simmering desire that had flared the first time they met. No awkward moments, no averted eyes, no unspoken regrets had arisen, and it seemed to Kiana as if she had known Rex for a much longer time than the short, intense duration of their adventure.

In the forest they had lain together after making love, listening to the rain pummel the roof of the tent. Far into the night they had talked, laughed, held onto each other while sharing their secrets and dreams. Kiana had divulged the painful details of her mother's death, describing the strain that eventually developed between her and Ida in the years that followed. Rex had broken his stoic silence, confirming her suspicions that he was feeling guilty about not being with his brother and his parents during the difficult time his family was facing. He felt torn. He wanted to see his brother, but he didn't want to leave Kiana and was firm about not abandoning the search. Kiana had urged him to go home immediately, and now, as they climbed the steps to the Houston Museum, Kiana selfishly wished Rex had not followed her advice and made reservations to return to D.C. the following night.

A primly dressed matron in sensible shoes and horned-rimmed glasses greeted them in the museum entryway.

"Welcome," she said in a pinched, nasal tone. "I'm Lea Bowser, acting director of the museum."

Rex and Kiana shook her hand and made their introductions.

"Joe Dawson is not here?" Kiana asked.

"No," Lea said. "Unfortunately, he's out of the country right now but I am happy to help in any way I can."

"Good," Rex said. "We're not going to be in town very long, and if you can help us, we'd appreciate it."

"No problem. You've never been here before?"

"No," Kiana said. Rex nodded.

"Well, I'm glad you stopped by. Let's go to the west wing. I know you'd like to see a little of our collection while you're here."

She tucked a manila folder under her arm, then motioned for Kiana and Rex to follow her across the sunny museum entryway. "Are you enjoying Chattanooga? Where are you staying?"

"The Colonial Inn," Kiana replied. "And we just got in yesterday afternoon. Haven't had a chance to see much of the city."

"Lovely place," Miss Bowser replied, moving efficiently across the room to a red door. "Go over to Lookout Mountain, if you can." She pushed the door open and held it for Rex.

Quickly, the threesome came to the west wing of the building and halted at the expansive entrance. Kiana stared wide-eyed at the rich decoration in the interior of an area that resembled an eighteenth-century mansion, complete with half walls, fake windows, and muted floral carpet.

"As you can see," Lea Bowser began, "we specialize in decorative arts and antiques from the eighteenth through the twentieth centuries. Our collection is displayed in natural settings. Living rooms, dining rooms, libraries, and so on. It makes for a much more realistic experience, don't you think, to see the glass and porcelains and silver as they would have been placed and used in a real home?"

"This is lovely," Kiana said, stepping toward an alcove. The entrance had been secured by a swag of burgundy velvet rope, and the area was arranged like a cozy Victorian parlor—complete with oxblood red walls, an ornate rosewood mantelpiece, an Eastlake chair, and a grand piano draped in true Victorian fashion with a deeply fringed shawl. A vase of pale pink roses sat atop it.

"Only the extremely rare pieces are displayed in glass cases or kept behind protective barriers." Miss Bowser curved her index finger in a beckoning motion. "Like the Queensware. Follow me."

At a lighted floor-to-ceiling display case along the back wall of the exhibit hall, Miss Bowser came to a halt. "This is the largest collection of Queensware in the United States."

Rex whistled lowly through his teeth, looking up to the highest shelf, then down to the lowest, taking in the vast assortment of goblets, compotes, salt and pepper shakers, celery vases, butter dishes, syrup jugs, and tumblers that shimmered before them like a treasure chest of precious jewels. "This is fabulous!"

"Isn't it?" Miss Bowser agreed. "I wasn't the curator for this exhibit. Mr. Dawson acquires and curates all the glass. Of course, we're very proud of our collection."

Kiana examined the collection eagerly. "How did the museum find all of this?"

"From estate sales, individual donations. The director has made several trips to England over the years."

"The design of Queensware is so similar to Soddy Glass," Kiana noted. "The scalloped bases, the tapering ribs that run half-way up the pieces."

Miss Bowser nodded and moved down the walkway a few feet. She stopped in front of another lighted cabinet. "Here are the only pieces of Soddy Glass that Mr. Dawson has been able to acquire for the museum. We're hoping to expand our collection in time, but it's so rare and so expensive," she broke off in a short laugh, "and our budget is so strained."

"I can understand that," Rex replied.

"You said Mr. Dawson is out of the country?" Kiana prompted, curious about the source of the twenty or so examples of the familiar glass that she had grown up peering at in her grandmother's old curio cabinet.

"Yes, he's finishing up a three-month tour of European glass factories. He's in London now. Should be leaving tomorrow, I believe. He'll be back by the end of the week."

Kiana glanced from the Soddy Glass to the wall of brilliant Queensware. "It's amazing. The only differences between the two types of glass are the way the borders have been decorated."

"Right," Miss Bowser agreed. "Every piece of Queensware has a wide, plain border. It was left that way so that the king could have his coat of arms engraved there. Do you know the story of the origin of Queensware?"

"Yes," Kiana said. "My mother did some research on it, and from her journals I learned about the DeRossette brothers and their unfortunate commission for King George."

Miss Bowser chuckled. "Unfortunate, then, yes. But not so unfortunate for the Americans who purchased the unwanted collection. The original set that was commissioned for the king is now scattered all over the world. Any part of it is as rare as a snowstorm in Jamaica, and let me tell you . . . we have only two-hundred thirty-seven articles from that original commission of one thousand. Some items have been located and remain in private collections, the rest will most likely never be found."

"Don't you find it unusual that the only difference between Queensware and Soddy Glass are the African motifs applied to the plain borders?" Kiana broke in.

"Precisely," Miss Bowser agreed. "It's as if the same pattern mold had been used for both types of glass. Soddy Russell appears to have threaded his primitive motifs in various colors directly onto the plain rims and bulbs of Queensware."

Kiana looked at Rex, then back to her guide. "Why did he do it? How could he have gained access to original Queensware molds to make his creations? *If* that's what he did."

Miss Bowser smiled and sadly shook her head. "It's a mystery, I agree. But sit down," she said, pointing to an area where two benches faced each other. She looked at her watch. "It's almost time to open up, but I'll share with you what I can about the history of Queensware." She touched Kiana's arm before she sat down and gave her an earnest nod. "I'm glad to know you are undertaking this research. Maybe you will be the one to finally figure out what the experts have been trying to explain for years."

"Do you mind if I tape you?" Kiana asked, one hand on the record button of her micro recorder.

"No, not at all," Miss Bowser replied, crossing her legs, opening the manila folder on her lap. She looked over at the wall of glass, then at Rex, who was perched expectantly on the edge of his seat, then began to speak.

"Between 1850 and 1859, Queensware glass was exported from Manchester, England, to three cities on the eastern seaboard of the United States . . . Boston, New York, and Philadelphia. Daniel DeRossette was the agent over here and he received and distributed the shipments from his plantation north of here in Sequatchie Valley. As far as historians can tell, Queensware was never produced in the United States."

"But DeRossette had made plans to build a glass factory in America, hadn't he?" Kiana interrupted, hoping her mother's story would pan out.

"Why yes," Miss Bowser replied, arching a thin eyebrow. "I see you've really done your research." Not to be deflated, she sat up taller and went on. "The records indicate that DeRossette had contracted to buy out a factory in Pennsylvania and was working on plans to modify it to his father's specifications."

"What factory?" Rex asked.

"The Porter Glass Works."

Kiana flinched, then reached over and grabbed Rex's hand. "I knew there had to be a connection."

"What happened to his plan?" Rex asked.

"The story is that he sent for a cousin to come over and manage the new factory but his ship sank on the voyage over and he was killed. Daniel was so devastated that he sank into deep despair, eventually abandoning not only his plans to have a factory in the North, but his entire import venture as well."

"What became of Daniel DeRossette?"

"An awful thing, really," Miss Bowser said. "He was killed in 1859 in a slave uprising on his plantation. Everything was burned to the ground."

"What was his place called?" Rex asked.

"Magnolia Crossing," Miss Bowser verified. "It was said to have been somewhere in Sequatchie Valley . . . one of the very few agricultural endeavors in that part of the state to be supported by slave labor. Few planters managed to make a go of it, but De-Rossette apparently was one who did. Now, let me warn you, don't go off hunting for Magnolia Crossing. Many researchers have. Not a trace of it exists."

"Where was Daniel DeRossette buried?"

"Oh, my." She looked through her folder of papers. "I believe his body was shipped back to England for burial in the family plot." Miss Bowser nodded, then closed her folder and stood. Smoothing the wrinkles in her beige linen skirt, she said, "That's about all I can tell you. I hope it helps."

Kiana also rose and positioned herself in front of Lea Bowser, wishing the woman had more to offer. "What was Daniel De-Rossette's cousin's name? The one who drowned on his way to America?"

Miss Bowser reopened her folder and shuffled through the pages, then without looking up, told Kiana, "His name was Rossel DeRossette."

Ida waited until the last customer had left Watts Antiques before getting out of her rental car and crossing the street. As soon as the bell on the front door jingled, Marvin Watts emerged from the back of his shop.

"Thought you were coming yesterday," he said, standing in the doorway, his ever-present cigarette dangling from his mouth. He shifted his stance as if to block Ida's view of the open back room, a smirk on his lips.

Ida approached the waist-high counter that stood between them, flung down her purse, and suspiciously looked Watts over. She cleared her throat impatiently, then told the antique dealer, "There was bad weather in Saint Louis. Unavoidable delay."

"You should have called. I don't like keeping my 'work' in the shop overnight."

"Afraid your greedy friend might pay you a surprise visit?"

Watts took a drag on his cigarette, then rolled his eyes in disgust. "He knows better than to try to hit me up for the money you owe him. He's not as shifty as some people I know."

Ida tapped her manicured nails on the glass counter. "Well, I'm here now," she snapped, not about to waste any more time quibbling with Marvin Watts. He'd served his purpose and it was definitely time to get him out of the picture. "I want everything you have."

Watts blew a cloud of smoke toward the whirling ceiling fan in the center of the shop and nonchalantly raked Ida from head to toe. "Everything? I think we'd better talk about that."

"Why? I quoted you a fair price. Not getting greedy, are we?"

"Not greedy. But I still have to make good on the promise I made to my buddy who did your dirty work."

"Did? I don't think that's the right word. Attempted, maybe."

"Whatever," Watts grumbled. "I expect you to fork over the rest of the money . . . and as far as this shipment is concerned, I was looking it over last night. Flawless. Really, my best work yet."

Ida stared at him in disbelief. "So now you want to renege on our agreement?" She threw back her head in laughter. "Don't press me. I really don't owe you a dime."

Watts's jowls slackened and he twitched his shoulder nervously.

Ida's voice softened in a mocking tone. "I know all about the transaction you made in December. I thought we had an agreement—if any authentic Soddy Glass surfaced, I was to be informed. Immediately."

"I don't know what you're talking about."

"Yes you do!" Ida hissed. "You were paid thousands of dollars by an auctioneer from Houston for a rather large collection of originals. You mean you've forgotten about that?"

"It was a legitimate sale."

"Legitimate! Ha!" Ida's mouth twisted in a sarcastic grin. "Not only was I cut out of any profit, you were too stupid to realize that you wrecked the best little scam you ever were involved in. The plan was to release the reproductions in Washington, New York, Chicago, and Los Angeles. Remember?"

"Yeah," Watts tossed back, "that's why I sold the real thing to the woman from Houston. How was I supposed to know you had a nosy kid sister living there?"

"What did you tell Kiana when she came here?" Ida said fiercely.

"Nothing," Watts said. "Not a thing."

"Good!" Ida said with satisfaction. Then, "You are a real idiot. If Kiana had never seen that glass in Houston, I would not be in this mess!" She reached for her purse. "Go get the shipment."

Watts eyed her suspiciously, not moving.

"Go get it!" Ida ordered, unzipping her soft leather handbag.

"I want to see the money, first," Watts stalled.

"This is all you are going to see," Ida threw back, slipping her hand inside her bag to calmly pull out her gun. Leveling the .25-caliber piece on Watts's chest, she ordered again, "I want you to go in the back room and get the items I ordered you to make and put them in the trunk of my car."

Watts didn't even blink. In fact, he grinned patronizingly, then said lazily, "Not without the cash."

"Cash? Oh, please. You've got the nerve to ask me for money after cheating me out of thousands of dollars *and* jeopardizing my plan!" She shoved the gun forward. "I don't think so."

Still Watts didn't move. "You're not taking a thing out of this shop until you put my money on the counter," he threatened. "Don't think I won't stop you."

Ida circled the counter, coming closer. "Just try, Watts." She motioned with the gun. "In the back. Show me what you've got."

Watts dropped his cigarette into the overflowing ashtray and held up his hands, backing slowly into the cluttered workroom behind the counter. "You're gonna be real sorry you did this, Ida."

"What the hell do I care?" Ida tossed back. "I never plan to see you again. We've come to the end of our rather imperfect relationship."

"You don't need to hold a gun on me," Watts coaxed in an appeasing voice. "I'm a reasonable man. Put the gun away."

Ida's eyes narrowed under her sculpted brows as she boldly pressed the tip of the gun flush against Watts's ribs. "Shut up! I don't need any lip from you. Maybe I don't feel like being reasonable! You low-life cheat," she growled, eyes as cold as stones.

With a jerky sidestep, Watts jumped back, bringing his right hand down in a straight, forceful chop.

Ida reflexively pulled the gun back, and to her own surprise pulled the trigger, squeezing off a single shot.

"Jesus!" Watts screamed, clutching his hand. "You crazy broad! What the hell are you trying to do?" He examined the wound, cringing to see a hole through the center of his palm. He clamped his good hand over it as blood trickled through his fingers, glaring in rage at Ida.

Shaken, though desperate not to let him see how rattled she was, Ida spoke with bravado. "You shouldn't have pushed me! Why'd you have to make me shoot you? God!" she muttered tightly, relieved she'd only hit his hand, but frightened that some-one passing by might have heard the gun go off.

Still holding the gun on Watts, she yanked a piece of white cloth from a pile of rags atop a nearby crate and threw it at his feet. "Pick that up. Wrap up your hand. It's just a scratch, for God's sake. You're not going to die. Do it! Now!"

She waited, trembling, until Watts wound the cloth over the wound, then she summoned up her gruffest voice. "That's better. Now. Do as I said and get that crate of goods in my car. And if you call the police, you better be prepared to have a long talk with the judge yourself."

Chapter Thirty-two

WHEN the gleaming Pontiac Star Chief came into view, Kiana was more frightened than excited. The car sat in the front yard of Muriel Quinn's tiny house like a hulking, armor-clad protector. After her telephone conversation with the mystery lady yesterday, Kiana had the distinct feeling that the tremor in the old woman's voice had been borne of distrust, not age.

Rex stopped at the edge of the quaint country road that was lined with a riot of colorful wildflowers, glanced over at Kiana, then gave her a weak, though supportive half smile. "Here we are. At the source."

Kiana took in the time-weathered A-framed cottage that had been plunked down in the middle of a neglected vegetable garden. Tangled among the remnants of last year's corn and mustard, were tender green vines of a new season of summer squash.

"Well, maybe, we're getting closer," she answered, apprehensive about getting her hopes up too high.

"Come on," Rex said. "Let's see what Muriel Quinn has to say."

Kiana slid across the seat and exited the Blazer on his side. "Keep your fingers crossed that she hasn't changed her mind. She sounded kind of shaky on the phone."

Muriel Quinn peeked around the edge of her partially opened door. Her eyes instantly riveted on Kiana. For several long seconds she absorbed her in puzzled curiosity while Kiana remained perfectly still, trying to appear unruffled by the woman's intense scrutiny.

Rex waited, watching Muriel closely until she began to ease the door more fully open.

"Miss Quinn?" Kiana began, "I'm Kiana Sheridan. This is Rex Tandy. I telephoned yesterday."

Muriel shifted her eyes from Kiana's face to her hands, then over to Rex before moving completely into the narrow opening. She was wearing a flowered smock and white polyester slacks and had a lace handkerchief clutched in one hand. She wiped it across her cinnamon-colored cheeks two times before she spoke. "Hello," she said flatly.

"Hello, and thanks for agreeing to see us," Kiana replied.

"You don't have to ask us in," Rex volunteered. "We can talk right here if you prefer."

Kiana nodded. "As I mentioned yesterday, I'm doing some family tracing and I'm very interested in learning more about the glass you sold to Marvin Watts in Nashville. It's rather important that I know where it came from."

Muriel gave Kiana and Rex a hesitant shake of her head, pulled the door wide open, and began to speak. "You're Louise Sheridan's daughter, all right." Her cautious expression shifted to somber recognition. "My, my, I would have known it even if you hadn't told me. Goodness, you favor her so."

Astounded by the unexpected remark, Kiana stammered her reply, "What do you mean? You knew my mother?"

Muriel paid no attention to Kiana's questions. "The cheekbones. The eyes. The same coloring. And you've got her slender fingers, too. Child, if you didn't have those braids in your hair, I would have thought your mother was standing on my porch."

Rex came alongside Kiana and held her by the arm, steadying her as he asked, "How did you know Kiana's mother?"

Muriel unlatched her shiny aluminum screen door and pushed it toward them. "Come in. Come in. Let me get you young folks some iced tea, then I'll tell you exactly what I told Louise Sheridan almost twenty years ago."

Lea Bowser stared intently at the woman sitting in her office. The story the stranger was telling her was compelling, and though she felt the lady might be a little too anxious to sound convincing, Lea was too caught up in the tale to interrupt it. Intrigued, she sat quietly, listening to the woman's explanation of her mission.

"It has taken quite a bit of effort and expense on my part to track down these pieces for Mr. Dawson," she said.

"I'm very sorry, but Mr. Dawson is in Europe, Miss . . . ?" Lea asked, embarrassed to have forgotten the woman's name so quickly.

"Miss Wilson. Ida Wilson."

"Yes. Well, he left no instructions about a pending acquisition of Soddy Glass, though I must admit we'd like to have it." Lea reached into the open crate on her desk and removed a beautiful honey-colored trumpet vase. She turned it up to the light, waiting for the oval fish to emerge on the bottom. "Looks authentic," she told Ida.

"It is," Ida replied coolly, sniffing in slight reproach. Though she gave the outward appearance of being totally in control, inside she was quaking with surprise and fear. If this woman couldn't help her, Ida wanted out. Fast. It had never crossed her mind that Dawson would not be at the museum, checkbook open, anxious to acquire what she had boldly placed on Lea Bowser's desk. "Here," Ida said pulling an envelope from her purse, "is a certificate of authenticity from Marvin Watts . . . Watts Antiques?"

"Oh my, yes. In Nashville." Lea quickly took the document and scrutinized it carefully. "Heavens. This is a fabulous collection. I'm certain Mr. Dawson will be interested."

"I'm sure you will see in your records that Mr. Dawson and I have been working on this acquisition for some time. I was the one who helped him locate and acquire the Soddy Glass that is on display here now."

"Really?" Lea got up and went to a file cabinet, took out a folder, and leafed through its contents. "So you were, Miss Wilson." Lea shut the file drawer and returned to her desk. "I wish I could do something, but my hands are tied. I don't have the authority to make such a costly or important acquisition. It would have to go before the board, be appraised."

"But Mr. Dawson has already verbally approved it."

"He's in Europe!"

"Can't you call him?" Ida pressed.

"Oh dear, I don't think I can do that. He's most likely in transit . . . on his way back."

"When do you expect him?"

"Let's see, today is Friday. He'll be in New York tonight." She flipped through the pages of her desk calendar. "He's not scheduled to be back in the museum until Monday, but he usually calls and checks in when he gets to New York. Sometimes he comes straight back, or he might decide to spend a day or two in the city before returning to Chattanooga."

Ida bristled. She had come too far and gone through too much to let this pinched-nosed biddy wreck her plans. "That's too bad," Ida said. "You know, I could take the collection to the Heritage Gallery in Pittsburgh. Do you know Adela Richards?"

"Yes. I do. And I know she'd love to have it." Lea Bowser looked nervously at the crate. "Tell you what. When Mr. Dawson calls from New York tonight, I'll tell him you are here. If he wants to move forward, we'll proceed. Where are you staying?"

"I haven't checked into a hotel yet," Ida said tightly, infuriated by the delay. All she wanted to do was unload the stuff as quickly as possible and get out of Chattanooga. She had other matters to take care of and she'd already lost too much time. But why chance dragging Watts's latest creations to a stranger in Pittsburgh if she could sell it to Dawson and be on her way? "What are you suggesting?" Ida asked Lea.

"Can you give us a few days? Wait until I talk to Mr. Dawson before leaving town. Call me late tomorrow afternoon."

Ida rose, considering Lea's request as she slowly put the lid on the crate. Hanging around Chattanooga with a trunk full of fake Soddy Glass was definitely not a good idea, but turning down Lea Bowser's offer might make her look too desperate. The wait would cost her a day or two, but she'd better play this one out. "All right, Miss Bowser," Ida agreed in her most charming voice. She extended a sweaty hand. "I know Mr. Dawson will want to add to his already fabulous collection. The Houston Museum must have these pieces."

"I agree," Lea said, shaking Ida's hand.

Ida picked up Watts's certificate of authenticity and slipped it into her purse. "You can expect to hear from me in twenty-four hours."

The furniture inside Muriel Quinn's house looked as if it had been carved by Tennessee mountain men over a century ago. The birch chairs, pine tables, and red maple chests sat on rough wooden floors beneath a low-beamed ceiling from which oil burning lamps were suspended. The rustic design of the odd little structure made Kiana feel as if she had slipped, quite accidentally, back into the cabin where her great-great-grandmother, Adiaga Kante, might have lived.

Sitting with her feet propped up on a floral chintz footstool, Muriel Quinn tilted in her ladder-back rocker, folded her hands across her small round stomach, and began to speak.

"Your mother found me . . . right here where I am now . . . some twenty years ago. She sat on the very same sofa where you now sit and I told her the story I'll tell you. I am sorry to hear that your mother is deceased. She was a very smart, interesting young woman. I can remember how excited she was about her search and how much she wanted to unravel the mystery of her great-grandmother's disappearance."

Kiana was overwhelmed. Fate had placed her and Rex on the freeway at exactly the right moment to encounter Muriel Quinn. It was eerie to think that her mother had been in this room on a similar mission, and Kiana prayed that, this time, she would be able to bring the search to an end.

After telling Muriel what she had learned so far, Kiana started right in with her questions. "What do you know about the glass? About Magnolia Crossing? Adi and Price?"

Muriel's face relaxed as she studied Kiana and it seemed as if she were reaching far back into her memory to pull up the story. "I can tell you about Porter Glass Works because it belonged to my great uncle, Eric James Porter. I can tell you how I came into possession of what you tell me is called Soddy Glass. And I can tell you what I know about Marcela DeRossette, the Black Angel. But I can't tell you a thing about any slaves named Adi or Price or what might have become of them."

A flicker of disappointment pricked Kiana, but it quickly passed as she leveled her eyes on Muriel's face. She pressed the button to record the interview. "Let's start with your background," she said. "How are you connected to Magnolia Crossing? Or are you?"

Muriel shifted in her rocker, settling in. "Very indirectly, I assure you. I have an older sister named Portia. She and I were born in a hollow at the northernmost tip of Walden Ridge called the Sequatchie Valley. It divides the lower portion of the Cumberland Plateau into two parts . . . the eastern section is Walden Ridge. The hills. You might have called us hillbillies at one time," she said, chuckling. "Portia and I are descendants of those little children you now know were taken to the hills by Marcela DeRossette."

Kiana looked at Rex, heart pounding. "But," she began.

"I know what you're about to ask," Muriel broke in. "All the children Marcela took into the hills were white." She laughed softly, then lifted her hands, palms up. "Over time, things change," she said. "When Marcela lost the Negro children to the Freedman's Bureau, she was devastated. Leaving city life forever, she started over in a place she named Dove Hollow and swore it was the exact spot where her old plantation had been. By the time I was born, there were no traces of a plantation having been there, but the story goes that Marcela had come home."

"So Dove Hollow sprang up over the ruins of Magnolia Crossing?" Kiana whispered. "That must be why no one knows where it was."

"Appears that way," Muriel agreed.

"And where exactly *is* Dove Hollow?" Rex asked.

"Far up the ridge, deep in a valley. Difficult to find unless you grew up in these parts."

Rex pressed her to clarify. "The children Marcela took into the hills eventually intermarried with blacks?"

"Exactly. After the Civil War a lot of ex-slaves and freedmen were still living in the hills."

"I'd think the caves all through this area offered better living quarters than what some of them had on the plantations," Rex observed.

"Oh, yes," Muriel agreed. "Especially for those who had been living under brutal conditions in the lower south. After Emancipation, many former slaves were living like animals. Though free, they had nothing. They wandered the roads, starving, ragged—knowing they were not safe. So they remained hidden in the mountains, afraid to go down into the cities. When the Black Angel arrived and started up her little settlement, they did come to her—probably out of hunger, curiosity, desperation. Many eventually settled in Dove Hollow and intermingled with the white children. A village was born. I can vaguely remember people with light-brown skin living there when I was very young, but by the time I was a teenager, the place was virtually all white. I think that's one reason I left. I never felt at ease there. Never felt truly wanted."

"And your sister, Portia?" Kiana asked.

"She's still alive . . . living in Dove Hollow. You see, she is much lighter in complexion than I am. Very fair. She loved the isolated hollow and the folks there seemed to accept her as one of their own."

"What happened to your parents?"

"When Portia and I were just babies, our parents left us in Dove Hollow with an elderly aunt so they could go to work in my great-uncle's glass factory in Pennsylvania. They never did come back."

"And the glass?" Kiana prompted.

"When I made my decision to leave the hollow, Portia gave me the crates of glass. She said they had been sent to her from our great-uncle, Eric Porter, when he shut down his factory, the Porter Glass Works. Portia had all his papers and stuff from the old company. I remember when the wooden crates arrived. There were quite a few, stacked in our little cabin, taller than I was at the time. Probably still there. Portia told me the glass was valuable and if ever I needed money to sell it. It was all I took from that place when I left and to this day I've never been back."

"Is there more of it? Does Portia have any? Why did you go

into Nashville to sell it?" Kiana ran her questions together in her excitement, as she rapidly pieced the story together.

Muriel frowned, then laughed at Kiana's enthusiasm. "I am sure Portia has a lot of it. She was never known to be generous or fair. If she gave me three crates, she must have kept six. That's the way she was." Muriel removed her feet from the claw-footed stool and placed them flat on the floor. She leaned over nearly double to peer into Kiana's face. "I had no education, so I struggled to make it. A white lady I worked for left me the car. And you know it never crossed my mind that Portia had told me the truth when she said that glass was valuable. I was very desperate for cash last fall, and when I was talking to a lady in town about finding somebody who could tell me if that stuff was worth anything, she said to call Marvin Watts's Antique shop in Nashville, 'cause he was supposed to be an expert. I did. He bought it. And when I came back home I had enough money to maybe live out the rest of my days." She put her feet back up. "That is if I'm careful how I spend it."

"Can you tell us how to get to Dove Hollow?" Rex asked.

A shadow of concern passed over Muriel's face. "Sure, I could, but I don't recommend you make a visit. Those folks don't take to outsiders and frankly I think you might be in danger if you go snooping around, digging up things long forgotten. The residents of Dove Hollow don't want the color of their past thrown up in their faces, if you know what I mean. It's not a good idea to start asking a lot of questions."

"So Portia wouldn't talk to me?" Kiana asked.

"Oh, God no! She'd more'n likely run you off with that old Kentucky rifle Aunt Betty kept hanging over the fireplace. Don't go. Please."

Kiana slumped back on the sofa and cast a furtive glance at Rex, who, as if reading her mind, pressed Muriel.

"Miss Quinn," Rex said, "if you'll just tell me how to get there, I'd be very grateful. What happens after that is my responsibility. But you can see that we have to talk to Portia."

"I'd feel just awful if anything happened to you young folks." She blinked nervously, then gazed thoughtfully at the rough-beamed ceiling. "You must take my warning seriously and be careful what you say, if you find anyone willing to talk to you."

Kiana quickly dug into her bag and pulled out a small spiral notebook. After opening it to a blank page, she extended it to Muriel. "Can you draw us a map?"

Muriel studied her hands, then reluctantly took the notebook and began to sketch a series of twisted lines.

By the time Lovell Field Municipal Airport came into sight, Kiana still had not shaken the feeling that once Rex boarded his plane to Washington, D.C., she might never see him again. She worried that he would get so immersed in his family's problems that he wouldn't be able to come back to Chattanooga. Though she genuinely believed he ought to go home, she was perilously close to asking him to stay.

Her selfish thoughts flared every time she realized how much he meant to her and how much a part of her life he had become. A plea for him to stay would reveal her insecurity, and that was the last thing she wanted him to know. A short separation was not going to change their feelings, so she might as well dismiss her unfounded worries before they undercut the concentration she was going to need to hold herself together while he was gone.

Kiana was very keyed up over the information Muriel Quinn had provided and was anxious to strike out for Dove Hollow immediately. Without forbidding her to go on without him, Rex had expressed his grave concern, so she'd decided to wait for his return. Their time together was not only moving them steadily toward the origin of Soddy Russell's legacy, it was propelling them closer emotionally. Kiana hated the fact that Rex's departure would interrupt the momentum that was building.

They were working well together, like partners charged with solving an impossibly complicated crime. They played off each other's strengths, had stopped criticizing weaknesses, and were finally functioning as a team instead of the two strong-willed, independent, stubborn souls they had been when they first started out. Whether bumping over back roads, hunting and pecking their way through unfamiliar territory, or rummaging through dusty books and ledgers in courthouse basements and libraries, their respect and concern for each other's way of doing things was now demonstrated without fanfare or fuss.

Not surprisingly, Kiana and Rex found themselves talking of other research projects and she was looking forward to traveling with him on his next Underground Railroad Tour, which he said would go into Canada. Sometimes they let their imaginations run completely wild, conjuring up scenes of them—a husband-and-wife team—managing their own tour business, escorting groups of African-Americans all over the world to allow them to trace their ancestries. Though Africa might be considered the motherland of most blacks, the exotic mix of nationalities and races blended in the genes of most African-Americans could mean trips to almost every country in the world.

Kiana sneaked a peek at Rex's virile profile and smiled. The dark interior of the Blazer masked the confusing mix of joy and misery on her face. Maybe Rex's brother's problems would not keep them apart too long. From the beginning, the tour had had its twists and turns—this separation was only one more.

Yes, it had been quite an adventure, filled with land mines as if someone were deliberately hindering her progress.

Kiana thought again how oddly Marla Sherer had acted when she had called her and questioned her about the abrupt cancellation of the tour. Marla had actually gotten huffy and snapped at Kiana, saying that she was under no obligation to divulge her reasons. Kiana's money would be refunded. Case closed.

And the near-accident on the freeway? The slashing of their tires? Who was the man in the battered white van and was he still on their trail? she worried. After much discussion of who he might be and why he had targeted them, she and Rex had finally dropped their attempt to solve the mystery, but remained cautiously observant while on the road. Since their arrival in Chattanooga no more problems had surfaced, and Kiana was beginning to believe things might stay that way. It was another reason why she wanted to push on without delay.

Rex stopped at the passenger drop-off area, then shut off the engine. "I'm going to try like hell to be back tomorrow night. Plan on picking me up, okay? It might be late, but I'll call you at the hotel and tell you which flight I'll be on."

Kiana put her arms around Rex. "Don't worry. I'll be waiting for the call."

He kissed her lightly, then said, "Please be careful. Keep the hotel door bolted. Don't go off by yourself into any strange places, okay?"

Kiana leaned over and kissed him back. "I'll be fine. Lonely, but fine."

Rex slid his hand behind Kiana's neck, pulled her to him, and kissed her more fully, dispersing her earlier fears. "I'm going to miss you something awful, too," he murmured. "But wait for me to get back before you do anything . . . serious. Please?"

"Aye, aye, Captain," Kiana said in jest, putting two fingers above her right eyebrow. "I wouldn't dream of disobeying your orders."

Rex playfully grabbed her hand and removed it from her face, holding her fingers tightly. "I'm serious, Kiana. We're getting close. But I believe somebody doesn't want us to unravel this mystery."

"So it seems," Kiana replied, a sense of dread coiling inside her.

"While I'm gone, try to find out more about the house where Marcela DeRossette had her orphanage. Dig around in the library and see if you can find any more references to DeRossette or Magnolia Crossing. But *don't* take off for Dove Hollow alone."

His request grated sharply on her sense of independence, but when she saw genuine concern glimmering in his eyes, she nodded in assent.

"Muriel Quinn wasn't kidding," Rex warned. "People living in remote hollows like the one she described can be hostile to strangers who come asking questions. As soon as I'm back we'll go to Dove Hollow together and find Portia Quinn."

"I won't do anything foolish," was all Kiana could manage. Her heart twisted painfully when Rex opened the door. When he got out, she slid over into the driver's seat and kissed him through the open window.

"Gotta go," Rex said, caressing her cheek.

"Call me tonight? No matter how late?"

"You know I will. As soon as I get home."

Kiana sat watching Rex until he disappeared inside the terminal. She pushed the ache of separation down deep into her stomach and started the engine. As she swung away from the curb and headed back toward town, her thoughts returned to the most vital question that still remained unanswered.

Who *was* Soddy Russell? Had he been a light-skinned black man? A white man? Had he been related to Daniel DeRossette? Or to Price, the slave-father of her great-grandmother, Lucy Russell?

Kiana pressed a button and let the window back up, cutting off the blast of humid night air that was rushing into her face. She flipped on the radio to some easy country music and hummed along as she thought about those questions.

The mystery of how authentic Soddy Glass got to the auction block in Houston had been resolved, but the link between it and Kiana's family remained elusive. Was the answer trapped in the magnificent, purple mountains looming ominously in the distance? Or in the hollows carved among the craggy peaks? And why should the connection be of the least bit of importance to anyone other than herself?

Chapter Thirty-three

THE excitement of making such a rare and important acquisition in Joe Dawson's absence, forced Lea Bowser's concentration from the new museum brochure she was proofing. Her thoughts slid back to Kiana and Rex. She set aside her paperwork, reached for the phone, and dialed information for the number for the Colonial Inn.

When Kiana groggily said hello, she had hoped to hear Rex's sexy voice teasing her fully awake, but instead she was greeted by a nasal apology for having called so early.

"Miss Bowser?" Kiana said, surprised that the woman had tracked her down.

"I'm sorry to call so early," Lea started. "I know it's Saturday and you're probably sleeping in . . . but I couldn't resist letting you know about the outstanding pieces of Soddy Glass I am negotiating to add to the museum's collection."

Kiana jolted awake, sitting up in her bed, listening as Lea related the discussion she'd had with the woman who brought in the pieces and her subsequent telephone conversation with Mr. Dawson in New York.

"What did Mr. Dawson say when you told him?"

"Oh, he's very excited. Gave me approval to proceed. He's on his way back to Chattanooga today. The deal should be completed by Monday afternoon. I know the glass won't be ready for public viewing for quite some time, but I thought . . ." her voice trailed off.

"You'd let me see it?"

"Yes. You have such a personal interest. I think it could be arranged."

Kiana's breath was trapped behind tightly compressed lips. What was going on? Why should this glass surface now? Surely this pending acquisition had not been arranged by Muriel Quinn. Portia, perhaps? That didn't make sense either.

"Miss Bowser," Kiana said, "are you at liberty to tell me the name of the person who brought this Soddy Glass to you?"

"Hmm," Lea paused. "She didn't ask that her identity be protected. A very elegant woman, seemed a little distracted, though. She knows the value of her collection, that's obvious."

"Her name?" Kiana prompted.

"Oh! It well . . . it was a Miss Wilson. Ida Wilson. From Washington, D.C."

Kiana sucked in a gasp of a breath. Ida Wilson? As in Mrs. Bonard Wilson, she thought. Surely not! "What did the lady look like?" Kiana managed hoarsely, her voice a rough whisper.

"A very attractive African-American woman. Beautiful oval eyes, almost Asian. Fair skinned. And she has the most unusual finger-waved hair-do—not old-fashioned looking, quite stylish. Very chic."

Kiana slumped down on her back, her head sinking into the pillows. She stared at the light fixture above her in horror. Ida! How could she have come into possession of authentic Soddy Glass? Why was she in Chattanooga, of all places? What was going on? Kiana's thoughts whirled as she struggled to make sense of what Lea Bowser had just said. "Do you know how to get in touch with Miss Wilson?" Kiana asked.

"No. She didn't tell me where she's staying, but she is going to call me later this afternoon. I assume she's staying in a hotel in town, where I couldn't say."

With a jolt, Kiana threw back the covers and slammed her feet to the floor. She didn't know what the hell Ida thought she was doing, but it was clear that she didn't want Kiana to know about it. Portia Quinn! Had Ida gotten to her first? The answers to all of this must lie with her—within the records of the Porter Glass Works. Gathering her composure, Kiana spoke, "Miss Bowser. Thank you so much for calling. I certainly will get back to you about coming by to view the addition to the collection, but I have to go out of town for a few days. I'll call when I get back."

"Good," Lea said. "Do that. It's exquisite! You will be very impressed."

"I'm sure I will," Kiana replied, then added, "Miss Bowser?"

"Yes?"

"Mr. Tandy and I prefer to keep a pretty low profile while doing our research. Some people don't like publicity, or might want to remain anonymous, you know? I'd appreciate it if you didn't mention to Miss Wilson that you discussed this matter with me."

"Of course," Lea said.

"Thank you," Kiana replied, hanging up the phone. Within thirty minutes, she had showered, dressed appropriately for the trip she was about to undertake, and was on the elevator heading to the hotel garage. Crumpled in the palm of her hand were Muriel's scribbled directions to Dove Hollow.

Rex paced the pink-and-gray marble floor outside of Courtroom number 9, unable to offer any words of reassurance to his parents, who sat anxiously holding hands in silence on a nearby bench in the hallway.

After listening to the testimony of three witnesses and a surprisingly positive character reference from Lionel's high school English teacher, Rex remained cautiously optimistic that his brother would not be charged with participating in the sale of drugs. Rex's stomach churned when he thought about the videotape in his closet at home and knew he should have handed it over to Lionel's attorney, but he was not going to complicate matters by placing Lionel at the scene of the crime. If things went badly today, he'd reveal the existence of the tape, but not until after the judge had ruled.

When the bailiff poked his head into the hall and announced the judge's imminent return to the bench, Rex linked arms with his mother and father and led them back to their seats. Sitting stiffly in the first row of pewlike benches in the small courtroom, Rex held his mother's hand, squeezing it reassuringly when the judge ordered Lionel to stand.

"After listening to the testimony of all of the witnesses in the case of the Federal District versus Lionel Tandy, I have found that the evidence does not prove that the defendant was directly involved in the possession or sale of illegal drugs."

Lionel looked over his shoulder and grinned at Rex, who winked and nodded his head.

The judge spoke. "Therefore, the defendant, Lionel Everett Tandy, is to be released, but I must remind him and his parents that he will be closely supervised by the court. Lionel," the judge said, giving his defendant a stern look, "I can see exactly where you are headed if you don't make some changes. Young man, you have a supportive family and a future ahead of you if you're willing to divest yourself of all connections with gangs and walk the straight and narrow. Do you understand what I mean?"

"Yes, sir," Lionel answered.

"Good. You are released into the custody of your parents and I don't ever want to see you back in my court." He banged his gavel. "The defendant is free to leave."

The courtroom quickly cleared. Rex hugged his brother tightly, kissed his mother and father good-bye, and managed to beg off sticking around for a few days despite his mother's tearful plea. It was important that Lionel know Rex cared enough to be there for him, but Kiana needed Rex, too.

After thanking Lionel's court-appointed attorney for doing such an excellent job, Rex hurried down the courthouse steps, flagged down a cab, and headed to Washington National Airport for a three-fifteen flight back to Chattanooga.

Kiana stood at the forested rim of the valley and stared at the terraced slopes. Lush and green with vegetation, they were dotted with figures bent over hoes, squatting on haunches, or trudging wearily behind mule-driven ploughs that looked as if they could have come straight out of a Civil War museum. What struck Kiana as equally odd was that all the workers in the fields were women.

Intently focused, they pruned, chopped, tilled, and harvested as their bonneted heads bobbed up and down in a silent rhythmic dance. Not one of the women glanced her way or diverted a moment's attention from her task. Kiana shifted her gaze from one worker to another, intrigued by the sameness of the figures in the valley. They were dressed exactly alike, in long gray dresses with white collars and cuffs with dark blue sunbonnets shielding their faces. They were average in size, neither tall nor short, not heavy or slim, but as similar in build and stance as members of a family might be.

Kiana placed a steadying hand on the rough bark of a yellow poplar as a faint somersault lurched inside. She tried to catch her breath. When the paved road had run out, she had pressed ahead, guiding the Blazer over a narrow dirt trail that eventually tunneled into an impassable path too small to squeeze the vehicle through. Abandoning it, she had continued on foot, pushing brambles and thorny hawthorn out of her way, cutting tangled vines with her Swiss pocketknife in order to make her way through. The journey had been as difficult as Muriel Quinn had warned, yet Kiana was not sorry she had struck out alone and she wasn't about to turn back now. When she had burst out of the forest and seen the valley spread out below, Kiana had immediately thought of Adi and her arrival at Magnolia Crossing.

She may have passed over this route, stood at this spot, Kiana thought, calmed by the possibility that she had now discovered the hollow where Adi may have lived one hundred and forty years ago.

A shaft of sunlight filtered through the branches in mottled patchy shade, gilding the picturesque scene below. Kiana shaded her eyes and squinted at what looked like a ghost town out of the pioneer West nestled on the floor of the valley.

A scattering of bearded men in full white smocks moved methodically along the main street. They looked as weathered and gray as the old-fashioned structures, and ambled along as if time had no meaning. There were clapboard houses that had baked in the sun and shivered through chilling winters. Their sides were peeling, their roofs were sagging, their doorways were flung open to the tall bluegrass that was feathered by a very light wind.

The structures in the central area of the hollow were lined up uniformly along a main street, their roofs and storefronts connected by a raised boardwalk that ran the length of the town. There were signs designating a general store, a barber, a hardware shop, a dentist, and what appeared to be an old family cafe. In the distance, a zigzag of narrow streets contained log cabins and wood-frame buildings that spread out to the base of the sloping hillsides where spiked ridges of pines towered above the hollow.

Sitting slightly out of town, to the west, was what looked like a church with a tall bell tower and what more than likely was a school. Beyond those structures, there were shanties and low, one-story buildings, all constructed of wood, scattered about in no particular pattern across an expansive area hemmed in by the woods.

Jolted by a sensation of being whipped back in time, Kiana gulped in a swallow of cool mountain air, then strode determinedly forward.

Midway down the terraced slope she entered a stand of staked grapevines. Kiana shoved aside a verdant tangle of broad flat leaves and heavy budding fruit to find herself facing one of the women. Startled, Kiana froze in her tracks. The woman briefly looked up from the blade of her hoe. There was a slack emptiness to her chalk-white face. When she bent to resume her work, she began humming a low, resonant drone of a tune that seeped from her lips in a frightening tremor.

Kiana eyed the disinterested woman in surprise. "I . . . I'm looking for Portia Quinn," Kiana stammered, terrified more by the eerie tune and the absolute lack of emotion the woman was exhibiting than the prospect of being turned away. "This is Dove Hollow, isn't it?" Kiana asked, hoping to evoke some response. But the field worker kept her head lowered, ignoring Kiana's question. She jabbed at the earth with quick, sharp movements, sending up a spray of rich black soil that landed on Kiana's scuffed Reeboks.

After an awkward few seconds with no reply, Kiana shrugged. Forget her, she thought, stepping out of the woman's way, turning on her heel to continue down the hillside. She had only gone a few feet on the convoluted path when the sound of humming grew louder. Stopping, Kiana cocked her head to listen to a rich low drone that sounded rather like a muffled whistle. It sent cold shivers over Kiana's perspiring arms.

Spinning around, Kiana lifted her eyes to the sloping hills and saw that all of the women in the fields had stopped working and, with hoes in hand, were advancing toward Kiana.

Stunned, Kiana stared back at the chalky white faces that remained immobilized and blank inside the deep recesses of their old-fashioned sunbonnets. She silently cautioned herself not to panic, though her insides quivered like Jell-O.

Clenching the straps of her heavy backpack, Kiana turned away from the ominous sound that was gathering momentum as it pulsed through the light mountain air. As she fled toward the village, the humming grew louder. Kiana grew more tense, until she increased her pace from a moderate trot, to a slow jog, then broke into a frantic sprint.

The soft fertile soil felt like soggy sponges beneath her feet. Kiana stumbled on the winding footpath and fell, facedown, in the dirt. She jumped up, looked around, and swallowed the scream that was lodged in her chest. They were definitely after her! The sinister hum vibrated across the valley as if spiraling out of the heavens.

Kiana ran, pushing branches and vines out of her way, frantic to get to the village. Her heart thundered against her ribs. Muriel had been right. They did not want strangers in Dove Hollow. Oh, God, she lamented, what will I do if these crazy people refuse to let me out of here? Racing forward, she blindly clawed her way through a dense clump of prickly holly, cringing as its pointed leaves scraped her face.

Without looking back, she plunged unthinkingly into a wild patch of thorny raspberry bushes that snagged her skin and tangled in her hair. Tears rushed into her eyes, but she blinked them away, and tore the branches from her braids. When she reached a clearing at the foot of the hill, she stopped.

A shot rang out.

Kiana screamed and dropped to her knees. A shadow fell on the ground beside her hands and she looked up to find a heavily bearded man with a double-barreled hunting rifle held tautly against his beet-red cheek standing over her.

"Don't shoot me! Please!" Kiana yelled, dropping her backpack to the ground, lifting both hands in surrender.

The man lowered the rifle only a fraction, raked her slowly with a beady dark eye, then put it back to his face.

Chest heaving, Kiana snatched gulps of air into her lungs, desperate to gauge how much danger she was in. The man wore a floppy felt hat that was sweat stained and soiled. He had bushy gray hair extending from his temples over the lower part of his face, and it prevented Kiana from seeing much more than his angry, dime-size eyes. She remained perfectly still, allowing the grizzly mountain man to take his time assessing her.

"What you want?" he growled suspiciously, tightening the rifle to his eye.

"I'm looking for Portia Quinn," Kiana stated in the firmest voice she could summon, praying that some sympathetic soul might hear her and come rushing to her aid. "Portia Quinn's sister told me I could find her here."

There was a loud click. The mountain man cocked his rifle. "Portia Quinn's got no sister. What you want? Why are you here?"

Finding hope in the fact that he was willing to talk, Kiana rushed to clarify the situation. "I'm Kiana Sheridan . . . from Houston, Texas. I'm doing some research. It's a . . . a private family matter. I—"

The man guffawed in disgust and scraped the dirt with a shove of his boot. Kiana watched him closely as he flitted his eyes from her braided hair to her nose, to her heaving chest. "Your kind ain't got no family here." He stepped closer, holding the rifle straight out before him as if he were thrusting a bayonet. "And your kind ain't welcome here, either."

Kiana shot to her feet, then took a tentative step backward.

He advanced with a long, swift stride.

"I'm not here to make trouble," Kiana began softly. "I'd just like to speak to Portia Quinn. Only for a moment. Then I'll leave." She continued to back up, the man continued his pursuit.

"You'll leave now!" he shouted, making an upward jerking motion with the barrel of his rifle. "Now! You understand? Git outta here!"

Kiana flinched, her mind racing. From the corner of her eye she could see the women from the fields coming up behind her. In a rustle of long skirts, they fanned out and made a circle, enclosing Kiana and the mountain man in the center. They held their mud-caked hoes just as the man held his rifle, straight out in front, as if ready to charge.

Kiana kept her hands raised, but was beginning to think that the mountain man surely was a good enough shot to have killed her already if that had been his intention. The women could have overtaken her on the hillside, if they'd rushed her all at once. Apparently these people weren't ready to do her permanent harm, so Kiana decided to press her luck. "I *will* go. I will. I didn't come here to upset you. But please tell me where I can find Portia Quinn. All I want—"

A gun shot exploded above her head. Dropping once more to her knees, Kiana covered her head with her arms, bending her face to the ground.

This is the end, she thought, cowering without shame in the dirt, waiting for the next blast to rip right through her body. But what she heard was the sound of horse's hooves pounding the earth, and felt the vibrations beneath her knees. Kiana cautiously lowered her arms and lifted her chin.

In the center of the circle, towering above the mountain man on a big black mare was a tiny gnomelike woman dressed from neck to foot in ruddy brown buckskin. She wore a raccoon cap on her head. Beneath her furry cap, a weather-ravaged face peeked out, its patchwork of creases and lines finely etched into a complexion that at one time must have been as fair and creamy as the petals of a blooming magnolia.

"What's going on?" the rider shouted.

Kiana looked at the narrow planes of the woman's forehead. They sloped down to bright blue eyes that were set in hollows above aging jowls that hung slack on either side of a still vibrant face. Over her buckskin leggings, the rider wore canvas gaiters that were laced from her boots nearly to her knees, and around her neck there was a heavy gold medallion. In one hand she held a smoking pistol, with the other she clutched her reins.

"Put that rifle down, Ethan!" she hollered at the man, who immediately did as he was told. The rider urged her mount closer to Kiana, leaned over to one side, and locked eyes with her. "You lookin' for Portia Quinn?" she asked.

Kiana opened her mouth to reply but clamped it shut when the woman's anxious mare neighed loudly, then reared up on its hind legs.

Grinning, the woman quieted her horse, then sidestepped closer. "Well," she said, "I'm Portia Quinn. What the devil do you want with me?"

Chapter Thirty-four

WHEN Ida awakened on Sunday, she was shocked to see a bright ribbon of sunlight peeping through the half-closed drapes. She squinted, sat up on one elbow, and glanced at the clock beside the bed. It was 3:00 P.M. and Lea Bowser had not yet called. Ida was beginning to wonder if something had gone wrong.

The tension of waiting, coupled with the stress of her encounter with Marvin Watts had finally caught up with Ida and now she was anxious to finish her business with the museum and be on her way. By this time tomorrow the deal should be done, and once the check had been converted to cash, she was going straight to Dove Hollow to claim what was hers.

Ida stretched languidly, calmly examining a chip in her pearlized fingernail polish as she tried to envision the shock on Kiana's face when she learned she'd been outsmarted. Ida picked up the itinerary Kiana had faxed her and studied it, calculating that she and Rex ought to be in Knoxville right now, still miles away from Chattanooga. If her timing were right, Ida knew she could stay one day ahead of her meddlesome stepsister.

So far, everything had gone off just as she'd hoped, except that little incident with Marvin Watts. The fool! He should have realized she meant business and was serious about having her way.

She'd invested too much in this scheme to let him botch it now.

After a luxurious soaking in a perfumed bath in the sunken tub in her suite, Ida jolted her system back into action with a cold shower. Dressed in cream-colored silk lounging pajamas, Ida settled down on the thick quilted bedspread with her attaché case. After emptying Louise Sheridan's papers onto the bed, Ida picked up each thick yellow page and studied it carefully. She squinted at a map, comparing her stepmother's hand-drawn lines to the colorful ones on the map she had picked up at the National Car Rental stand.

"God, this place is really in the boonies," Ida murmured as she traced a lacquered fingernail over the route she would have to take from Chattanooga into Dove Hollow. It was a twisted, contorted route leading north from Chattanooga on U.S. 127 toward Walden Ridge. Then it turned west through Pikeville, until it doglegged in a northeasterly direction to a narrow dirt road at the tip of the Cumberland Plateau. From there it twisted through what looked like densely forested, hilly country into an area that appeared to be at the very end of the Sequatchie River. The directions were very complicated and the route looked dangerous, but Ida remained undaunted by the prospect of going. Even if she had to inch her way up steep mountain passes or bump along on single-lane dirt roads, she'd get there. Ida dreaded hiking the last two miles of the journey on foot more than the drive. She studied Louise Sheridan's sketch of the underground caves she'd have to enter, and shuddered. Close dark places she did not like, but this was one descent Ida knew she'd have to make.

Ida sank back in thought. Perhaps the road to Dove Hollow had been cleared, even paved by now, she mused. Louise's notes had been made over twenty years ago, things might have changed since then.

Ida took a sip from the bottle of iced Perrier that was sitting on the bedside table, then got up and went to her closet. After pawing through the silk and linen separates hanging there, and examining the soft Ferragamo sandals she had hastily thrown into her bag, she decided she'd better go shopping.

"If I've got to get down in the trenches to get this stuff, I'd better get ready for it," she decided, shoving the maps and notes back into her attaché case before locking them inside her hotel room safe.

"I don't have a sister," Portia gruffly told Kiana.

"Muriel Quinn? She's not related to you?" Kiana boldly tossed back.

Portia's mouth flew open in surprise, then she slowly drew her lips together, inhaling deeply through her nose. "Get on back to work!" she shouted at the curious onlookers. "All of you! I can take care of this." With a scathing sweep of her eyes, she repelled the women, who lowered their bonnet-covered heads and inched back in fearful respect.

With the crowd dispersed, Kiana felt shaken and wary, but not afraid of the tiny woman who lowered herself from her horse with a thud. When her feet hit the ground, Kiana calculated that Portia Quinn could not have been much taller than four and a half feet, and no younger than seventy-five. Her tiny legs were bowed beneath a barrel-shaped body and on her back she carried the weight of a dowager's hump. Kiana stared at the woman who looked more like an elfin figure from a children's storybook than the crusty mountain woman she apparently was.

"Who really sent you here and why?" Portia hissed.

"I told you, your sister Muriel gave me directions."

"You'd better leave. Now. Before something starts that I can't stop."

"Then you do admit that Muriel Quinn is your sister?"

Portia glanced nervously around. "Why do you want to know?"

Latching onto the obvious curiosity in Portia's reply, Kiana flew ahead with her request. "Muriel told me that you would have the answer to a question I've come a long way to ask."

Portia tugged her fuzzy cap more securely onto her head, and holding her horse's reins started walking away. "I don't have any answers," she said, dismissing Kiana.

The undisguised softening of Portia's tone touched Kiana. She seized the opportunity to make her point. "I must thank you for rescuing me, and I *will* go away and leave you alone if you will only answer one question." Kiana hurried to catch up with Portia, then stopped. "Please. Don't go. Just one question."

Portia didn't break her stride, which was considerably brisk in light of her age. She trotted along with her mare in tow, leaving Kiana staring after her. Her gaze remained focused on the hard dirt path that wound like a red snake away from the center of town. Kiana started off in pursuit. Before rounding a bend in the road that would have put her out of Kiana's sight, Portia stopped and looked back, scowling to see Kiana still there.

"You better go back where you came from!" Portia called.

"I can't. Not now. One question. Please?" Kiana responded, running forward. She quickly closed the stretch of dusty road that lay hard and red between them.

Portia glared at Kiana when she came to a stop. "If it'll get you out of this hollow alive, all right. What do you want from me?"

In a dry whisper, Kiana asked, "Who was Soddy Russell?"

Portia jerked her head up sharply, a flash of recognition sparking her watery blue eyes. Her shoulders recoiled in wary confusion, but she didn't turn away.

"You know," Kiana said. She waited expectantly, then stepped closer and asked the question again. "Who was Soddy Russell?"

Portia's hand shot out and landed on Kiana's arm. "Why do you want to know that?" she croaked, visibly distressed by the mention of the artist's name.

"Because Soddy Russell was my great-great-grandfather, and I believe he once lived in this valley." Firmly rooted in place, Kiana stood her ground, her arm burning under Portia's firm grip.

With the tail of her coonskin cap swaying back and forth, Portia solemnly shook her head. She appeared caught, as if trapped by Kiana's unexpected resurrection of a matter considered long dead. She licked wrinkled lips, then forced her question, "Is that what you've been told?"

Kiana nodded.

In a fluid motion, Portia let her taut face relax and she eased her hand from Kiana's arm. Slipping it around her waist, she admitted, "It's been a long time coming. I should have known you . . . or some soul like you . . . was gonna show up one day and force me to put the story back like it ought to be." Leaning heavily against the younger woman, Portia resumed her walk. "Come on home with me, child. It's not too far. And while we're walking, I want you to tell me everything you know about me, my sister, and Dove Hollow."

The house was a square wood and cement-chinked cabin, low and squat to the ground with a red brick chimney at the back that only rose three feet above the roofline. Overhead, the tangled branches of white ash, sugar maple, magnolias, and American beech formed a leafy canopy, and from every window inside the cabin, Kiana could see the tall straight trunks of the many yellow poplars that made up the cove where Portia Quinn said she had been born and lived all her life.

The mug of creamy brown liquid that Portia set down on the octagon-shaped table in front of Kiana neither looked nor smelled like tea. It had the appearance of hot chocolate, but gave off the fragrance of roasted cloves.

"What is this?" Kiana asked, picking up the thick mug, holding it under her nose to savor the exotic aroma.

"Indian chocolate," Portia replied, taking a quick sip from her own steaming cup. "Made from milk, sugar, and the creeping water avens root. A country folks' drink, I guess you'd say." Portia plopped down opposite Kiana in an oversized wing chair that was covered with a quilt. In her gnarled hands she cradled the bittersweet elixir. "It has mysterious properties," she said.

Kiana skeptically raised an eyebrow.

"Oh, yes," Portia assured her, "once you drink it, you will be able to converse with folks miles away. You'll hear them speaking in whispers."

An irrepressible chuckle rose in Kiana's throat. She sniffed again at the liquid, then hesitated before putting the mug to her lips. "Do you really believe that?" she asked.

Portia's wrinkled face lit up with a beaming smile that immediately put Kiana at ease. "Take a sip," she advised. "Sit back and listen to what I have to say. You'll find out for yourself."

Kiana did as she was told, gingerly drawing a small amount of the Indian chocolate onto her tongue. She rolled it around in her mouth, then swallowed the slightly astringent-tasting liquid. "Not bad. Rather like sugared tonic," she said, unable to give a better description of the unusual flavor.

"It will grow on you. Take your time." Portia set her cup on the table, then scooted back so far into the wide-seated chair that her feet dangled high above the warped wooden floor. "Now that you have told me what you know, I have no choice but to tell you the rest of the story."

She removed her coonskin cap and tossed it to the floor, then ran a small hand over her pale pink head that was shiny and bald in patches, obviously trying to decide where to start. After a moment, she told Kiana, "When Marcela DeRossette brought her white children to the burned-out plantation, Magnolia Crossing, she was joined, not only by many of Daniel DeRossette's ex-slaves, but by slaves who had fled into Tennessee from states in the lower South. One such slave was Marcela's brother, Thom. He came with his woman and their three children. Thom was my great-grandfather, so I am the great-niece of Marcela DeRossette. It was from her lips that the story of Magnolia Crossing was first told, and how it eventually passed on to me."

"So most of the people now in Dove Hollow are descendants of the white children and the slaves of Daniel DeRossette?" Kiana clarified.

"Exactly. But you've seen them. Now they are white." She let out a cynical grunt. "As they have convinced themselves I am, also. Generations have eroded their roots, so they have chosen to forget where they came from and don't want strangers coming around to remind them of who they are. At one time nearly every family in Dove Hollow could trace its lineage directly to a former slave."

Anxious to get to the heart of her search, Kiana prompted, "Tell me, what do you know about Soddy Russell?"

Portia lifted a hand in caution. "In good time, dear. First I must tell you who Daniel DeRossette really was."

Kiana tucked her feet beneath her and let the Indian chocolate and Portia's vivid words transport her back to the parlor where long ago Daniel DeRossette was sitting.

The lamp was burning low but DeRossette pressed on with his writing. He pulled another sheaf of paper from the pigeonhole in

his desk and hastily scribbled another notice. Adi and Price and
their baby were gone. Unless he posted public notices of a reward
for their return, his neighbors would be very suspicious. After writing his final notice, he capped his pen, turned down the lamp, and
went to stand at the window of his study.

"I hope you are far into the mountains, Adi. I hope you and
Price are so deep in the woods that no bounty hunter will ever
find your trail because the saddest day of my life would be the day
you are brought before me in chains."

He turned from the window and mounted the stairs to his
lonely bedroom on the west wing of the mansion. He took off his
jacket, his brocade vest, his French silk shirt and handed them to
Zeke, his manservant.

"Zeke," DeRossette began, "I'm very tired. Please make sure
I'm not disturbed too early."

"Yes, Massa Daniel," Zeke replied as he hung up his master's
clothes, then helped him into his nightclothes.

After DeRossette was settled in bed, he spoke to Zeke again.
"Hand me that box on the table before you leave. I have one more
letter I must write."

Zeke did as he was told, then quietly left his master propped
up in bed with a quill pen once more in his hand.

DeRossette wrote quickly, as if time were running out and his
days at Magnolia Crossing were numbered. He began the letter.

February 12, 1859

Dear Father,

I cannot rest until clearing my mind of the weighty deception
I have perpetrated on you. Cousin Rossel's ship did not capsize at
sea on its way to America. In fact Cousin Rossel is not dead. He is
here in America, helping me fight against the perpetuation of this
god-awful American institution called slavery. I wrote you once of
all the trouble I have had with a sickness on my place. I must tell
you—it was no sickness that took the slave children away, it was
Rossel. His ingenious plan to ferry the children to freedom has been
working well, but I fear the other planters in the valley are now on
to my activities. Questions are being asked and though I attend the
proslavery meetings and, I am most ashamed to admit, have had to
turn in a fugitive slave or two to satisfy the urgings of my peers, I

am afraid that it is becoming more difficult each day to keep my ruse alive. I feel obligated to let you know what is going on for it is certain that war will soon tear this nation apart. If misfortune should befall me or Rossel, I wanted you to know that we have tried, Father, really tried, to do our part to speed the eradication of slavery from this land. Arrangements have been made with a Mr. Porter in Pennsylvania to ensure that our bodies are returned home for final resting near you, if such is ever necessary or even possible.

Your loving son,
Daniel.

Kiana flinched, the pieces were rapidly falling into place. "Rossel DeRossette was Soddy Russell?"

Portia smiled vaguely, nodding. "An excellent deduction, child." She winked at Kiana. "The story that Rossel was killed in a shipwreck was concocted by Daniel to allow his cousin to fully participate in the Underground Railroad without being linked to him."

"But *who* was he?" Kiana pressed. "How could he have been my great-great-grandfather? The glassmaker? The father of Lucy?" She shook her head in confusion, then asked, "Do you know?"

"Yes. I know what happened, and why. It was handed down to me through my mother and now it's time I passed it on to you. Muriel told you our parents worked for the Porter Glass Works, didn't she?"

"Yes," Kiana replied.

"Well, so did Rossel DeRossette. That's how he financed his Underground Railroad activities. He had been trained by the gifted glassmakers in Manchester, England, and was himself a master craftsman. After secretly arriving in Philadelphia on a ship that safely navigated the Atlantic, he took the name Soddy Russell and soon hired on at the Porter Glass Works."

"Rossel DeRossette made Soddy Glass?"

"Most assuredly. It is clear that he crafted the patterns, re-creating the African Kante symbols that your great-great-grandmother, Adiaga Kante, had drawn, then slipped into the baskets of the babies Rossel DeRossette brought out of slavery."

"Yes!" Kiana exclaimed, nearly rising from her seat in excitement. "I see how it happened. The tribal designs of Princess Ijoma's ancestors were passed to Adi. The artistic rendering of the designs was executed by Rossel DeRossette, better known as Soddy Russell."

"Exactly," Portia agreed. "On his clandestine journeys into the South, Rossel helped many slaves escape, not only from Magnolia Crossing, but from plantations all through the South. People believe he gave many of his pretty glass objects to the newly freed men and women when they reached free soil. As they moved on, usually farther North or out West, they took his creations with them."

Though preoccupied with her own thoughts, Kiana commented, "I remember reading that in the homes of free black families, a Soddy Glass vase or bowl was often prominently displayed on a table or in a window." Kiana lowered her voice to a whisper, then stated, "This is all very interesting, but it still leaves a major question. Was Rossel DeRossette Lucy's father?"

"Oh, no! The slave, Price, was Lucy's father all right," Portia quickly answered. "Let me explain what happened."

Kiana sat back, sipping the fragrant Indian chocolate. She was beginning to like the taste a little more with each swallow. A heaviness seemed to come over her, a sweet pull that swept all tension from her body. With a contented sigh, Kiana leaned against the hand-tufted pillows propped along the back of the sofa and concentrated on Portia's story.

Chapter Thirty-five

ADI stumbled up the steep mountain path behind Soddy Russell, a bent arm raised to shield her face from the back-slap of low branches that he was forcing out of their way. In the other arm Adi cradled baby Lucy, a tiny bundle of newborn flesh and swaddling cloth that grew heavier with each step.

When Russell abruptly halted at the end of the pitch-black tunnel they'd been traveling for the past two days, Adi's knees buckled and she fell. It had been ten weeks since they fled Magnolia Crossing and Adi was past the point of feeling pain. While her body cried for the chance to lie down and close her eyes, if for only a moment, her mind remained charged with the prospect of making it to free soil. Sheer exhaustion numbed her, but the press of Price's hands on her back and shoulders, bringing her upright, gave her strength and reassurance. He would not let her fail. Not now. With only three hours of darkness left, they had one last gorge to pass through before daylight sheened the eastern mountain slopes.

Adi lifted her eyes to the small quarter moon that was partially shadowed with fast-moving clouds, and prayed for the strength to continue. In the near total darkness she felt, more than saw, the movement of Russell's raised hand as he alerted them to be quiet. Adi stiffened in her tracks. Price pressed close behind, allowing her to lean heavily against him to stay on her feet, to prevent her from making the tiniest sound.

The wafting howl of a wolf shattered the quiet night and Adi trembled, worried that the animal might burst from the tangled forest in which they stood and attack them—kill baby Lucy, then drag her precious body back into its lair to eat.

After a short pause, Russell started forward again, his movements through the underbrush as quiet and practiced as the stealthy creep of a Cherokee hunter coming up on his prey.

Adi managed to put one foot in front of the other, willing her aching body forward. Her mud-caked linsey-woolsey skirt dragged at her stiff legs and slowed her steps. She moved as quietly as possible along the well-worn Indian trail that was surprisingly more level and easier to travel than the rocky mountain path they had been on while skirting Mountain City.

Determined to keep up, Adi hurried along. Russell had warned her and Price that this was considered a dangerous, but necessary route. Slave hunters were known to scout the area heavily, and they knew the terrain very well. Though it was the quickest route to freedom, it was also the place where many slaves met the agents their masters had sent after them, or even death itself. The starlit passage was also the quickest route to the Cherokee Indian camp.

Adi squeezed her eyes shut for a moment, blinking away the pull of sleep, fearing she might stumble at any moment and break the momentum of their trek. Thank God Lucy hadn't been difficult to train into sleeping soundly all through the night and nursing only when they took shelter at dawn's light. Tonight Adi's breasts were painfully heavy with milk. The front of her dress was soaked. All she wished for was a few minutes to feed her baby daughter, but dared not ask Mr. Russell to break his rule and stop before morning's light.

Hugging her infant tightly to her chest, Adi focused on keeping up. For weeks they had been moving higher and higher into the big mountain range the Cherokee Indians called *Shaconage*—the place of blue smoke. It was frightening, exciting, and sometimes even beautiful—as it was on the nights when the sky glowed deep velvet blue, and was dotted with a canopy of blazing stars. Adi had been tempted many times to reach out and try to touch the brilliant North Star that guided them in their flight.

As they had moved farther and farther away from Magnolia Crossing, Adi had been comforted by the isolated protection of the creepy dense woods, while remaining well aware of how vulnerable they were to attacks from wolves, bears, bobcats, copperhead snakes, and the ruthless slave hunters.

In the quiet, lonely forests, sometimes a misty gray fog would descend like a shroud around them, providing protection all day to allow Adi a chance to scavenge for roots or tubers to eat. Price had taught her which berries, leaves, and bark were edible and which they dared not touch, and though rabbits, squirrels, wild turkeys, and possum were plentiful and easy enough to catch, Russell warned Price not to make a fire in the hills for fear of instant detection. So they had grown used to a vegetarian diet that the big black bears that roamed alongside them would have considered a feast.

By sleeping in leafy coves and dry caves during the day and traveling under the cover of darkness, they had pressed ahead, at a terribly slow pace, always afraid of the unexpected appearance of strangers. Tonight, Russell had assured Adi and Price that once they reached the end of the gap through which they now traveled, they would find a safe haven at an encampment of Cherokees who had settled in the hills to avoid capture by the government during the great removal west. Sympathetic to the plight of the slaves, the Indians welcomed many fugitives into their settlement, where the frightened runaways could eat and rest and remain until arrangements were made to get them to the next station on the Underground Railroad.

Funny, Adi thought as she willed her legs forward, that such a luxurious term like "railroad" was used to describe their manner of escape. No trains whizzing down tracks would ever carry them north, but the kindness of strangers, the protection of darkness, and the fiery urge to live free was what ferried them toward freedom.

When they were able to stop, Adi diligently searched their resting spot for a dry place to sit and nurse her baby, a place where she did not have to worry that a snake might slither into Lucy's blanket and suck the baby's breath away. A place where she could put her arms around Price and take comfort in his presence. But that was nearly always impossible. There was no time for her and Price. Now, Adi's head throbbed, her insides churned raw, and she worried that the flow of birthing blood, which had quickly stopped after Lucy's arrival, might start up again and never stop, draining her life away before she ever got to freedom.

At the crest of a steep ridge Russell stopped and looked down. The moon made a silver valley of the deep gorge that lay ahead. Adi's heart quickened. She saw no evidence of an Indian camp. Despairing, unable to hold on any longer, she collapsed and lay like a crumpled flower on the ground.

Price hurried to her side and crouched down, folding her into his arms.

Russell pointed to a spot off the path where high ferns crowded together beneath a tall fringe tree and indicated that Price put Adi there, then he set off to see if it was safe to enter the Indian camp. Slave catchers liked to snoop around the Indians, threatening to turn them over to the government for removal to the West if they didn't give the slave hunters food and information about Negroes they'd seen on the trails.

Price's jaw clenched in fear as he took the squirming bundle from Adi's arms and cradled it in his own. He urged Adi to her feet. Guiding her beneath the safety of the shaggy fringe tree, he told himself they'd be just fine until their conductor, Mr. Russell, returned.

Once Soddy Russell had disappeared over the jagged crest of rocks that dropped off into the gorge, Price took off his patched jacket, and spread it on the ground. He helped Adi to lie down on it, then he sat by her side until she fell into a black, fitful sleep.

With Adi safely asleep, Price got up and crept across the glade. He sat with his back pressed to a giant umbrella magnolia and carefully placed baby Lucy on his knees. Gently, he pulled back the swaddling cloth and stared with prideful wonder at the moonlit face of his daughter.

A tree frog croaked a sporadic mating grunt, a barred owl hooted in the bare-branched red bud across the path. Price smiled at the vivid sounds of life in the forest as he held his baby's tiny fingers in his. He leaned over and rubbed his nose across her cheek, wishing he could sing her a song. He'd learned all types of songs during his life as a slave. While picking tobacco, cotton, corn, or slopping hogs and feeding chickens, he'd sung. The words were engraved in his heart as they were in the souls of every slave. Those in bondage sang songs of salvation to help survive the heat of the day, the sting of the master's whip, the hopelessness of backbreaking sunup to sunset labor. And there were also songs sung to pass a message of warning, to relay a rare bit of good news, or to simply remind the slaves that God was watching them and one day bondage would end.

Price longed for the day when he would be able to teach such songs to Lucy, not for her to sing in bondage, but to sing as joyful reminders of the life she had been fortunate to escape. But instead of singing, Price just rocked his knees back and forth, his heart leaping when Lucy curled her perfect little mouth into a dark red rosebud, then yawned as if she had done a full day's work.

With a contented sigh, Price closed his eyes, letting his head tilt back against the rough tree trunk, and dared to let images of a future in freedom seep into his mind. His chest swelled with anticipation and impatience. How much longer would this journey last? he wondered, rocking his baby from side to side. And what would freedom feel like? The heady thought swirled through him like smoke rising from a campfire, lifting him from the ominous darkness into a light-filled vision of liberty. He smoothed Lucy's cheek with a callused finger, but jerked it back in alarm when the loud snap of a breaking branch jolted him keenly alert.

Price's head swung around. Someone or something was coming. He held his breath, listening, looking, trying to force an image from the vague shadows that filled the space behind him.

Another snap. A loud crack. The damp earth beneath his buttocks trembled. He gripped baby Lucy and flung her protectively against his chest, muffling her tiny mouth against his shirt. Price's heart pumped so fast and hard he was sure it could be heard, but he grit his teeth, swallowed his fear, and prayed that the moonlight, in which he had seen his daughter's beautiful face, would not betray him now.

Chapter Thirty-six

A YELLOW pinpoint of light the size of the flame at the end of a sulfur match flickered among the trees. Horrified, Price watched it carefully, trying to deny what he knew must be true. Another dot of fire erupted, then the unmistakable thud of horses' hooves resounded in muffled thunder.

Price jumped to his feet and raced to Adi's side. "Adi! Adi! Wake up!" He shook her brutally hard, flinching when she only groaned and, out of habit, reached up to take the baby from Price. Holding Lucy up and away from her, he whispered tightly, "There's night riders comin'! I can see their torches!" He yanked her to her feet.

Adi glared at Price in wide-eyed terror, then shifted her gaze to look over his shoulder. Two tiny golden dots were wavering in the dark, advancing nearer by the second. "God help us!" she prayed in a low broken voice.

"Come! Hurry!" Price urged, spinning Adi around. They raced for cover, crashing headlong into the wilderness.

Price expected to hear baying hounds at their heels, but the only sounds coming to him were triumphant shouts of discovery as the men zeroed in on their prey. "There they are!"

"Up ahead."

"Cut them off to the left! Don't let them get too deep in the woods."

The earth beneath Price's feet quivered under the pounding assault of the horses' hooves as the slave catchers increased their pace.

"Halt!" one of the riders boomed. "You two! I said halt!"

Price bent his head and plunged into a twisted clump of mountain laurel that had grown like a tangled barrier rimming the upper crest of the mountain. Sharp branches jabbed him in the face. He bit his tongue to keep from crying out, and took longer strides to penetrate the undergrowth.

Unable to look back and see where Adi was, he extended a hand backward, urging her to take it. "Hold onto me. Hurry, Adi! Just come on!" His low whispers were frantic urgings to keep her from lagging too far behind. Price worried that Adi might not be strong enough to keep up with him.

The rustle of horses breaking branches as they tramped through the thicket spurred Price and Adi to run faster. Darting from tree to tree, they worked themselves deeply into the forest, pausing only once to peer from behind an ancient white oak to see how close the men were. Two men sat tall in their saddles, flaming torches held high. Their faces were as white and luminescent as two pearls set against black velvet, and on their heads they wore big black hats. Across the shoulder of one of the men hung a coiled length of rope.

Price took Adi's hand and squeezed it reassuringly, then tugged her away from the tree. Creaking over twigs and dry leaves on the floor of the forest, they ran on, their hands clasped together in silent prayer.

Suddenly, Adi and Price burst from the scratchy laurel and were shocked to find themselves standing in a half-circle clearing that fronted the edge of a narrow rocky gorge. Price stopped abruptly. At their feet was an enormous black void that seemed to stretch on forever.

Adi trembled at his side. Price flung a muscular arm around Adi's waist and held her fast, glancing nervously from the gaping black hole before them to the trembling bushes that quivered in the moonlight at their backs.

Within an instant, the slave hunters burst out of the thicket in a flurry of flailing hooves, upraised rifles, and hissing, flaming torches.

Adi shied forward, cowering against Price, terrified by the wild prancing of the snorting, fiery stallions.

"Jump! Adi! Jump," Price yelled, tucking Lucy beneath his chin. He doubled over in an attempt to avoid the slap of a razor-sharp whip that one of the men snapped his way. Driven to the brink of the ledge, Price shrieked, "Jump. Adi! Jump!"

"No!" Adi screamed. "I can't! No! Price!"

The whip slashed across Price's face, its keen tip drawing blood on his cheek. He shrieked and jumped closer to the rocky ledge to avoid another lashing. But the whip came down atop Price's bare head and he screamed as loudly as he could, as if sending a message to Soddy Russell. Would he or the Indians hear his cry? Could the conductor do anything to save them?

Adi pressed herself against Price, trying to hide from the cracking bullwhip that was now directed toward her. When it hit her, she shrieked and spun around, eyes widened in horror as she faced her attacker.

Price reached for Adi, but he tripped and lost his footing. The earth seemed to have opened up to swallow him whole.

"Adi!" he yelled. "Adi!" He had one hand outstretched toward her, the other was wrapped around Lucy. He felt himself falling and grabbed a tuft of bramble bush jutting from the side of the mountain. It quickly gave way. Price looked for Adi, screamed, then let go, careening toward the rocky soul of the deep black hole below.

"Price!" Adi started toward him, but was stopped when the whip split the back of her dress, then wrapped its snaky coil about her upper torso.

Price hit the bottom of the gorge just as he heard the shattering blast of a shotgun. He rolled over onto his back. Icy water in the cold mountain creek rushed over him, stinging his face with a spray of rock and gravel, washing the blood from his cheek. His eyes fluttered open. He saw torches still flickering at the top of the gorge. He heard guttural laughter ring out.

A spasm of hatred convulsed inside Price. His body grew

numb, but his soul was aflame. Lying in the cold water, he whispered Adi's name over and over until he was nearly hypnotized. Paralyzed with grief, frozen by the cold water, he lay flat on his back unable to move, but when the soggy little bundle clutched in his arms began to squirm against his chest, Price finally dragged himself and Lucy to the bank where he broke down and cried.

At daybreak the hungry wail of his daughter forced Price's eyes wide open. His mind jerked back into consciousness. Lucy was soaking wet, cold as ice, and demanding her mother's milk. Price tucked the baby inside his shirtfront and clawed his way up the sheer drop-off to stand on unsteady legs.

A foggy mist hung over the clearing, but Price gasped aloud at what he could see. There was a body crumpled at the edge of the cliff. Price set Lucy under a nearby tree and crept closer, heart beating wildly as he prepared himself to look down upon the face of his beloved Adi. The mist curled in wavy drifts, then separated. Price stopped and gazed down at the form, immediately realizing that the stone-cold corpse at his feet was that of their conductor, Soddy Russell. He had a gaping gunshot wound in the front of his head.

Price's blood rushed through his veins like boiling water. He took off running, going back to the main trail, into the cove, over to the western side of the mountain where the worn Indian trail fed up into the hills. He found nothing. There were no signs of Adi or what may have happened to her.

Hollow with grief, Price returned and knelt beside Russell's body. His face was stained with silent tears and his mind was so thick with loss and confusion, he barely heard Lucy's demanding cry.

If he returned to Magnolia Crossing how could he possibly get Adi out again? If he went on without her how could he possibly live with himself?

Price bent in sorrow above the slain man as if willing Soddy Russell to tell him what to do. Lucy's thin whimper rose to a screeching wail, forcing Price into action.

"Please, forgive me, Mr. Russell," he whispered, reaching over to remove the conductor's coat. When he discovered a sheaf of papers, Price removed them and stared blankly at them, wishing Adi were there to tell him what they said, but they looked important enough to prove helpful, so he stuffed them into his shirt pocket.

After freeing Lucy of her soaking-wet quilt, Price wrapped her in the dead man's jacket, calming her enough to bring her wail to a whimper, and coax her tiny thumb into her mouth.

Next, Price took a pouch of tobacco, a pocket watch, and a handful of silver change from Russell's body and put the items in his pocket.

"You'd a told me to do this, Mr. Russell," Price muttered, "you'd a wanted me and Lucy to go on to freedom." He wiped a rush of tears from his eyes, then dragged Soddy Russell's stiff body into the thick underbrush and covered it with a pile of branches. "We're gonna make it. For you. For Adi. Yes, sir, me and my Lucy *will* live free."

Price removed his baby girl from the bed of dry leaves where he'd left her, took a deep breath, then fled down the steep side of the rocky gorge, praying the Indians would be friendly.

Kiana wiped a tear from her cheek as she stared out the window, trying to digest Portia's revelations. The sky was fading into a light purple haze. Night would soon be upon them. She had been so absorbed in listening to the tale, she had forgotten about Rex, about meeting him at the airport, about how black the night could be in the country—as inky black and impenetrable as tar. If she hurried she might be able to get out of Dove Hollow while it was still barely light, but how could she leave now? With so many unasked questions? Impossible, she decided, wiping a bead of perspiration from her upper lip.

"So . . . the fugitive slave, Price, assumed Soddy Russell's identity," Kiana finally murmured.

"Yes," Portia said. "After living three months among the Cherokees, Price decided Lucy was old enough to travel with him, so they left the safety of the Indian camp and started on the last leg of their freedom journey. He made it to Virginia, and from there he was assisted by station masters on the Underground as far as Pennsylvania. His goal was to get into Canada, but Lucy fell ill and he was forced to stop at Centerville near the Pennsylvania-Ohio border."

Kiana shivered. "That's where I was born, where my grandmother, Lucy's daughter, still lives today."

Portia let a smile curve her lips as she put them again to the rim of her cup. "Yes, Price settled there, but it was not long before he had second thoughts. In 1862, he was reported to the U.S. Marshall as a possible fugitive. The marshall and two bounty hunters came to his tiny shack one day and questioned him. Many Northern marshalls were not very keen about trying to enforce the Fugitive Slave Act, and truly wanted no part of the nasty business of trying to return slaves to their masters. The marshall in western Pennsylvania was more friend than foe to the runaways, so when he discovered the papers Price had taken off Soddy Russell, he didn't question them. The marshall declared Price to be a free man who worked as hired labor at the nearby Porter Glass Works. The disgruntled bounty hunters left the area and never bothered Price again. Feeling safe as long as he used the name Soddy Russell, Price stayed put, built himself a house in Centerville, and lived there the rest of his life. Everybody in the little town believed his story that he had been a glassmaker at the Porter Glass Works, and Price, aka Soddy, became well-known and respected in the area. And that's how it happened," Portia concluded. "I guess you already know the rest."

Kiana sat stunned, absorbing Portia's tale, then turned questioning eyes on the woman. "The rest? Well, no, I don't. What happened to Adi?"

A flicker of a frown touched Portia's brow. "As for Adi, my great-aunt, Marcela DeRossette, told my mother that she had been standing by the east gate of the property the night the bounty hunters brought Adi home in chains. From her neck to her hands to her feet. It was a very sad day."

A flush of apprehension shot through Kiana. "She was whipped?"

"Worse," Portia replied. "Let me tell you what happened."

With her head lowered, Adi forced one foot in front of the other, watching blood seep from beneath her toes and mix with the hard-caked mud on the tops of her feet. She had no more tears to shed, and as she blinked dry eyes to ward off a pesky swarm of horse flies, she struggled to stay upright. With her hands chained and neck collared, she felt as if she were already dead, and as long as Lucy and Price remained lost to her, she had no will to live.

Where are they, she wondered, hastening her step when the leather cord tethered to her waist tugged her forward. Surely Price was alive. He was too strong and proud to have died, besides he had to take care of Lucy now. Adi tried to picture her baby and her lover, but her mind was so tired, so confused, that their images escaped her no matter how hard she concentrated on summoning them up. In a panic, she looked skyward, but was unable to find their faces in the swirl of clouds overhead.

When Adi lowered her face to the horizon again, there was Magnolia Crossing—spread out below her as it had been the first time she set eyes on the place. The closer she came to the big house, the more determined she became not to shed a tear or beg Master Daniel for forgiveness.

Let him whip me, brand me, tie me to a tree in the sun, she thought, but I'll never stay. Now that I know the secret tunnel out of this valley, I will never rest until I see Price and my baby again.

As they proceeded down the hill toward the big house, Adi concentrated on her memories of sitting under a canopy of stars with baby Lucy at her breast, of Price at her side, of the sense of family she'd experienced, ever so briefly. No matter what happened those memories could never be taken away.

On the property, Marcela rushed out the back door of the big house and positioned herself beside the east gate. Soon, other slaves came out of their cabins and gathered in clumps to watch Adi's arrival. Stationed in front of the house on the circular bricked drive were the saddled horses and open buggies that had brought neighboring farmers to the plantation. They were anxious to watch Daniel DeRossette punish his runaway slave.

At the clearing between the cookhouse and the barn, the bounty hunters stopped. Within seconds, Daniel DeRossette appeared, followed closely by a dozen or so men.

"You found her!" he shouted, rushing forward. He had a bull-whip in his right hand.

Adi froze. It was an awful sight, seeing Master Daniel carrying such a cruel weapon. She backed up, but one of the hunters pushed her forward, propelling her to her knees in the red dust.

"Take this, Tom," DeRossette said as he handed the whip to the overseer. "Thirty lashes. Yes. That should teach her a lesson. Go on. Whip her," DeRossette ordered. "And make each lash truly count."

Boldly, Adi looked her master dead in the face, but now it was he who averted his eyes.

"Hang her!" one of the planters shouted, hurrying into the center of the circle of men. "We need to show these niggers what will happen if they run off like that! Hang her!"

DeRossette whirled around. "No. There will be no hanging on Magnolia Crossing."

Another of the men grabbed DeRossette by the arm. "And why not? Why should your darkies be treated special?"

"I've never supported lynching, Mr. Charles. You know I have spoken against that since the day I came here."

"Yes," Mr. Charles agreed. "And I've always suspected that you sympathized too damn much with the lot of the niggers. Now I see it's true."

"That's right!" a voice shot from the rapidly enlarging crowd.

"Not true," DeRossette cried out in a panic. "I will punish her! Whip her. Brand her, if you will, but there will not be a hanging here!"

Several men surged forward and grabbed Adi. They yanked her from the bounty hunters, tore off the neck irons, then stood her on an overturned crate.

"Hang her! Hang her!" they chanted.

Adi screamed and tried to pull away. DeRossette extended both arms and placed himself between Adi and the riotous gathering. "You will not hang this girl." He looked from the enraged planters to his slaves, then eased backward to stand beside Adi. "I have tried to be a fair master. A human being, not a monster like so many of you standing here now. The Negroes are not animals, not chattel —but labor, no more, no less. I will never be able to see my blacks in the inhumane light that you evil men do, and your accusations against me are neither warranted nor fair. I am not afraid of any of you." He lowered his voice and focused on Marcela. "And I have hoped that my slaves have never been afraid of me."

When he finished, Marcela broke into a howling sob, for the end was surely in sight. Ofia stood with her mouth hanging open, her thin arms wrapped over her chest, and Rusty, the old man, just nodded his head.

"You traitor!" A planter stepped forward and knocked De-Rossette to the ground. "Examples need to be set. Niggers need to have the fear of God placed in their souls, and there's only one way to do it. A lynching." The man placed his foot on DeRossette's chest. "And that goes for nigger lovers, too."

A roar of approval shot from the vigilantes. The slaves raised their voices in abject horror. The white men cried out for vengeance. The black men prayed that the life of their reluctant master be spared.

DeRossette struggled to get up, but was pressed back to the ground by his neighbor's polished boot.

"Let's get on with it," one man shouted.

The tallest of the two bounty hunters tossed his length of rope over the lowest limb of the old white oak that shaded the grounds where the slave children played. The other followed suit. Once both ropes were swinging, hangman's knots were tied. Adi was left standing on the tall wooden crate, DeRossette was set upon a bounty hunter's horse. Ropes were quickly placed around their necks, and as the goading cries and sorrowful wails surged from the crowd and split the afternoon, Adi screamed and screamed and screamed, as if purging herself of life—as if she could deprive the white men of the satisfaction of taking it from her.

The box was kicked from beneath her feet. The horse was slapped on the rear. The thick ropes snapped tautly into place as the two bodies fell, and the cracking sound of breaking bones could be heard above the fury.

Then all hell broke out. Before the planters had time to get their rifles, the slaves broke ranks and rushed the men, using machetes, pitchforks, clubs, whatever they could get their hands on, piercing, chopping, slashing at the men until blood covered the dusty clearing and bodies fell to the ground.

Several wagon loads of other planters arrived and soon shots rang out. The slaves scattered, some running off toward the woods, others toward the main house with torches in their hands. Within seconds, the verandas all around the house were belching smoke and flames.

Desperate to flee the destruction and save her life, Marcela gathered as many of the slave children to her as she could and fled to the cellar door. She opened it, then looked around before descending into the underground cave. From where she stood all she could see was red—blood staining the red earth, fires raging through the house, the barns, the smokehouse, and even the pitiful corridor of slave cabins.

"God help us all," she muttered as she and the children disappeared beneath the trapdoor.

Fire raged at Magnolia Crossing for days . . . until every scrap of the place was burned down to dust, and every slave was either dead or had escaped. The uprising was what destroyed Magnolia Crossing and forced Marcela from the valley.

"How horrible," Kiana said, images of Adi and DeRossette swinging from lynching ropes burning in her mind. She could imagine the stench and confusion that must have reigned—the gruesome sight of corpses scattered over the land, of charred flesh, and smoldering ruins. "Marcela went to Chattanooga?" she managed to ask.

"Yes, and there she stayed until returning to start the settlement here at Dove Hollow." Portia drummed her stubby finger on her knee, took a deep breath as if clearing away the unwanted memories, then looked up and winked at Kiana. "I'll bet I know what your next question is. Where is the glass? Eh?"

"Yes. Where?" Kiana put a finger to her chin, waiting.

Portia slipped out of her chair and went to the window, assessed the twilight, then turned back to Kiana. "Surely, you'll be staying the night," she stated more than asked.

"Looks like I don't have much of a choice," Kiana answered, doubting she would be able to find the path back to the Blazer even in daylight. She wished she could call the hotel and leave a message for Rex, but, not surprisingly she supposed, Portia did not have a telephone.

"Good," Portia said. She came back to stand beside Kiana and quietly gazed at her guest. "Tomorrow we will take a short trip."

Kiana glanced up in question. "A short trip? Where?"

"You want to know what happened to the glass Rossel De-Rossette created?"

"Yes, of course."

"Then I will take you to a place where you will find the answers to all of your questions, though you may not be pleased by what you learn."

Chapter Thirty-seven

AFTER waiting forty-five minutes in the passenger pickup area, Rex went back inside the terminal and telephoned Kiana. When she didn't answer, he returned to his spot next to the sliding glass doors, stood there for thirty minutes, then left.

During the cab ride to the hotel, Rex stared gloomily out the window. The ebullient mood created by the dismissal of Lionel's case, coupled with his anticipation of seeing Kiana had made the long trip easier to bear, but now he was fearfully worried. What if the man who had attacked them in Nashville had followed them to Chattanooga? Had he seen Rex kiss Kiana good-bye, then made her his next target? A knot of uneasiness settled at the back of Rex's throat and he struggled to keep control of his emotions.

It was nearly midnight—too late for Kiana to be out of the hotel unless she had had car trouble on her way to the airport. He searched both sides of the highway for any sign of an accident, wondering if she had even gotten his message.

Fear of losing Kiana gripped him. She was an attractive, passionate, complex woman, but how well did he really know her? She was free to come and go as she pleased, but he had to believe she would not have deliberately left him stranded. For the past two days he had been consumed with thoughts of the future, and those thoughts always included her.

The ferocity of his attraction to Kiana made him physically ache to hold her in his arms. Images he'd never forget stayed with him—Kiana in his arms on the dance floor, clinging to him in her hotel room, trembling beneath him on the floor of the tent.

He had tried calling her twice from the airport in Washington, and once from St. Louis while waiting for his connection. Each time he had dropped his quarter into the pay phone, his heart had raced and his palms had gone sweaty as if he were an adolescent making his first date.

Rex felt a thread of apprehension begin to tighten. What was going on? What had been so important that it had kept her from meeting him?

At the hotel, Rex tentatively unlocked the door. The drapes were drawn and it was pitch black inside. Since no light had been left burning, Rex assumed Kiana must have been gone since early in the day. After flipping on the light, he saw that her suitcases were still there. Her cosmetics and toiletries remained strewn over the bathroom counter. At the desk, he snapped on the small lamp. No blinking message light on the telephone. No message scribbled by the phone for him. He examined the papers and notes Kiana had left piled there, picked up the spiral notebook in which Muriel had drawn the map to Dove Hollow, and flipped through it once. Then twice. The map was gone. Small pieces of shredded paper were still in the wire coil, indicating that the last page had been ripped out. In a panic, he shoved the clutter off every surface. No car keys either.

Rex went to the window and yanked the drapes back. The Blazer was nowhere to be seen. The roller-coaster rush of emotions that had coursed through him all evening, gathered into a cold lump of reality, numbing him. He jammed his fists to his hips, focusing on the slumbering black mountains in the distance. If Kiana was in Dove Hollow, there was no way he'd find her tonight.

Marvin Watts balanced the receiver of his cordless phone between his ear and his shoulder, using his good hand to raise the green shade covering the front door of his shop. Sunlight flooded the room, but did little to lift his spirits. After a visit to the emergency room and a night spent popping pain pills every three hours, he wished he'd stayed at home, but Sundays were usually pretty busy days in his shop and he needed every dime he could make.

Halfheartedly, he listened to the nasal voice on the other end of the line. "Yes. This is Marvin Watts."

"Lea Bowser here . . . the assistant director of the Houston Museum in Chattanooga."

Watts's mood quickly lightened. If he had, or could locate, whatever the museum was looking for, he might make himself a handsome commission. "Hello. Yes, I remember you, Ms. Bowser. I helped with that lovely Queensware exhibit you have."

"You certainly did, and once again, I need your help."

"What can I do for you? Something in particular you're trying to locate?"

"Not exactly. I just need some information."

"Yes?" Watts replied, listening closely as Lea Bowser told him about the pending acquisition of Soddy Glass. She had a letter of authentication from him and wanted to verify that he had examined the collection.

Watts stiffened, furious that Ida was already trying to strike a deal. Why the hell hadn't she at least gone out of state? he wondered.

Lea continued talking as he hurriedly thought about what to do.

"Do you have the glass at the museum?" he asked.

"No," Miss Bowser replied. "But as soon as Mr. Dawson arrives, we plan to move forward. Quickly."

"Hmph," Watts grunted, examining the strips of gauze that crossed the bullet wound in his palm, the back of his hand, and were wrapped tightly all the way up to his wrist. Yes, Ida had definitely gone too far this time. "There must be a mistake. I never authenticated that glass. In fact I don't think I've seen any Soddy Glass in . . . oh, four or five years. If I were you, I'd be careful. What did she say her name was?"

"Wilson. Ida Wilson."

"Well," Watts breathed, a sly grin splitting his face. "Better stall on buying anything from Miss Wilson until you have time to check her out."

Kiana jumped down first, then Portia dismounted, leaving the brown mare heaving after a spirited trot. Portia reached up and unstrapped a bulging saddlebag and tossed it to the ground. After taking the horse's reins, she led her mount to a shady stand of white pines, tethered her securely, then gave her a cube of sugar.

Kiana walked a few yards deeper into the tall mountain grass and stopped at a barrier of oaks and pines that was bordered with blooming rhododendron. She assessed the tangled, overgrown acreage that extended from where she stood up the steep incline that led up to the rim of the valley. High above, she saw a ring of flowering dogwood swaying in the wind. Chickadees chirped in the trees nearby and a red squirrel scampered up a straight tall pine.

"This is it?" she asked Portia, unable to see any traces of the old plantation.

Portia came up behind Kiana and stopped. "Yes. This is the spot where the main house used to be." She pulled on her leather gloves, tromped past Kiana, and pushed aside a clump of prickly brambles. Pointing into the dense undergrowth, she said, "In there—about twenty feet—is the opening to the old cellar . . . and the tunnels that were under the big house." She plunged into the brambles, beckoning Kiana to follow. "Over here. Yes." She leaned down and pulled aside a mass of creeping crossvine that had blanketed everything in its path with its broad green leaves.

Kiana edged closer, and stared in awe at the wide plank trapdoor that was set with huge rusted hinges. There was an open padlock hooked to one side of a thick metal latch.

"This is it," Portia said. "The door to the cellar. When Muriel and I were young, we used to open it and dare each other to venture down into the cellar, but we were too scared to do it. Our aunt Marcela told us that one of the tunnels leads straight up the wall of the valley and will take you all the way to the forest atop that ridge." She pointed skyward as she spoke.

"I read about such a passage in my mother's book," Kiana said. "So you've never been down there?"

"Not exactly," Portia said, letting go of the bushes. "But I paid a man five dollars to put the glass I inherited from my uncle down there." She urged Kiana out of the thicket.

"What happened to him?" Kiana asked.

"Dead. He's been dead for many years. But he did tell me that he saw a deep lagoon in there, and spanning it was an arch of limestone rock—rather like a bridge. In order to get out of the valley using the tunnel, he said you'd have to cross that stone bridge and it looked real fragile."

Portia and Kiana returned to a grassy spot beneath a basswood tree. Sinking down, they sat in silence for a few moments drinking in the tranquillity of the setting, listening to the buzzing bees that were hovering around a clump of sweet yellow jasmine.

Portia pulled off her raccoon cap and rubbed it between both hands. "You want to know about the glass?"

Kiana nodded.

"All right." Portia plucked the bloom off a pink lady slipper and twirled it as she spoke. "One of the reasons Daniel DeRossette chose this unlikely place to settle was to take advantage of the underground caves and natural passageways in the floor of this valley. He used the caves for storage, but also—and as you now know—the tunnels provided excellent routes for his cousin to use as he helped slaves escape."

Kiana's heart raced. "Why wasn't Muriel told all of this?"

"When she left Dove Hollow, I kept most of the pretty glass for myself. I was just plain greedy and did not want my sister to benefit from what may now be lost forever." She clucked her tongue in a mocking gesture of regret. "You know what greedy people wind up with, don't you? Nothing. Nothing at all."

A puzzled expression drew Kiana's brows together, but Portia lifted her hand in a choppy wave. "My crates of glass are probably still down there. Time passed and I grew old. Why try to go back in there? I asked myself a hundred times. I have no need of money. I'm eighty years old, Kiana." She shook her head. "I'm glad Muriel was able to benefit from her share, but I decided a long time ago to go to my grave with my crates of glass exactly where they belonged . . . with the ghosts of Magnolia Crossing. But . . . here you are." She grinned. "And here I am again."

A shudder swept over Kiana at the prospect of discovering not only the tunnel that Adi had taken out of the valley, but the cache of Soddy Glass she had set out to find.

"I want to go down there," Kiana told Portia, expecting the old woman to hit her with a barrage of protestations.

But Portia beamed her approval. "I was hoping you'd want to." She gripped Kiana's arm. "You're young. I don't have the legs or the strength to make the trek, but if you are willing, I'll help." She got up and went to the saddlebag, opened it, and took out a coil of thick rope, two battery-operated lanterns, some candles, a small hand shovel, and a pair of sturdy leather gloves.

"You came prepared, didn't you?" Kiana said with a laugh, tugging her Houston Rockets cap securely on her head.

"Oh, yes," Portia said as she tied the gear together in a bundle. "I knew you were the adventuresome type when I first met you in the road. You've been sent to help me rescue my treasure." She stopped and winked at Kiana. "Well, your treasure, now, young lady. All of this belongs to you, and I know you will find a way to share your legacy with others."

Kiana took one of the lanterns from Portia and flipped it on. Adi's flight from Magnolia Crossing was instantly recalled in a premonitory flash. What would she find below the ground? In the long lost passageway to freedom. Kiana's breathing grew fast and a foreboding filtered through her as she lifted the cellar door and peered inside.

"What's it look like down there?" Portia said from behind.

Kiana lowered the lantern into the dark space. "The steps appear to be rotted out in spots, but most are still intact. Kind of steep, but I think I can manage."

"Here," Portia said, handing Kiana the heavy bundle. "Toss this down first."

Kiana threw the gear to the bottom of the stairwell, then gingerly placed one foot on the first broad plank to test it. Holding onto Portia's hand, she put the other foot on the entrance step and let the staircase bear the full weight of her body. "Seems stable," she said.

"Be careful," Portia warned.

"These steps are fastened together with iron studs. Probably as sturdy as they were when the DeRossette slaves built this staircase," Kiana replied. "Besides, they've been protected from the weather all these years." She turned Portia's hand loose. "It's fine. Stay there," she advised. "I'm going down. Just to the foot of the steps and look around."

With her lantern held high, Kiana began her descent. The boards on the second and third steps creaked loudly, but did not shake. On the fourth plank, there was a groaning, splintering sound. On the fifth, Kiana was jolted fiercely. She froze as the supports beneath the structure abruptly shifted.

"Whoa!" Kiana shouted. The entire staircase tilted to one side. "This is not as sturdy as it looks."

"Come back up!" Portia shouted. "Please, don't go any farther."

Kiana pressed a hand flat against the cool wall of the cellar to steady herself and waited for the staircase to settle. Breath trapped in her lungs, she stared anxiously into the shadowy pit below. "It's okay now! I think it's settled. I can see the floor."

"Don't go on," Portia shouted. "You might not be able to get back up."

"Yes, I will. Don't worry," Kiana yelled back, determined now to get to the bottom. She moved a step lower. The structure held. She took another step, then called back to Portia. "It's not shaking anymore. I'm going all the way down." She held the lantern straight out in front of her, sheening the ebony shadows yellow. The passage to the cellar was hung with cobwebs, but it was dry, and she could see the edges of a clearing at the bottom of the stairs.

Kiana slid her free hand along the wall as she crept down. Blood pounded in her temples as she thought about the slaves who had traversed this final passage so long ago. Tentatively, she inched along, taking careful steps, making her way halfway to the bottom before she felt the structure begin to tremble again.

Kiana screamed.

The plank beneath her feet broke in two, plunging her straight down between its jagged edges. The back of her shirt caught on an iron peg, and there was a loud rip as the fabric tore away. Kiana shrieked in pain as her bare back scraped against raw timber.

The intricate understructure of the stairwell rapidly closed in on top of her with sharp blows to her head and shoulders. Falling boards clattered to the floor, sending up an explosion of dirt, musty rotted wood, and lethal dartlike splinters. The gritty blast roared upward and stung Kiana's face. Thick grime filled the inside of her nose.

"Kiana!" Portia shouted, reeling backward, one arm flung over her eyes to protect them from the cloud of dust that shot up. "Kiana! Answer me! Are you hurt?"

Entangled in the rubble of the collapsed stairwell, Kiana was able to scream her reply. "Portia! I'm scraped up, but I'm okay! Stay back!"

"Oh, my God! Hold on," Portia called, fanning at the dusty air to stare in horror at the heap of splintered wood piled in the cellar like a funeral pyre. Her eyes widened. "Don't move. Please don't move. I'll go get some of the men from the village to get you out. Can you hear me? Kiana?"

"Yes! I hear you," she replied. "Hurry."

Kiana coughed violently, then put a hand over her mouth to keep from inhaling more grit. Miraculously, the lantern had survived the fall and was lying at the bottom of the pile of wood, its dim yellow-white glow illuminating the dusty space. She assessed her predicament, determined not to panic. She was alive. Nothing hurt too badly. And Portia had gone for help.

Kiana tried to move, but pieces of rotted wood covered her chest and arms, burying her up to her neck. With a shove, she pushed some boards out of her way, gripped what was left of the main beam under the stairwell, and hoisted herself upward. Gingerly, she balanced herself on a sturdy piece of wood that was protruding out of the rubble. She sat with her feet dangling above the cellar floor and gazed in wonder at what lay below.

At the foot of the stairwell was a spacious circular clearing. Dark archways, like doors, were cut into the cellar walls. The tunnel openings, she thought, noticing that the cavities were no more than three to four feet high, roughly carved, and were hung with thick drifts of gray spiderwebs. In front of the largest opening, which faced to the north, there were two huge trunks. Their brown leather coverings had rotted away in patches and lay curled like ragged blankets thrown over their humpbacked lids.

Kiana gauged the distance from her perch to the floor, squeezed her eyes shut, then let go. With a thud, she landed on the earthen floor, and the impact sent a slash of pain across her right shoulder directly into her neck. She crumpled to the ground and lay very still, nearly paralyzed by the searing jolt. At last she eased to her feet and crept toward one of the trunks.

The domed trunk was not easy to open, but Kiana grasped the rusty lock and tugged until it sprang free. Startled, Kiana stared at the contents, shocked by her discovery. Another sharp pain gripped her shoulder. A streak of fire flashed up her neck into the base of her skull and exploded behind her eyes. Kiana fell to the floor, unconscious.

Chapter Thirty-eight

REX pulled his rented Chevy Geo off the road and laid his forehead on the warm steering wheel. A fast-moving tractor trailer truck whizzed by and caused the tiny compact car to quiver in its wake. He looked up, squinted at the sign indicating his arrival at Crossville, and tried desperately to recall the curve of the lines, the highway numbers, and the names of the towns Muriel had drawn on her map.

He could remember seeing highway numbers 30, 127, and 101 on it, but after rushing up and down each one for the past two hours, he'd come across nothing that resembled the dirt road turn-off that Daisy had said would lead to Dove Hollow. He'd driven through Pikesville twice and had asked for directions from six different people, only to be met with blank stares. No one had ever heard of the place.

In frustration, Rex silently cursed Kiana for going off without him, while his heart pounded in fear that she might be in real danger. Muriel's warning echoed in his head as he pulled the directions to her house from his pocket. If he planned to find Kiana, he had no choice. He'd have to ask Muriel for help.

After making a U-turn in the deserted intersection, Rex stepped on the accelerator and raced down the highway, still puzzling over what had prompted Kiana to act so recklessly. It was a mystery to him, but one thing was certain—if Kiana were still in Dove Hollow, something must have gone terribly wrong.

It was 5:30 when the call Ida had been waiting for all day finally came through. She had left a message for Lea Bowser hours ago, and at last the woman was calling her back. Ida sank onto the hotel bed and zapped the evening news into silence.

"Yes, Ms. Bowser. This is Ida Wilson." She tightened her lips as she listened to what the museum director had to say.

"Could you bring the collection by this evening?" Lea Bowser asked.

Ida broke into a broad smile. "Of course. I take it Mr. Dawson has approved the acquisition?"

The phone was silent for a moment, then Lea spoke. "Not exactly."

"What's wrong?" Ida pressed her hand to her stomach.

"Nothing, I assure you. But I'd like to have an independent evaluation of the authenticity of the glass."

"Why?" Ida snapped coldly.

"Standard procedure. I talked to Marvin Watts, but our policy is to have our own appraisers make the final authentication."

Ida tried to analyze the tone. Marvin Watts? she thought. What lies did he tell to get back at me for putting a hole through his hand? She knew she'd better play it cool or she'd be in worse trouble than she was. "An independent evaluation?" she replied. "Why, of course, when?"

"This evening, if possible. I have an appraiser here now. He can start immediately."

Ida dared not overreact or underestimate the risky situation she was in, so she calmly told Lea Bowser, "No problem. I'll bring the collection right over. I can be there in half an hour."

"Thank you," Lea replied.

"*No.* Thank you," Ida tossed back in an icy, calculating voice. Lea Bowser's call had saved her from walking into a trap. If anyone found out she'd been palming off reproduction glass as the real thing, all her dreams would be ruined. She'd always thought she could afford to wait to get her hands on Portia's secret treasures until the old woman died. But now she had no choice—she had to come up with some original Soddy Glass—and fast.

After hanging up the phone, Ida stripped off her silk caftan and pulled on the clothes she'd bought at the mall that morning—black denim jeans, a heavy cotton parka, sturdy ankle-high boots, and a black scarf that she draped around her neck. She jammed the rope and flashlights into a Neiman Marcus shopping bag, then frantically stuffed the rest of her clothes into her suitcases. When everything was packed, she called the front desk to inform them that she was checking out.

"No. I don't need any help with my bags, but could you have the valet bring my car around? I'd like to get on the road before dark."

"Pass Cane Creek Falls, Rockhouse Falls, go south on 285 to 101," Rex muttered as he tore away from Muriel's yard. "At the Cumberland-Bledsoe County line, head east and stop at the second dirt road. It'll be on the northern side of the valley, opposite from the spot where Kiana would have entered."

Rex grit his teeth as he sped toward Dove Hollow. Muriel said he would approach the isolated hollow from the upper rim of the valley. There was an old Indian trail that the Cherokees had used to go down into the valley from the north. After entering the gorge he was to look for a small waterfall. Behind it was the entrance to a tunnel, which Muriel had said would lead him under the site where the big house used to be, but she warned him not to use it. He should go across the fields and circle back to the center of town and to ask for Portia Quinn.

Kiana's failure to return that morning had Rex in a frantic state. Tossing aside Muriel's warning, Rex made up his mind to try the tunnel. It might be dangerous, but it would be the fastest way to find Kiana.

Though it was still light, Rex flipped on the headlights and hunched determinedly over the steering wheel, glad he had had the foresight to remove his camping gear from the Blazer before he left for D.C. With the aid of his Coleman lantern and his oversized flashlight, he hoped he'd be able to find the back passageway into Dove Hollow before it got too dark.

The first thing Kiana heard when she opened her eyes was the faint sound of water dripping somewhere in the tunnels. Stiffly, she raised her head from the cellar floor and looked around. Light streamed through the opening above her head, but it had lost its daytime glow. She shivered, sat fully upright, and looked at her watch. Six-fifteen. On her knees, she crawled across the floor to position herself beside the open trunk.

Kiana looked over the rim and stared in awe at the top tray. It was lined in royal blue velvet, set with sterling silver hinges, and held a double row of brilliant Queensware goblets. With a trembling hand she picked up one of the heavy crystal glasses and held it toward the light that was still coming from the overturned lantern. She ran a shaky finger over the royal crest of King George III, then twirled the goblet around, weighing it in the palm of her hand. Daniel DeRossette might have drunk his wine from the rare, magnificent piece.

Kiana lifted off the top tray and discovered three more layers of Queensware glass. Each piece was etched with the royal crest and nestled in a custom-made blue velvet niche, gleaming as if Adi had just washed it. Quickly, Kiana opened the second trunk and found more of the same.

The raucous ring of cicadas initiating their evening clamor began outside. Kiana looked up at the hole above her and wondered what had happened to Portia. She had gone for help hours ago, and surely ought to have returned by now.

Kiana moved her head back and forth, rubbing the sore spot on her neck, hoping she hadn't misjudged Portia. Could the woman have deliberately left her to die in the cellar in order to keep the glass for herself? Kiana shook her head. Probably not. No one had forced Portia to bring her here in the first place, or tell her the true story of Soddy Russell's legacy.

It was rapidly getting dark outside, and Kiana knew she'd soon have to try to find her own way out. The lantern still gave off a generous amount of light, so Kiana went to the pile of broken wood and pulled Portia's bundle of gear free. She untied it and took out the small hand shovel, then picked up the lantern and held it high. The Queensware discovery was exciting, but which one of the shadowy passageways would lead her to Portia's cache of Soddy Glass?

Kiana decided to try the tunnel that stretched out behind the trunks, and she managed to penetrate the narrow passage for about ten feet. It came to a dead end, blocked by a pile of rubble. She dug at the pile of rocks to see if she could break through, but it was impossible. Giving up, she returned to the circular clearing in the cellar and tried the next three passages. Each was as impassable as the first, crammed with years of crumbling mud and stone.

When Kiana entered the fifth tunnel, she immediately noticed the ceiling was higher, the breadth more generous, and it allowed her enough room to walk upright and hold the lantern high. Kiana crept along the musty path, winding her way through about twenty feet of tunnel. She heard the trickling of water over stone and smelled the dampness of the air. With each step, the sound grew louder and the walls more moist.

At an enormous arch, Kiana stopped. Drawing a sharp breath, she entered a vaulted cavern. On the opposite side of the cave she could see the continuation of the tunnel. Kiana walked slowly into the center of the underground room, then turned in a circle, gazing at the mysteriously beautiful limestone formations protruding from the walls. A natural bridge spanned a wide lagoon of black water and a narrow stream emerged from the rock, ran a few feet, then disappeared again, underground. Though the temperature had dropped dramatically, Kiana was warmly flushed by the shock of what she had discovered. Wiping her forehead with a grimy hand, she examined a pointed stalagmite rising beside the bridge.

Nearby, more water dripped down a limestone ledge and fell in a whispery cascade toward the deep black pool. She stepped closer to the bridge, then cried out, shocked by the most unusual sight Kiana had ever seen.

Flush against the sloping side of the terra-cotta wall were six life-size figures molded of clay. They were seated on a high mud altar with their long arms extended downward, their clublike hands resting on their knees. The earthen statues faced Kiana with flat eyes that were set among features that were definitely African. The high foreheads, broad noses, elongated chins, and full lips were so skillfully carved on the ancestral idols that Kiana inched away in fear. They were so lifelike, she felt they might open their mouths and speak.

At the feet of the molded forms, were several big clay jars and smooth black stones arranged in a semicircle, inviting worship, or prayer. The ghostly panel of ancestors presided over the cool dim cavern with a regal presence, making Kiana feel like an intruder.

She came closer, critically examining the altar. The figures had been carved, then placed in seated positions atop a shelflike ledge. Kiana went to the side of the structure, and crouched down, holding the lantern up to see into the hollow space. Her heart leaped into her throat. The figures were placed there to protect a cache of treasure. Wedged inside were several wooden crates. She tugged the first one out and grinned in delight.

"Yes!" she said rather loudly to herself as the top and the sides of the crate came into view. The initials PGW were stamped in blue ink.

With the tip of the shovel, Kiana pried open the crate and removed the first piece of glass she came to. It was a small dish with a scalloped pedestal base. Around the rim were a series of horned dogs with scrolling tails and tongues—Ijoma's favorite design. Kiana's hands shook so badly she feared she might drop it, but she carefully placed it back into the crate and pulled out a bowl with diagonal blocks of stripes set with tight coillike spirals. Then she removed four goblets covered with flat oval fish, their butterfly tails overlapping each other. There were four flat dishes with concentric circles set in the center, and several pieces in amber that had weeping, potbellied gods with teardrops on their faces.

Kiana stared at the center of each plate. A long breath drained from her lungs. She sank back on her heels in shock, as the irony of her discovery materialized. In her hands were the creations that had been inspired by the slave-Princess Ijoma of Bwerani and executed by the hand of a brave abolitionist.

All of Kiana's worries about being rescued from the pit, dissolved as she settled in to examine each piece. Several hours passed before she heard sounds of someone outside. Kiana jumped up from the floor of the cave, and with her lantern, hurried back down the tunnel toward the main entrance to the cellar.

"Portia?" she called, approaching the rubble. "Portia? Hurry. I've found it!"

A dark figure appeared in the entrance, then a thick rope was lowered. When the rescuer shimmied down the rope and dropped onto the remains of the entrance plank, a shower of dirt flew up, forcing Kiana to jump back and cover her eyes. The sound of wood shifting and falling to the floor filled the cellar. When the dust settled, Kiana was staring into Ida's face.

Chapter Thirty-nine

IDA grinned perversely, then let go of the rope. She stood with her legs wide, gun in one hand, the other in front of her as if to keep Kiana at bay.

"Hello, Kiana." She advanced toward her stepsister. "Did I hear you say you've found it?"

Kiana's mouth flew open. Shocked, she stumbled back, shoulders raised nearly up to her ears. "Ida! My God! What are you doing here?"

"You don't know?" Ida threw her head back, grinning, thrilled to have caught Kiana by surprise. "I can't believe my ears. With all your fancy degrees, I would have thought you were smart enough to have figured out that your mother's family owes me a lot."

"Owes you? For what?"

"For taking my father from me. For causing his death. For treating me like an orphan, as if I didn't belong."

Kiana stared at Ida as if she were a ghost. "Didn't belong? That's nonsense."

"You got that right! It's nonsense now, because Hester has made a generous attempt to repair the damage your mother did."

"What have you been telling Hester?"

"Nothing. The truth. She has changed her will to make

amends and I'm very pleased, Kiana. Very." Ida shifted to one side. "As a matter of fact, you're out of the picture. Everything will be left to me."

Kiana frowned. "That's crazy. I'm Grandmother's only blood relative. She wouldn't do that . . . not unless you tricked her into doing it."

Ida shook her head. "No tricks. You upset her terribly with your talk about reparations and digging up old family secrets. She's a proud, traditional kind of woman, Kiana, and she confided to me that she's ashamed of you and what you're trying to do. She has no desire to see you again."

Outraged, Kiana shot back. "How could you turn Grandmother against me?"

"Easy," Ida replied.

Kiana watched the gun in Ida's hand as it was waved back and forth. With her gaze riveted on the small chrome gun, she growled, "Cold and calculating, that's you. I wanted to believe you had changed. I wanted us to be like real sisters, Ida, but I can see that you've never wanted to do anything but put me down and enrich yourself."

"Listen!" Ida snapped. "You were sent off to college. I had no choice but to become a secretary. You and your snooty grandmother made me feel like an outcast, especially after I got out of prison. You think you can hold that over my head forever?"

"That's long forgotten!"

"Oh, don't give me that. I know what you think of me, and I just want what's mine. Because of your mother, I was left with nothing. Nobody! She ruined my life, Kiana."

"Ida, that's not true. My mother loved your father, and she loved you as if you were her own."

"She bewitched my father! She got inside his head and made him crazy. He never would have gone running all around the world to save other people's children if she hadn't influenced him. He would still be alive if he'd left her, as I begged and begged him to do. You think you're so much smarter than me. Well, we'll see about that now."

"What do you want?"

"The glass, of course." She lifted the gun to Kiana's face. "Where is it?"

Kiana backed up, but said nothing.

"Where is it?" Ida jabbed Kiana in the stomach with the pistol.

"Through that tunnel," Kiana said, jerking her head to the left.

"You go first," Ida ordered, waiting for Kiana to lead the way.

Once inside the vaulted cavern, Ida forced Kiana to her knees beside the open crates.

"Beautiful, isn't it?" she whispered, watching Kiana closely. "Almost as beautiful as the exquisite reproductions I managed to produce and sell all across the country. Prices are sky high, Kiana. I've done quite well, but there's still a lot of money to be made."

Kiana lifted her eyes to Ida's. "The vases I saw in Houston were not reproductions."

Ida chuckled. "Unfortunately, you're right. Watts let the real thing slip right past me that time, but you can bet he's sorry he did that."

"Watts? Marvin Watts in Nashville?"

"The same."

"He's involved in your dirty little scheme?"

"Not anymore." Ida circled Kiana, then told her, "He's history."

Kiana decided to try to reason with Ida. "You did time once, Ida. Surely you don't want to go back to prison."

"And I don't plan to," she snapped sharply. "Get up!"

Slowly, Kiana rose. Ida stepped closer, then slapped a gloved hand across Kiana's face, nearly knocking her to the floor. Kiana kicked at Ida, regained her balance, then fled back toward the entrance of the cave, still limping and a little woozy from the fall she'd suffered earlier.

Ida quickly overcame Kiana. Lunging forward she wrapped both arms around her and forced her down on the cool cellar floor. With her knee on Kiana's back, Ida struggled to hold her stepsister in place.

A loud scream tore from Kiana's throat. She flipped over, forcing her legs straight up in a gesture she had learned in a self-defense class in Houston—a move she had practiced many times, but had hoped she would never have to use.

Ida screamed, reeling back. The gun fell from her hand.

On her hands and knees, Kiana scrambled to get it, but Ida slipped in front of her and snatched it from her grasp. Waving the pistol between them, Ida yelled, "Get your ass up!" Then she bent to grab Kiana by the hair.

Kiana thrust a balled fist forward in a swift firm jab and landed a powerful blow to Ida's chest. A chilling wail erupted from Ida's lips as she sank to her knees. She let go of the gun. It clattered to the rock floor, spinning out of sight.

Clutching her stomach, Ida cursed Kiana, who jerkily got to her feet and tore off down the tunnel, trying to get back to the cellar entrance.

Where was Portia? Why hadn't help come? Would anyone hear her screams? She continued running, but soon Ida's rapid footsteps were thudding close behind.

Just when Kiana got to the pile of rotted wood below the trap-door opening, Ida lurched forward, grabbed Kiana by the belt loops of her jeans, and twisted her around. Kiana jerked sideways, managing to jab a fist into Ida's ribs as she struggled to get away.

"Help! Help me," Kiana cried, hoping her voice would carry up to the surface. It gave her a surge of energy, but it wasn't enough to push Ida away.

Kiana crashed to the ground. Ida pounced on top of her, trapping her with the weight of her body. Despite Kiana's scratching at her face, Ida managed to flip Kiana over, and yank a roll of silver duct tape from the pocket of her parka. Breathing raggedly, she began winding a length of the tape around Kiana's wrists.

"You're going for a swim, Kiana," she whispered, bending low to her ear. "Alone. Just like you used to do back on the farm." She pulled Kiana to her feet and forced her to walk back through the tunnel to the foot of the limestone bridge that spanned the black lagoon. "Surely this is deep enough for you to get lost in. For a long, long time."

When shoved to her knees, Kiana pressed herself against an outcropping of rock, refusing to move.

Ida yanked her by the arm.

Kiana resisted with all her strength. "You're not going to dump me in there!" she shouted. "Ida. Please. You can't get away with this. It's mad! People know I'm down here. Help is on the way."

"You mean that humpbacked dwarf I saw sprawled in the middle of the road?"

"Did you do something to Portia?" Kiana jerked back. "That nice old woman?"

"Nice? She was lying in the road. Looked like her horse might have thrown her. I didn't have time to stop and render aid, if that's what you're getting at. So don't count on her to save you."

"Someone will come looking for her—" Kiana started.

"Not before I'm long gone," Ida tossed back, poking Kiana with the tip of her boot.

"Think about what you're doing, Ida. You'll spend the rest of your life in prison for this."

"Shut up," Ida yelled. "Don't make this so damn difficult! I'll never go back to jail. Never!" She tugged Kiana by the arm. "You and your new lover boy! A research trip! You liar. Thought you had me fooled? I knew there was more to this sudden jaunt through Tennessee than you were letting on. All along you were planning to get your hands on the glass so you could cut me out of what's rightfully *mine*."

"That was never my intention." Kiana sadly shook her head.

Ida raked her stepsister with a bitter stare, then dragged her onto the bridge, cracking Kiana's forehead against the rocky surface. With both hands under Kiana's shoulders, she heaved her off the narrow bridge.

Kiana screamed as she hurtled through the air, but the impact of her body slamming into the cold black water soon silenced her. The next thing Kiana knew, water closed over her head.

Ida laughed aloud, satisfied.

After a few seconds, Kiana bobbed to the surface and began treading water, but with both hands tied she knew she wouldn't last very long. As her strength began to ebb, she grew dizzy and the image of Ida standing above her on the bridge shimmered and turned into a distorted fuzzy blur.

Ida remained calmly watching as Kiana thrashed around in the water. "You should have taken Grandmother's warning and stayed out of Tennessee, Kiana," she called down. "You brought this on yourself, you know."

"You will not get away with this!" A voice boomed into the cavern.

Kiana blinked. She could make out a faint light at the tunnel exit on the opposite side of the cavern. She slipped underwater, then floated back up. She saw Rex emerging from the dark hole, a lantern in his hand.

"Rex! Rex!" Kiana screamed, struggling to maneuver toward the side of the lagoon.

Ida spun around and glared at Rex. He raced toward her. She looked down, lunged for the gun, but Rex got there first and snatched the pistol from the ground.

Kiana frantically pedaled the water, determined not to go down. "Rex! Oh, thank God," she muttered before drifting down, again, beneath the cold black water.

"Kiana!" Rex stopped in the middle of the bridge and raised his hand to throw the gun into the pool, but Ida rushed him and tried to take it away. He jerked back.

Ida fell.

Rex stared in horror for a fraction of a second, unable to do more than watch. Ida disappeared in a flat loud splash that sent a spray of water over his face. He wiped his eyes, focused on Kiana, then dove headfirst into the water.

"She can't swim!" Kiana yelled, sputtering water that lapped into her mouth. Rex called something back at her but the water in Kiana's ears made him sound far away, hopelessly garbled.

Kiana could feel the splash of water as Ida fought the undertow. Then everything seemed eerily silent, except for the sound of Rex's hands slapping the water as he rhythmically made his way toward her. At last he grabbed her, lifted her up, and tugged the binding from her wrists. Once free, Kiana went limp against his chest, but soon caught her breath and swam to the steep wall of rock surrounding the quarrylike pool. Bracing herself against the wall, she watched, gasping for air as Rex dove underwater to find Ida.

Kiana shuddered as Rex disappeared into the inky hole.

After what seemed to be a very long time, he surfaced, shook his head, then swam over to her.

"It's too deep where she went down," he said. "There's nothing I can do."

He put his arm around Kiana and helped her swim to a place where they both could climb out. When they collapsed on the floor of the cave, Kiana burst into tears, clinging to Rex as her body quivered against his.

He held her for only a moment before urging her to her feet, guiding her into the narrow tunnel exit that would take them up to the rim of the valley.

Holding the lamp high, Rex led the way. Kiana followed closely, too numbed by the shock of what had transpired to feel the chill that had settled over her body. The ground beneath her feet began to rise sharply. As she trudged up the steep incline, the width of the tunnel began to broaden considerably, eventually becoming wide enough for her to move alongside Rex.

He reached over and clasped her hand, squeezing it warmly as they continued. The air soon lost its damp, musty smell. A breeze washed over their faces. They emerged from the stifling passageway to stand under a glittering blanket of stars. When Kiana looked up, the first thing she saw was the North Star. She laid her head on Rex's shoulder, realizing that it was the same star Adi and Price had followed more than a hundred years ago. When Rex slipped his arm around her waist, Kiana knew her search was over.

Epilogue

"GOOD morning. This is Thursday, March 24, 1994. Live from Studio 1A in Rockefeller Plaza, this is NBC News, *Today*, with Bryant Gumble and Katie Couric."

Kiana watched from the far side of the studio as Bryant Gumble greeted his unseen audience, made a few comments about the day's headline news, then offered a teaser about the upcoming guests.

Katie Couric grinned in her charmingly impish way, then said, "And I understand we also have Kiana Sheridan and Rex Tandy on today."

"Yes," Bryant replied. "Two very talented research/journalists who will be here to talk about their book, *Starlight Passage*, a mesmerizing story that has the art world, the antique world, and experts in black history squirming in their seats. It's quite an extraordinary tale that has completely turned upside down an artistic legacy." He tapped the desk with a pencil. "Great story. They'll be here with us after this message."

Kiana gripped her copy of *Starlight Passage* in perspiring hands and took a deep breath.

"Nervous?" Rex whispered, looking over at her.

"Not really," Kiana managed. "Anxious to get on with it, though."

A production assistant came up and ushered Rex and Kiana to

their seats, then began to adjust Kiana's mike. "Can you put that wire under your jacket?" she asked.

"Sure," Kiana said, shifting slightly to push the wire under her lapel.

"Girlfriend, I could not put it down," the production assistant told Kiana. She leaned over to check the placement of the book on the small table between Kiana and her host. "When Adi was hanged, I cried. Really cried. My husband thought I was out of my mind."

Kiana laughed. Rex rolled his eyes. The woman hurried out of camera range and the producer began the countdown to air time.

Very quickly, the interview started and Bryant Gumble smoothly guided them through their journey, asking questions of Kiana and Rex. An avid collector of black art, he was genuinely interested in the subject matter and was sensitive to the message underlying his guests' recent work.

"And how would you sum up the significance of what you discovered?" he asked. "About the past . . . the future as well."

Rex inclined his head toward Kiana, letting her have the final word.

"I think it's significant to understand that the quest for reparations is a complex undertaking, a journey infused with controversy. In this country, within the long forgotten layers of closely interrelated cultures, there are legacies that may never be fully untangled or claimed."

"But you managed to unravel one such legacy," Bryant commented.

"Yes," Kiana admitted, "but at great personal expense." Though Ida had set out to do her harm, Kiana couldn't help feeling devastated every time she thought of Ida's body, still unrecovered, submerged somewhere at the bottom of that gaping black pool.

"And where can the Soddy Glass be seen?" Bryant asked.

"It's on permanent display at the National Afro-American Museum and Cultural Center in Wilberforce, Ohio. A magnificent exhibit. Worth visiting."

Bryant smiled his agreement. "So, what's next for you two? Certainly you have another project in the works?"

Kiana glanced at Rex, then back to her host. "Well," she began. "It's about time we started on our own family legacy. . . ."

· A NOTE ON THE TYPE ·

The typeface used in this book is a version of Janson, a seventeenth-century Dutch style revived by Merganthaler Linotype in 1937. Long attributed to one Anton Janson through a mistake by the owners of the originals, the typeface was actually designed by a Hungarian, Nicholas (Miklós) Kis (1650–1702), in his time considered the finest punchcutter in Europe. Kis took religious orders as a young man, gaining a reputation as a classical scholar. As was the custom, he then traveled; because knowledge of typography was sorely lacking in Hungary, Kis decided to go to Holland, where he quickly mastered the trade. He soon had offers from all over Europe—including one from Cosimo de' Medici—but kept to his original plan, returning to Hungary to help promote learning. Unfortunately, his last years were embittered by the frustration of his ambitions caused by the political upheavals of the 1690s.